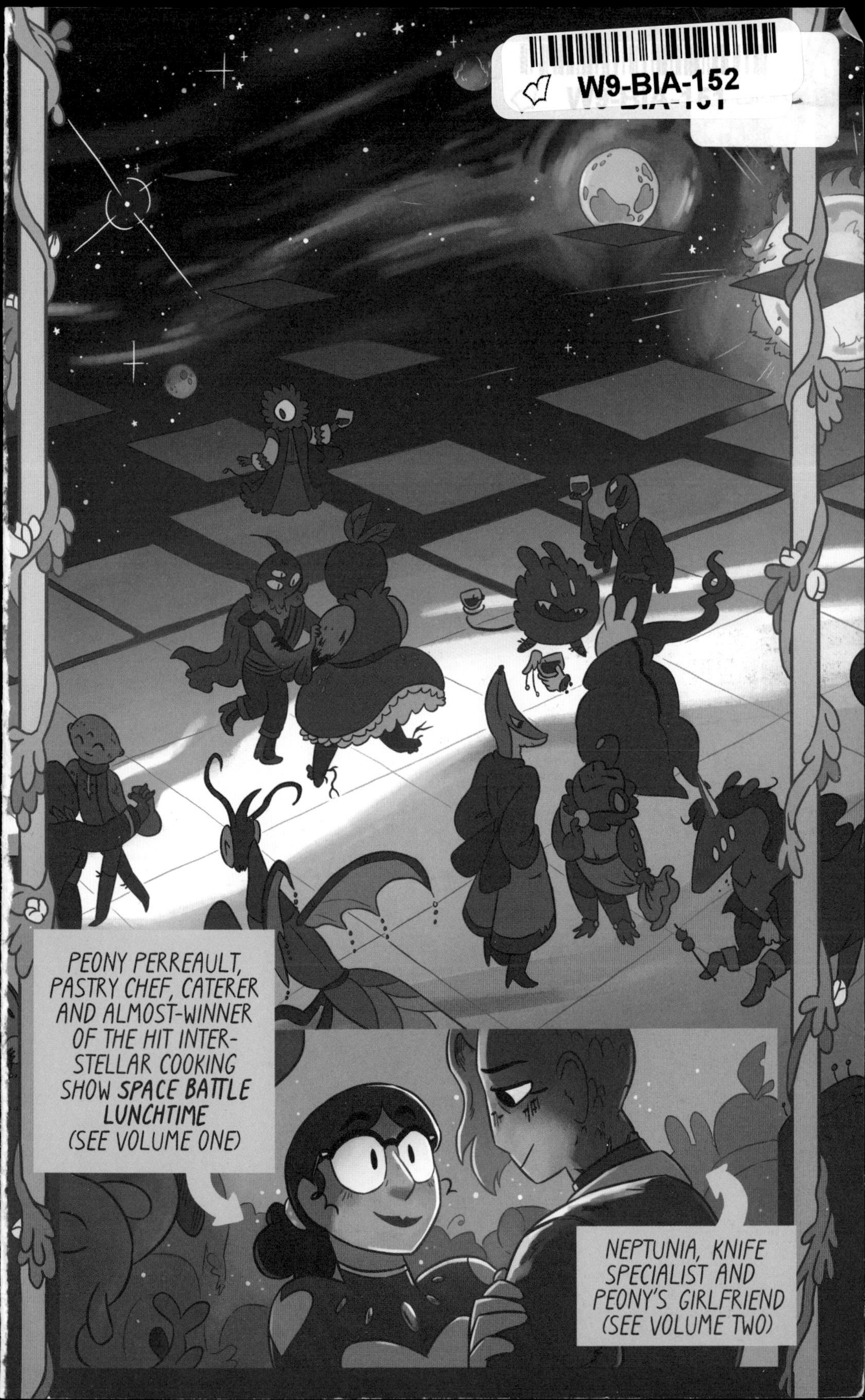
PEONY PERREAULT, PASTRY CHEF, CATERER AND ALMOST-WINNER OF THE HIT INTER-STELLAR COOKING SHOW **SPACE BATTLE LUNCHTIME** (SEE VOLUME ONE)
NEPTUNIA, KNIFE SPECIALIST AND PEONY'S GIRLFRIEND (SEE VOLUME TWO)

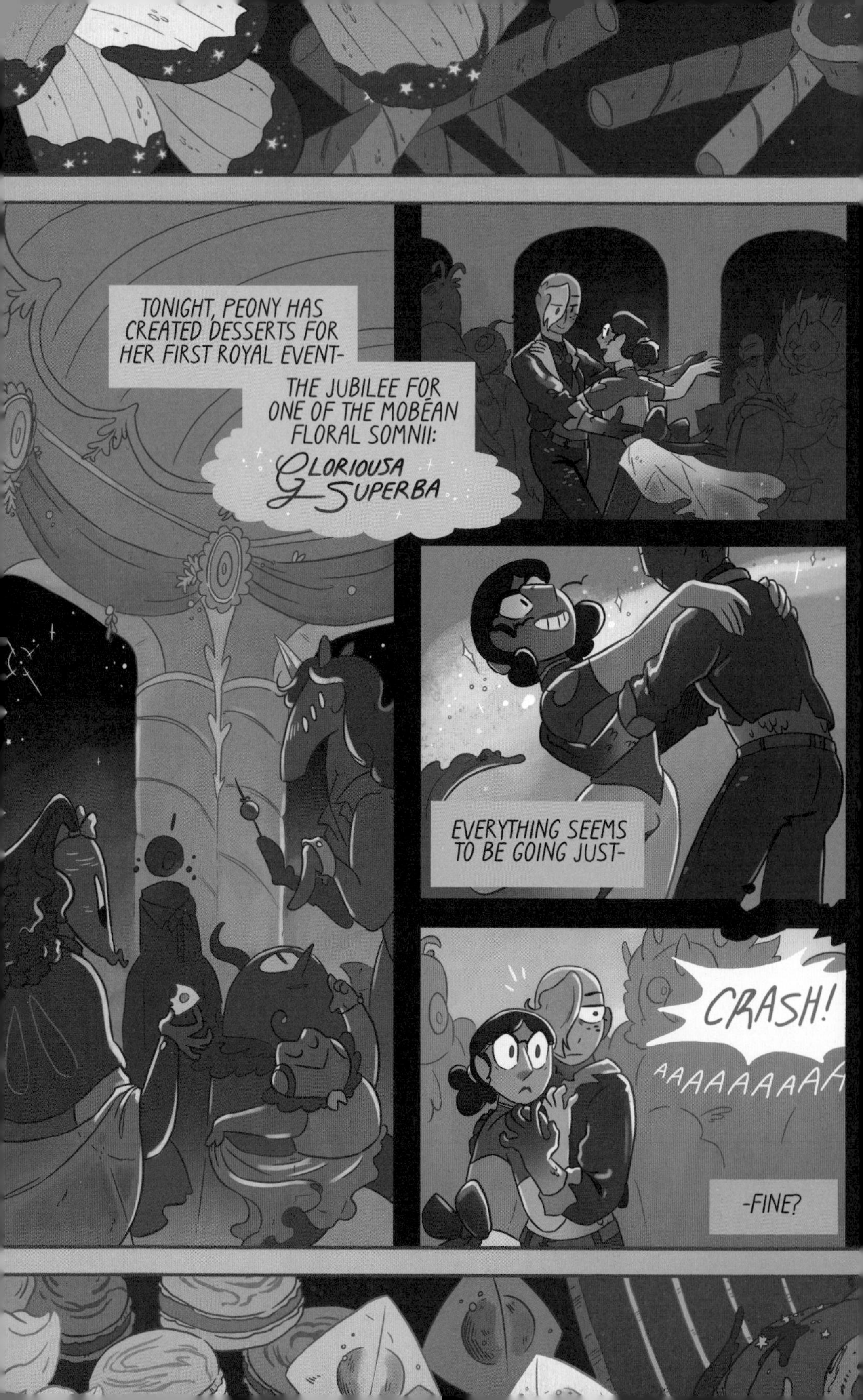
TONIGHT, PEONY HAS CREATED DESSERTS FOR HER FIRST ROYAL EVENT-
THE JUBILEE FOR ONE OF THE MOBÉAN FLORAL SOMNII:
GLORIOUSA SUPERBA
EVERYTHING SEEMS TO BE GOING JUST-
CRASH!
AAAAAAAAA
-FINE?

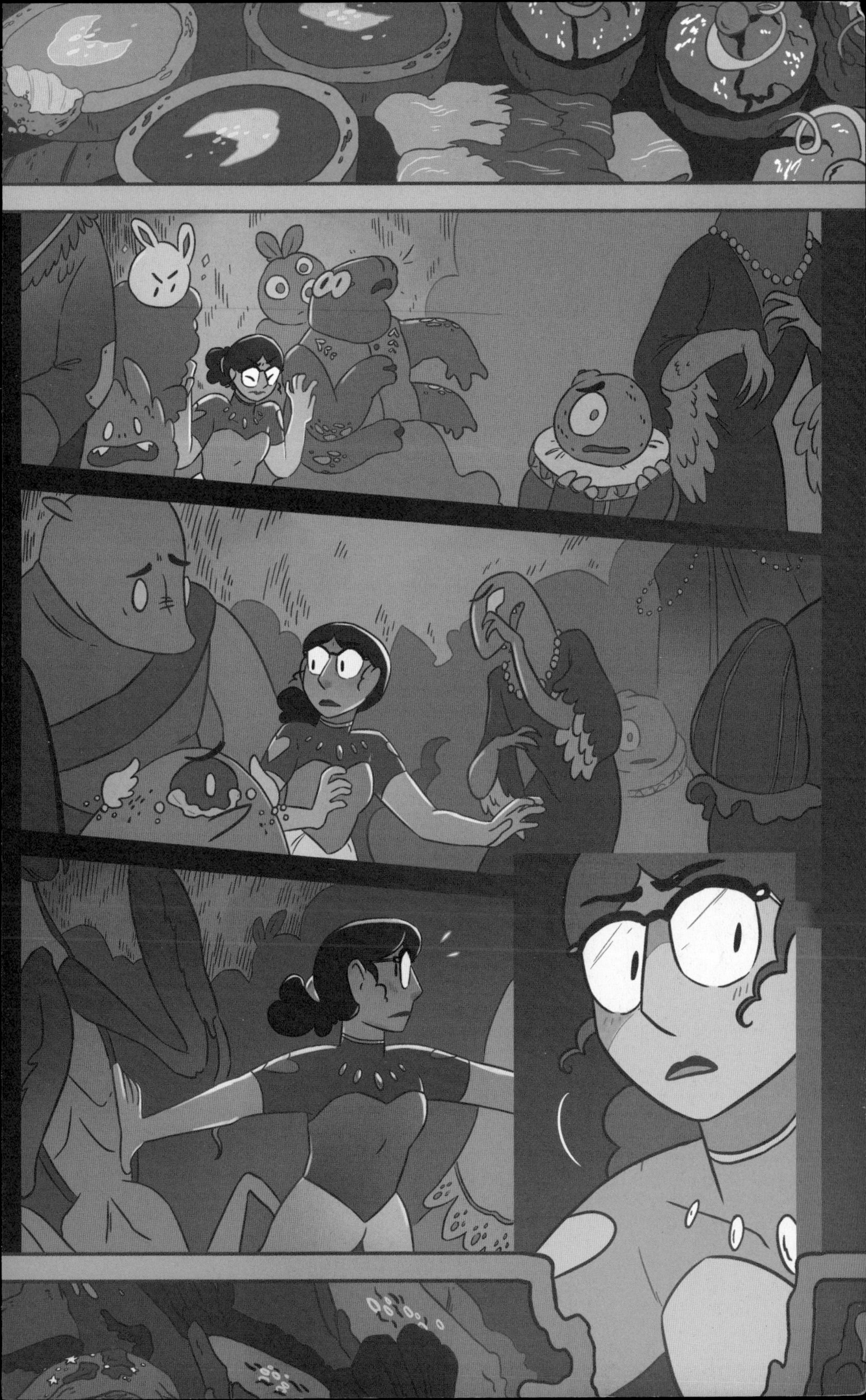

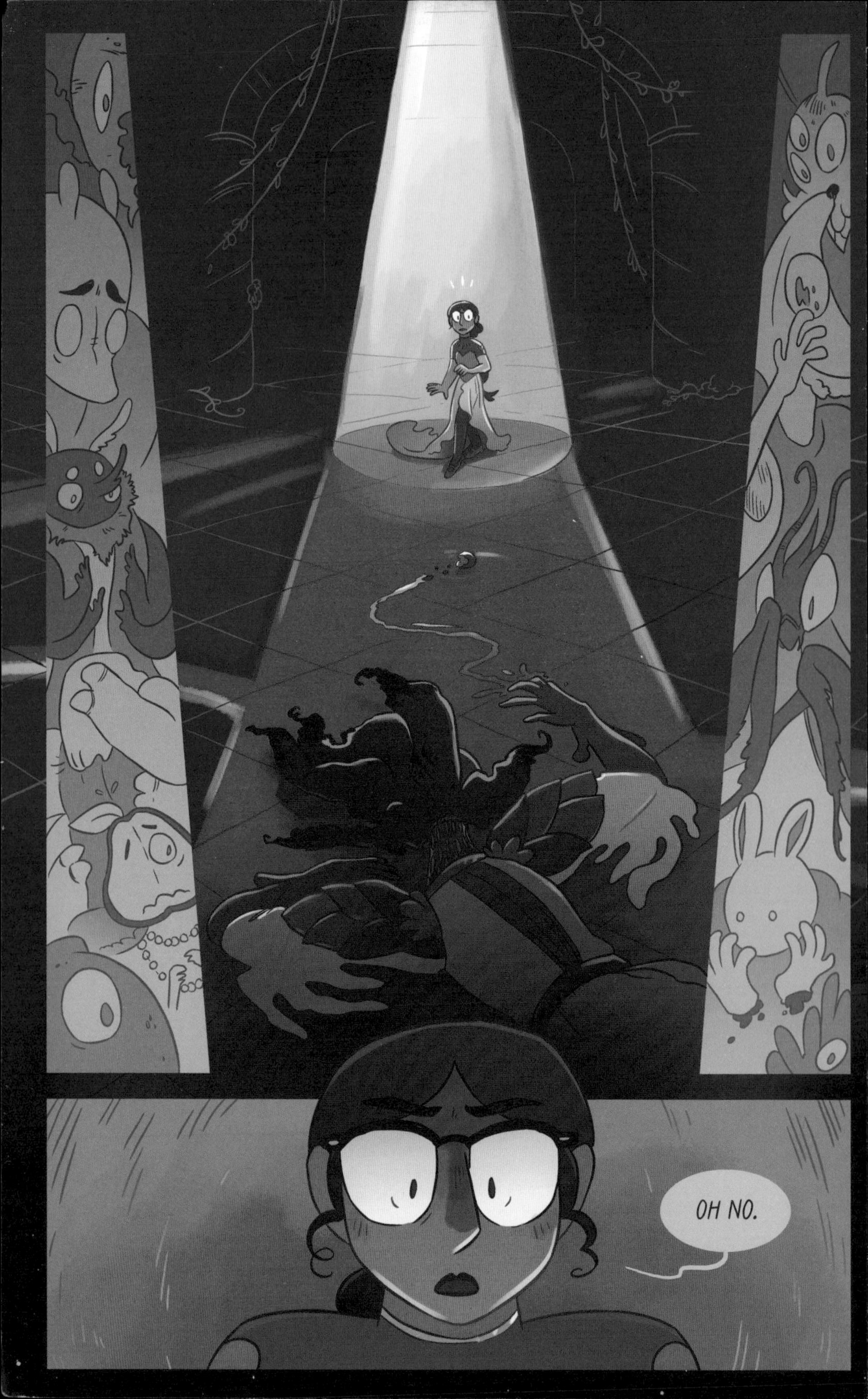
OH NO.

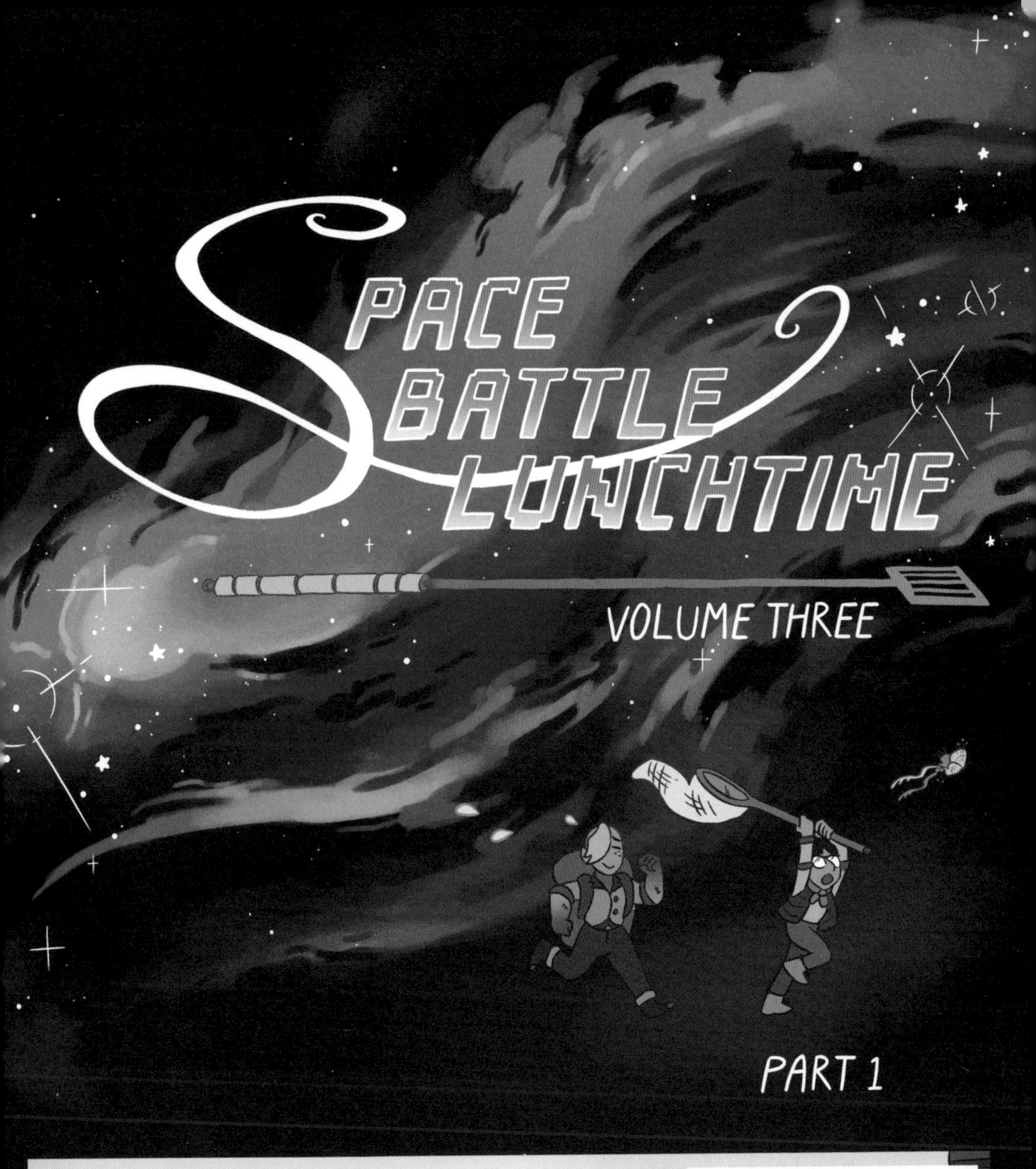
SPACE BATTLE LUNCHTIME
VOLUME THREE
PART 1

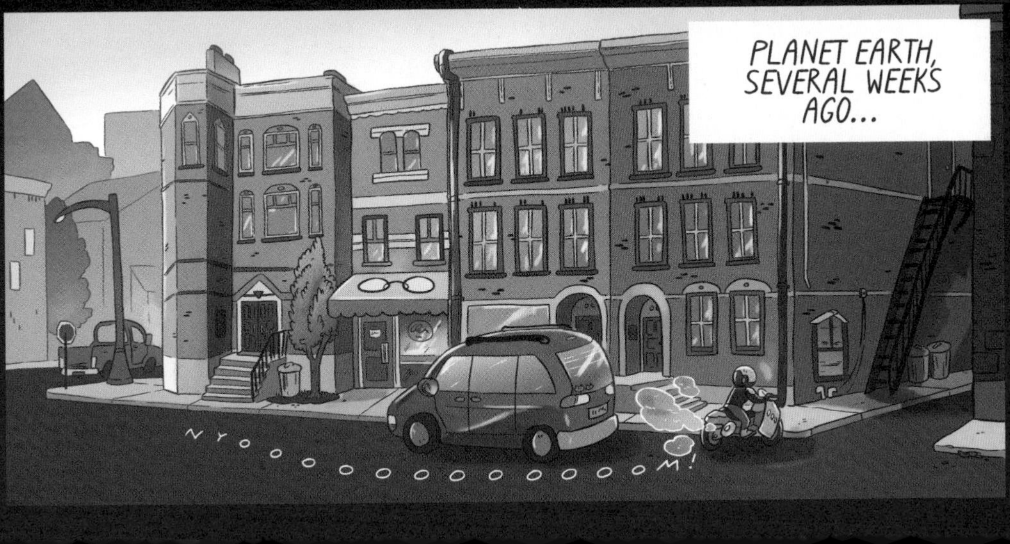
PLANET EARTH, SEVERAL WEEKS AGO...
NYOOOOOOOOOOOOOOOOM!

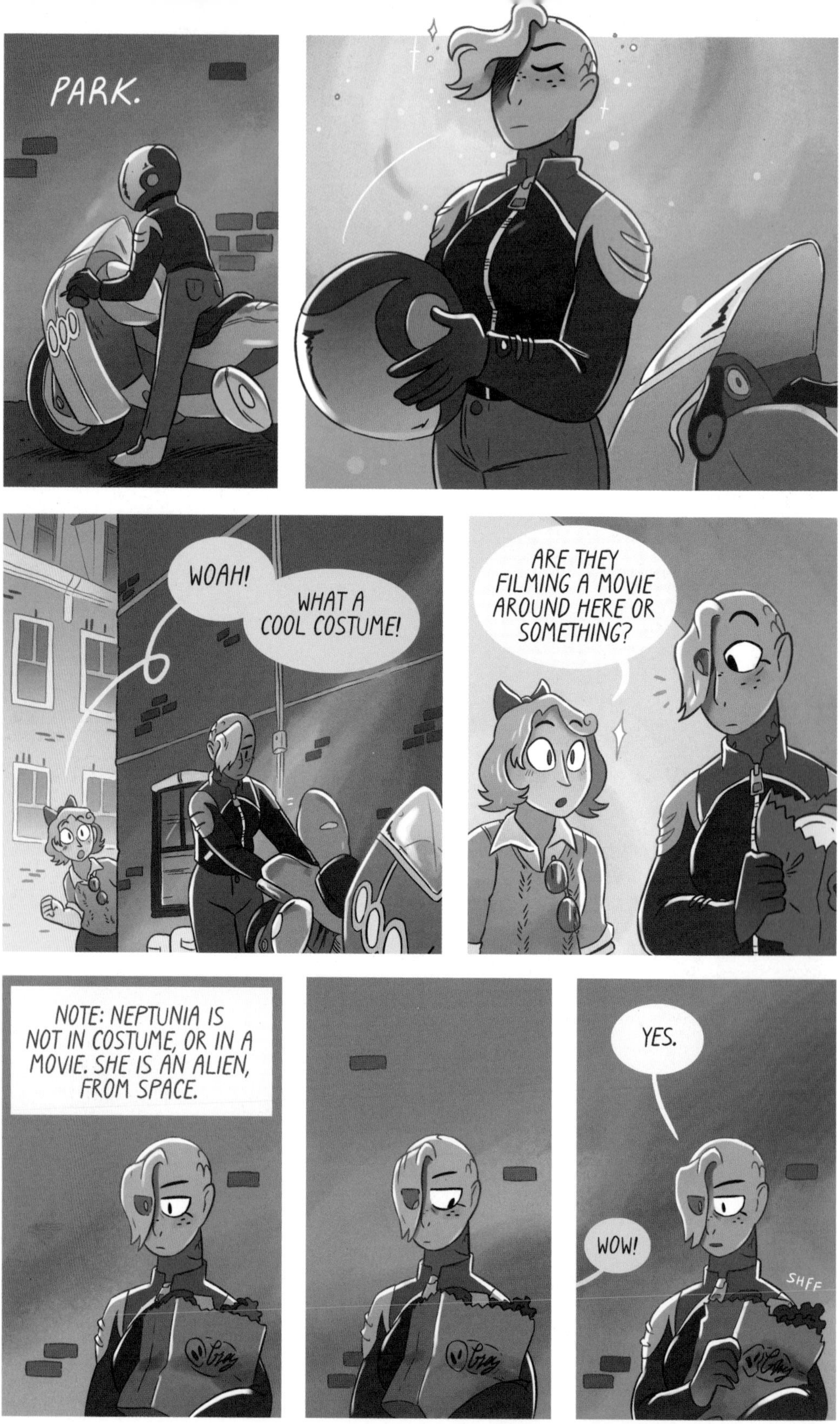
PARK.
WOAH!
WHAT A COOL COSTUME!
ARE THEY FILMING A MOVIE AROUND HERE OR SOMETHING?
NOTE: NEPTUNIA IS NOT IN COSTUME, OR IN A MOVIE. SHE IS AN ALIEN, FROM SPACE.
YES.
WOW!
SHFF

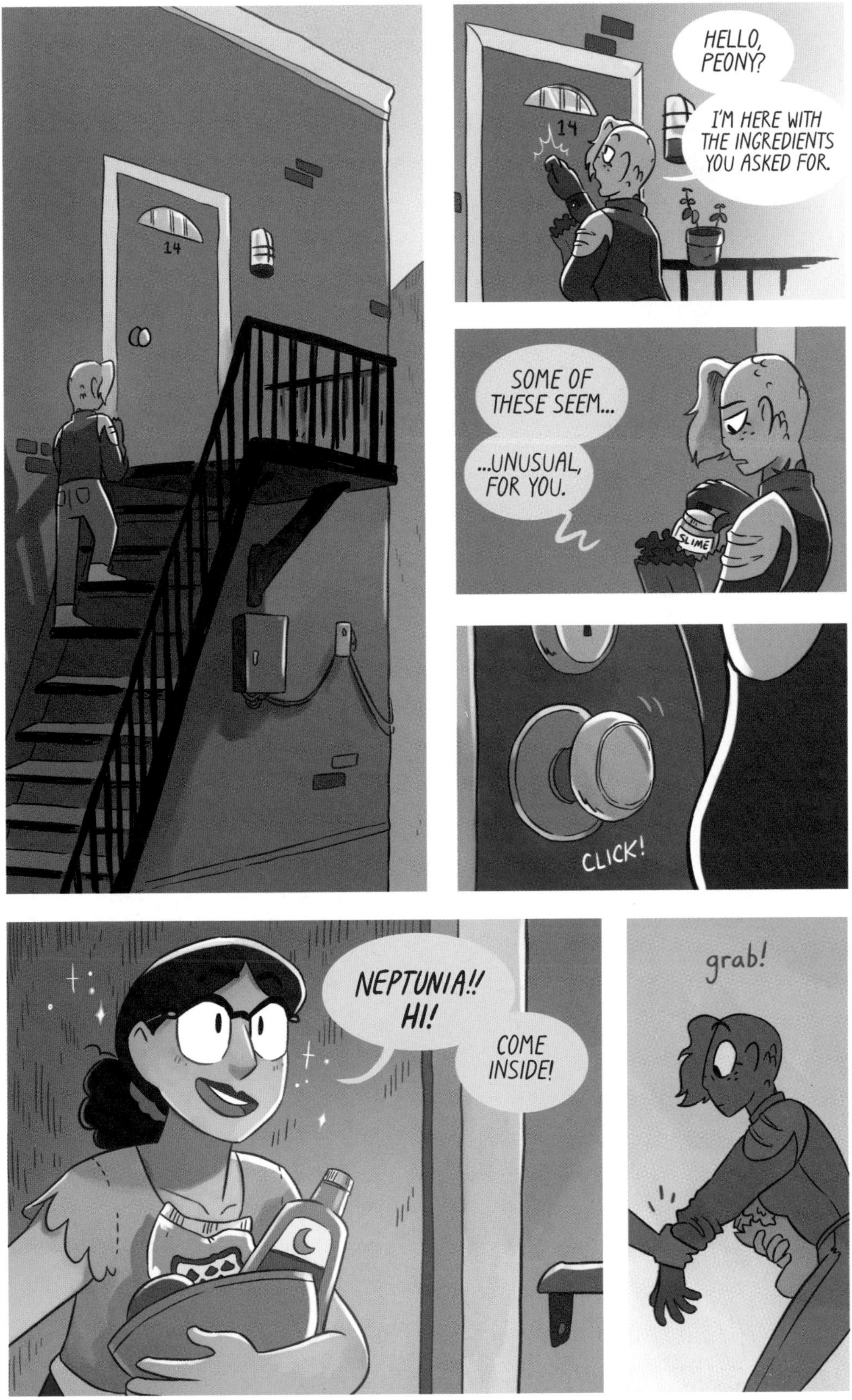

14
HELLO, PEONY?
I'M HERE WITH THE INGREDIENTS YOU ASKED FOR.
SOME OF THESE SEEM...
...UNUSUAL, FOR YOU.
SLIME
CLICK!
NEPTUNIA!! HI!
COME INSIDE!
grab!

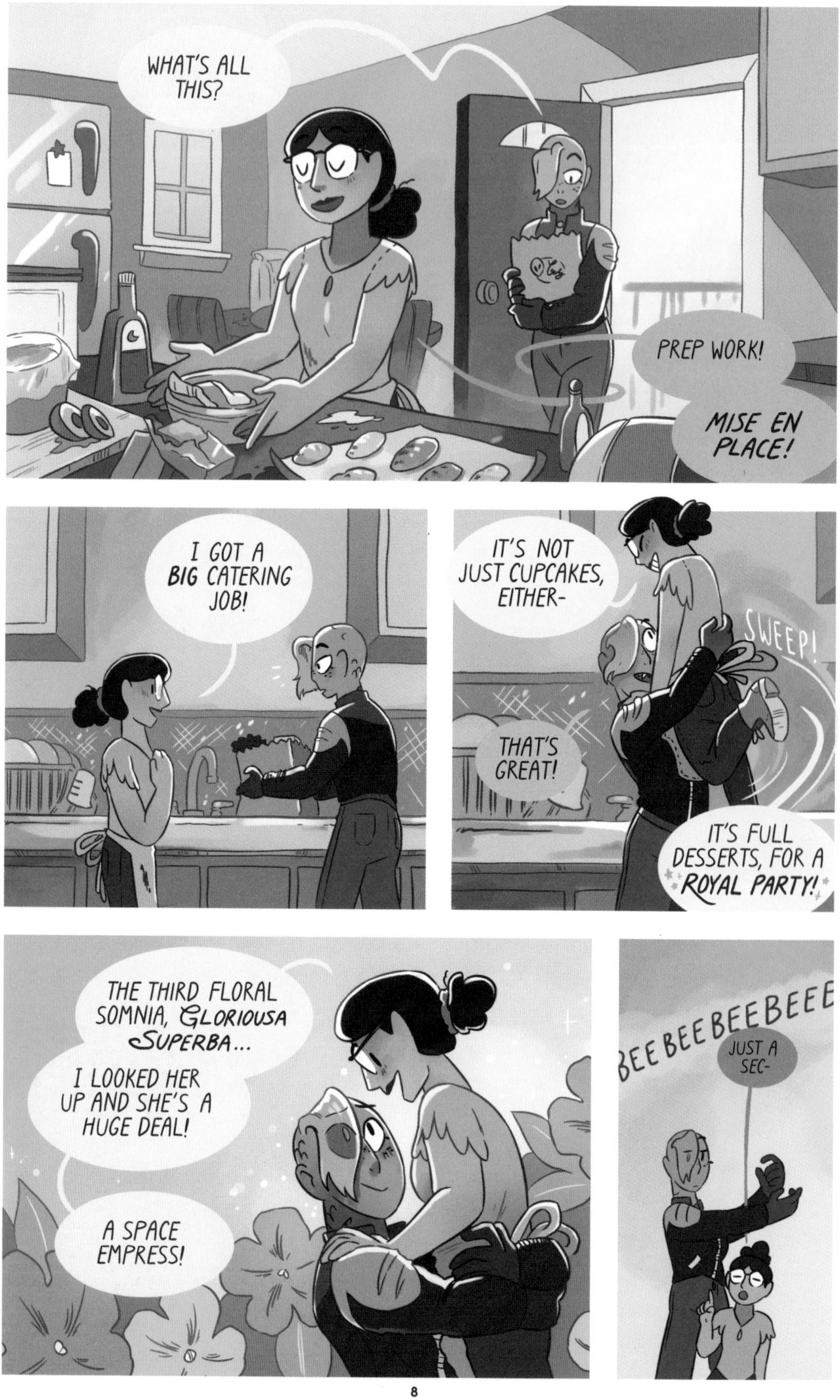
WHAT'S ALL THIS?
PREP WORK!
MISE EN PLACE!
I GOT A BIG CATERING JOB!
IT'S NOT JUST CUPCAKES, EITHER-
SWEEP!
THAT'S GREAT!
IT'S FULL DESSERTS, FOR A ROYAL PARTY!
THE THIRD FLORAL SOMNIA, GLORIOUSA SUPERBA...
I LOOKED HER UP AND SHE'S A HUGE DEAL!
A SPACE EMPRESS!
BEE BEE BEE BEEBEEE
JUST A SEC-

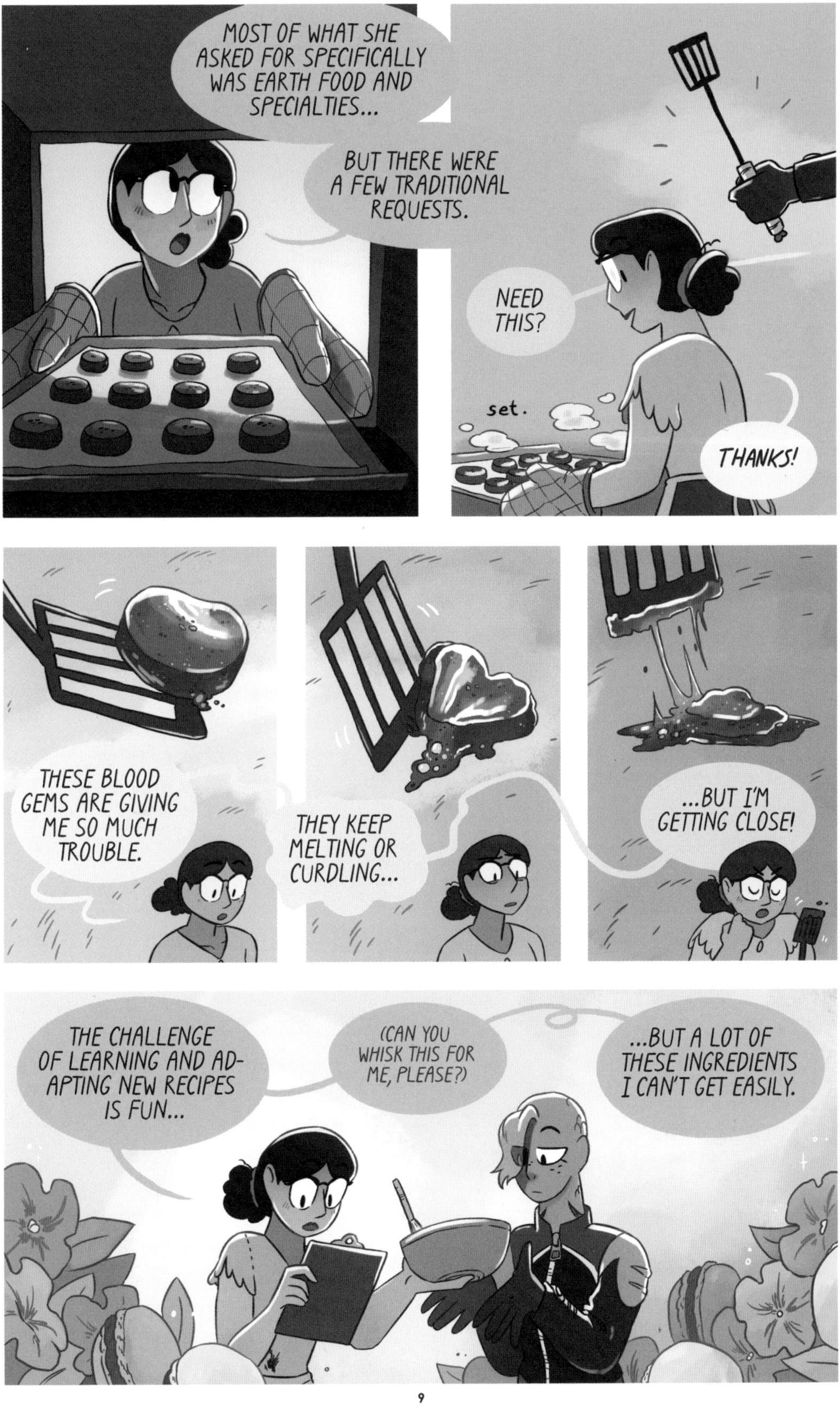
MOST OF WHAT SHE ASKED FOR SPECIFICALLY WAS EARTH FOOD AND SPECIALTIES...
BUT THERE WERE A FEW TRADITIONAL REQUESTS.
NEED THIS?
set.
THANKS!
THESE BLOOD GEMS ARE GIVING ME SO MUCH TROUBLE.
THEY KEEP MELTING OR CURDLING...
...BUT I'M GETTING CLOSE!
THE CHALLENGE OF LEARNING AND ADAPTING NEW RECIPES IS FUN...
(CAN YOU WHISK THIS FOR ME, PLEASE?)
...BUT A LOT OF THESE INGREDIENTS I CAN'T GET EASILY.

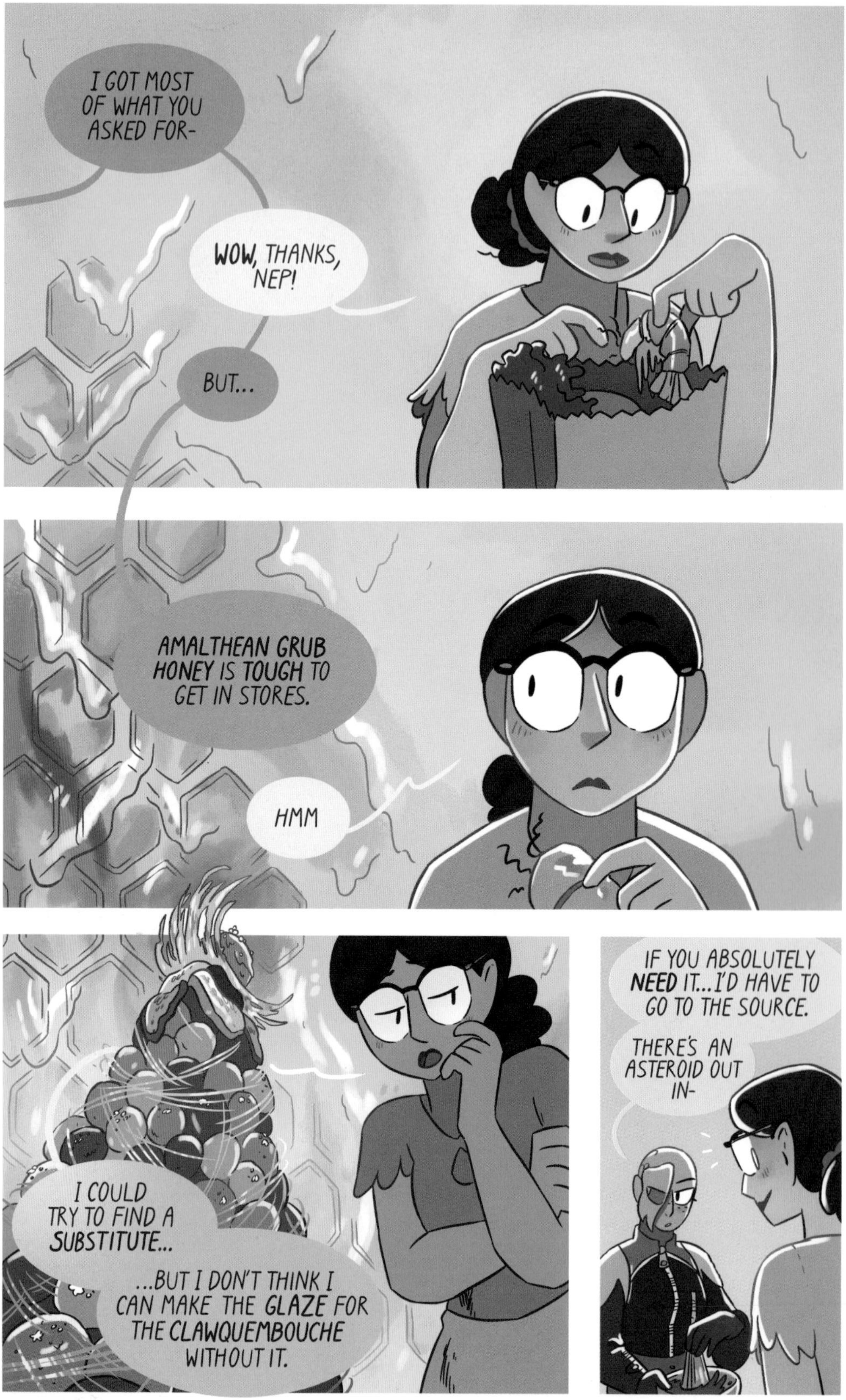
I GOT MOST OF WHAT YOU ASKED FOR-
WOW, THANKS, NEP!
BUT...
AMALTHEAN GRUB HONEY IS TOUGH TO GET IN STORES.
HMM
I COULD TRY TO FIND A SUBSTITUTE...
...BUT I DON'T THINK I CAN MAKE THE GLAZE FOR THE CLAWQUEMBOUCHE WITHOUT IT.
IF YOU ABSOLUTELY NEED IT...I'D HAVE TO GO TO THE SOURCE.
THERE'S AN ASTEROID OUT IN-

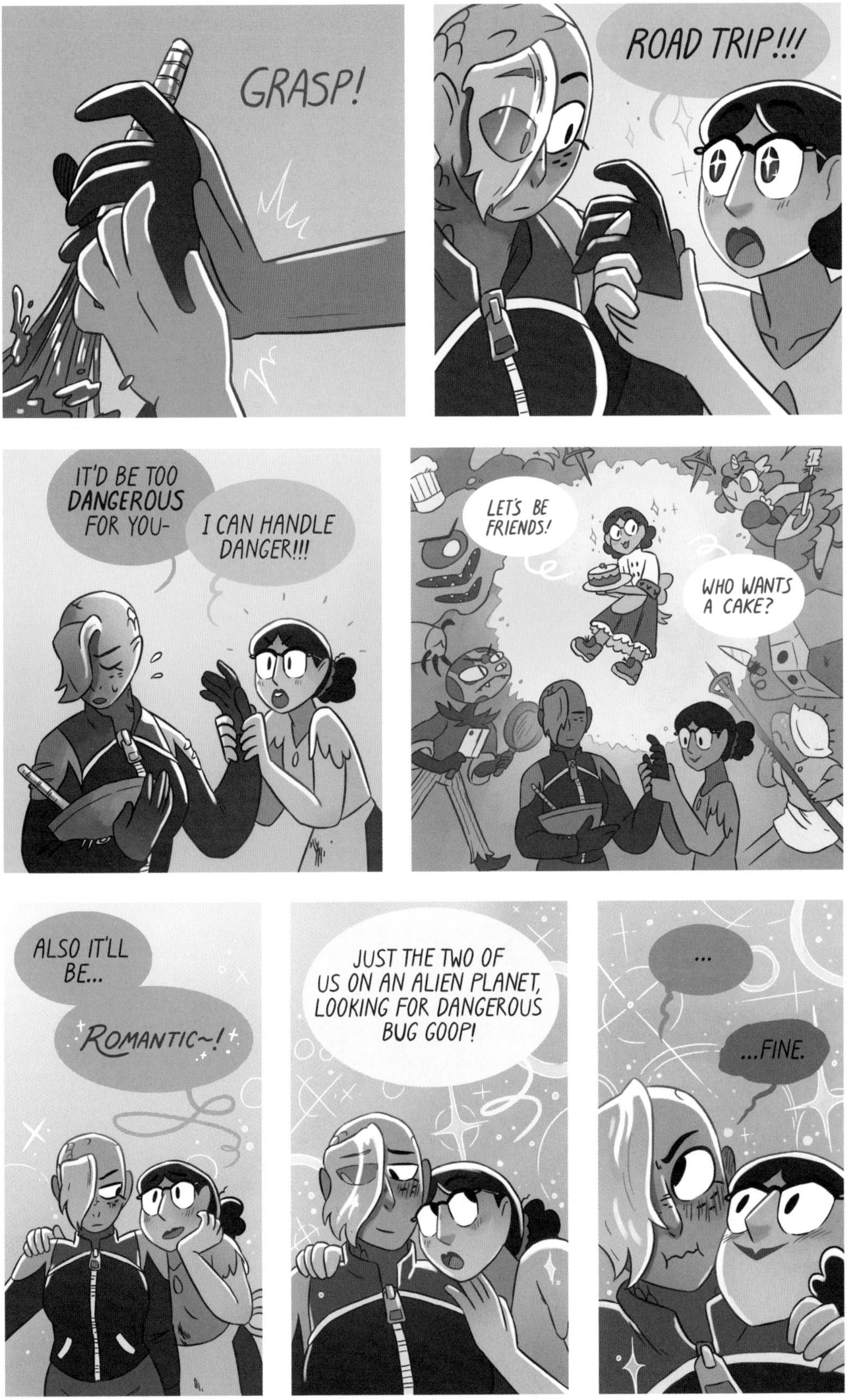
GRASP!
ROAD TRIP!!!
IT'D BE TOO DANGEROUS FOR YOU-
I CAN HANDLE DANGER!!!
LET'S BE FRIENDS!
WHO WANTS A CAKE?
ALSO IT'LL BE...
ROMANTIC~!
JUST THE TWO OF US ON AN ALIEN PLANET, LOOKING FOR DANGEROUS BUG GOOP!
...
...FINE.

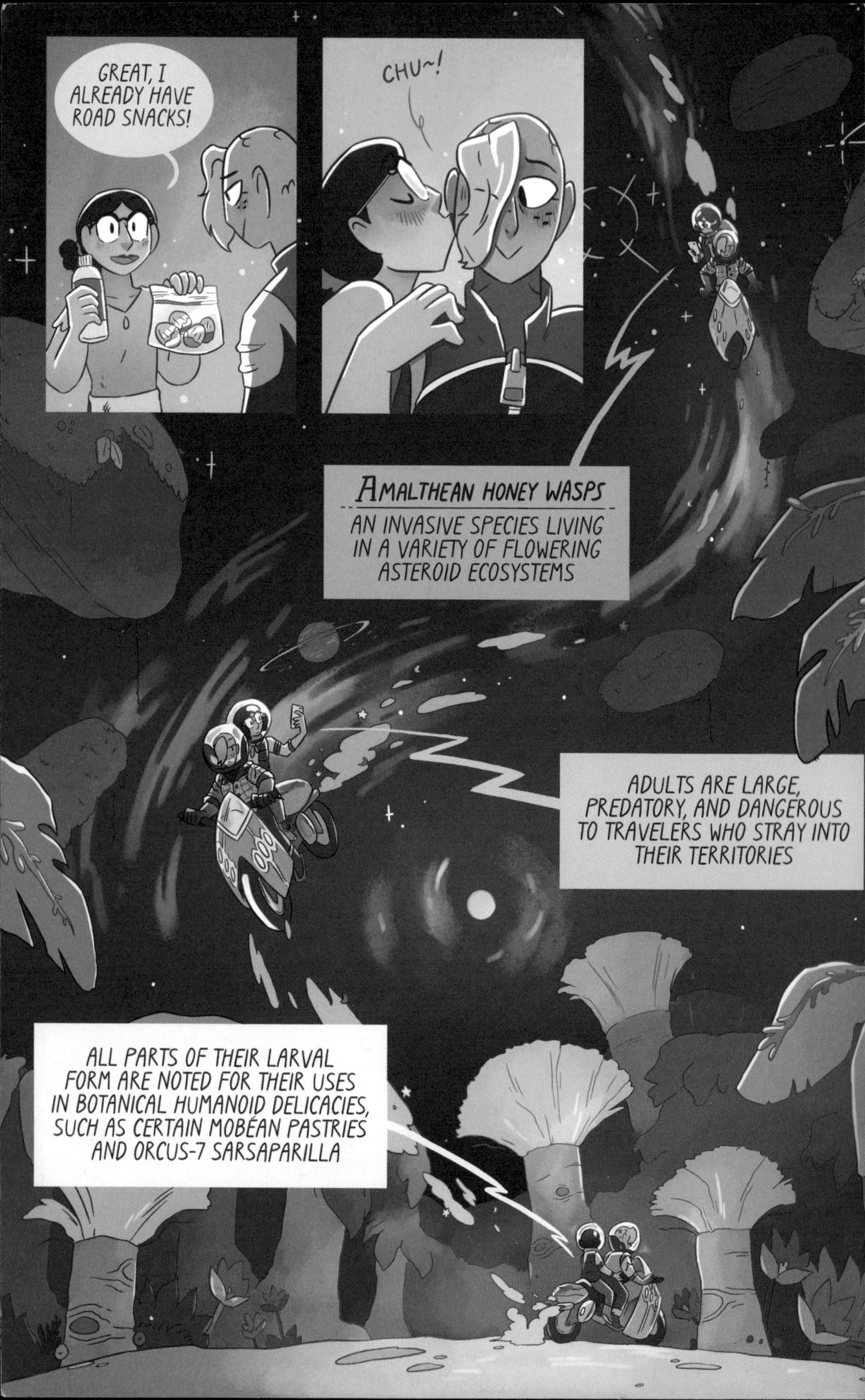
GREAT, I ALREADY HAVE ROAD SNACKS!
CHU~!
AMALTHEAN HONEY WASPS
AN INVASIVE SPECIES LIVING IN A VARIETY OF FLOWERING ASTEROID ECOSYSTEMS
ADULTS ARE LARGE, PREDATORY, AND DANGEROUS TO TRAVELERS WHO STRAY INTO THEIR TERRITORIES
ALL PARTS OF THEIR LARVAL FORM ARE NOTED FOR THEIR USES IN BOTANICAL HUMANOID DELICACIES, SUCH AS CERTAIN MOBÉAN PASTRIES AND ORCUS-7 SARSAPARILLA

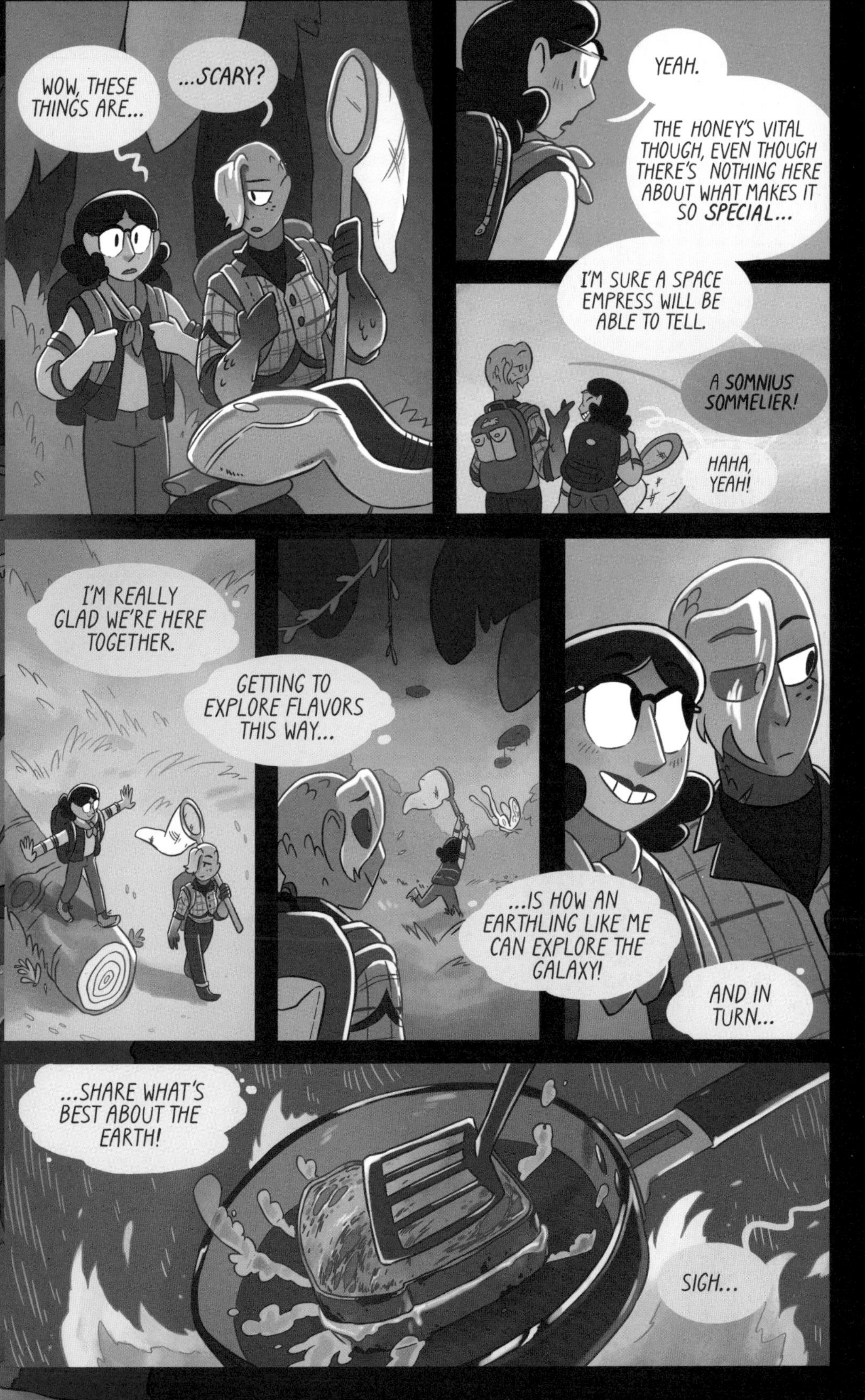
WOW, THESE THINGS ARE...
...SCARY?
YEAH.
THE HONEY'S VITAL THOUGH, EVEN THOUGH THERE'S NOTHING HERE ABOUT WHAT MAKES IT SO SPECIAL...
I'M SURE A SPACE EMPRESS WILL BE ABLE TO TELL.
A SOMNIUS SOMMELIER!
HAHA, YEAH!
I'M REALLY GLAD WE'RE HERE TOGETHER.
GETTING TO EXPLORE FLAVORS THIS WAY...
...IS HOW AN EARTHLING LIKE ME CAN EXPLORE THE GALAXY!
AND IN TURN...
...SHARE WHAT'S BEST ABOUT THE EARTH!
SIGH...

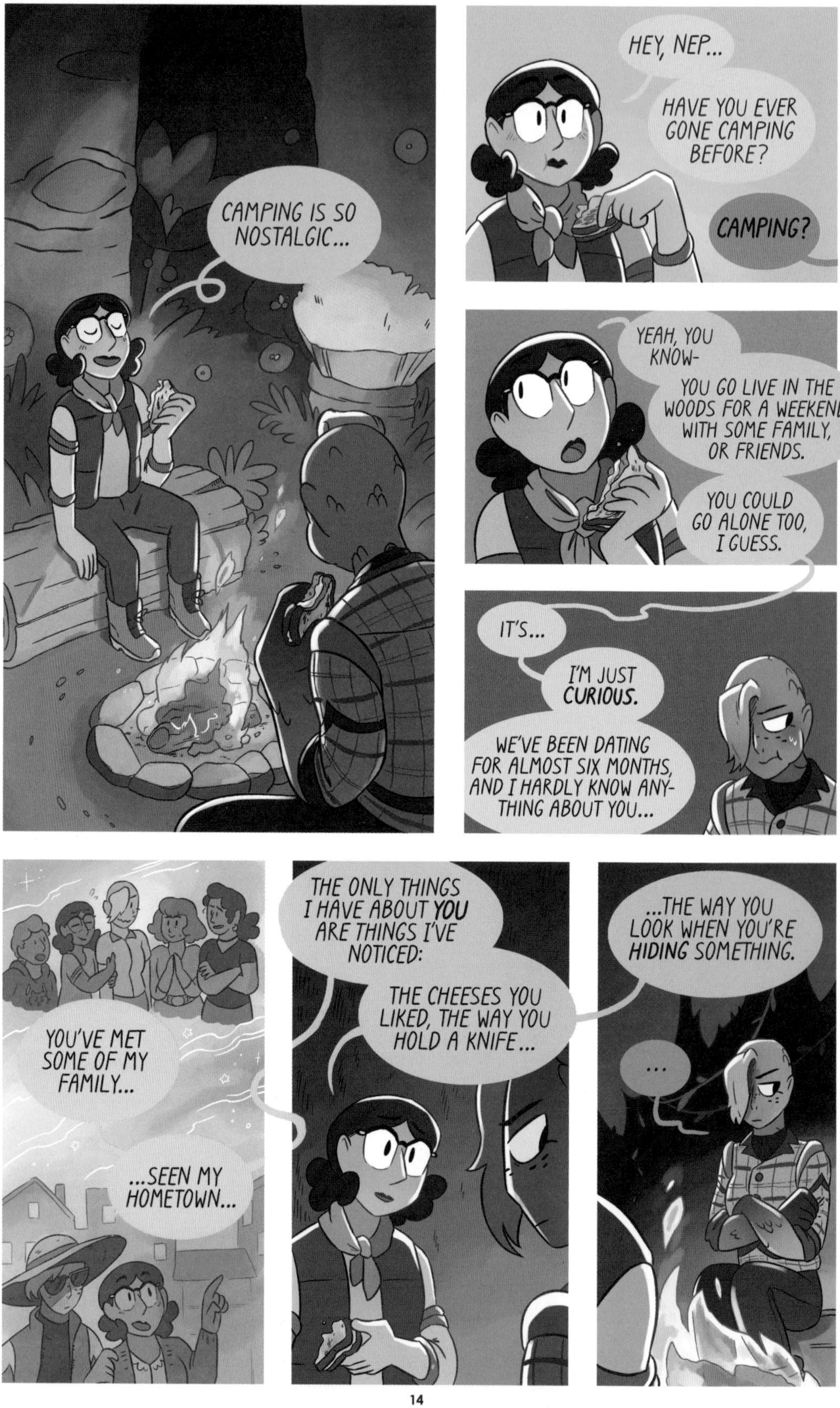
CAMPING IS SO NOSTALGIC...
HEY, NEP...
HAVE YOU EVER GONE CAMPING BEFORE?
CAMPING?
YEAH, YOU KNOW-
YOU GO LIVE IN THE WOODS FOR A WEEKEND, WITH SOME FAMILY, OR FRIENDS.
YOU COULD GO ALONE TOO, I GUESS.
IT'S...
I'M JUST CURIOUS.
WE'VE BEEN DATING FOR ALMOST SIX MONTHS, AND I HARDLY KNOW ANYTHING ABOUT YOU...
YOU'VE MET SOME OF MY FAMILY...
...SEEN MY HOMETOWN...
THE ONLY THINGS I HAVE ABOUT YOU ARE THINGS I'VE NOTICED:
THE CHEESES YOU LIKED, THE WAY YOU HOLD A KNIFE...
...THE WAY YOU LOOK WHEN YOU'RE HIDING SOMETHING.
...

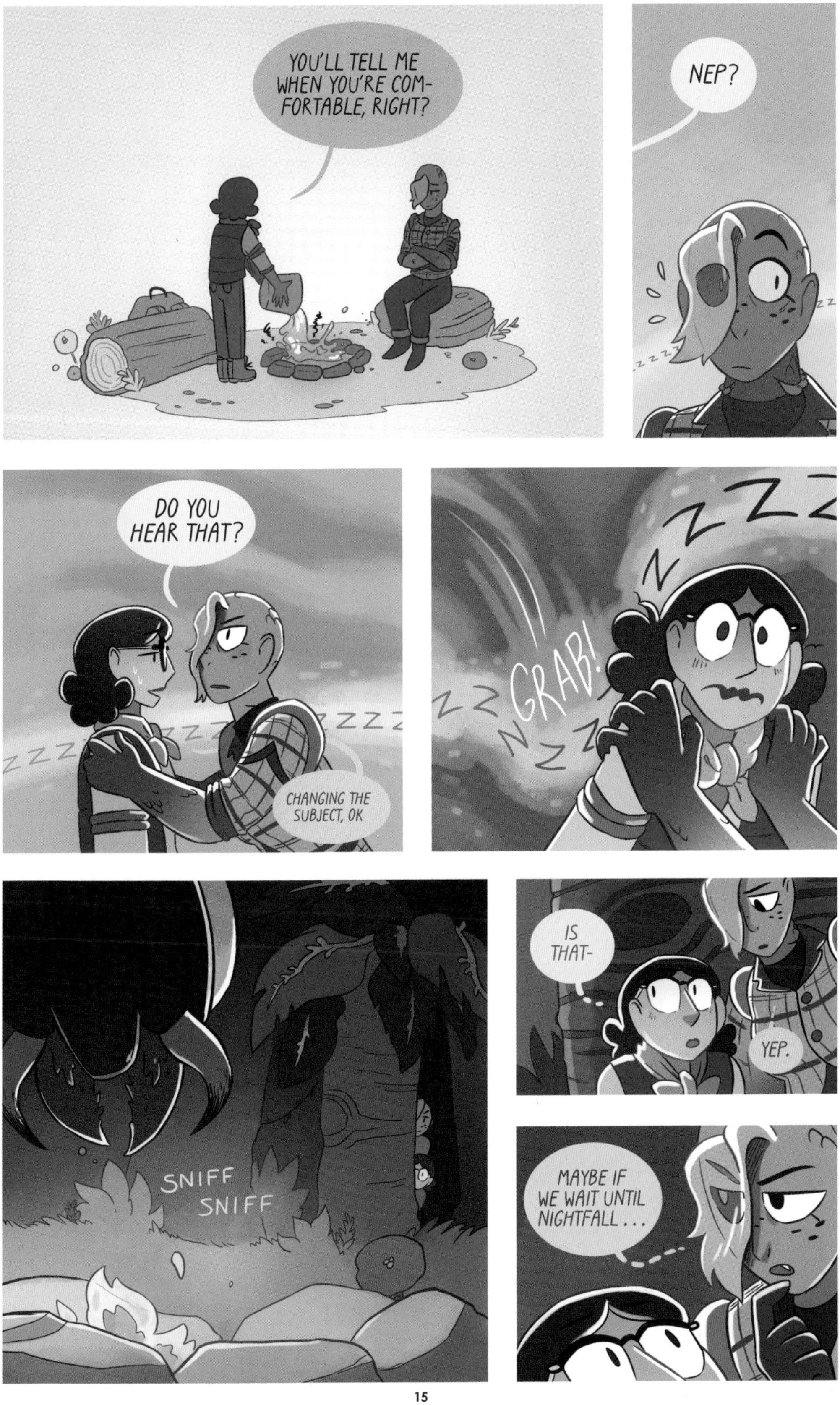
YOU'LL TELL ME WHEN YOU'RE COM-FORTABLE, RIGHT?
NEP?
DO YOU HEAR THAT?
CHANGING THE SUBJECT, OK
GRAB!
SNIFF
SNIFF
IS THAT-
YEP.
MAYBE IF WE WAIT UNTIL NIGHTFALL . . .

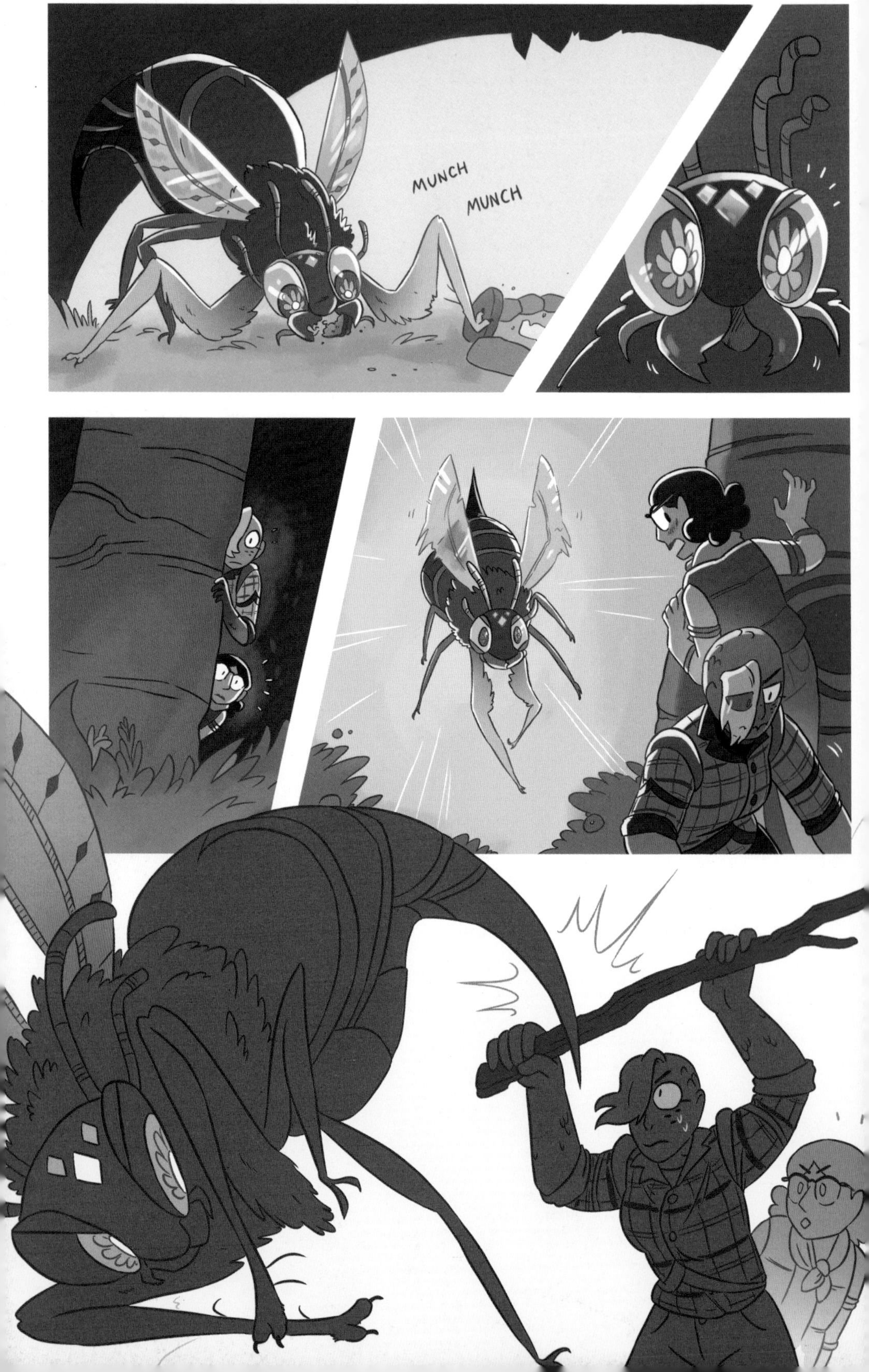
MUNCH
MUNCH

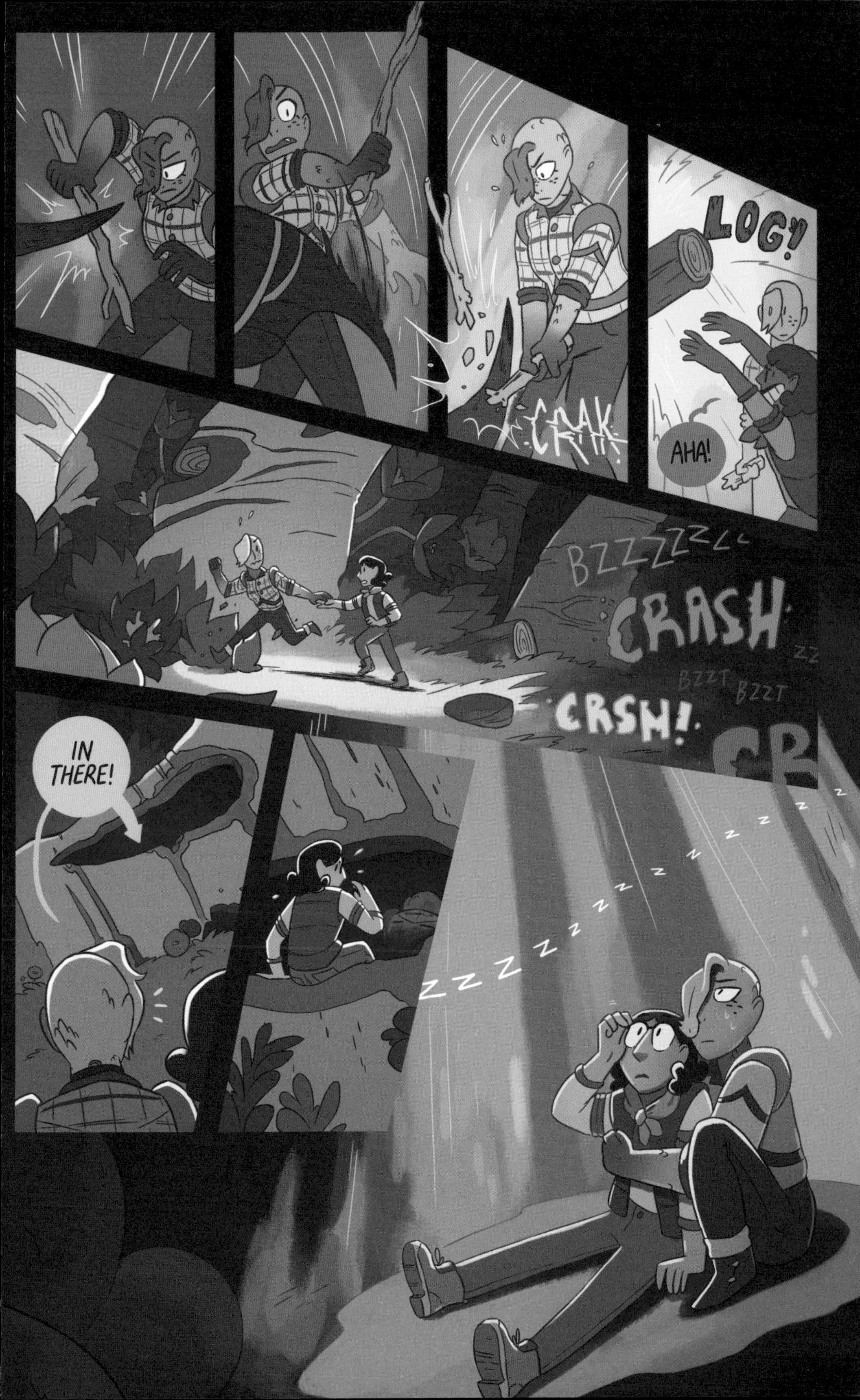

LOG!
AHA!
CRAAK
BZZZZZZ
CRASH
BZZT BZZT
CRSH!
IN THERE!
ZZZZZZZZZ

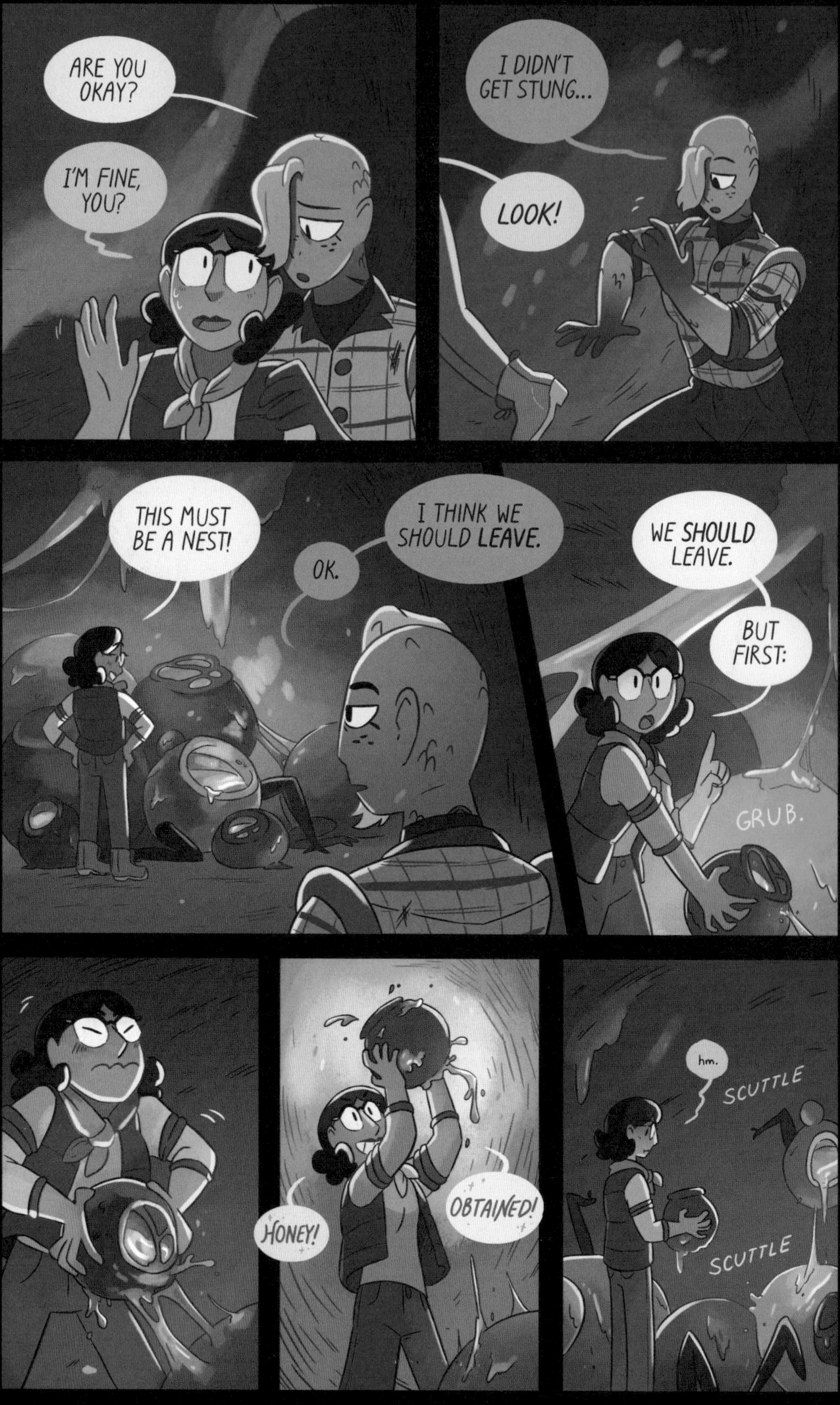
ARE YOU OKAY?
I'M FINE, YOU?
I DIDN'T GET STUNG...
LOOK!
THIS MUST BE A NEST!
I THINK WE SHOULD LEAVE.
OK.
WE SHOULD LEAVE.
BUT FIRST:
GRUB.
HONEY!
OBTAINED!
hm.
SCUTTLE
SCUTTLE

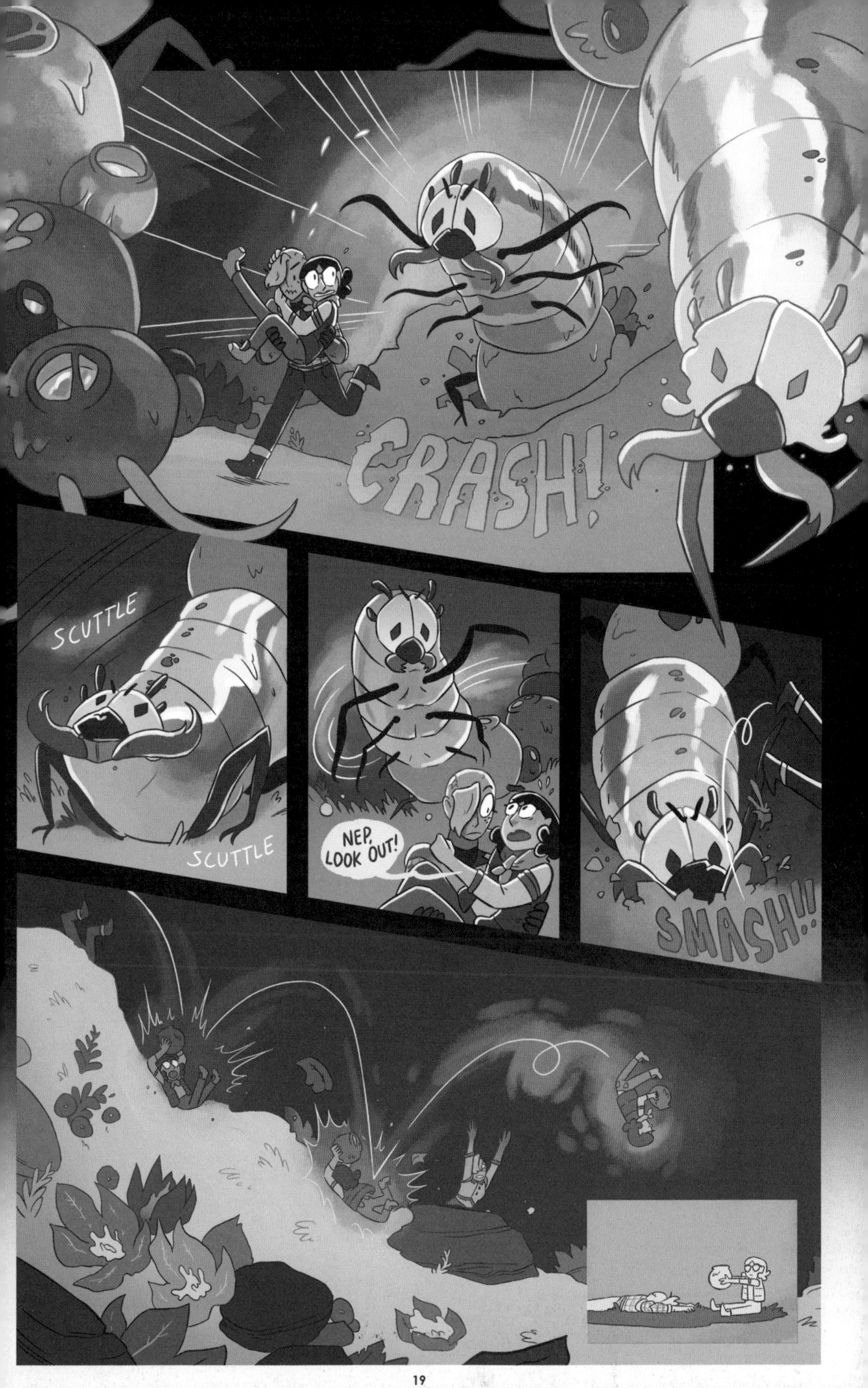
CRASH!
SCUTTLE
SCUTTLE
NEP, LOOK OUT!
SMASH!!

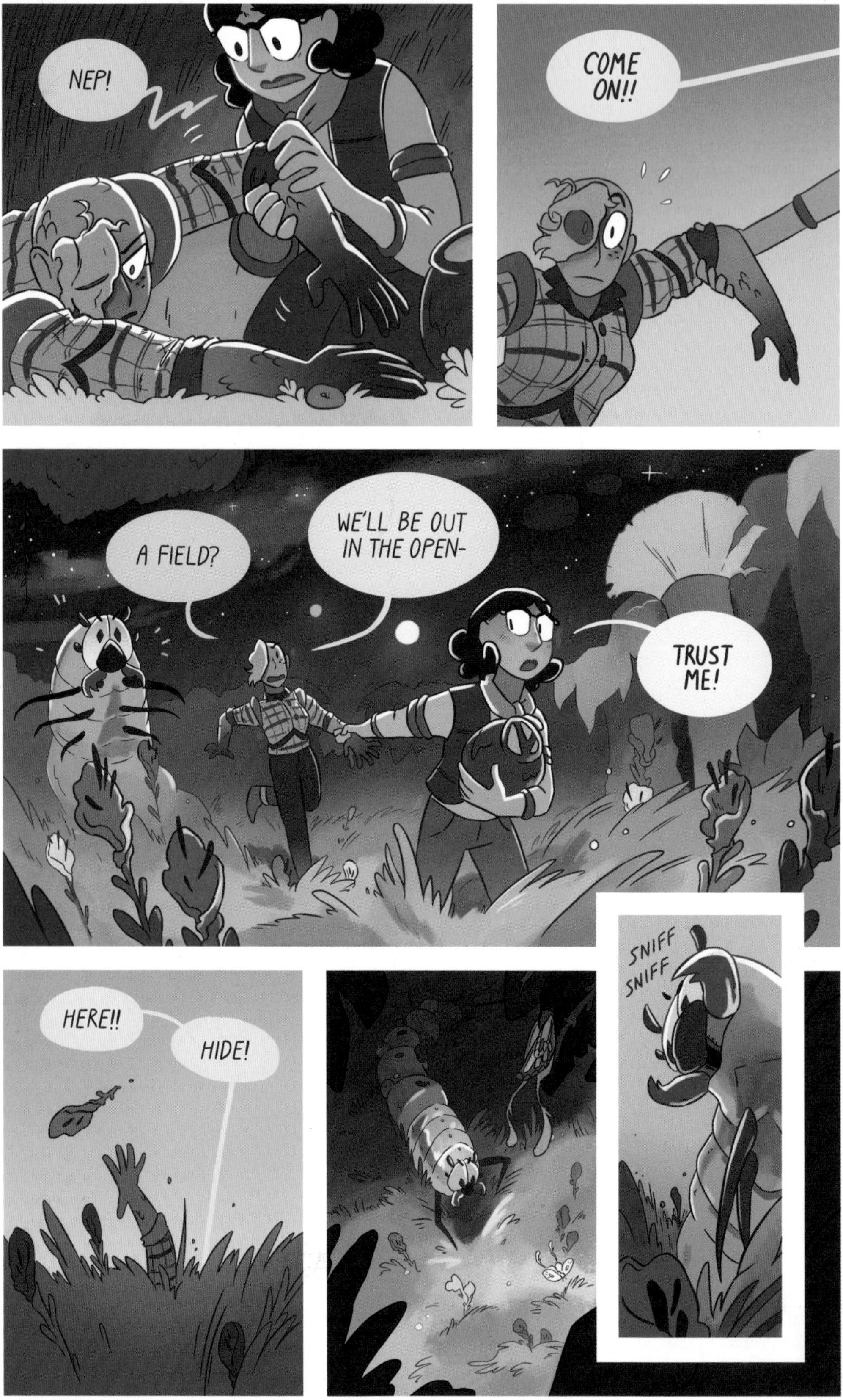
NEP!
COME ON!!
A FIELD?
WE'LL BE OUT IN THE OPEN-
TRUST ME!
HERE!!
HIDE!
SNIFF SNIFF

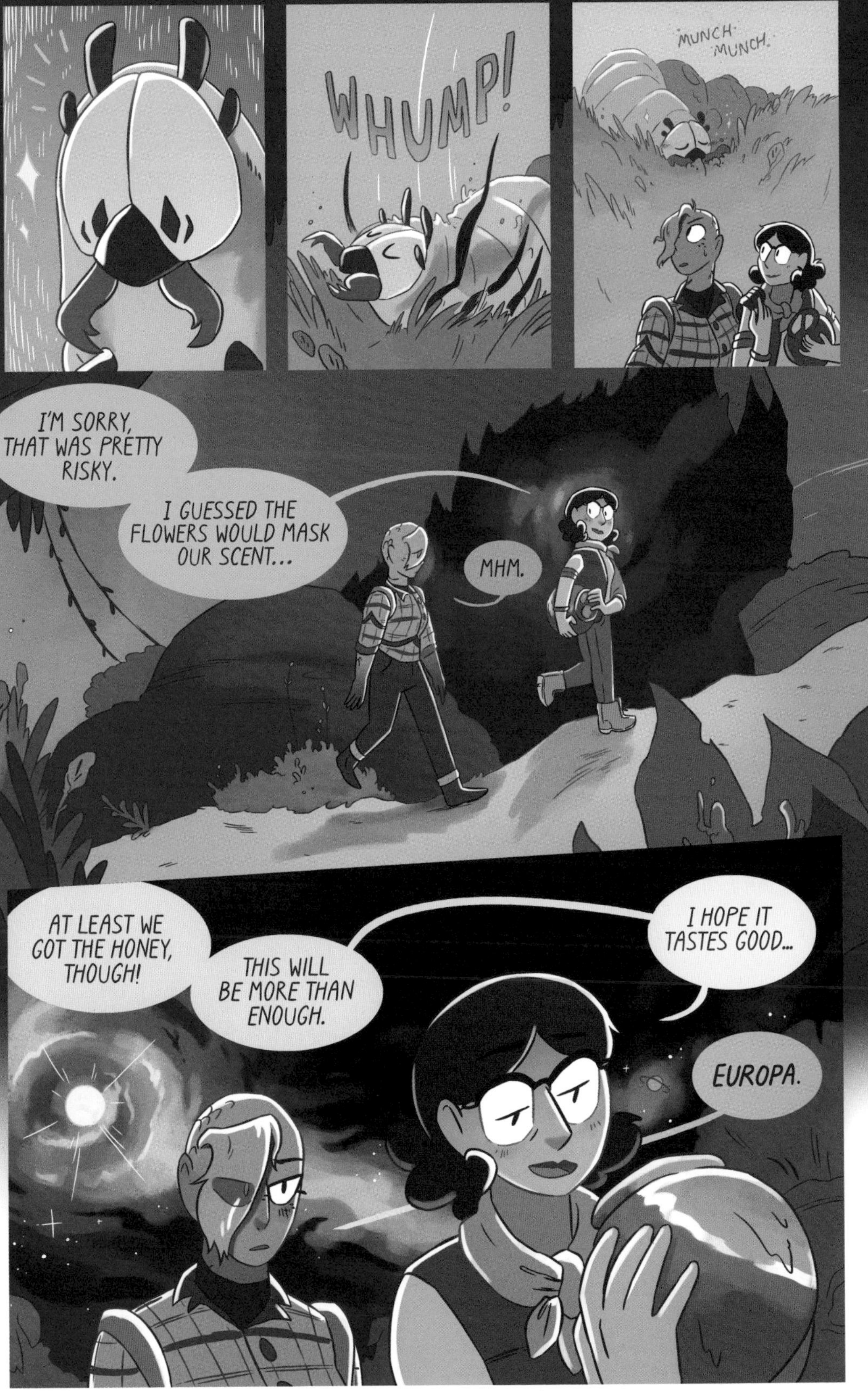
WHUMP!
MUNCH MUNCH
I'M SORRY, THAT WAS PRETTY RISKY.
I GUESSED THE FLOWERS WOULD MASK OUR SCENT...
MHM.
AT LEAST WE GOT THE HONEY, THOUGH!
THIS WILL BE MORE THAN ENOUGH.
I HOPE IT TASTES GOOD...
EUROPA.

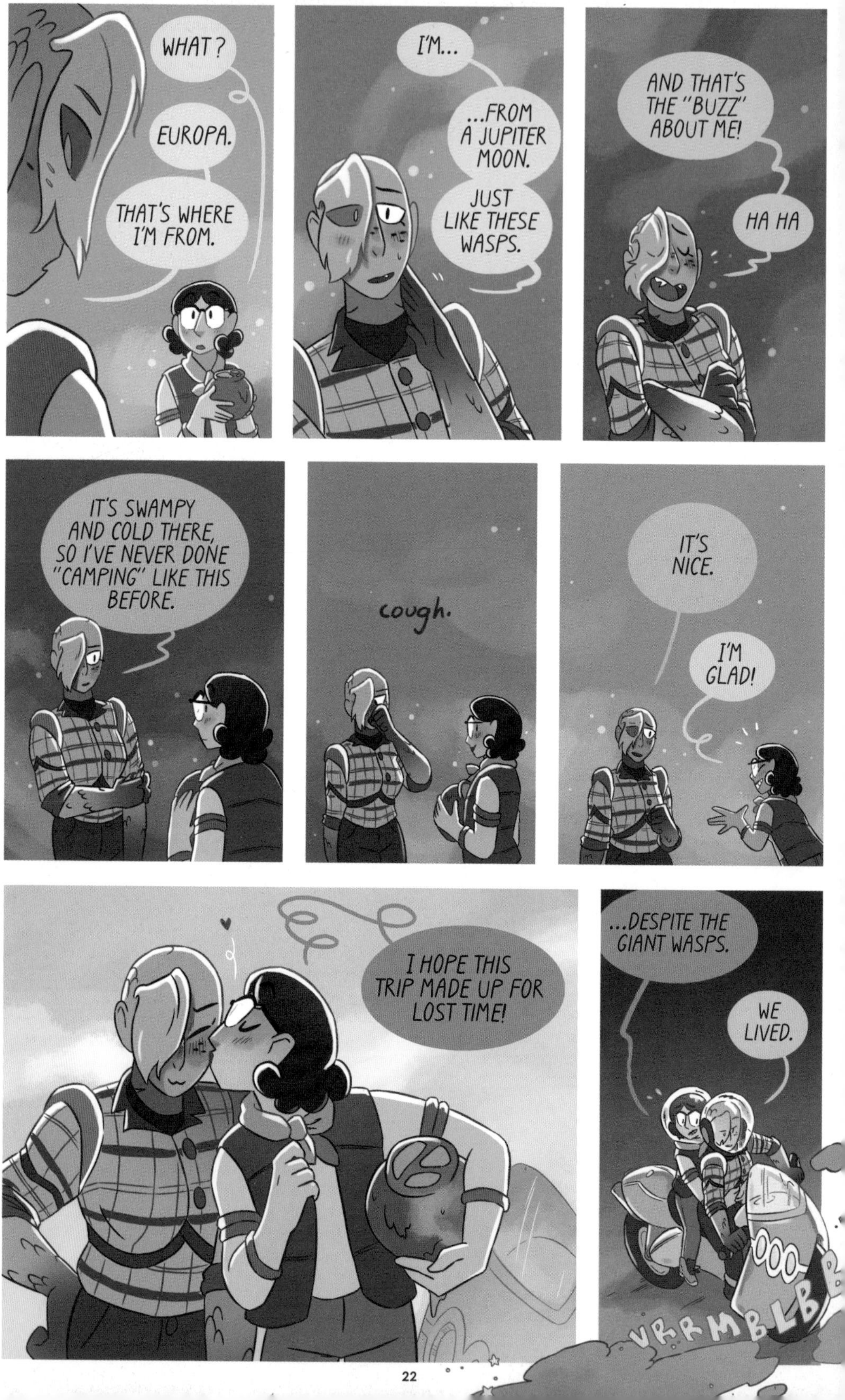
WHAT?
EUROPA.
THAT'S WHERE I'M FROM.
I'M...
...FROM A JUPITER MOON.
JUST LIKE THESE WASPS.
AND THAT'S THE "BUZZ" ABOUT ME!
HA HA
IT'S SWAMPY AND COLD THERE, SO I'VE NEVER DONE "CAMPING" LIKE THIS BEFORE.
cough.
IT'S NICE.
I'M GLAD!
I HOPE THIS TRIP MADE UP FOR LOST TIME!
...DESPITE THE GIANT WASPS.
WE LIVED.
VRRMBLB

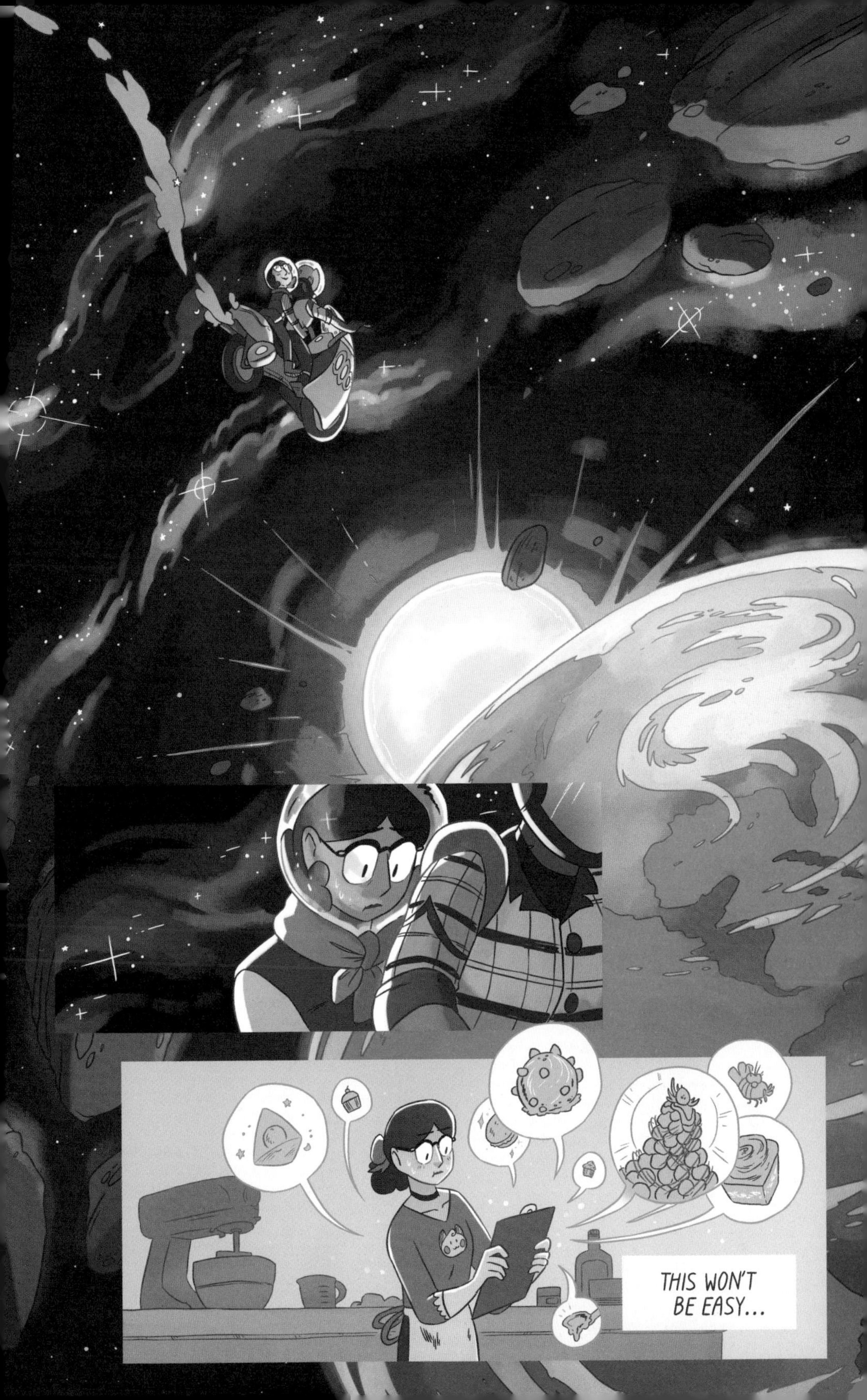
THIS WON'T BE EASY...

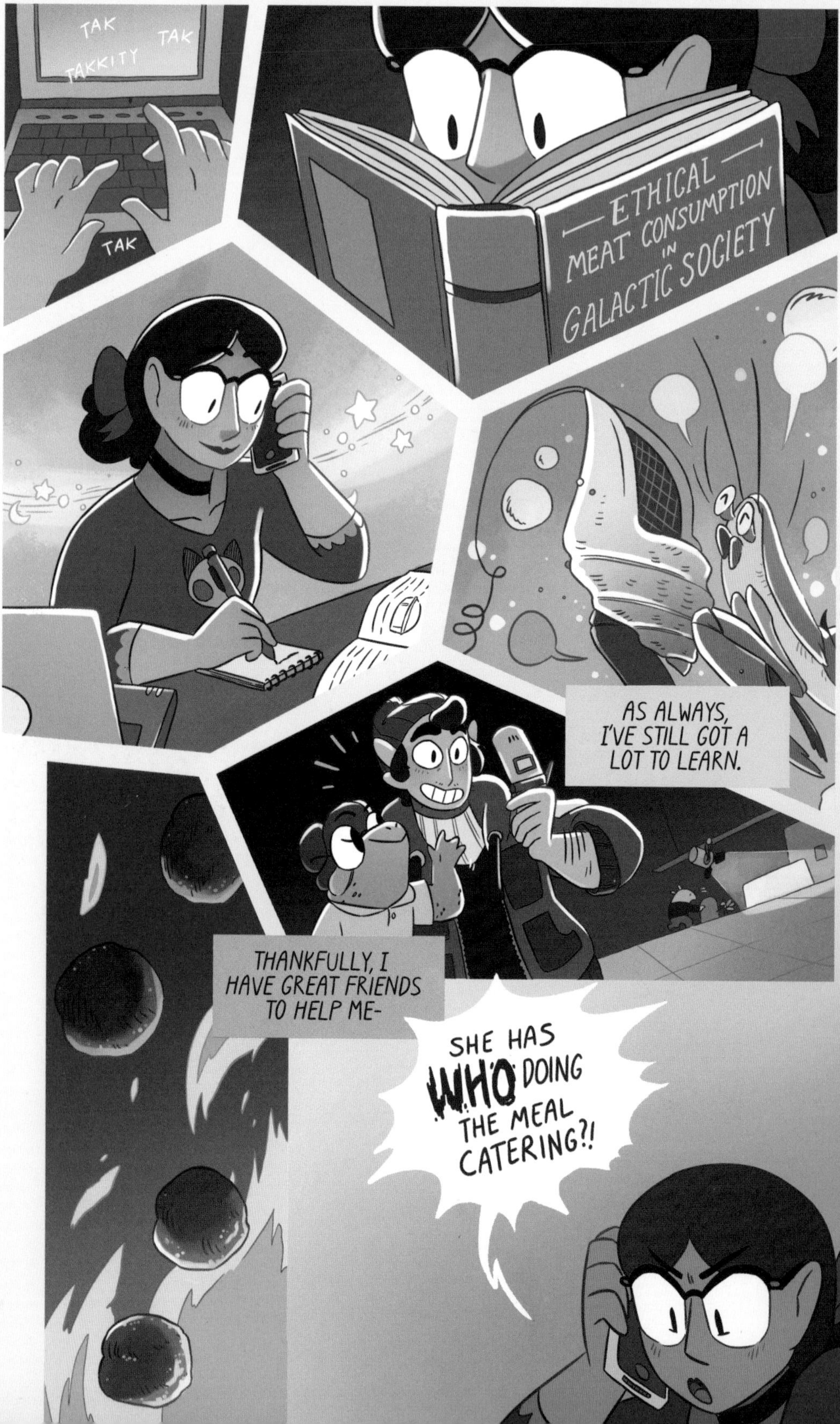
TAK
TAK
TAKKITY
TAK
ETHICAL MEAT CONSUMPTION IN GALACTIC SOCIETY
AS ALWAYS, I'VE STILL GOT A LOT TO LEARN.
THANKFULLY, I HAVE GREAT FRIENDS TO HELP ME-
SHE HAS WHO DOING THE MEAL CATERING?!

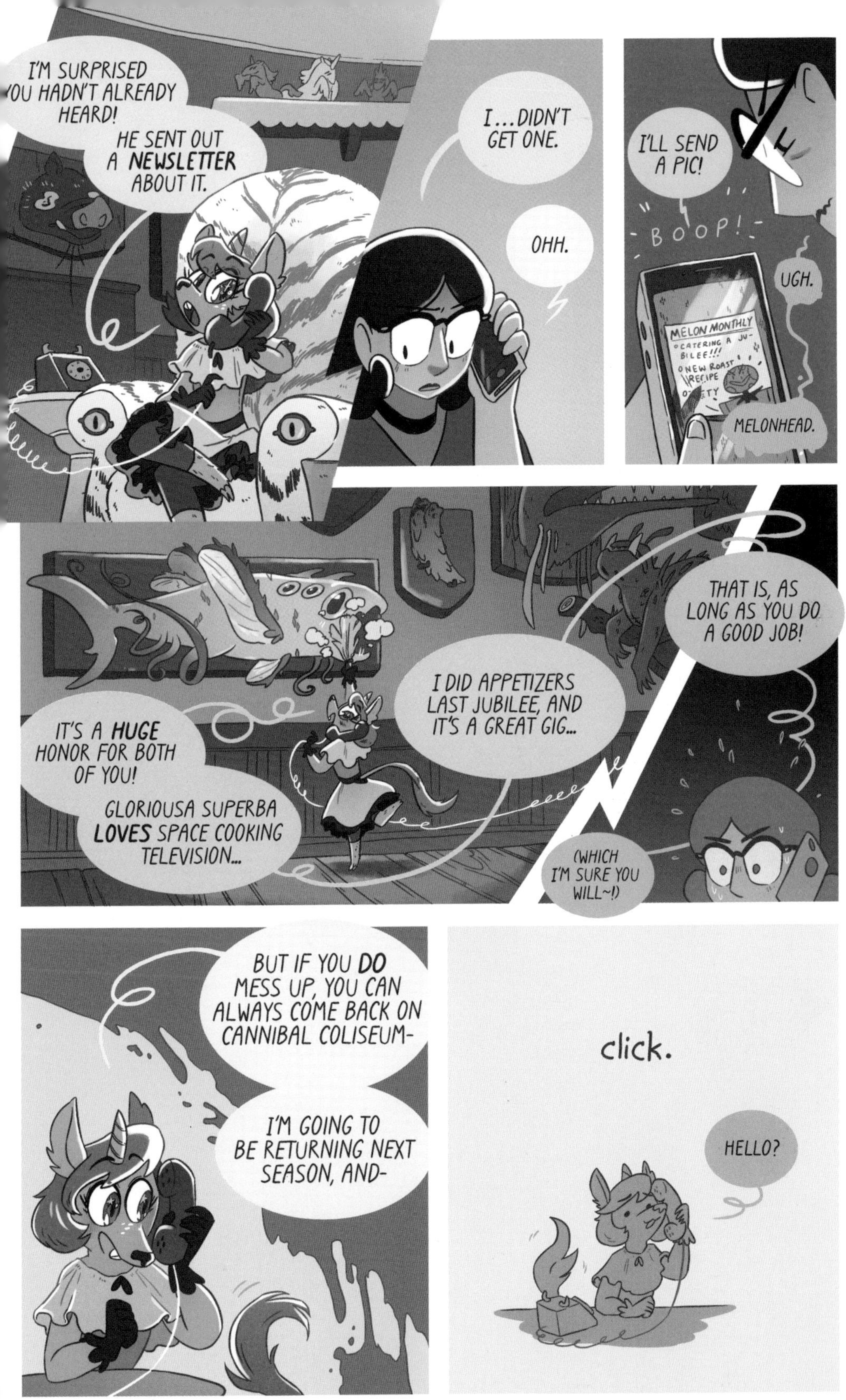

I'M SURPRISED YOU HADN'T ALREADY HEARD!
HE SENT OUT A **NEWSLETTER** ABOUT IT.
I...DIDN'T GET ONE.
OHH.
I'LL SEND A PIC!
BOOP!
UGH.
MELON MONTHLY
CATERING A JUBILEE!!!
NEW ROAST RECIPE
MELONHEAD.
IT'S A **HUGE** HONOR FOR BOTH OF YOU!
GLORIOUSA SUPERBA **LOVES** SPACE COOKING TELEVISION...
I DID APPETIZERS LAST JUBILEE, AND IT'S A GREAT GIG...
THAT IS, AS LONG AS YOU DO A GOOD JOB!
(WHICH I'M SURE YOU WILL~!)
BUT IF YOU **DO** MESS UP, YOU CAN ALWAYS COME BACK ON CANNIBAL COLISEUM-
I'M GOING TO BE RETURNING NEXT SEASON, AND-
click.
HELLO?

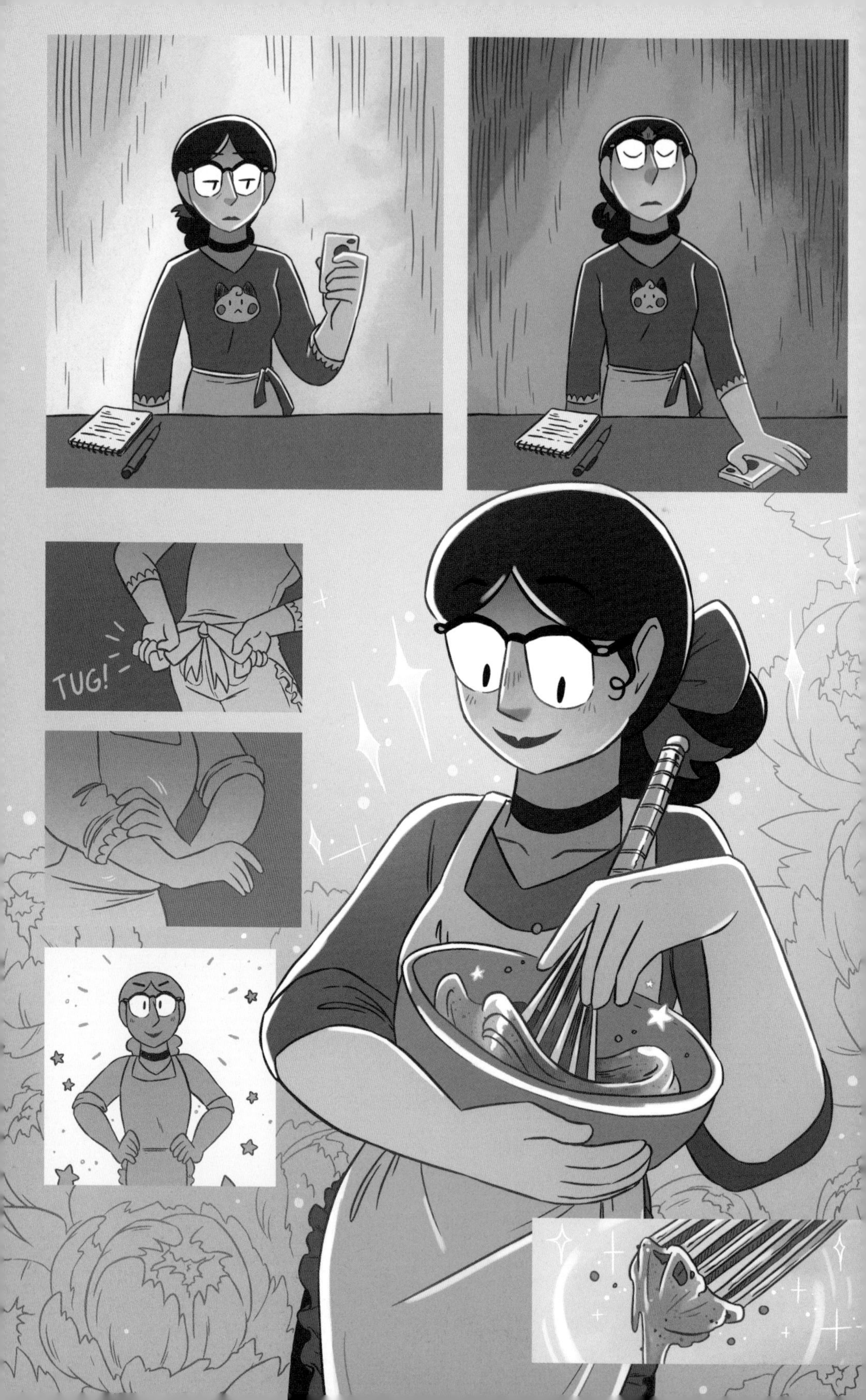
TUG!

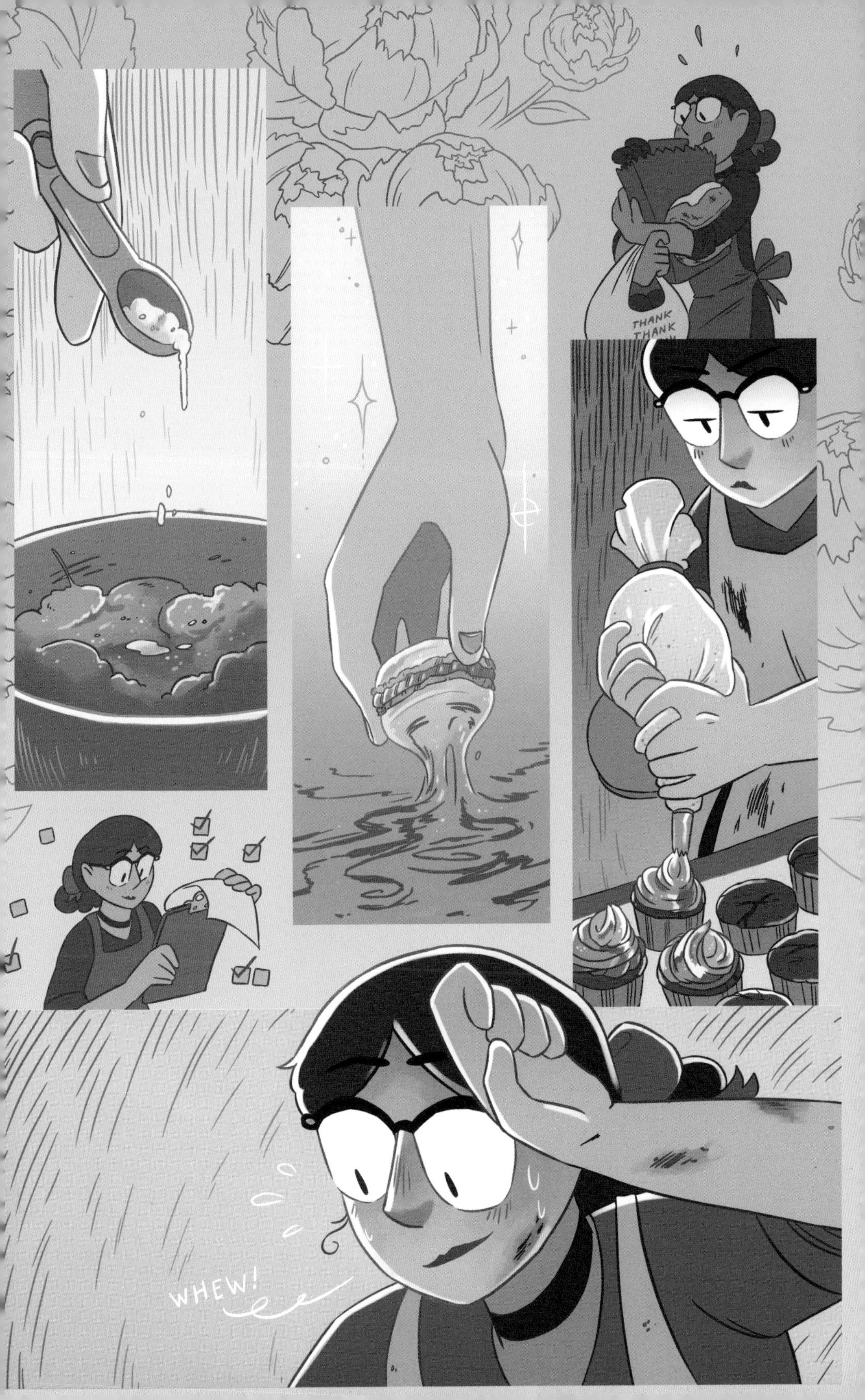
THANK
THANK
WHEW!

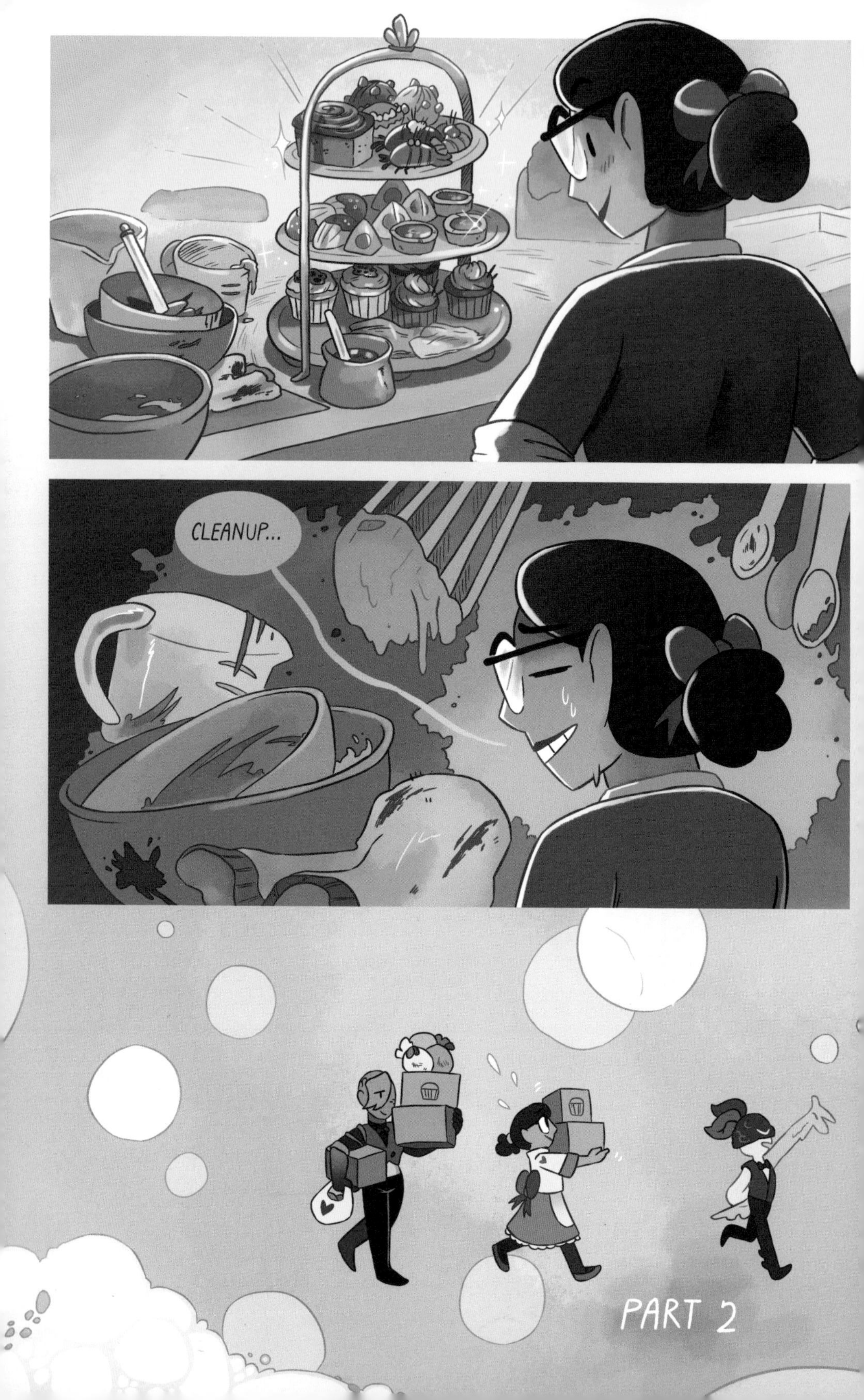
CLEANUP...
PART 2

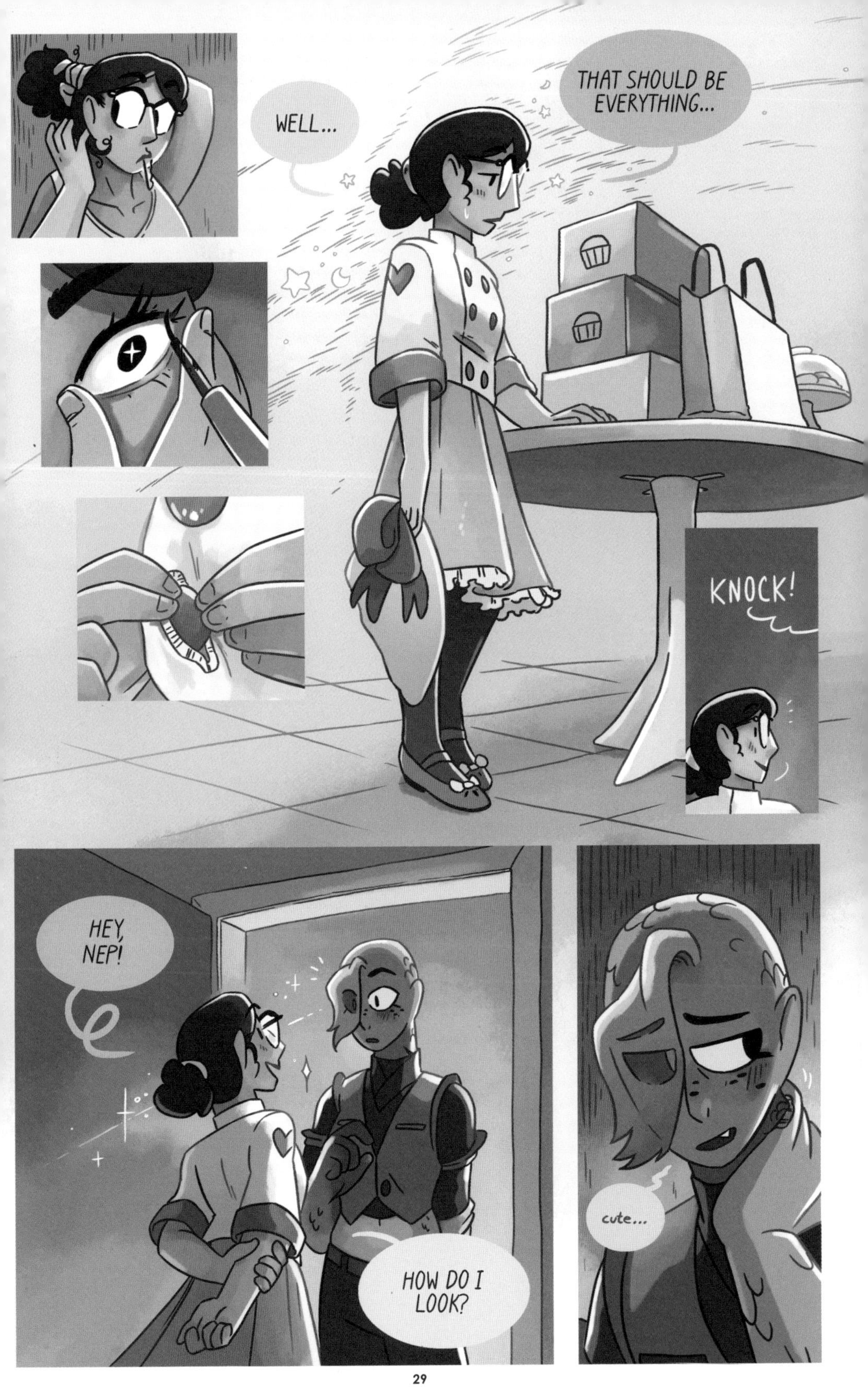
WELL...
THAT SHOULD BE EVERYTHING...
KNOCK!
HEY, NEP!
HOW DO I LOOK?
cute...

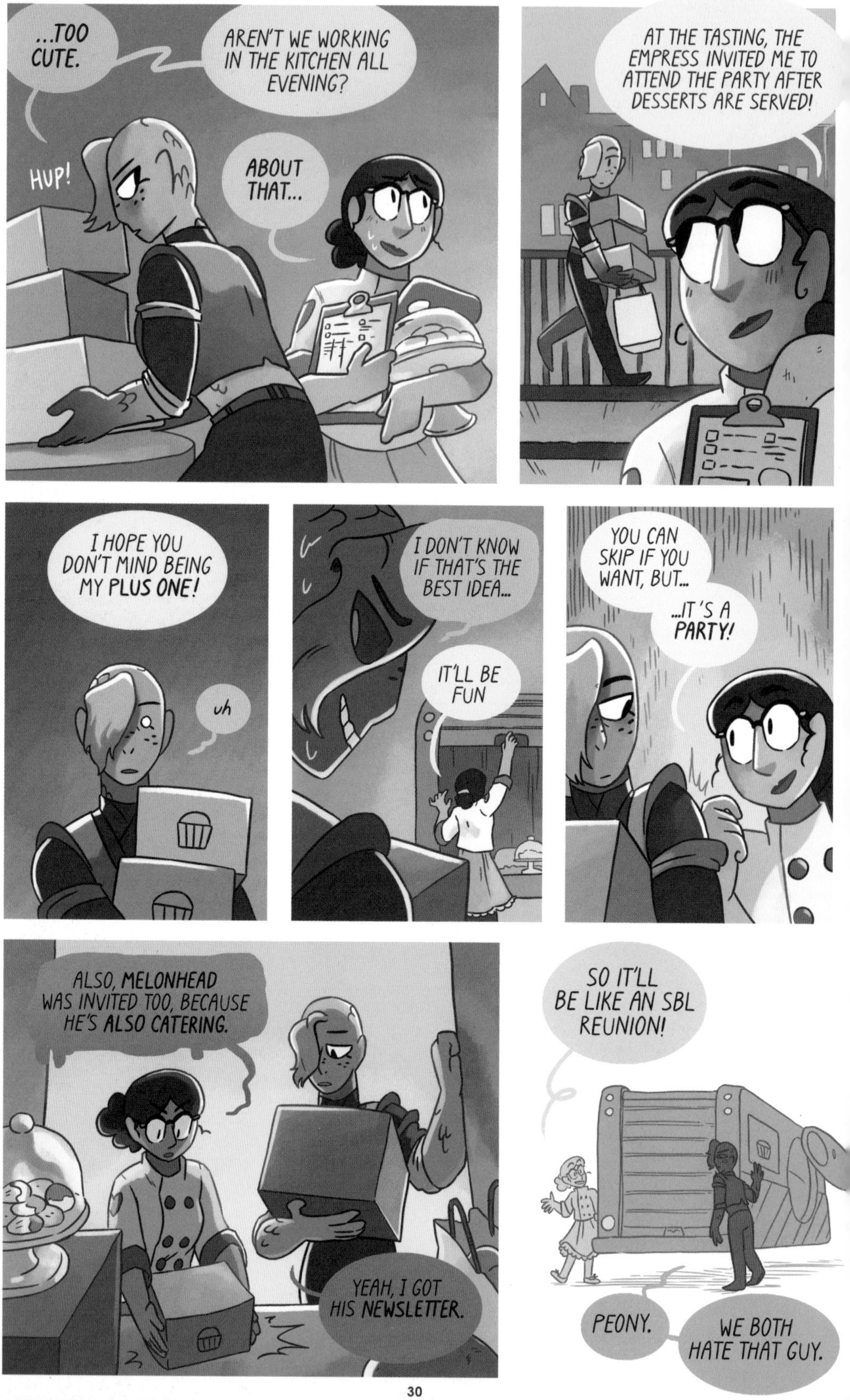
...TOO CUTE.
AREN'T WE WORKING IN THE KITCHEN ALL EVENING?
HUP!
ABOUT THAT...
AT THE TASTING, THE EMPRESS INVITED ME TO ATTEND THE PARTY AFTER DESSERTS ARE SERVED!
I HOPE YOU DON'T MIND BEING MY PLUS ONE!
uh
I DON'T KNOW IF THAT'S THE BEST IDEA...
IT'LL BE FUN
YOU CAN SKIP IF YOU WANT, BUT...
...IT'S A PARTY!
ALSO, MELONHEAD WAS INVITED TOO, BECAUSE HE'S ALSO CATERING.
YEAH, I GOT HIS NEWSLETTER.
SO IT'LL BE LIKE AN SBL REUNION!
PEONY.
WE BOTH HATE THAT GUY.

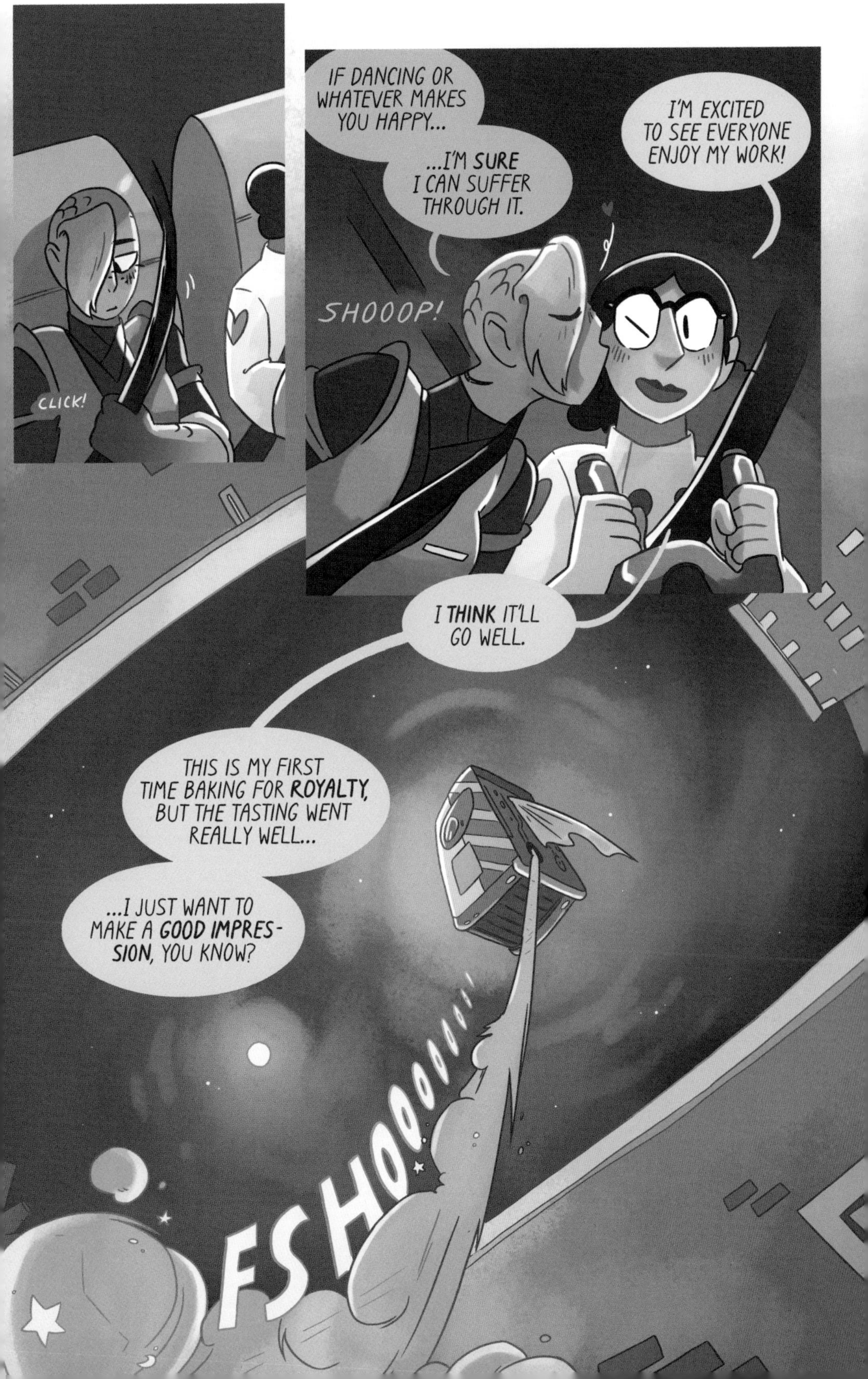
CLICK!
IF DANCING OR WHATEVER MAKES YOU HAPPY...
...I'M SURE I CAN SUFFER THROUGH IT.
SHOOOP!
I'M EXCITED TO SEE EVERYONE ENJOY MY WORK!
I THINK IT'LL GO WELL.
THIS IS MY FIRST TIME BAKING FOR ROYALTY, BUT THE TASTING WENT REALLY WELL...
...I JUST WANT TO MAKE A GOOD IMPRES-SION, YOU KNOW?
FSHOOOOOOOO

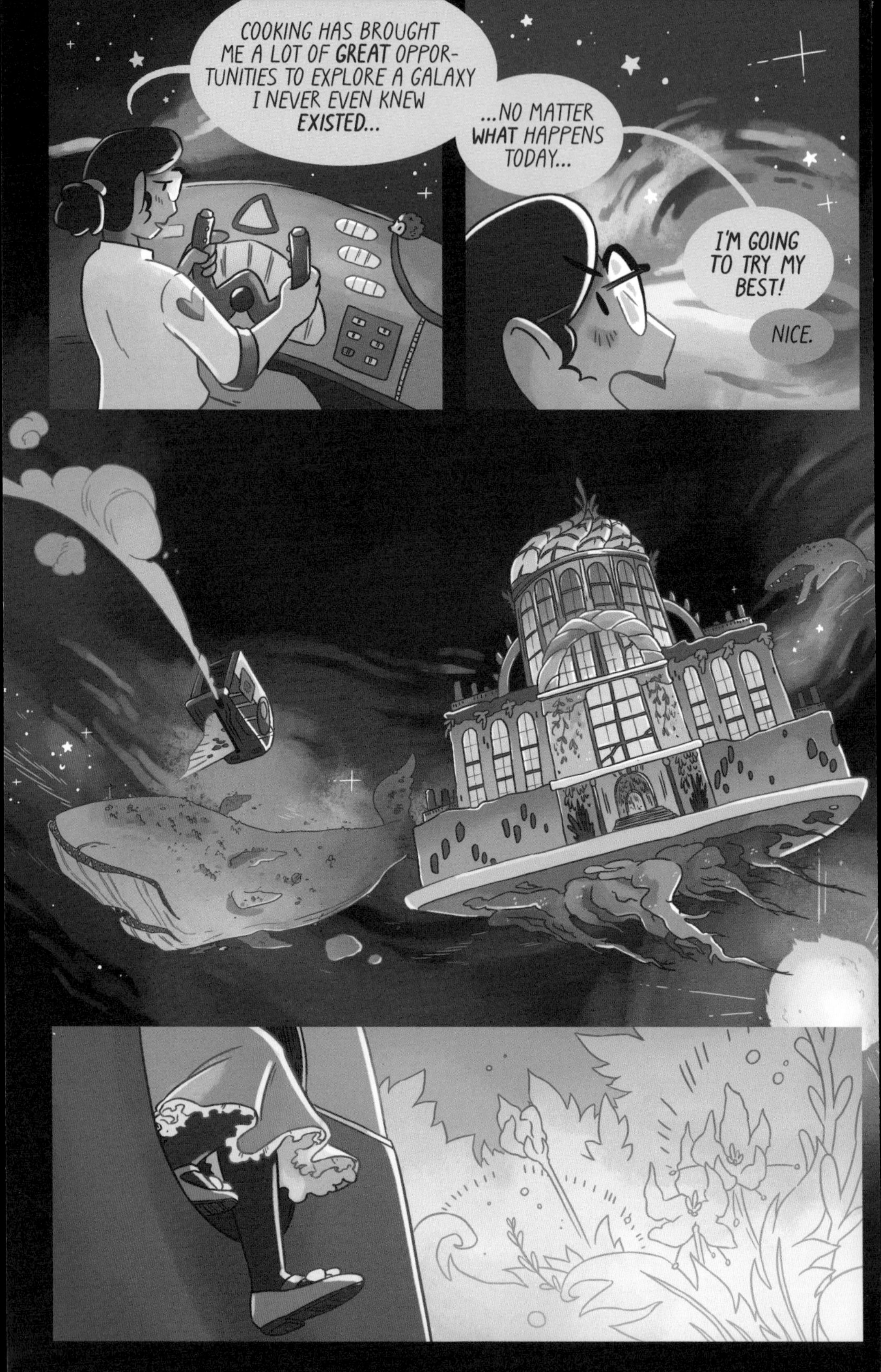
COOKING HAS BROUGHT ME A LOT OF GREAT OPPORTUNITIES TO EXPLORE A GALAXY I NEVER EVEN KNEW EXISTED...
...NO MATTER WHAT HAPPENS TODAY...
I'M GOING TO TRY MY BEST!
NICE.

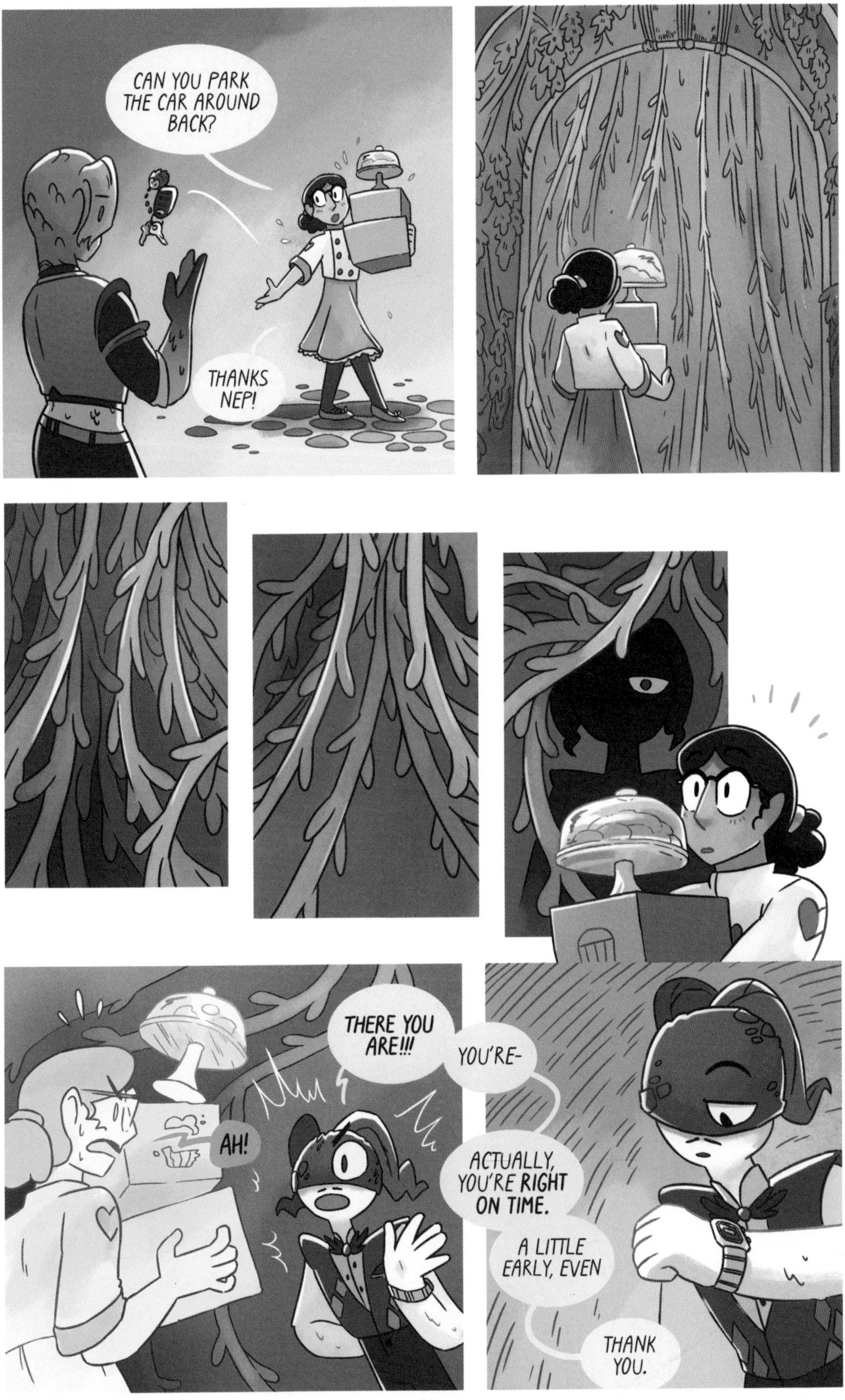
CAN YOU PARK THE CAR AROUND BACK?
THANKS NEP!
THERE YOU ARE!!!
YOU'RE-
AH!
ACTUALLY, YOU'RE RIGHT ON TIME.
A LITTLE EARLY, EVEN
THANK YOU.

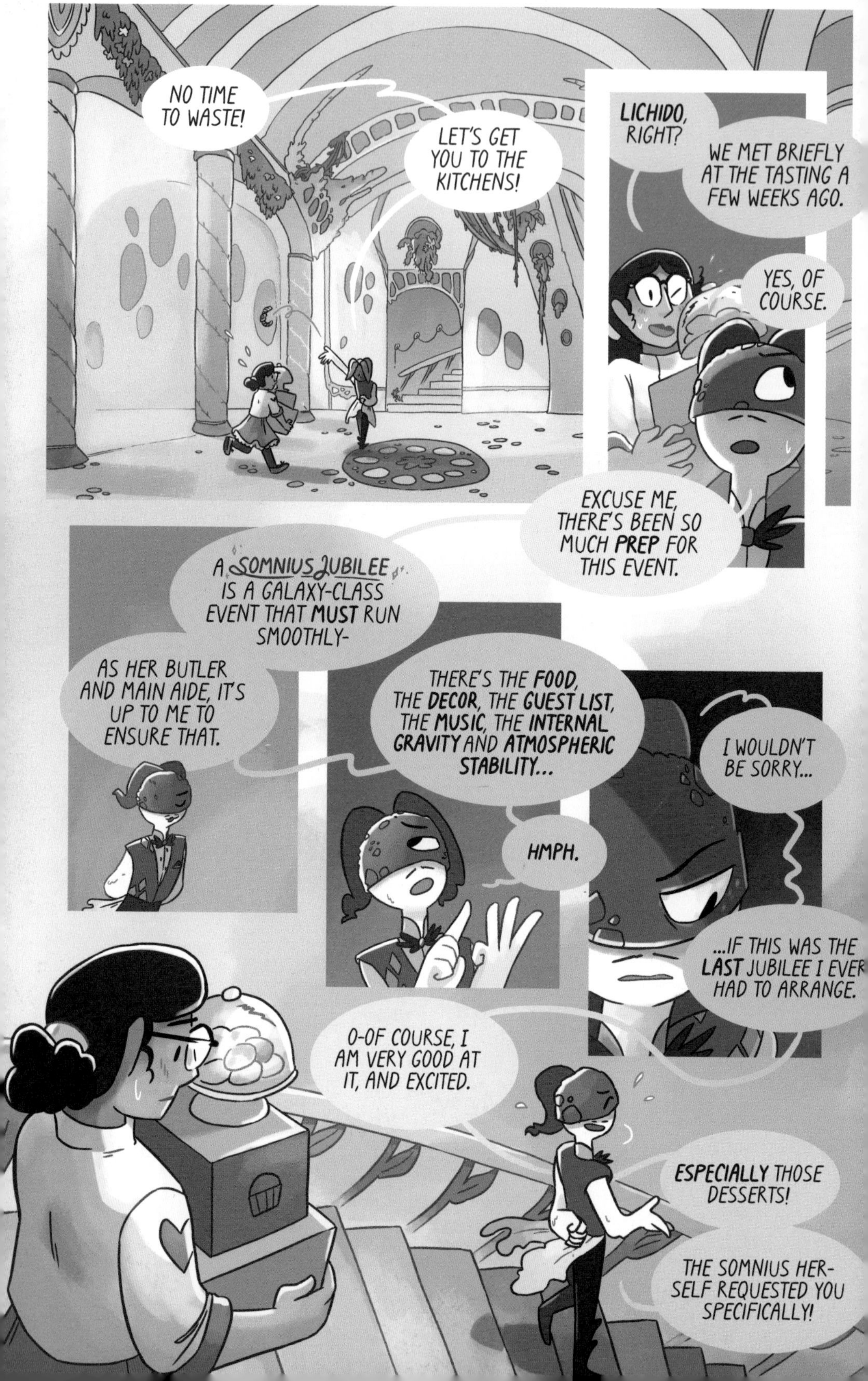
NO TIME TO WASTE!
LET'S GET YOU TO THE KITCHENS!
LICHIDO, RIGHT?
WE MET BRIEFLY AT THE TASTING A FEW WEEKS AGO.
YES, OF COURSE.
EXCUSE ME, THERE'S BEEN SO MUCH PREP FOR THIS EVENT.
A SOMNIUS JUBILEE IS A GALAXY-CLASS EVENT THAT MUST RUN SMOOTHLY-
AS HER BUTLER AND MAIN AIDE, IT'S UP TO ME TO ENSURE THAT.
THERE'S THE FOOD, THE DECOR, THE GUEST LIST, THE MUSIC, THE INTERNAL GRAVITY AND ATMOSPHERIC STABILITY...
HMPH.
I WOULDN'T BE SORRY...
...IF THIS WAS THE LAST JUBILEE I EVER HAD TO ARRANGE.
O-OF COURSE, I AM VERY GOOD AT IT, AND EXCITED.
ESPECIALLY THOSE DESSERTS!
THE SOMNIUS HER-SELF REQUESTED YOU SPECIFICALLY!

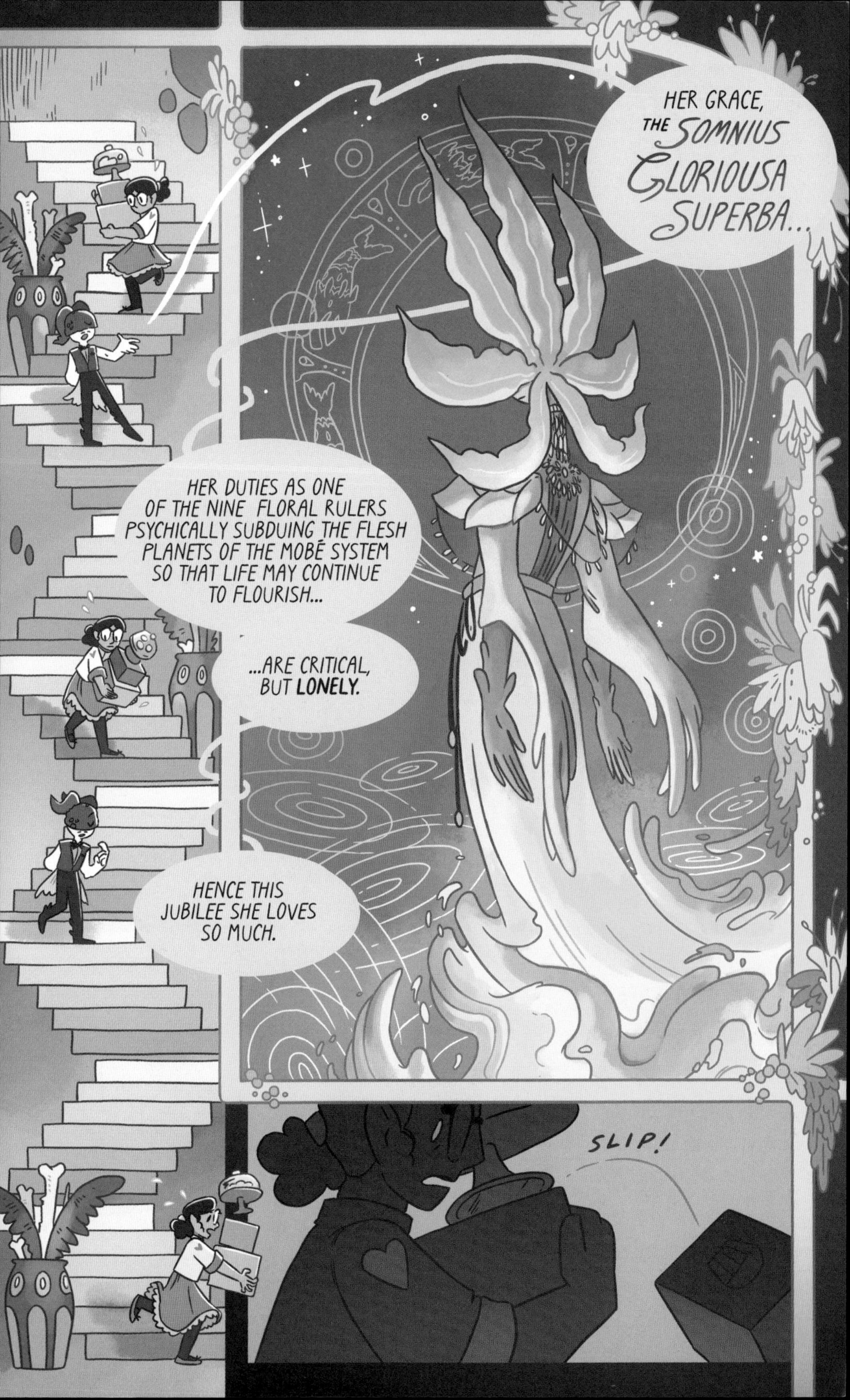
HER GRACE, THE SOMNIUS GLORIOUSA SUPERBA...
HER DUTIES AS ONE OF THE NINE FLORAL RULERS PSYCHICALLY SUBDUING THE FLESH PLANETS OF THE MOBĒ SYSTEM SO THAT LIFE MAY CONTINUE TO FLOURISH...
...ARE CRITICAL, BUT **LONELY.**
HENCE THIS JUBILEE SHE LOVES SO MUCH.
SLIP!

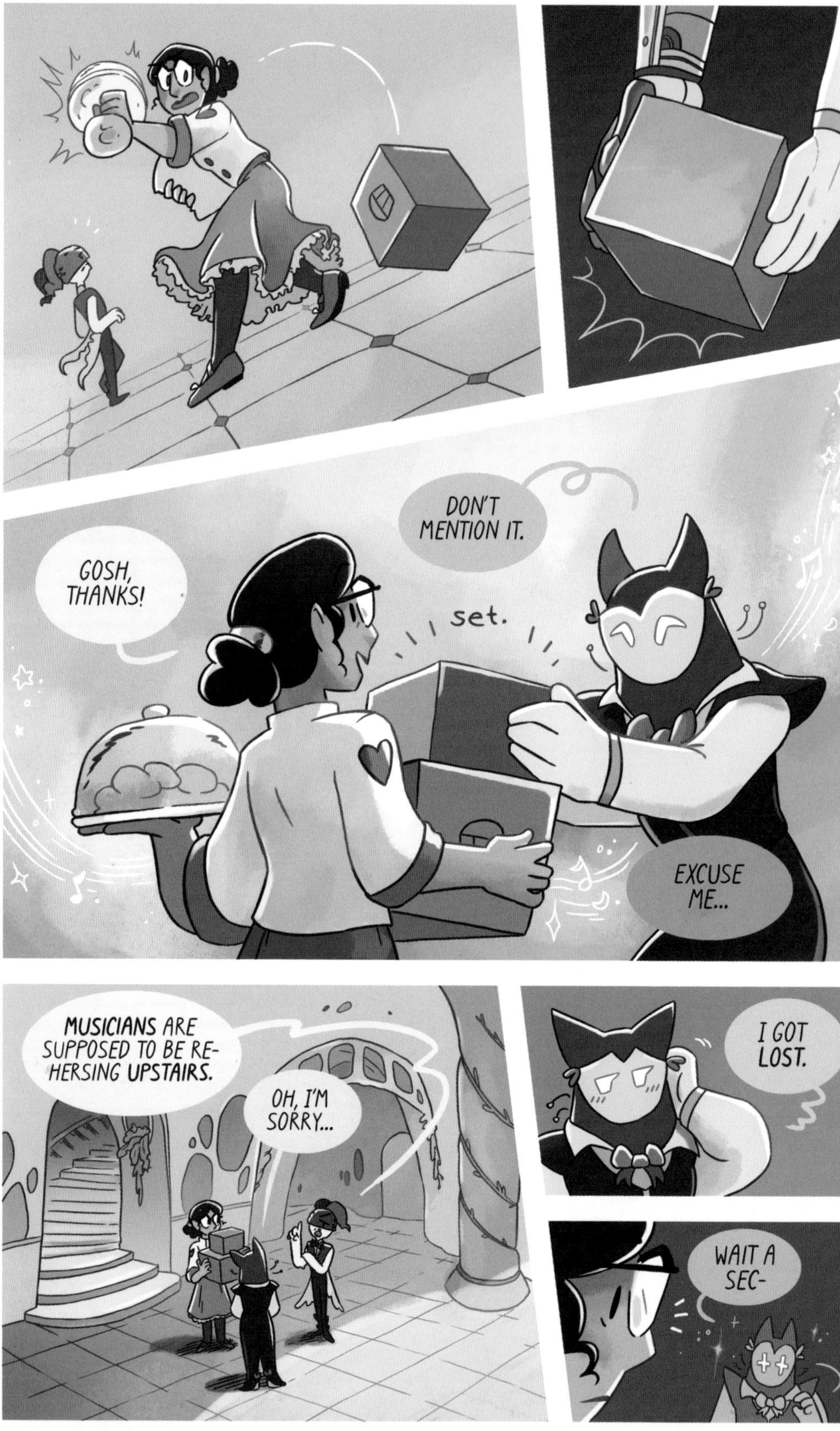
GOSH, THANKS!
DON'T MENTION IT.
set.
EXCUSE ME...
MUSICIANS ARE SUPPOSED TO BE RE-HERSING UPSTAIRS.
OH, I'M SORRY...
I GOT LOST.
WAIT A SEC-

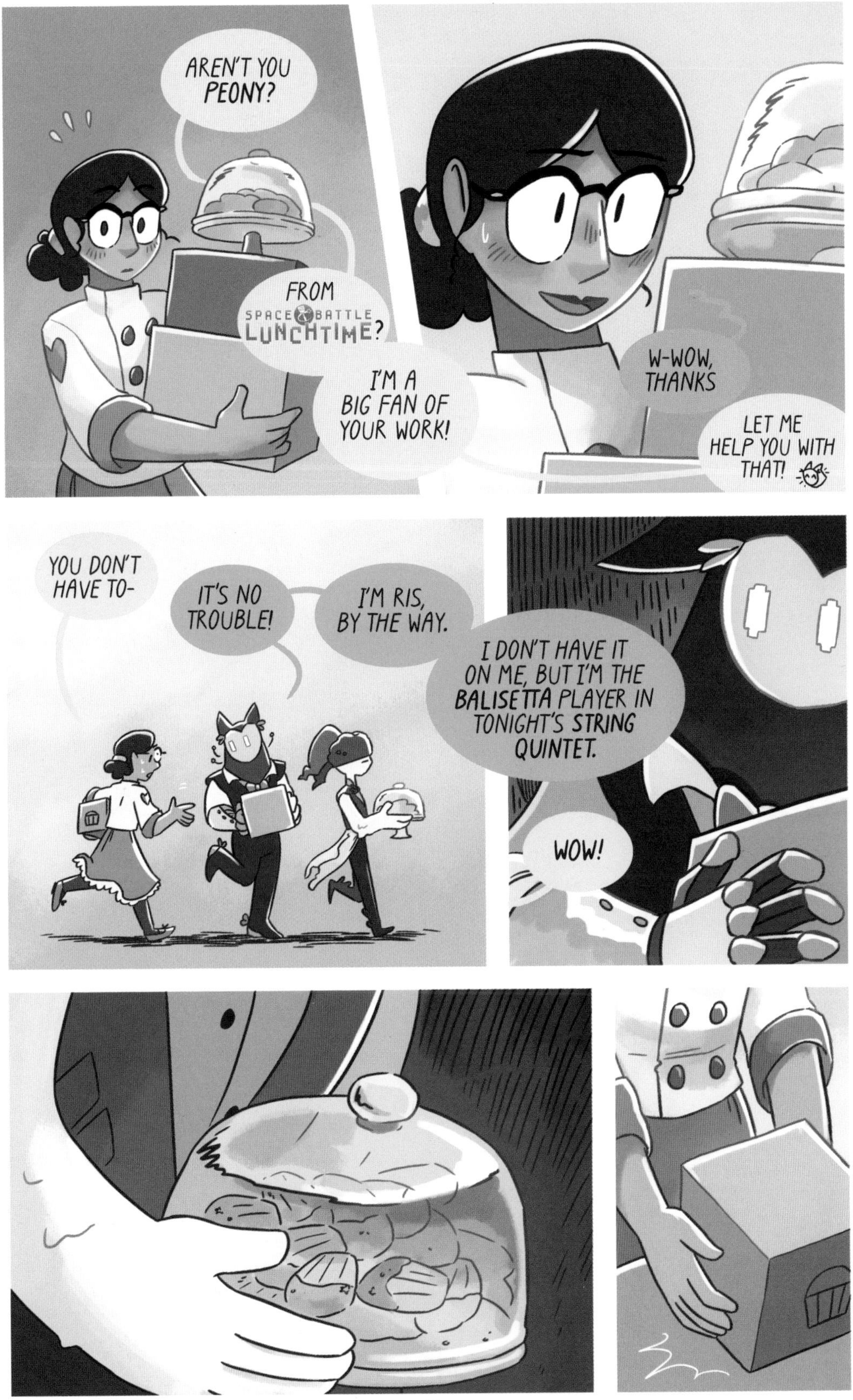
AREN'T YOU PEONY?
FROM SPACE BATTLE LUNCHTIME?
I'M A BIG FAN OF YOUR WORK!
W-WOW, THANKS
LET ME HELP YOU WITH THAT!
YOU DON'T HAVE TO-
IT'S NO TROUBLE!
I'M RIS, BY THE WAY.
I DON'T HAVE IT ON ME, BUT I'M THE BALISETTA PLAYER IN TONIGHT'S STRING QUINTET.
WOW!

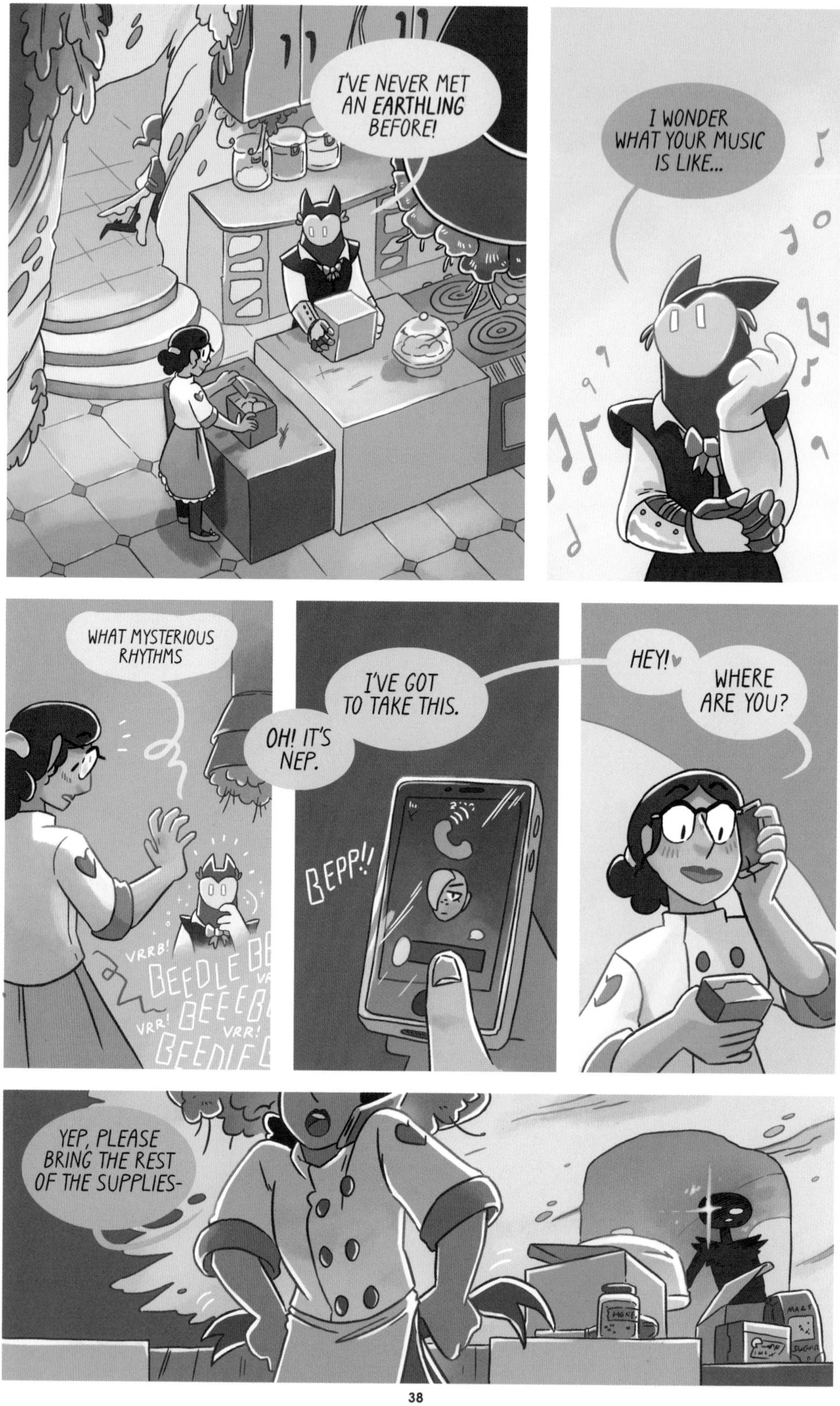
I'VE NEVER MET AN EARTHLING BEFORE!
I WONDER WHAT YOUR MUSIC IS LIKE...
WHAT MYSTERIOUS RHYTHMS
VRRB!
BEEDLE
VRR!
VRR!
OH! IT'S NEP.
I'VE GOT TO TAKE THIS.
BEPP!!
HEY!
WHERE ARE YOU?
YEP, PLEASE BRING THE REST OF THE SUPPLIES-

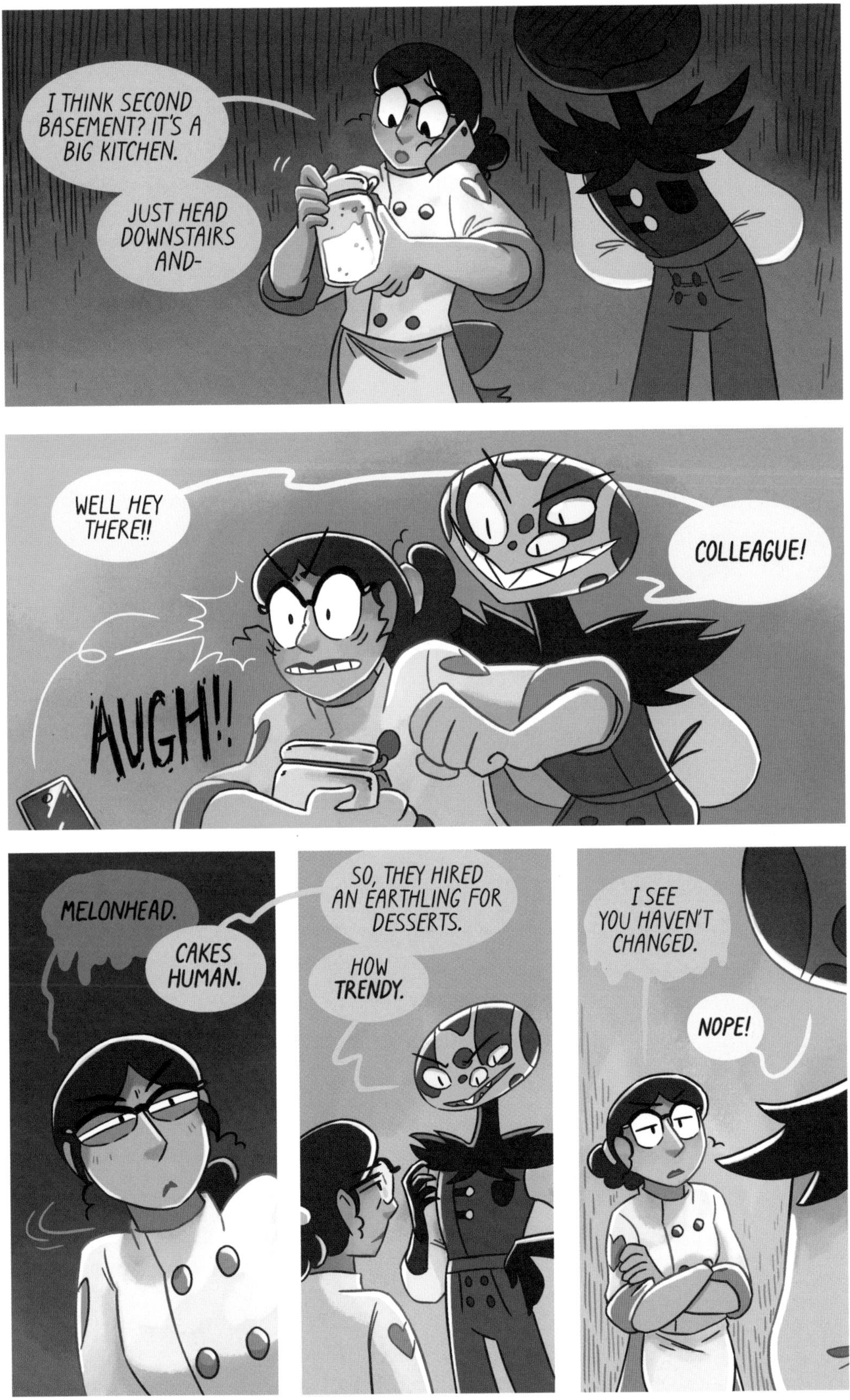
I THINK SECOND BASEMENT? IT'S A BIG KITCHEN.
JUST HEAD DOWNSTAIRS AND-
WELL HEY THERE!!
COLLEAGUE!
AUGH!!
MELONHEAD.
CAKES HUMAN.
SO, THEY HIRED AN EARTHLING FOR DESSERTS.
HOW TRENDY.
I SEE YOU HAVEN'T CHANGED.
NOPE!

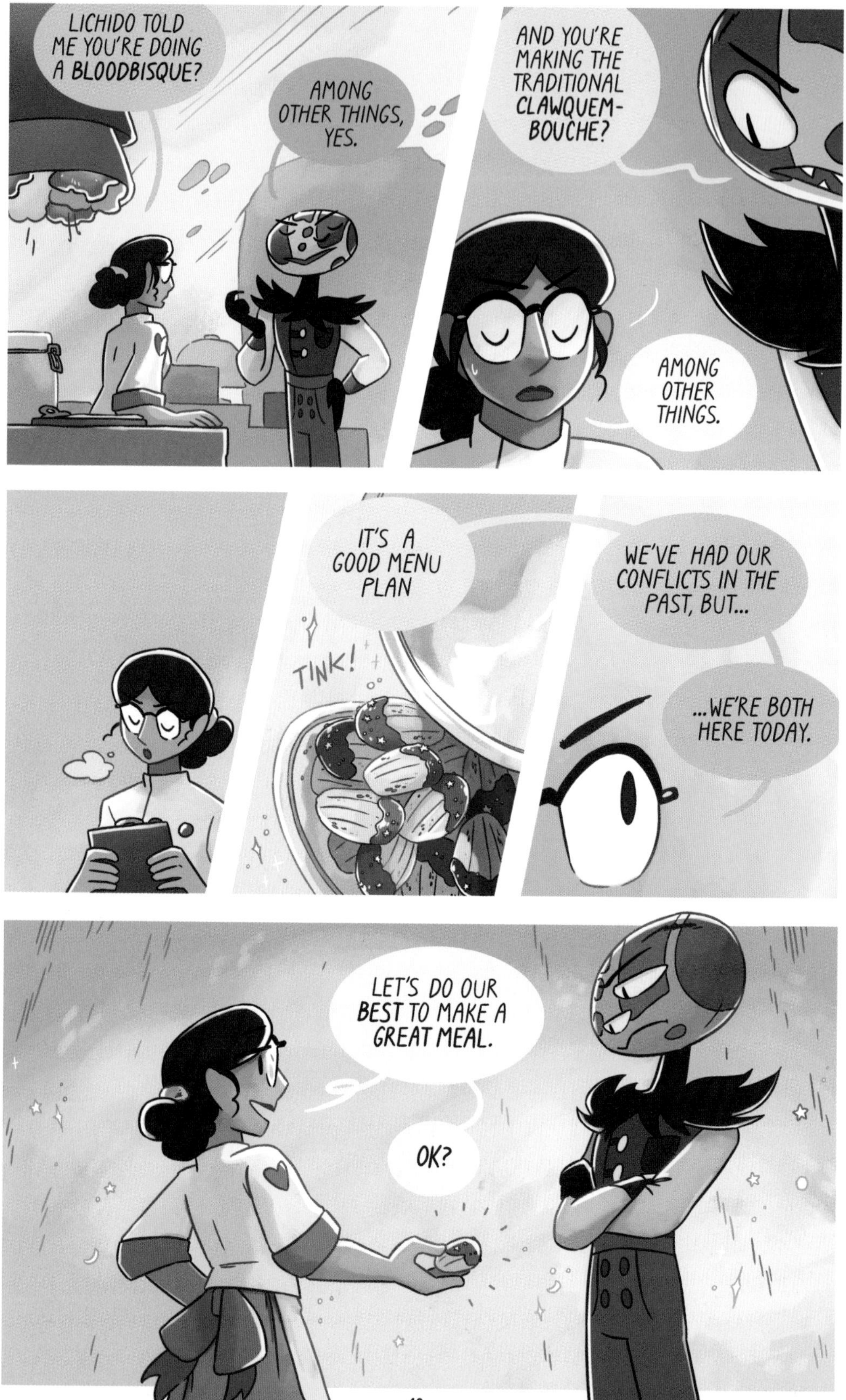
LICHIDO TOLD ME YOU'RE DOING A BLOODBISQUE?
AMONG OTHER THINGS, YES.
AND YOU'RE MAKING THE TRADITIONAL CLAWQUEM-BOUCHE?
AMONG OTHER THINGS.
IT'S A GOOD MENU PLAN
TINK!
WE'VE HAD OUR CONFLICTS IN THE PAST, BUT...
...WE'RE BOTH HERE TODAY.
LET'S DO OUR BEST TO MAKE A GREAT MEAL.
OK?

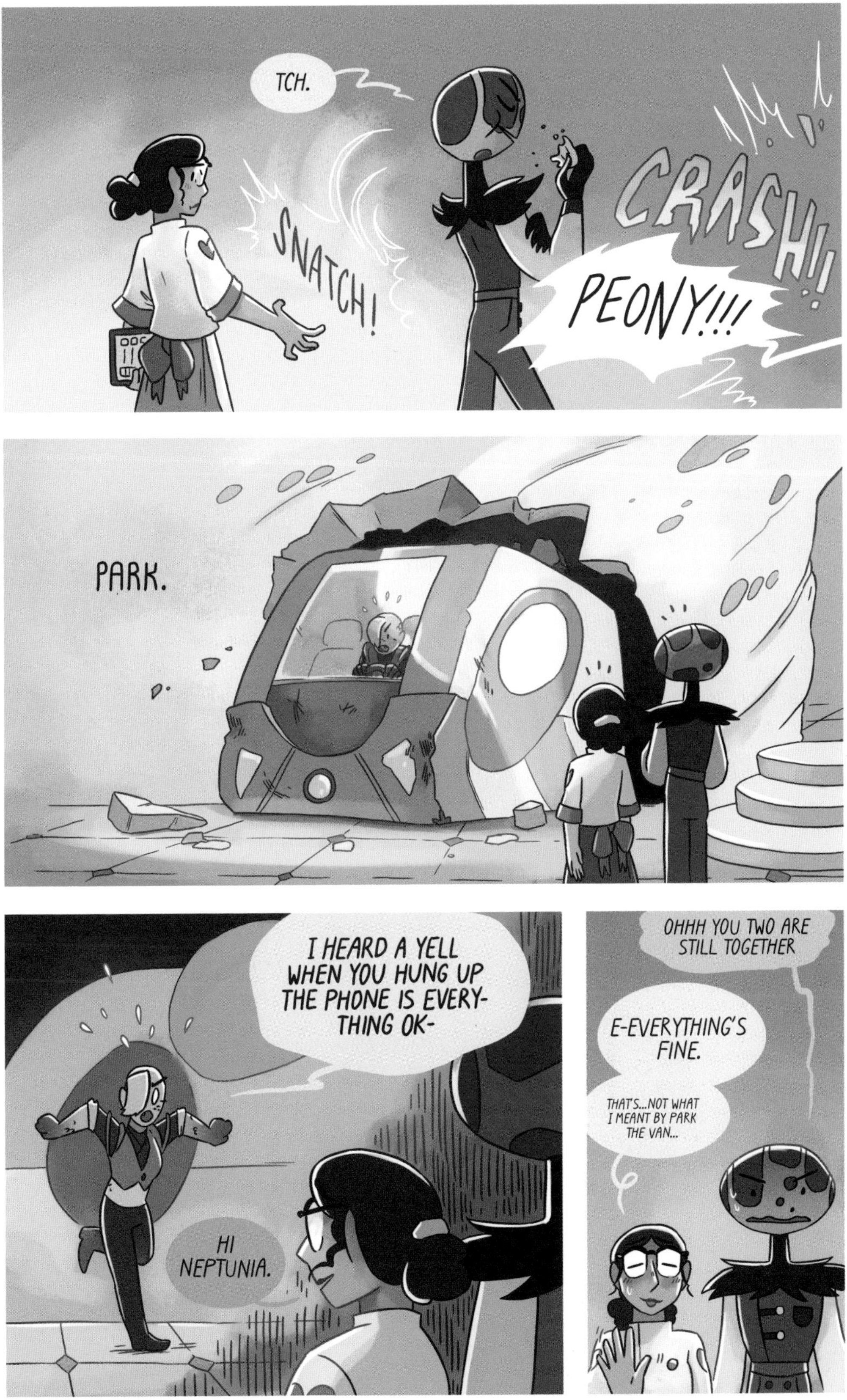
TCH.
SNATCH!
CRASH!!
PEONY!!!
PARK.
I HEARD A YELL WHEN YOU HUNG UP THE PHONE IS EVERY-THING OK-
HI NEPTUNIA.
OHHH YOU TWO ARE STILL TOGETHER
E-EVERYTHING'S FINE.
THAT'S...NOT WHAT I MEANT BY PARK THE VAN...

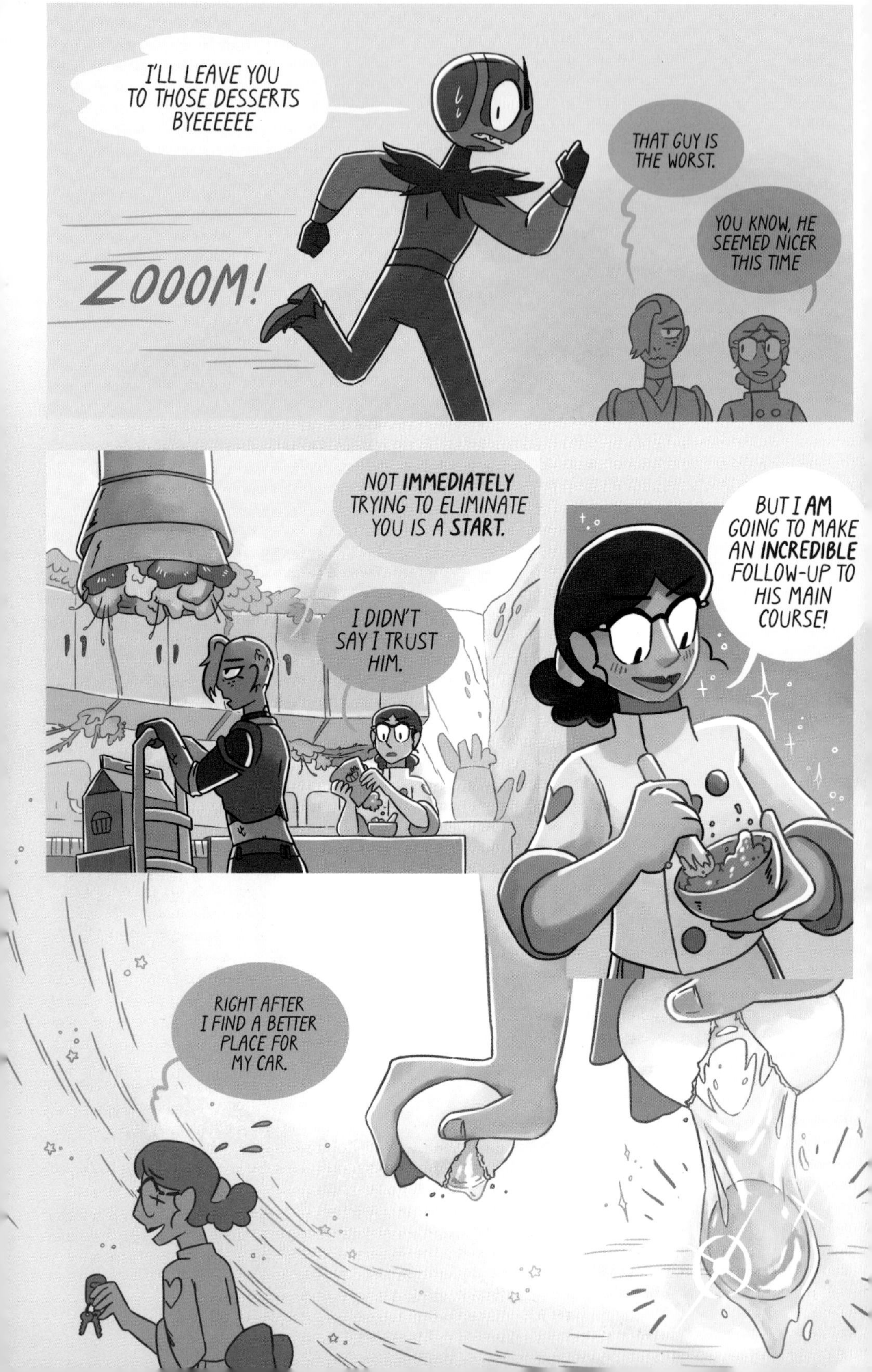
I'LL LEAVE YOU TO THOSE DESSERTS BYEEEEEE
ZOOOM!
THAT GUY IS THE WORST.
YOU KNOW, HE SEEMED NICER THIS TIME
NOT **IMMEDIATELY** TRYING TO ELIMINATE YOU IS A **START.**
I DIDN'T SAY I TRUST HIM.
BUT I **AM** GOING TO MAKE AN **INCREDIBLE** FOLLOW-UP TO HIS MAIN COURSE!
RIGHT AFTER I FIND A BETTER PLACE FOR MY CAR.

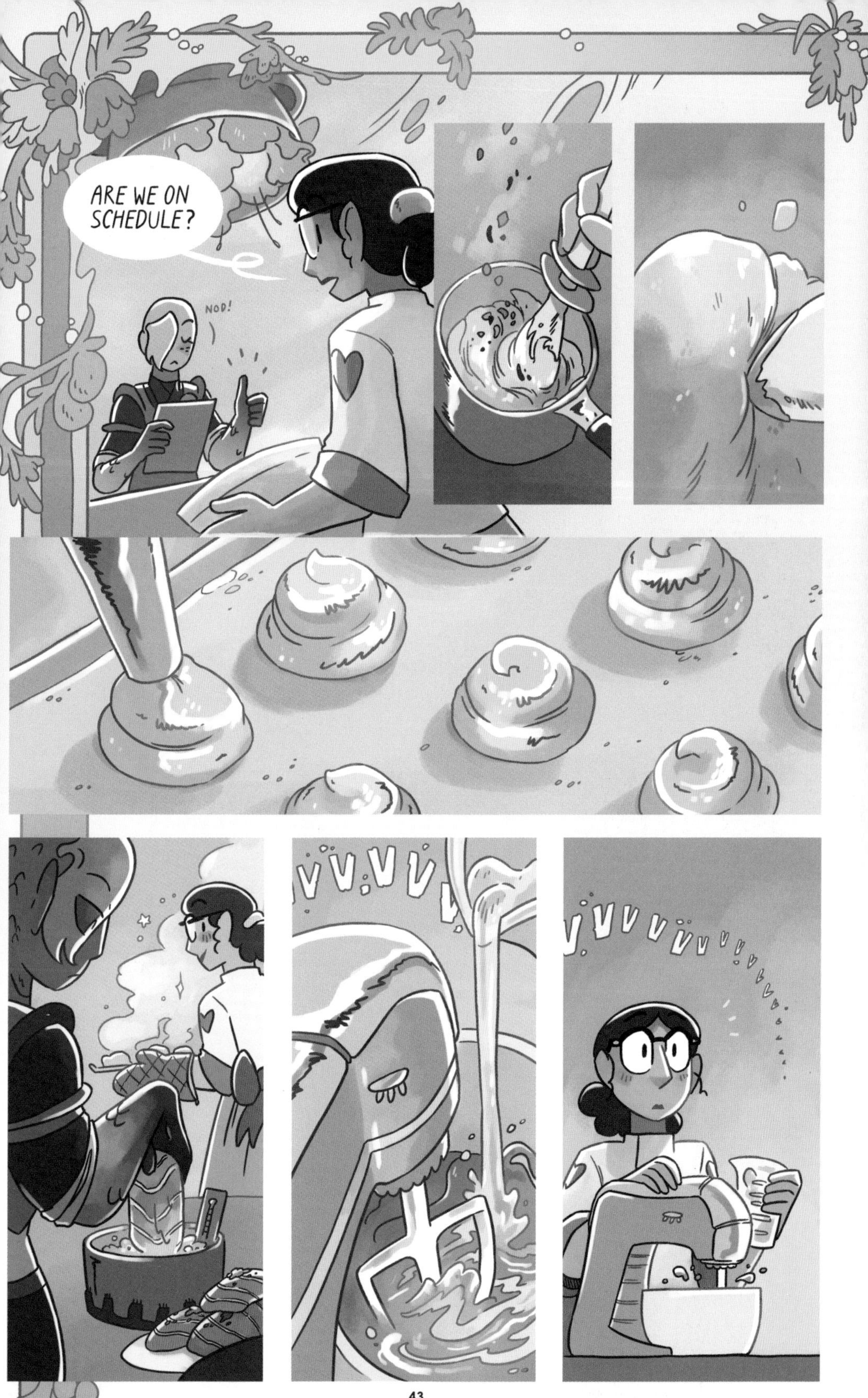
ARE WE ON SCHEDULE?
NOD!

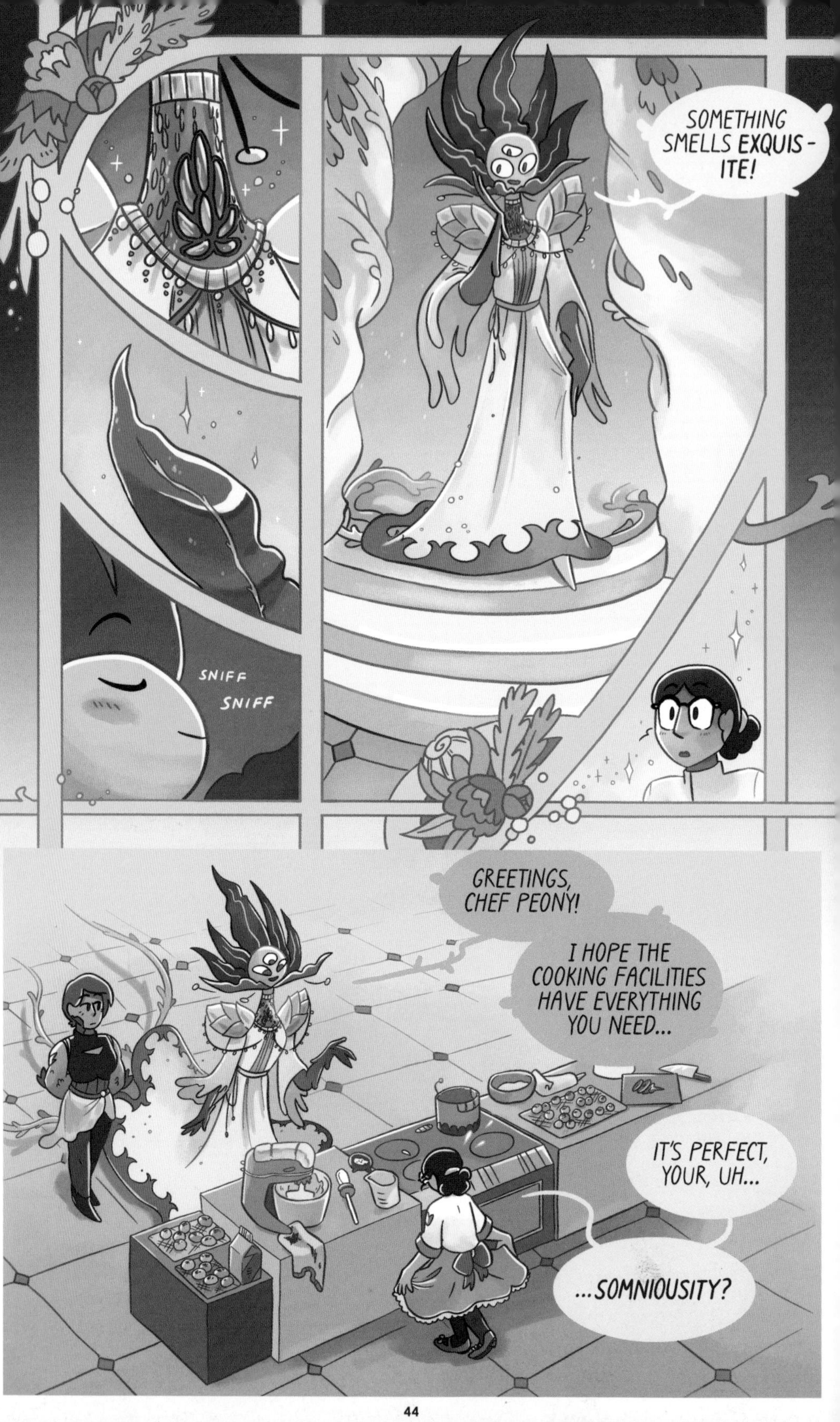
SOMETHING SMELLS EXQUIS-ITE!
SNIFF SNIFF
GREETINGS, CHEF PEONY!
I HOPE THE COOKING FACILITIES HAVE EVERYTHING YOU NEED...
IT'S PERFECT, YOUR, UH...
...SOMNIOUSITY?

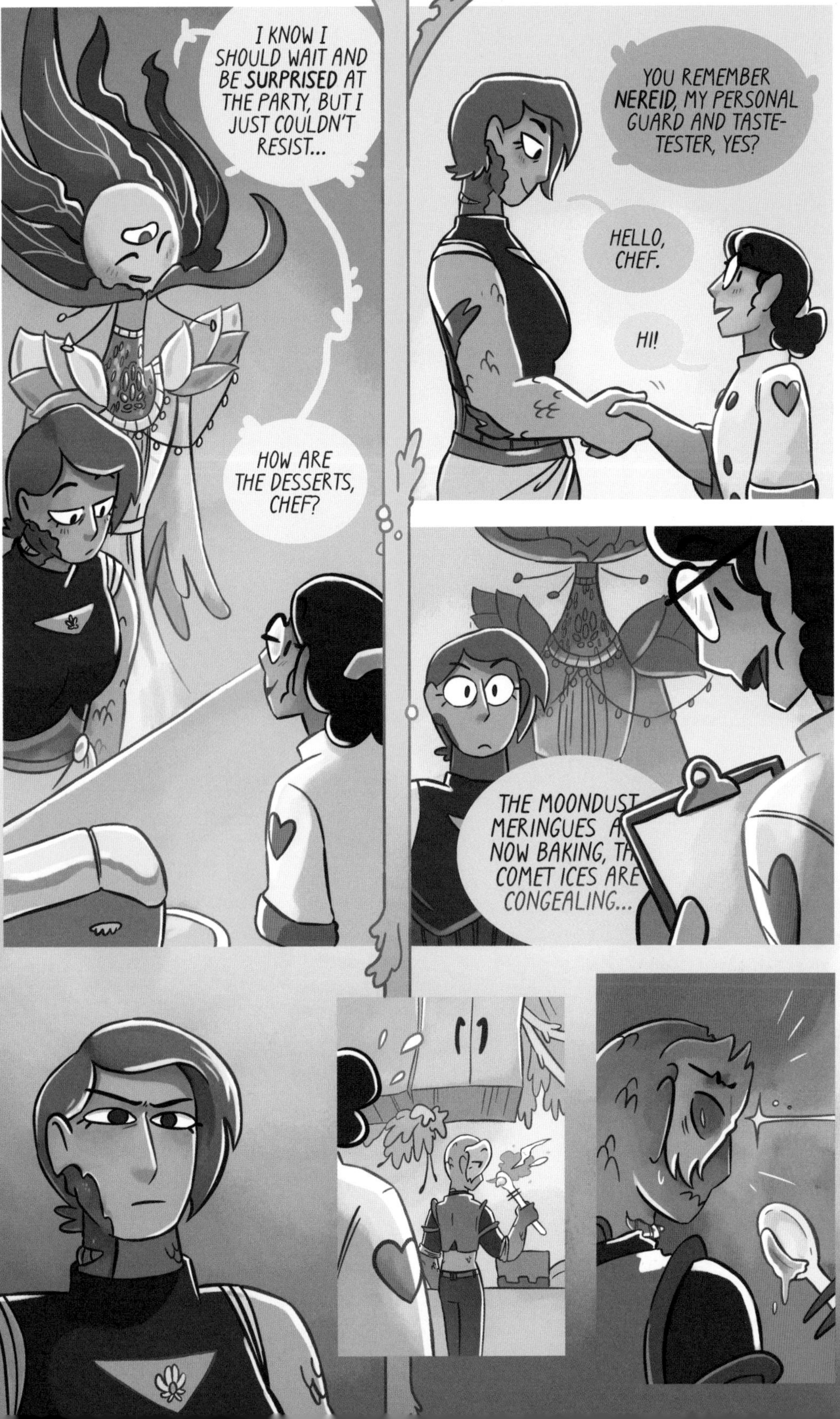
I KNOW I SHOULD WAIT AND BE **SURPRISED** AT THE PARTY, BUT I JUST COULDN'T RESIST...
HOW ARE THE DESSERTS, CHEF?
YOU REMEMBER **NEREID**, MY PERSONAL GUARD AND TASTE-TESTER, YES?
HELLO, CHEF.
HI!
THE MOONDUST MERINGUES A NOW BAKING, TH COMET ICES ARE CONGEALING...

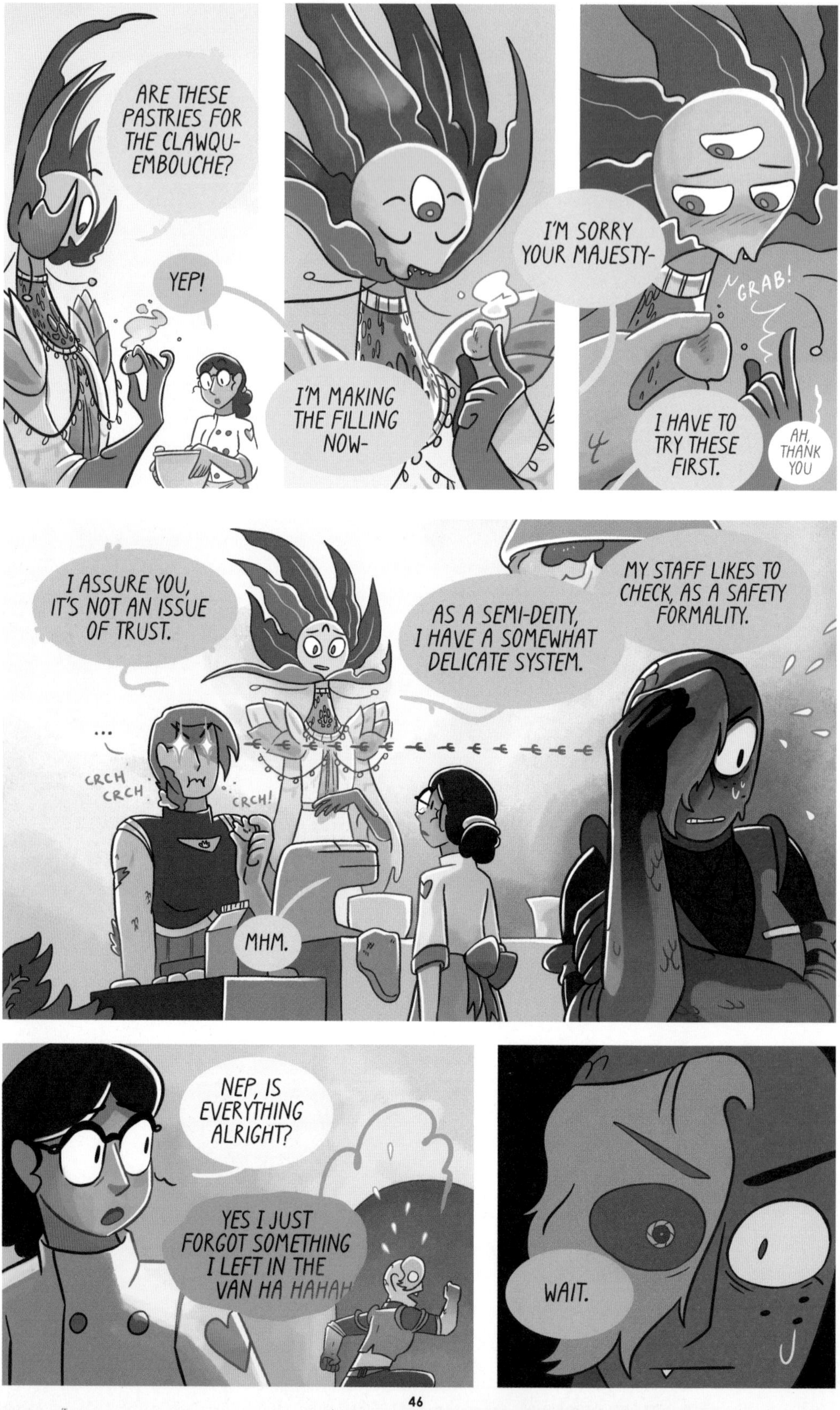
ARE THESE PASTRIES FOR THE CLAWQU-EMBOUCHE?
YEP!
I'M MAKING THE FILLING NOW-
I'M SORRY YOUR MAJESTY-
GRAB!
I HAVE TO TRY THESE FIRST.
AH, THANK YOU
I ASSURE YOU, IT'S NOT AN ISSUE OF TRUST.
AS A SEMI-DEITY, I HAVE A SOMEWHAT DELICATE SYSTEM.
MY STAFF LIKES TO CHECK, AS A SAFETY FORMALITY.
...
CRCH CRCH
CRCH!
MHM.
NEP, IS EVERYTHING ALRIGHT?
YES I JUST FORGOT SOMETHING I LEFT IN THE VAN HA HAHAH
WAIT.

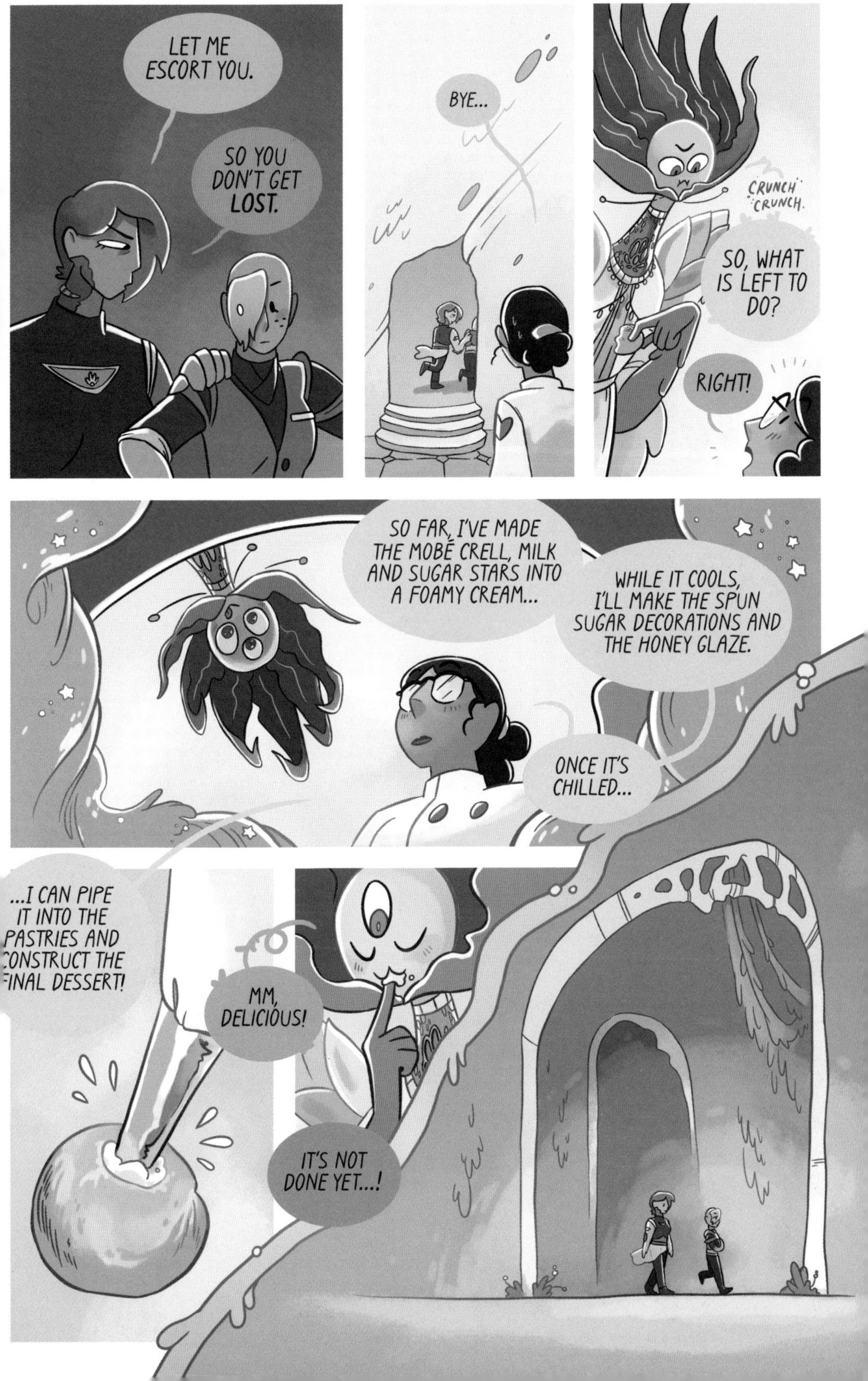
LET ME ESCORT YOU.
SO YOU DON'T GET **LOST.**
BYE...
CRUNCH CRUNCH
SO, WHAT IS LEFT TO DO?
RIGHT!
SO FAR, I'VE MADE THE MOBÉ CRELL, MILK AND SUGAR STARS INTO A FOAMY CREAM...
WHILE IT COOLS, I'LL MAKE THE SPUN SUGAR DECORATIONS AND THE HONEY GLAZE.
ONCE IT'S CHILLED...
...I CAN PIPE IT INTO THE PASTRIES AND CONSTRUCT THE FINAL DESSERT!
MM, DELICIOUS!
IT'S NOT DONE YET...!

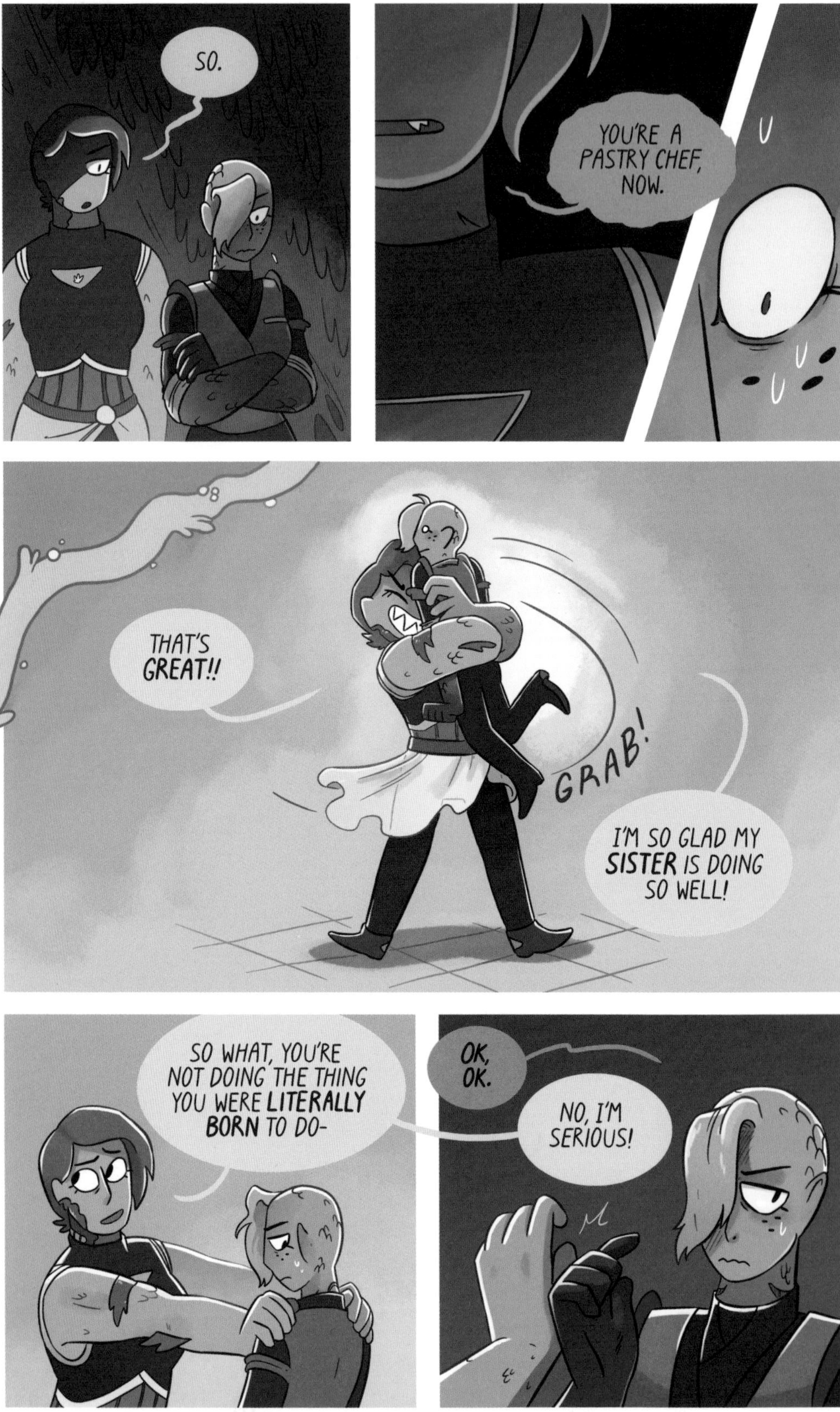
SO.
YOU'RE A PASTRY CHEF, NOW.
THAT'S **GREAT**!!
GRAB!
I'M SO GLAD MY **SISTER** IS DOING SO WELL!
SO WHAT, YOU'RE NOT DOING THE THING YOU WERE **LITERALLY BORN** TO DO-
OK, OK.
NO, I'M SERIOUS!

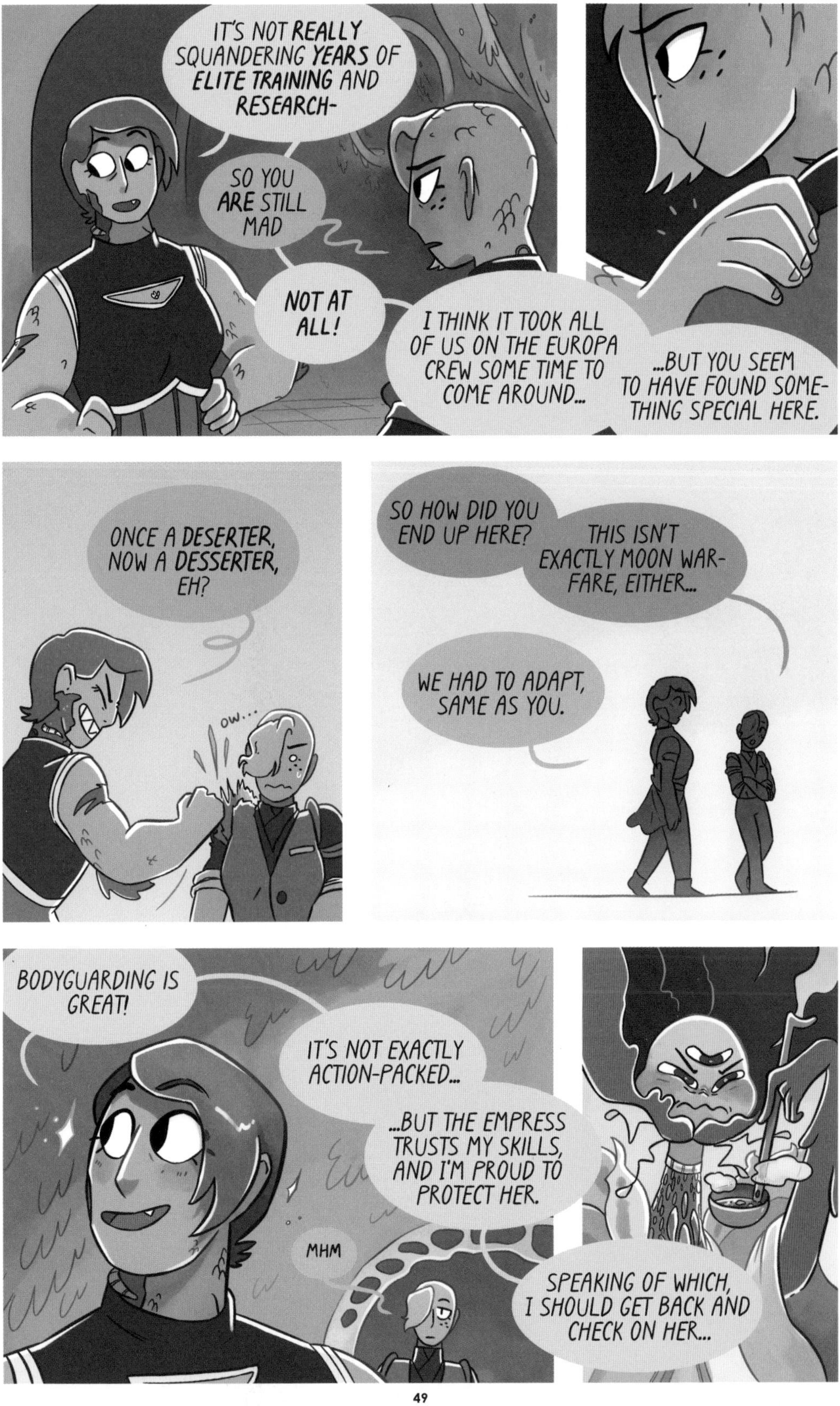
IT'S NOT REALLY SQUANDERING YEARS OF ELITE TRAINING AND RESEARCH-
SO YOU ARE STILL MAD
NOT AT ALL!
I THINK IT TOOK ALL OF US ON THE EUROPA CREW SOME TIME TO COME AROUND...
...BUT YOU SEEM TO HAVE FOUND SOME-THING SPECIAL HERE.
ONCE A DESERTER, NOW A DESSERTER, EH?
OW...
SO HOW DID YOU END UP HERE?
THIS ISN'T EXACTLY MOON WAR-FARE, EITHER...
WE HAD TO ADAPT, SAME AS YOU.
BODYGUARDING IS GREAT!
IT'S NOT EXACTLY ACTION-PACKED...
...BUT THE EMPRESS TRUSTS MY SKILLS, AND I'M PROUD TO PROTECT HER.
MHM
SPEAKING OF WHICH, I SHOULD GET BACK AND CHECK ON HER...

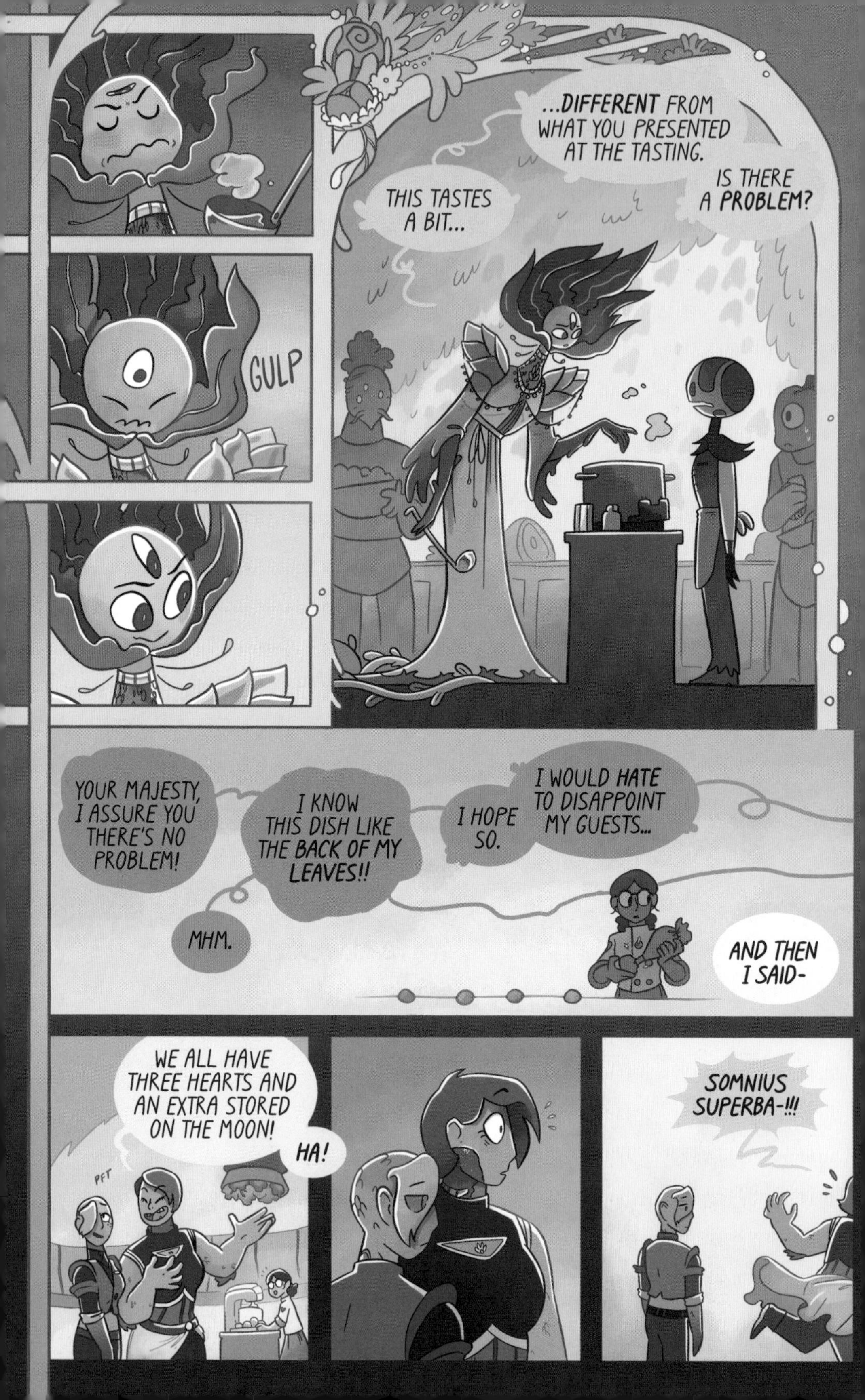
GULP
THIS TASTES A BIT...
...DIFFERENT FROM WHAT YOU PRESENTED AT THE TASTING.
IS THERE A PROBLEM?
YOUR MAJESTY, I ASSURE YOU THERE'S NO PROBLEM!
I KNOW THIS DISH LIKE THE BACK OF MY LEAVES!!
I HOPE SO.
I WOULD HATE TO DISAPPOINT MY GUESTS...
MHM.
AND THEN I SAID-
WE ALL HAVE THREE HEARTS AND AN EXTRA STORED ON THE MOON!
HA!
PFT
SOMNIUS SUPERBA-!!!

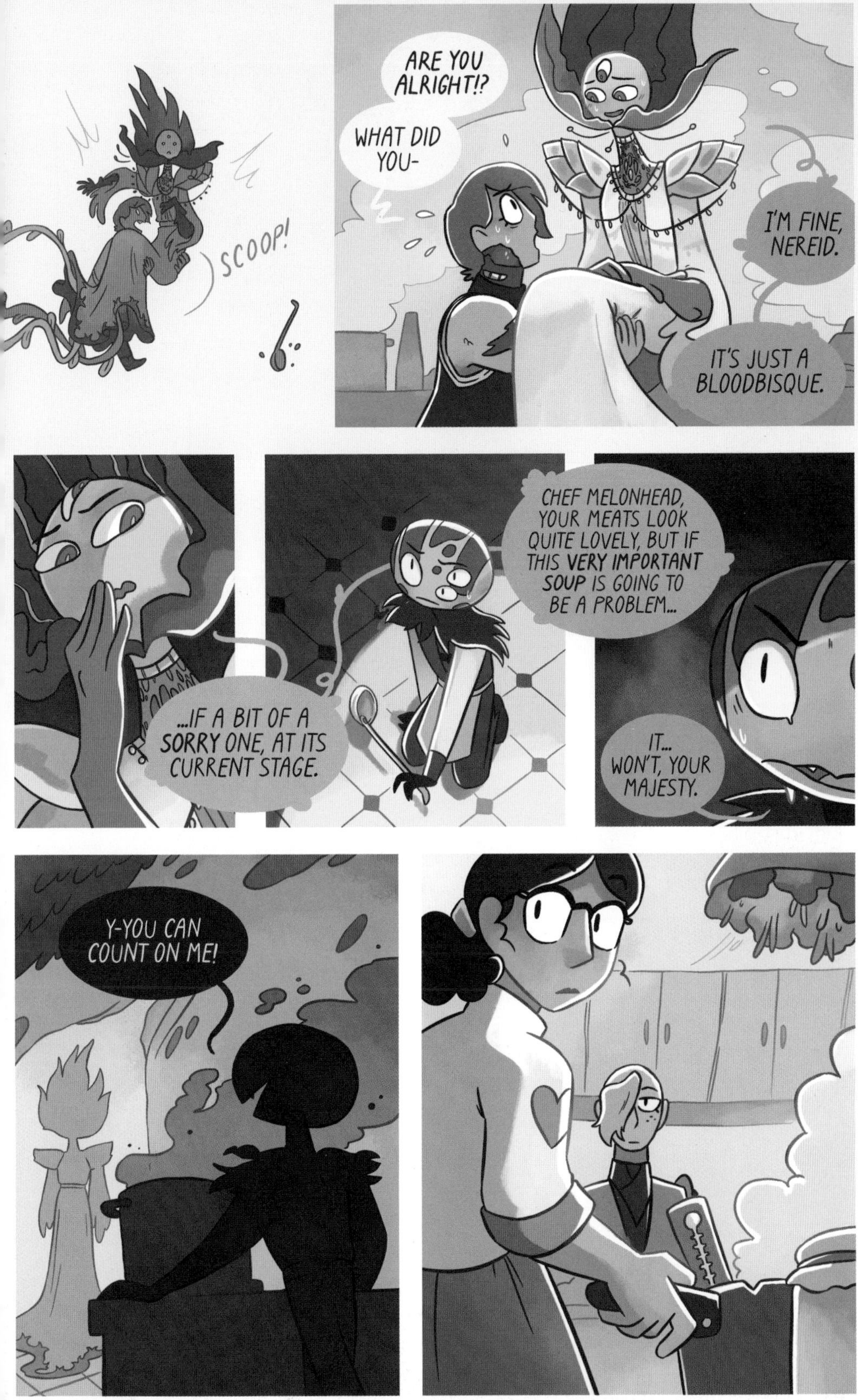
SCOOP!
ARE YOU ALRIGHT!?
WHAT DID YOU-
I'M FINE, NEREID.
IT'S JUST A BLOODBISQUE.
CHEF MELONHEAD, YOUR MEATS LOOK QUITE LOVELY, BUT IF THIS VERY IMPORTANT SOUP IS GOING TO BE A PROBLEM...
...IF A BIT OF A SORRY ONE, AT ITS CURRENT STAGE.
IT... WON'T, YOUR MAJESTY.
Y-YOU CAN COUNT ON ME!

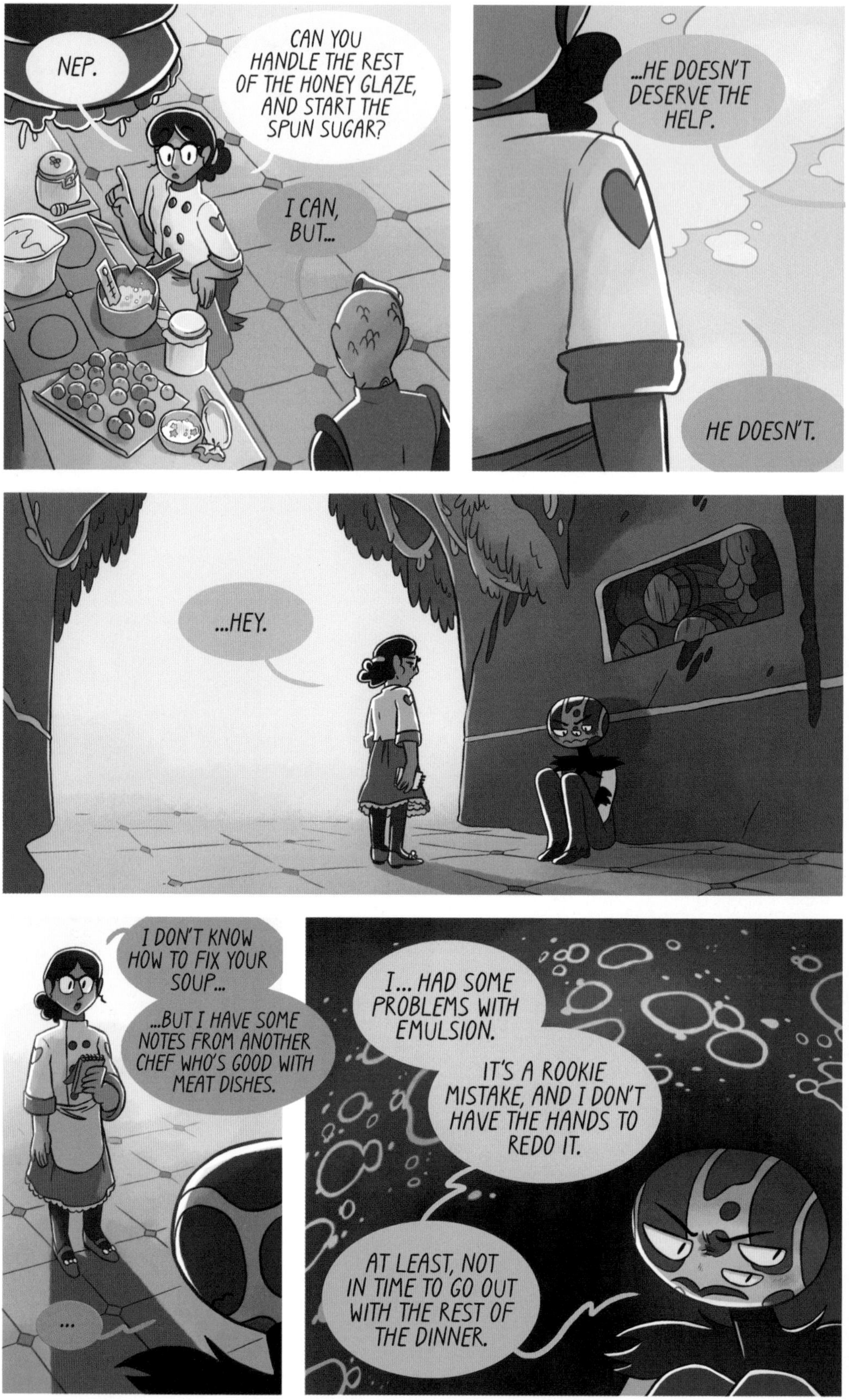
NEP.
CAN YOU HANDLE THE REST OF THE HONEY GLAZE, AND START THE SPUN SUGAR?
I CAN, BUT...
...HE DOESN'T DESERVE THE HELP.
HE DOESN'T.
...HEY.
I DON'T KNOW HOW TO FIX YOUR SOUP...
...BUT I HAVE SOME NOTES FROM ANOTHER CHEF WHO'S GOOD WITH MEAT DISHES.
...
I... HAD SOME PROBLEMS WITH EMULSION.
IT'S A ROOKIE MISTAKE, AND I DON'T HAVE THE HANDS TO REDO IT.
AT LEAST, NOT IN TIME TO GO OUT WITH THE REST OF THE DINNER.

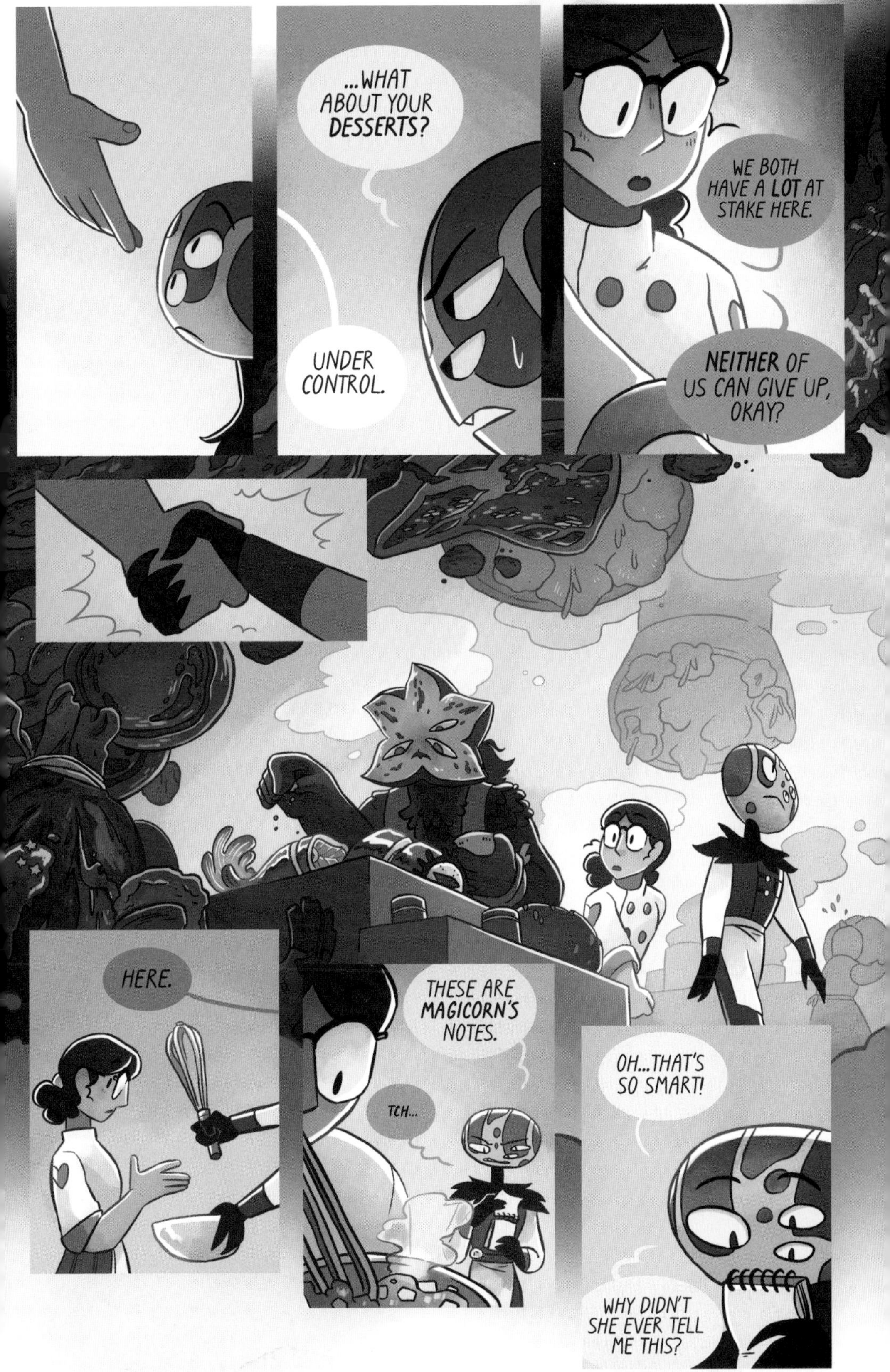
...WHAT ABOUT YOUR DESSERTS?
UNDER CONTROL.
WE BOTH HAVE A LOT AT STAKE HERE.
NEITHER OF US CAN GIVE UP, OKAY?
HERE.
THESE ARE MAGICORN'S NOTES.
TCH...
OH...THAT'S SO SMART!
WHY DIDN'T SHE EVER TELL ME THIS?

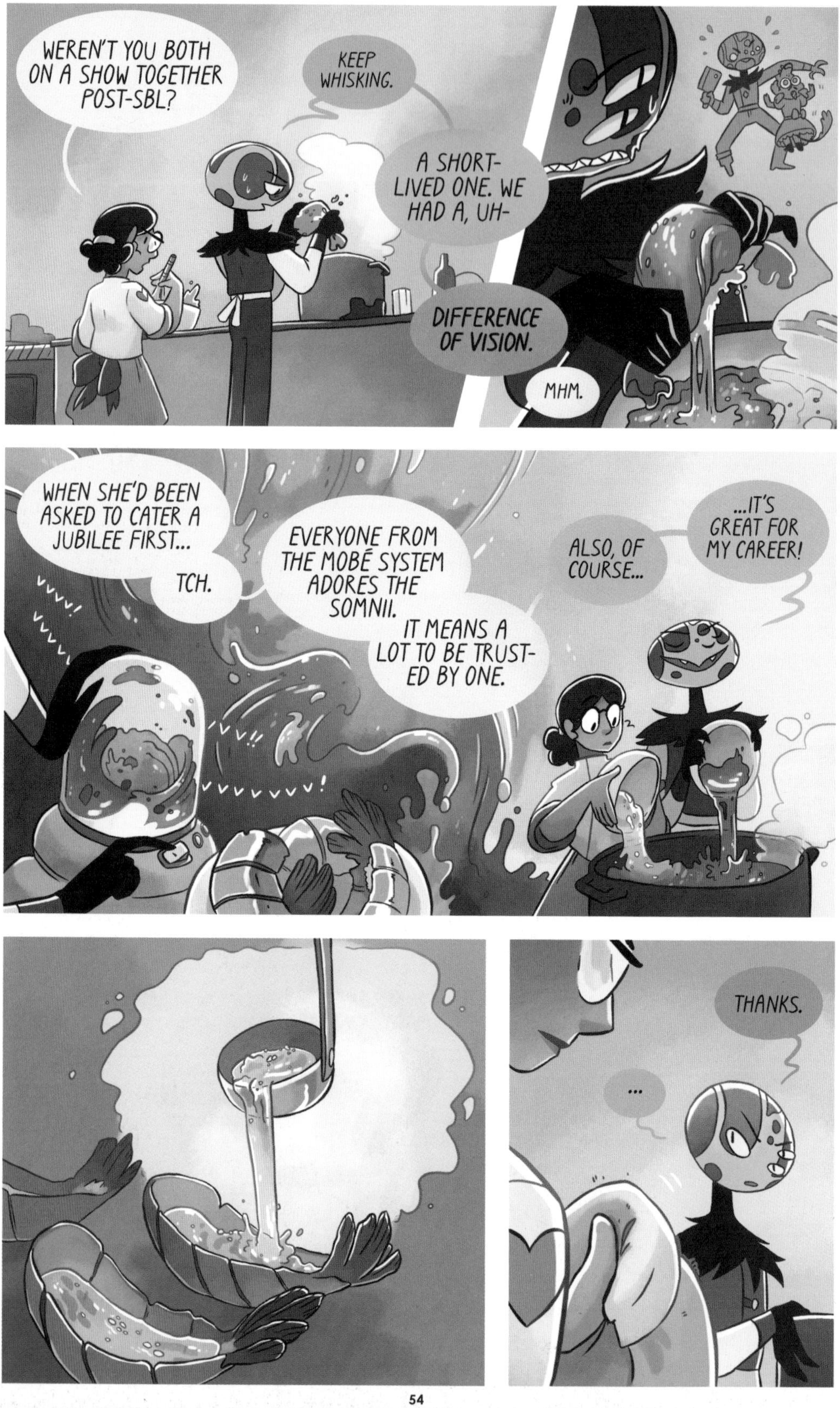
WEREN'T YOU BOTH ON A SHOW TOGETHER POST-SBL?
KEEP WHISKING.
A SHORT-LIVED ONE. WE HAD A, UH-
DIFFERENCE OF VISION.
MHM.
WHEN SHE'D BEEN ASKED TO CATER A JUBILEE FIRST...
TCH.
EVERYONE FROM THE MOBÉ SYSTEM ADORES THE SOMNII.
IT MEANS A LOT TO BE TRUSTED BY ONE.
ALSO, OF COURSE...
...IT'S GREAT FOR MY CAREER!
VVVV!
VVVV!!
VVVVVVVV!
THANKS.
...

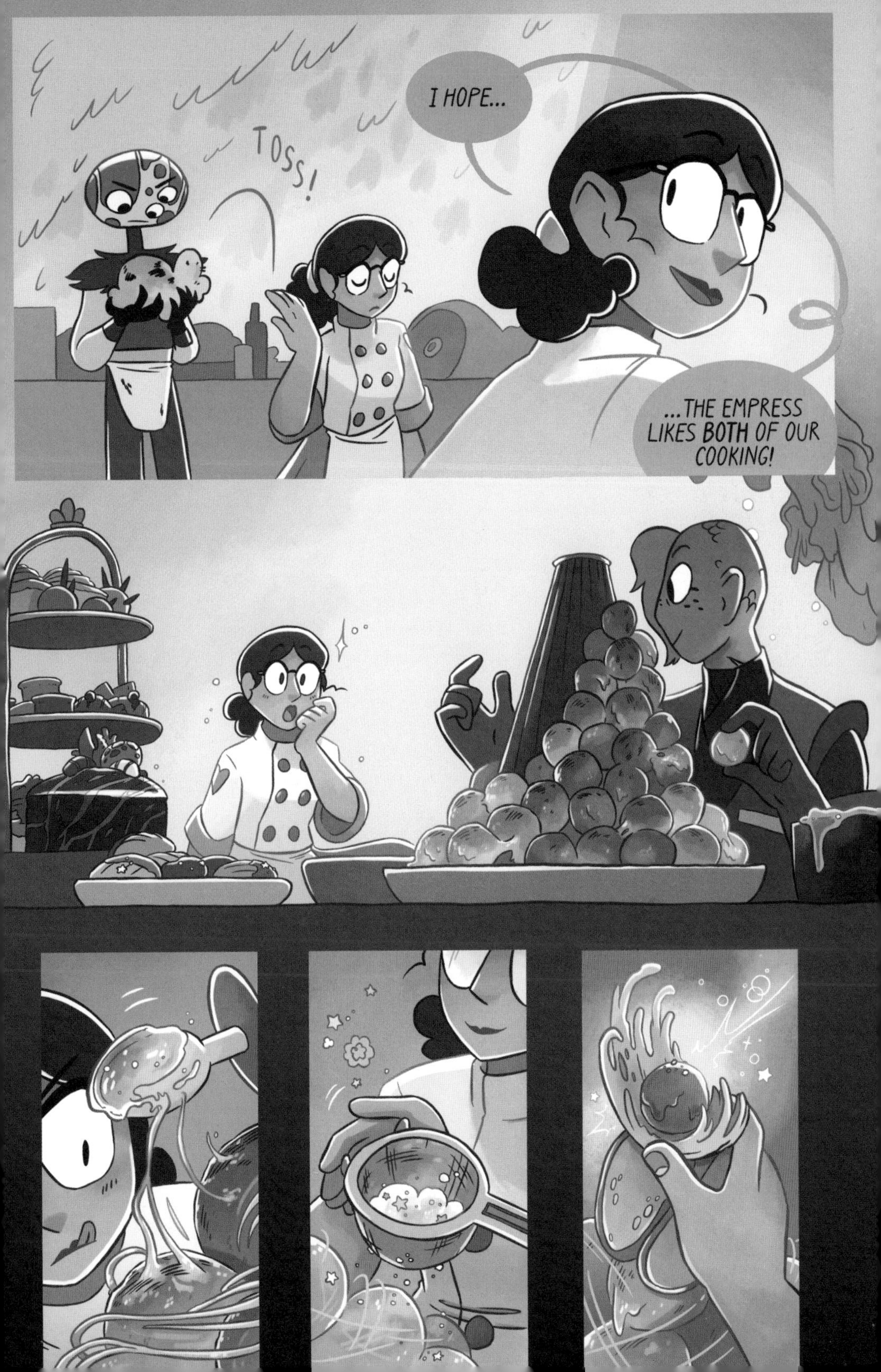
TOSS!
I HOPE...
...THE EMPRESS LIKES BOTH OF OUR COOKING!

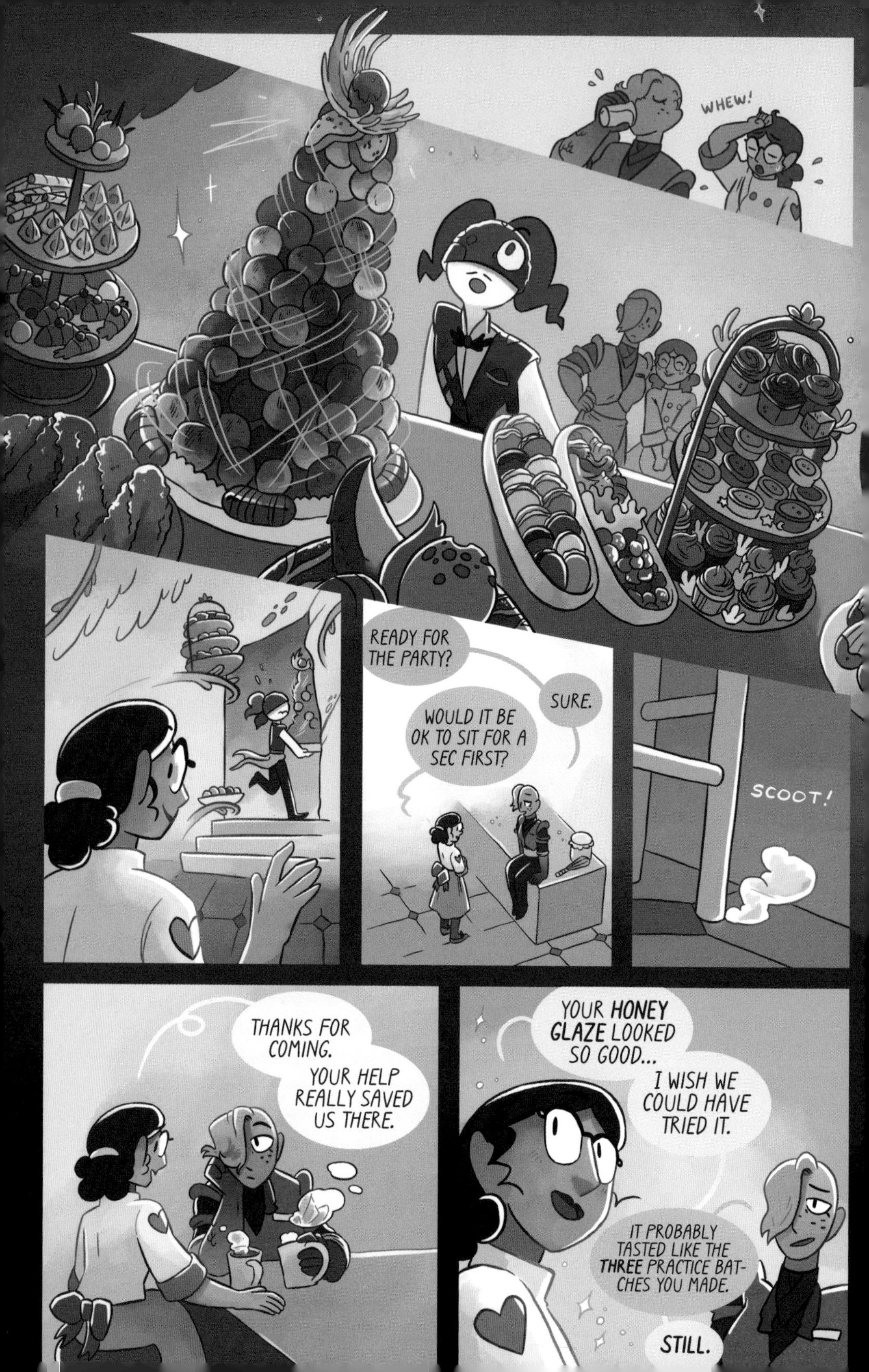
WHEW!
READY FOR THE PARTY?
SURE.
WOULD IT BE OK TO SIT FOR A SEC FIRST?
SCOOT!
THANKS FOR COMING.
YOUR HELP REALLY SAVED US THERE.
YOUR **HONEY GLAZE** LOOKED SO GOOD...
I WISH WE COULD HAVE TRIED IT.
IT PROBABLY TASTED LIKE THE **THREE** PRACTICE BATCHES YOU MADE.
STILL.

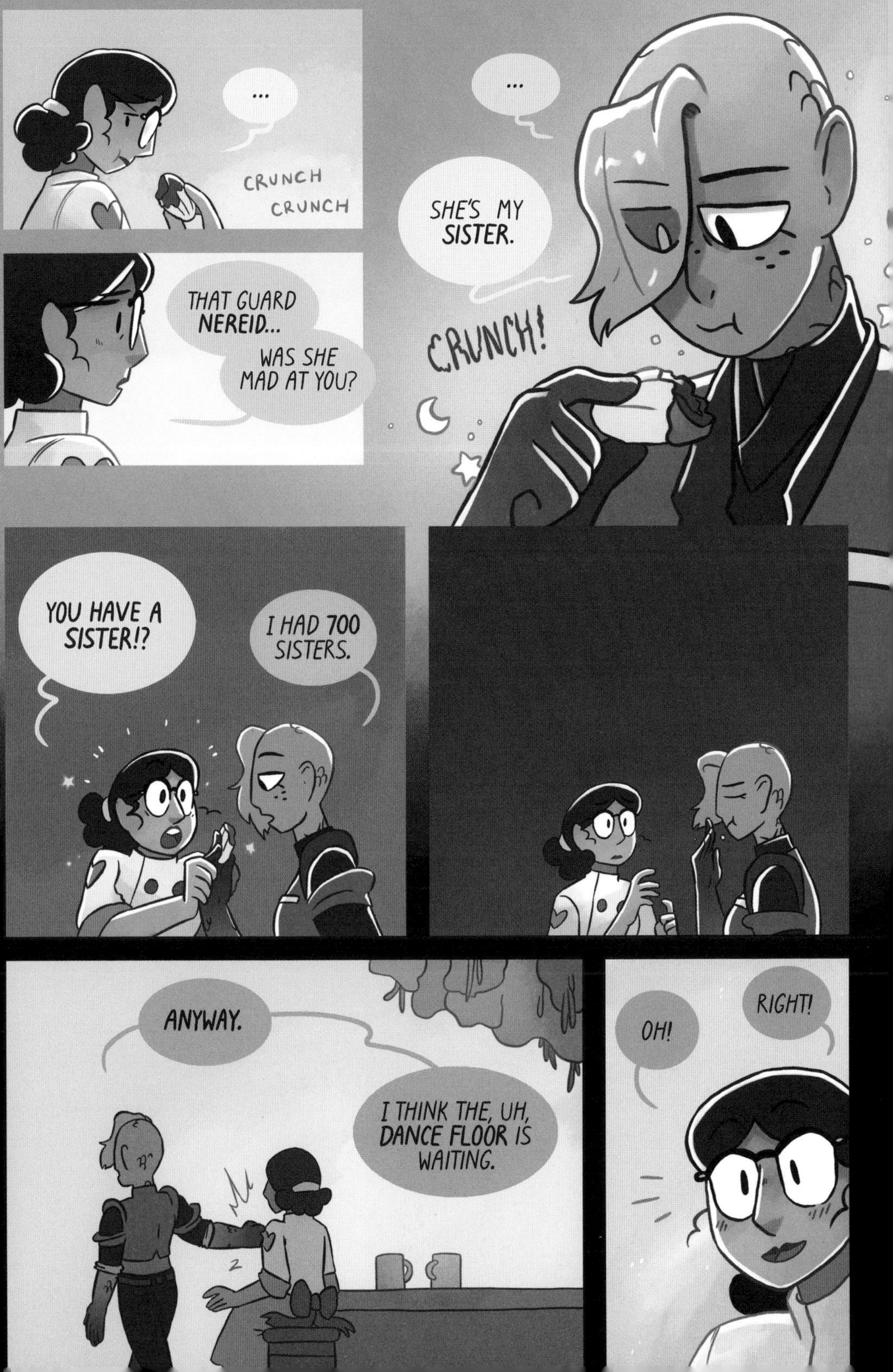
...
CRUNCH
CRUNCH
THAT GUARD NEREID...
WAS SHE MAD AT YOU?
...
SHE'S MY SISTER.
CRUNCH!
YOU HAVE A SISTER!?
I HAD 700 SISTERS.
ANYWAY.
I THINK THE, UH, DANCE FLOOR IS WAITING.
OH!
RIGHT!

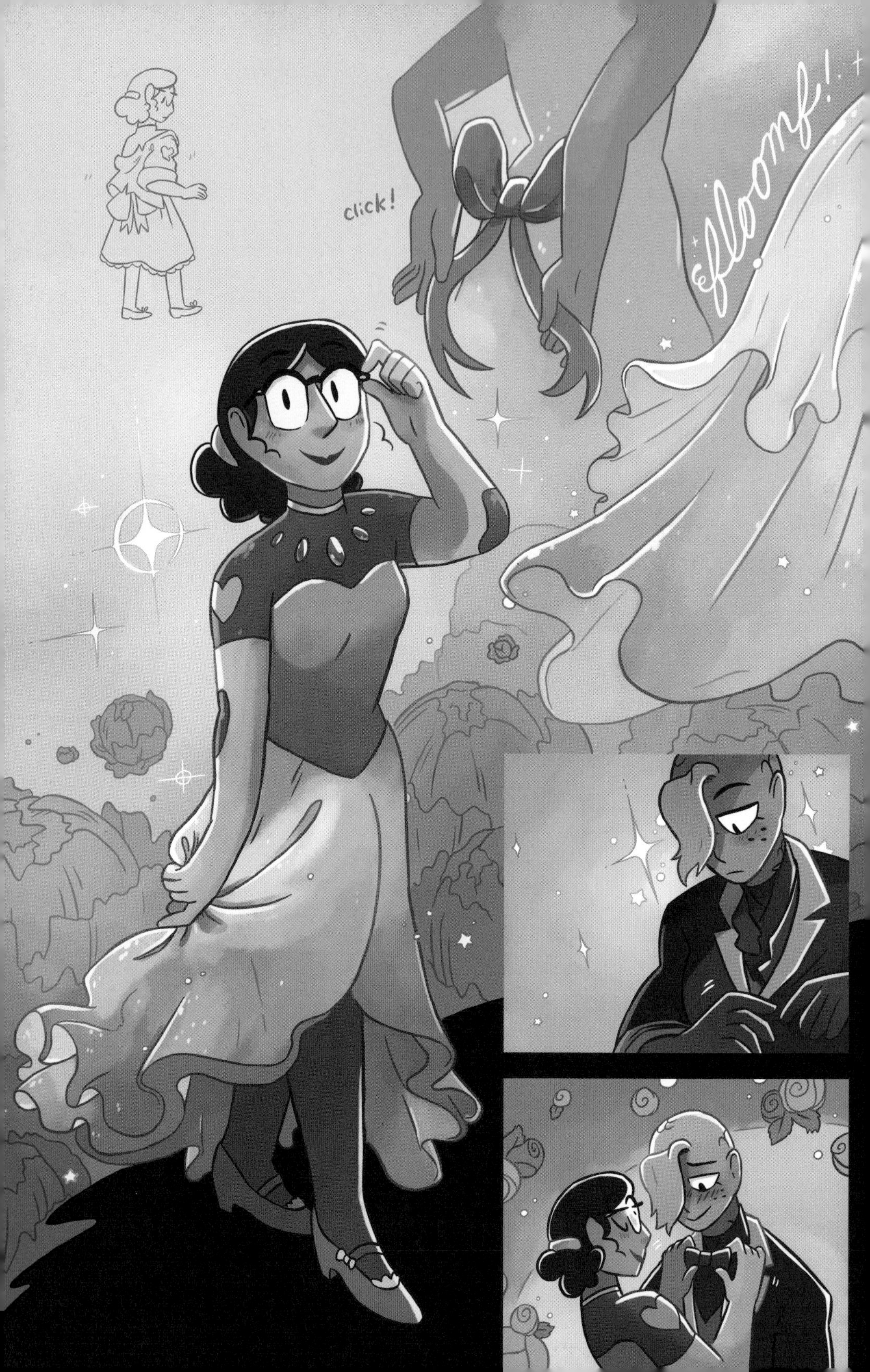
click!
floomf!

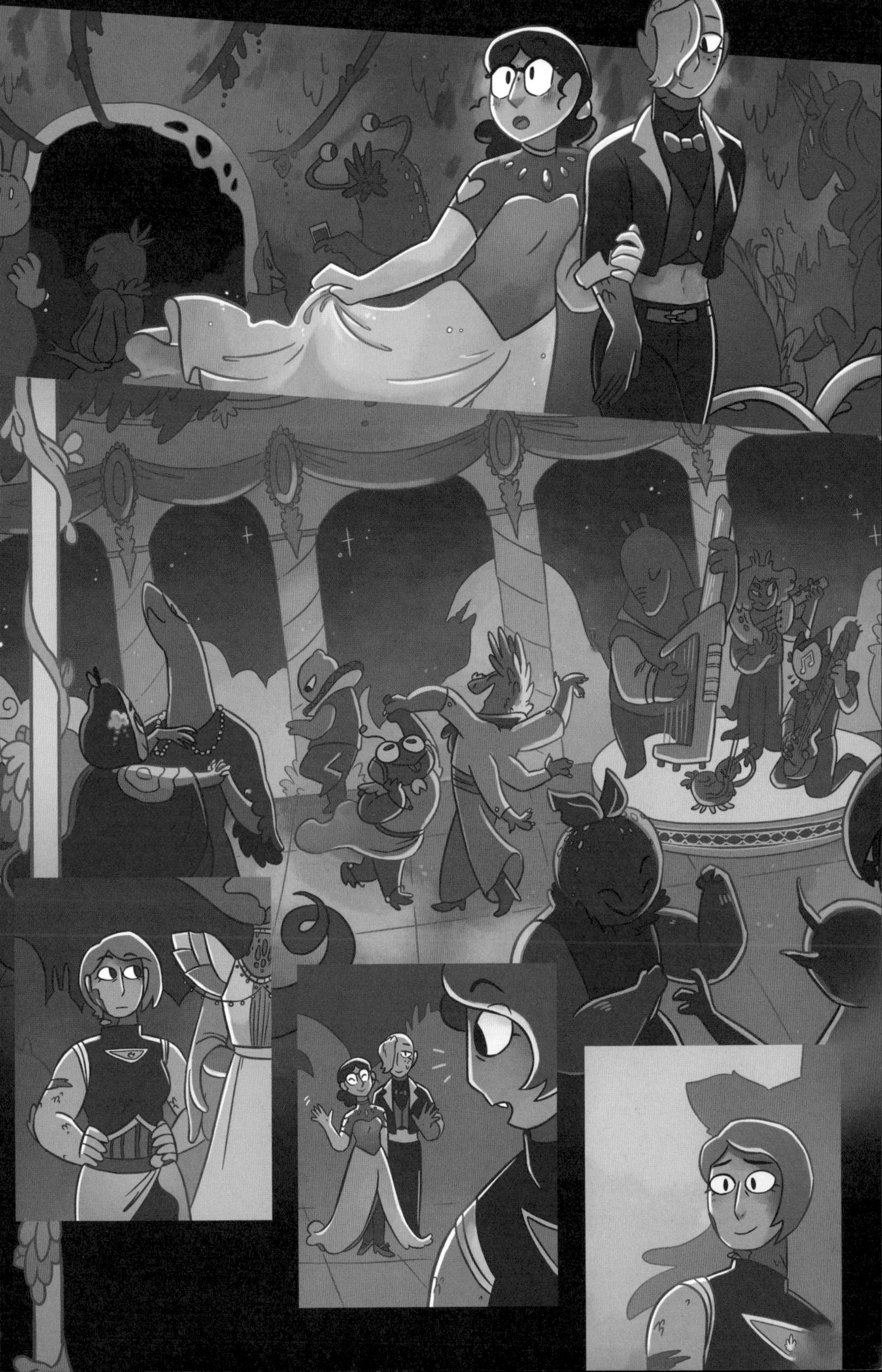

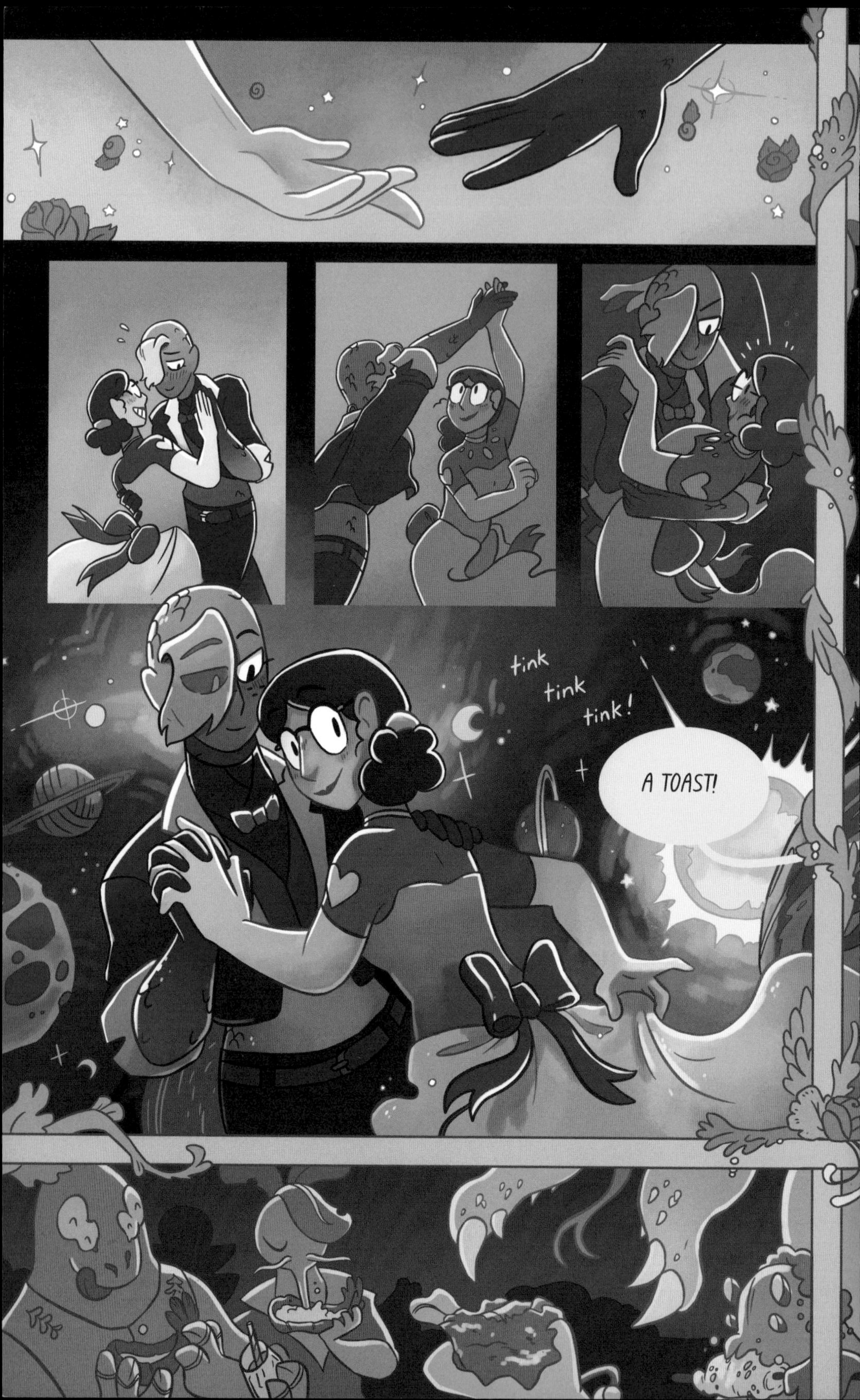
tink
tink
tink!
A TOAST!

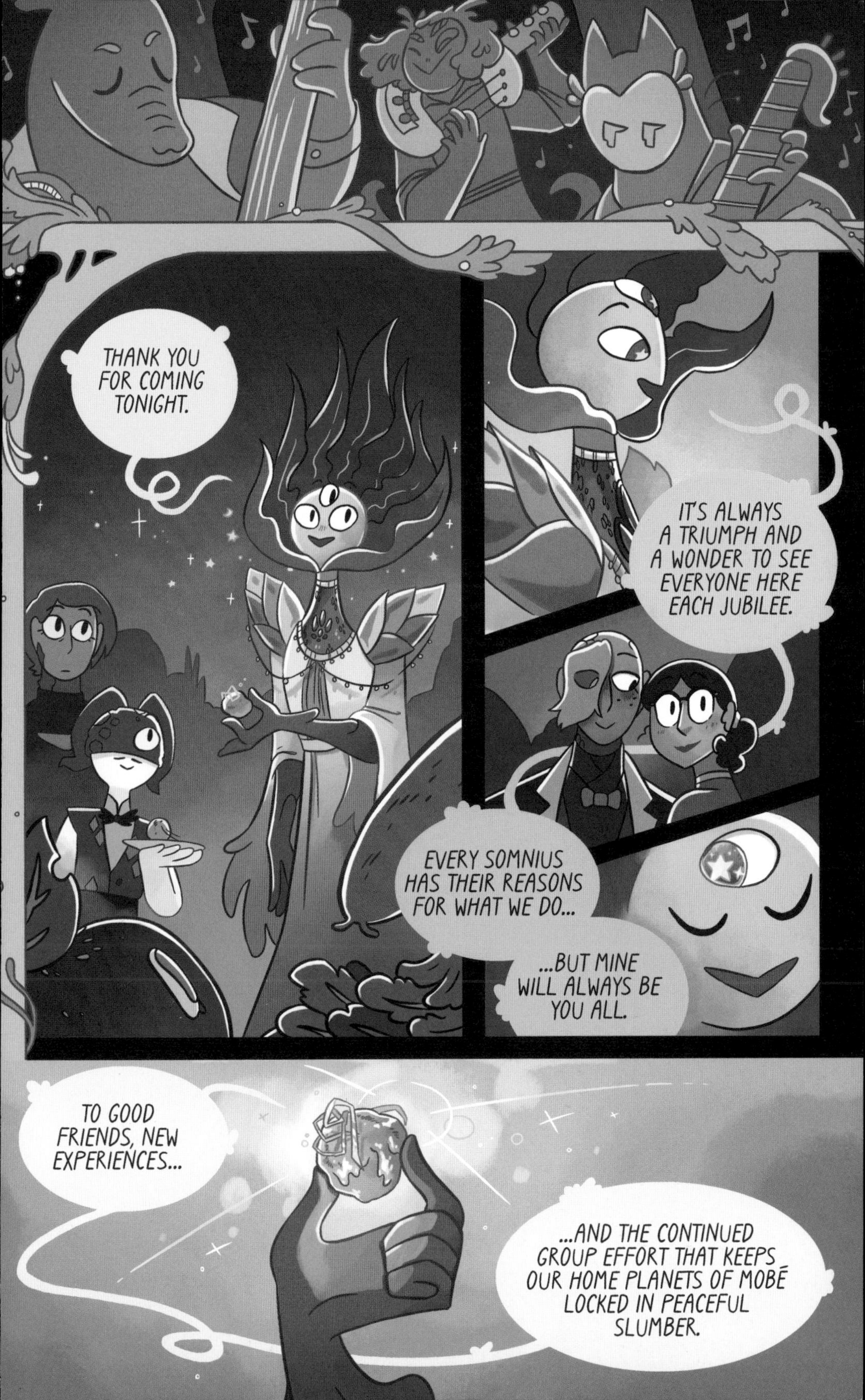
THANK YOU FOR COMING TONIGHT.
IT'S ALWAYS A TRIUMPH AND A WONDER TO SEE EVERYONE HERE EACH JUBILEE.
EVERY SOMNIUS HAS THEIR REASONS FOR WHAT WE DO...
...BUT MINE WILL ALWAYS BE YOU ALL.
TO GOOD FRIENDS, NEW EXPERIENCES...
...AND THE CONTINUED GROUP EFFORT THAT KEEPS OUR HOME PLANETS OF MOBÉ LOCKED IN PEACEFUL SLUMBER.

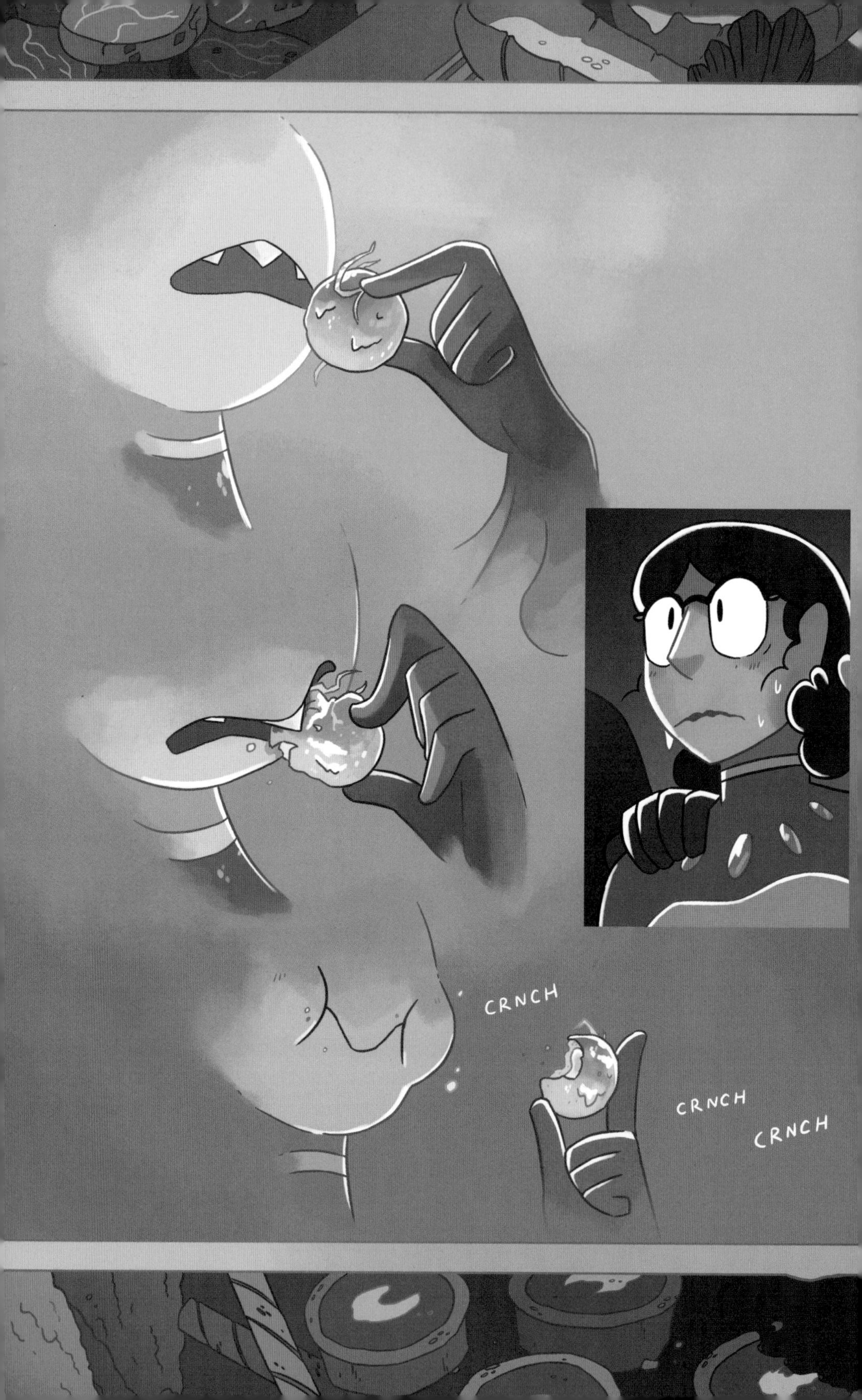
CRNCH
CRNCH
CRNCH

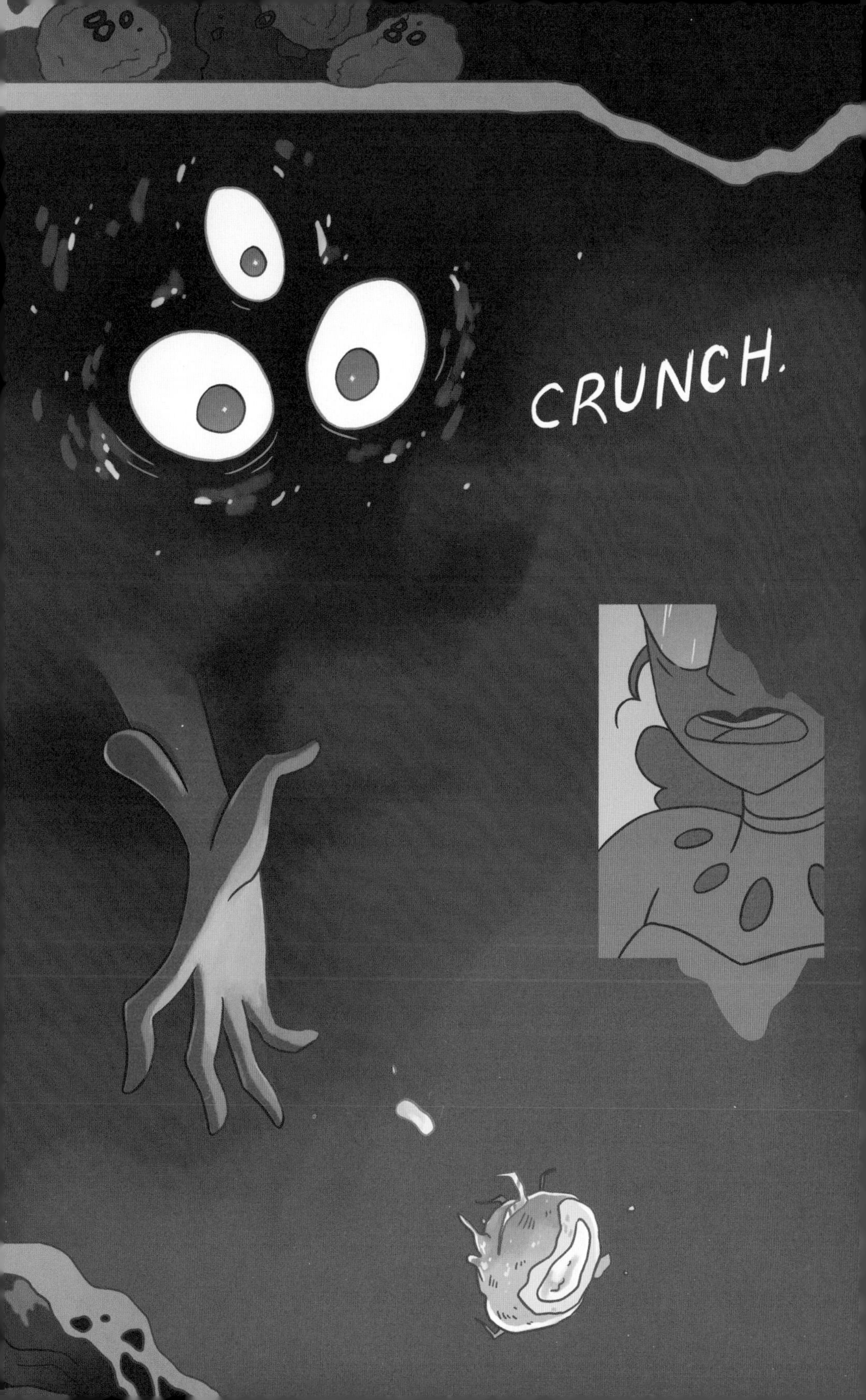
CRUNCH.

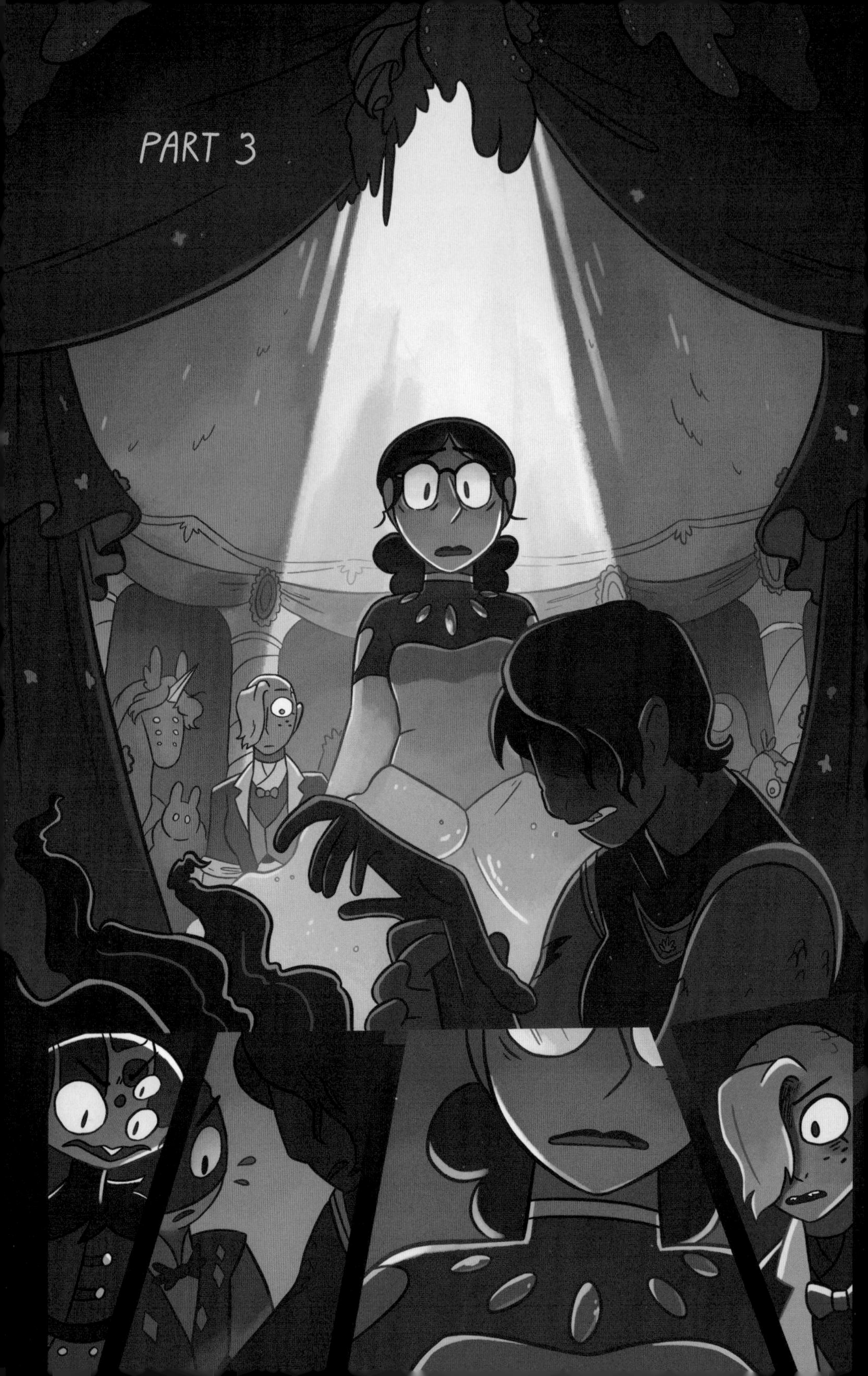
PART 3

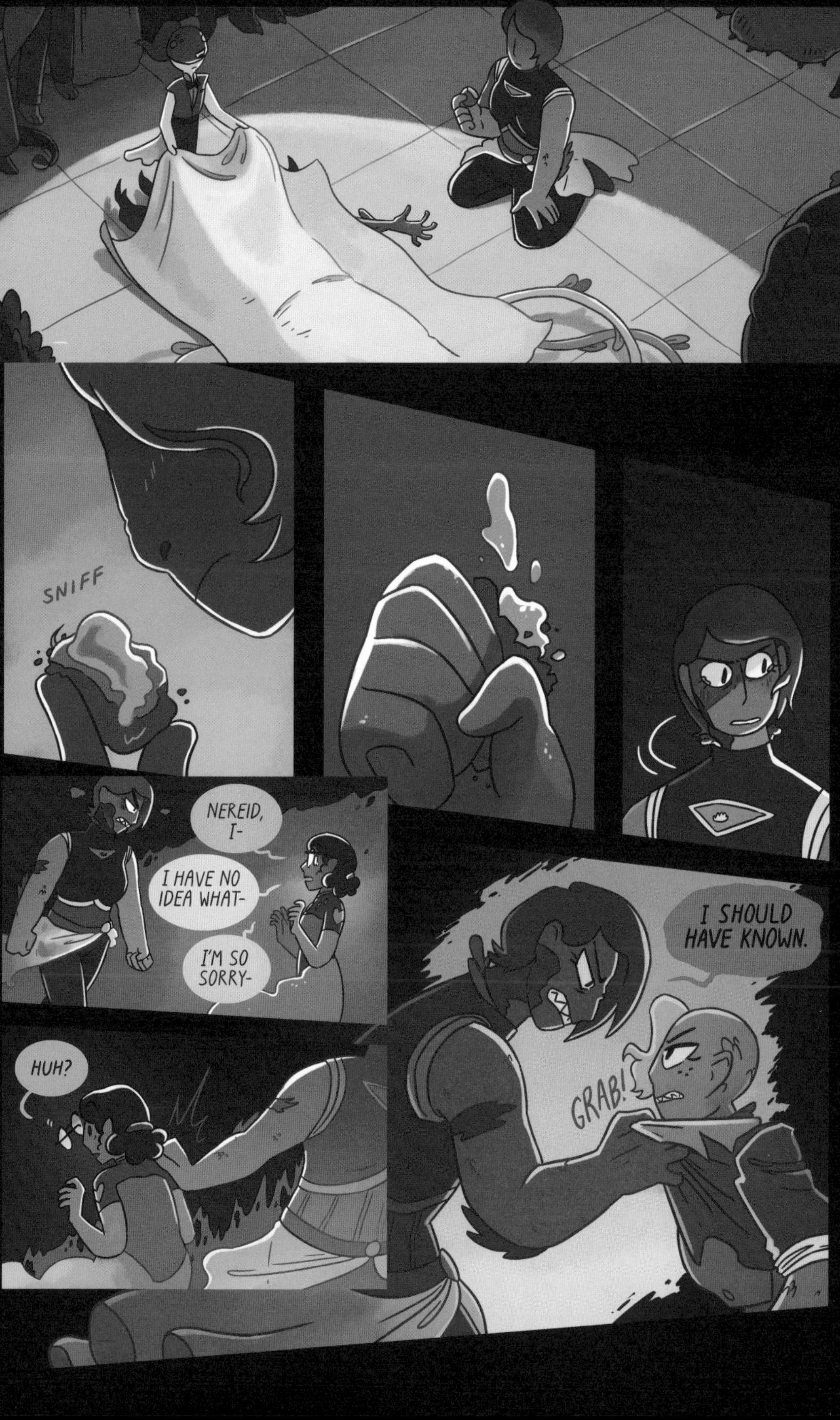
SNIFF
NEREID, I-
I HAVE NO IDEA WHAT-
I'M SO SORRY-
I SHOULD HAVE KNOWN.
HUH?
GRAB!

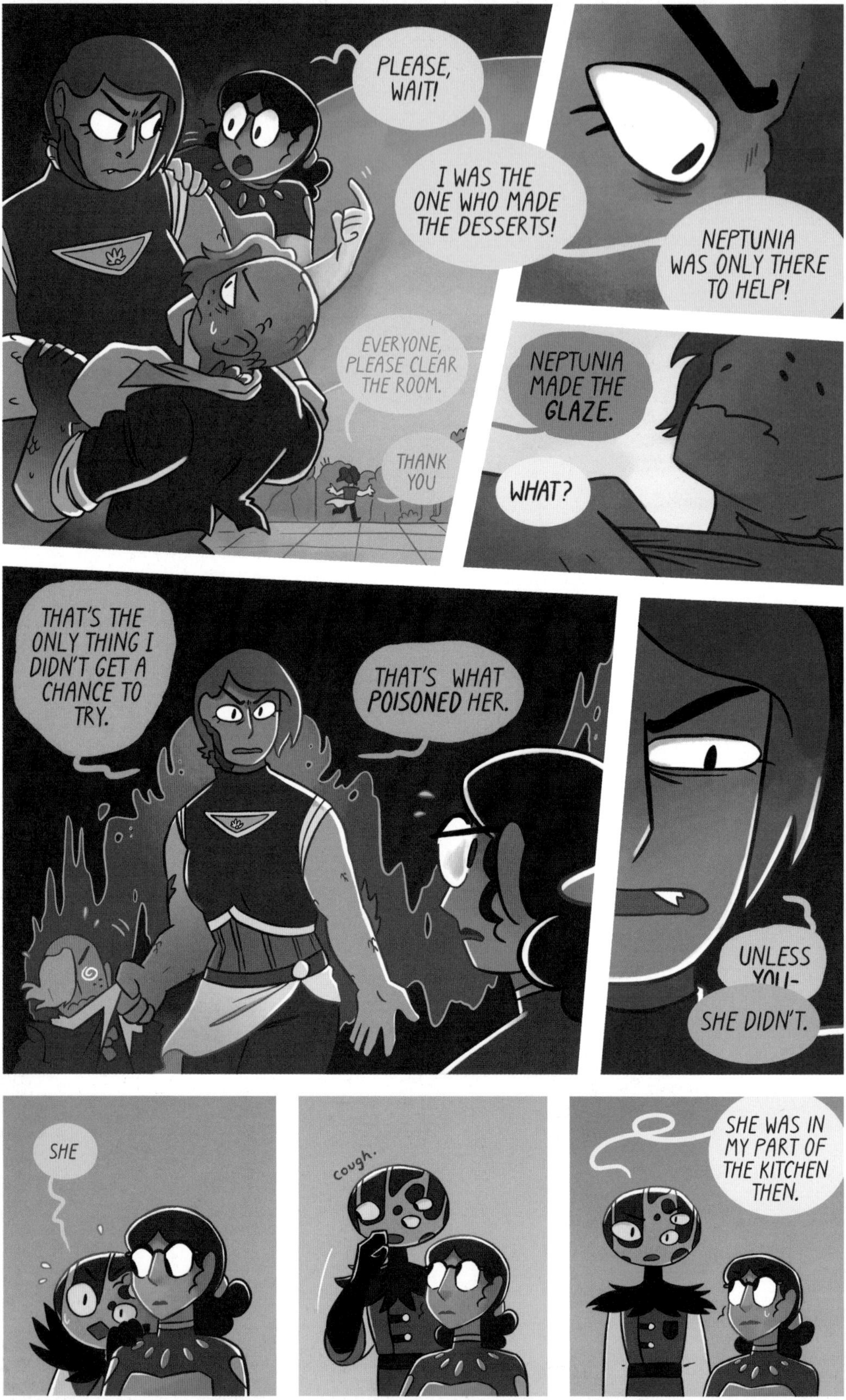
PLEASE, WAIT!
I WAS THE ONE WHO MADE THE DESSERTS!
NEPTUNIA WAS ONLY THERE TO HELP!
EVERYONE, PLEASE CLEAR THE ROOM.
THANK YOU
NEPTUNIA MADE THE GLAZE.
WHAT?
THAT'S THE ONLY THING I DIDN'T GET A CHANCE TO TRY.
THAT'S WHAT POISONED HER.
UNLESS YOU-
SHE DIDN'T.
SHE
cough.
SHE WAS IN MY PART OF THE KITCHEN THEN.

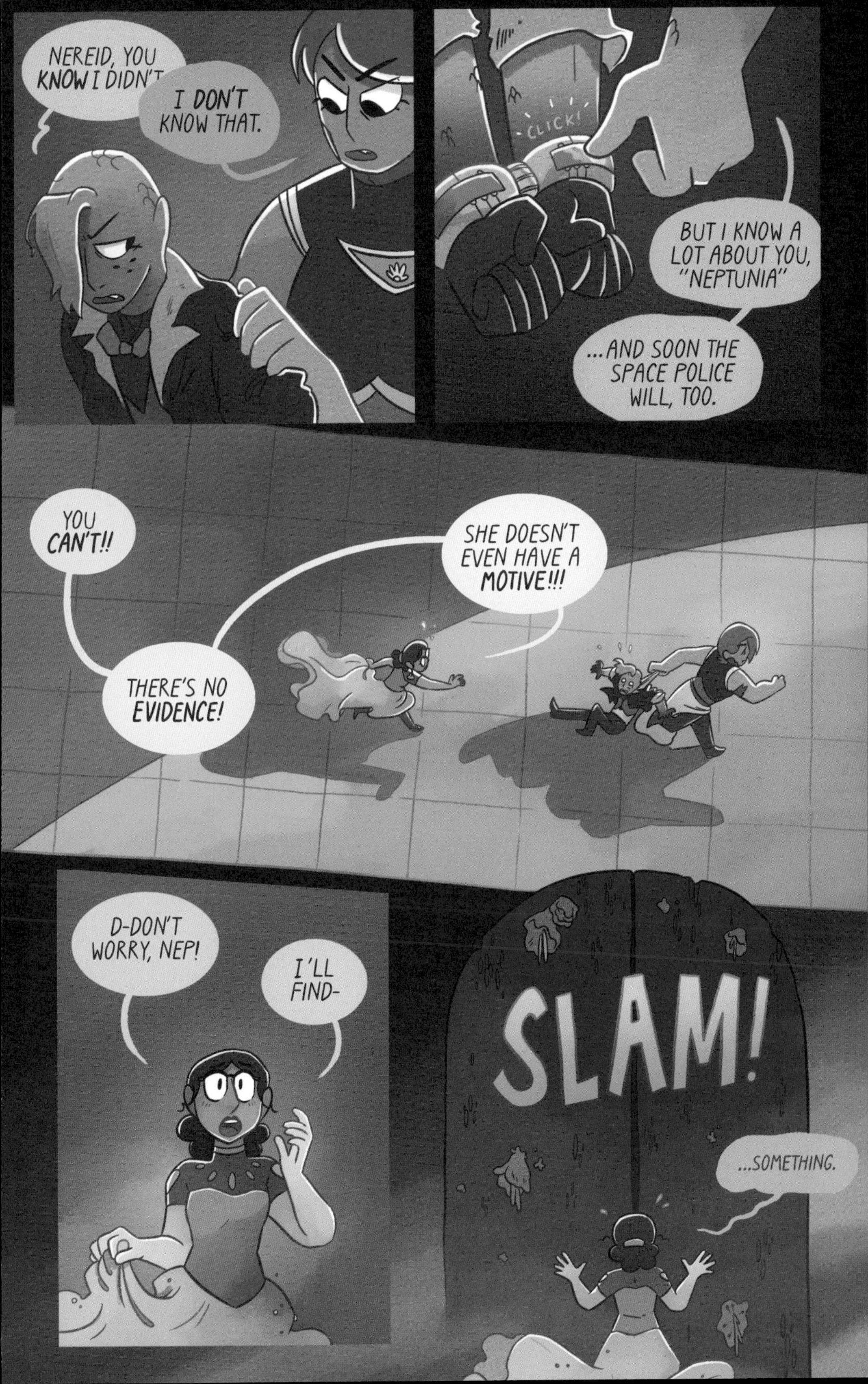
NEREID, YOU KNOW I DIDN'T
I DON'T KNOW THAT.
CLICK!
BUT I KNOW A LOT ABOUT YOU, "NEPTUNIA"
...AND SOON THE SPACE POLICE WILL, TOO.
YOU CAN'T!!
THERE'S NO EVIDENCE!
SHE DOESN'T EVEN HAVE A MOTIVE!!!
D-DON'T WORRY, NEP!
I'LL FIND-
SLAM!
...SOMETHING.

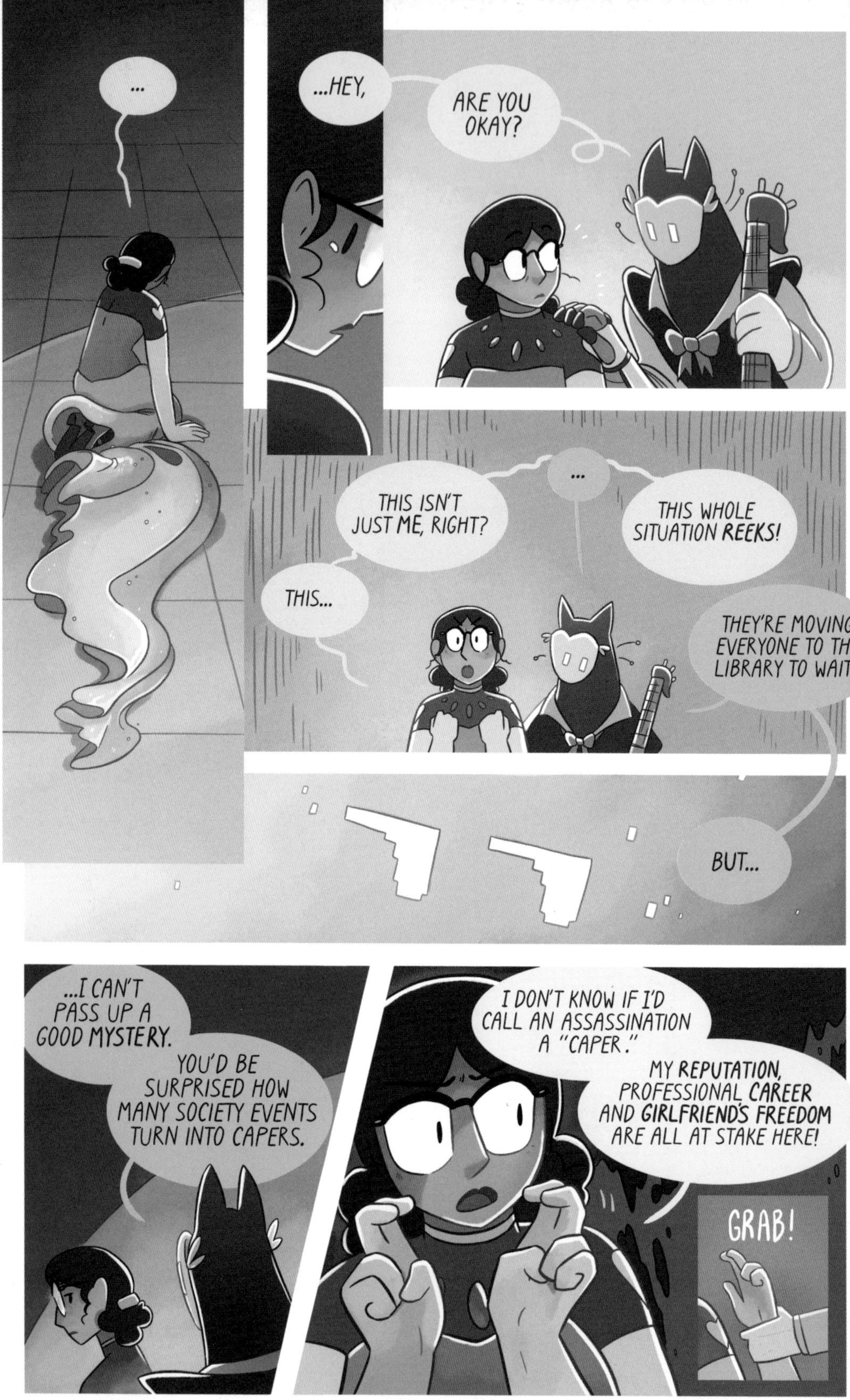
...
...HEY,
ARE YOU OKAY?
THIS...
THIS ISN'T JUST ME, RIGHT?
...
THIS WHOLE SITUATION REEKS!
THEY'RE MOVING EVERYONE TO THE LIBRARY TO WAIT.
BUT...
...I CAN'T PASS UP A GOOD MYSTERY.
YOU'D BE SURPRISED HOW MANY SOCIETY EVENTS TURN INTO CAPERS.
I DON'T KNOW IF I'D CALL AN ASSASSINATION A "CAPER."
MY REPUTATION, PROFESSIONAL CAREER AND GIRLFRIEND'S FREEDOM ARE ALL AT STAKE HERE!
GRAB!

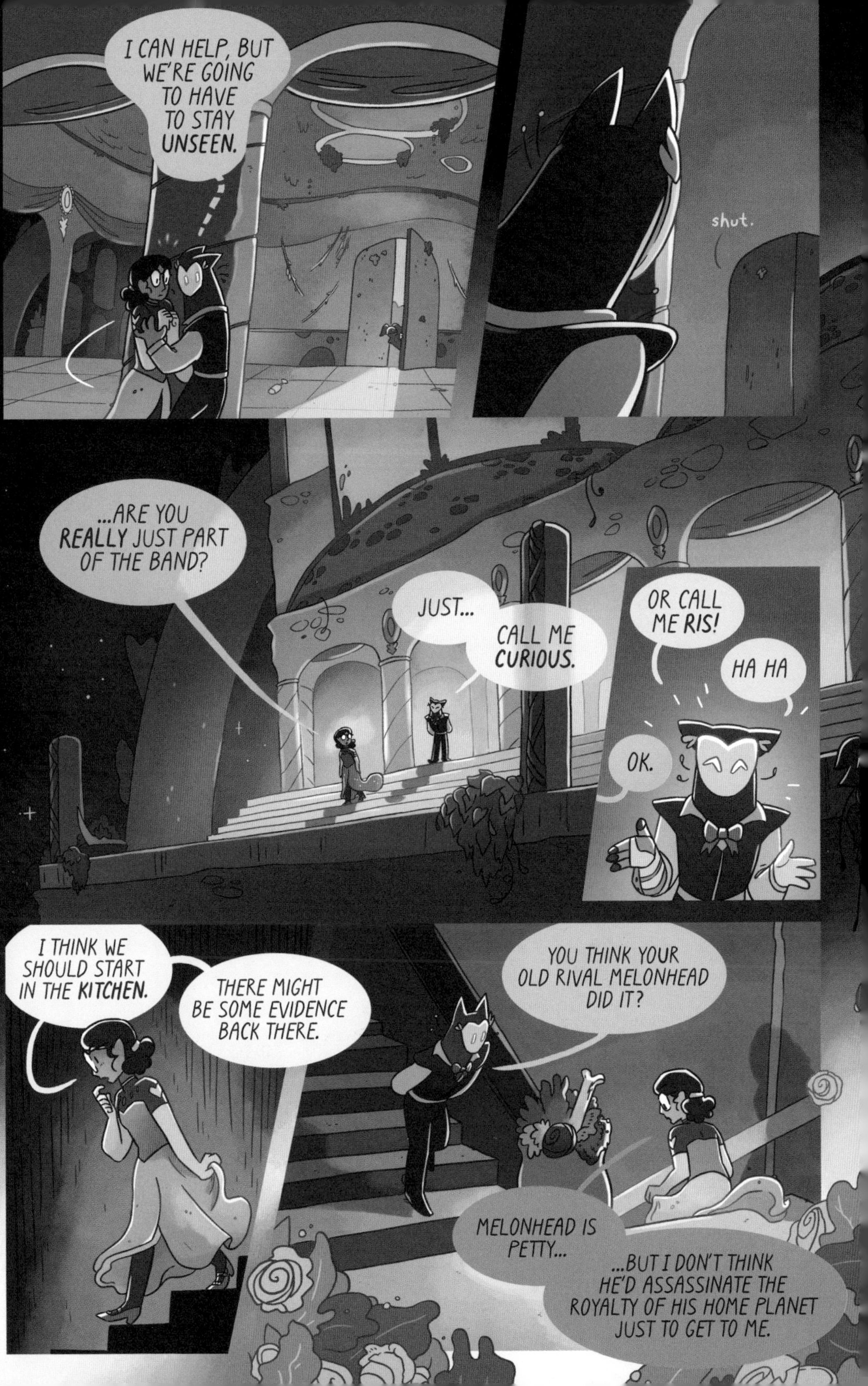
I CAN HELP, BUT WE'RE GOING TO HAVE TO STAY UNSEEN.
shut.
...ARE YOU REALLY JUST PART OF THE BAND?
JUST...
CALL ME CURIOUS.
OR CALL ME RIS!
HA HA
OK.
I THINK WE SHOULD START IN THE KITCHEN.
THERE MIGHT BE SOME EVIDENCE BACK THERE.
YOU THINK YOUR OLD RIVAL MELONHEAD DID IT?
MELONHEAD IS PETTY...
...BUT I DON'T THINK HE'D ASSASSINATE THE ROYALTY OF HIS HOME PLANET JUST TO GET TO ME.

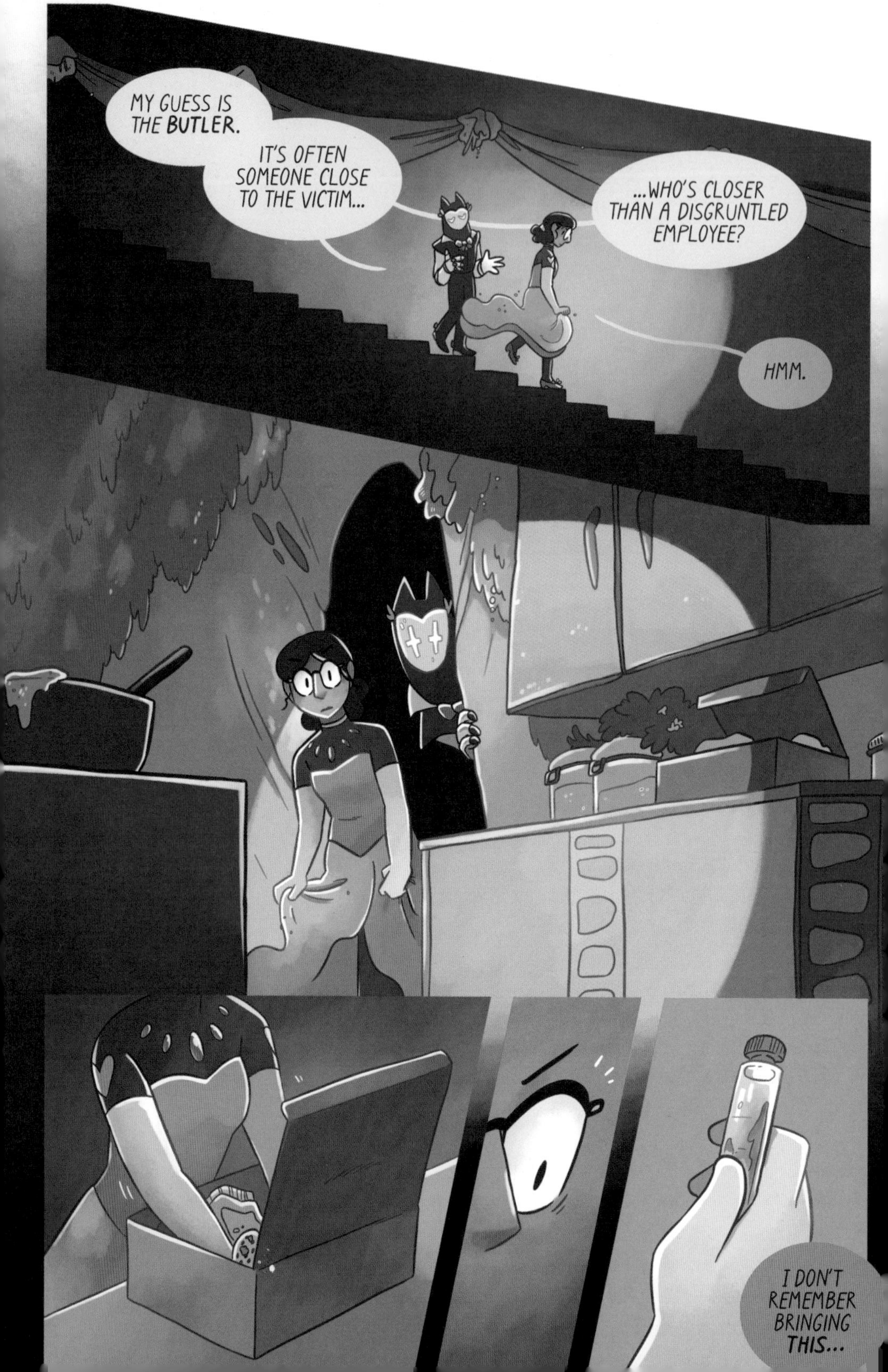
MY GUESS IS THE BUTLER.
IT'S OFTEN SOMEONE CLOSE TO THE VICTIM...
...WHO'S CLOSER THAN A DISGRUNTLED EMPLOYEE?
HMM.
I DON'T REMEMBER BRINGING THIS...

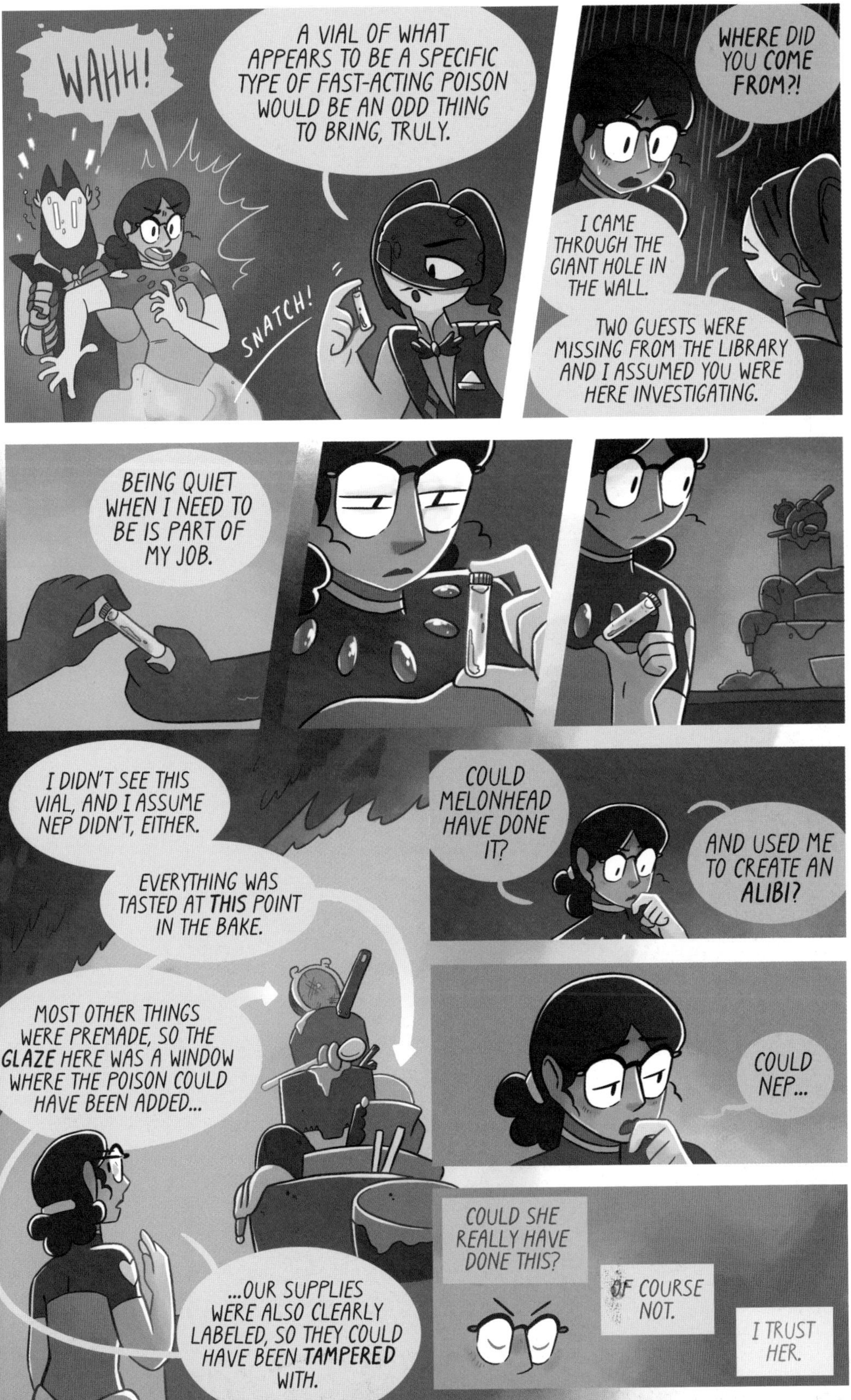
WAHH!
A VIAL OF WHAT APPEARS TO BE A SPECIFIC TYPE OF FAST-ACTING POISON WOULD BE AN ODD THING TO BRING, TRULY.
SNATCH!
WHERE DID YOU COME FROM?!
I CAME THROUGH THE GIANT HOLE IN THE WALL.
TWO GUESTS WERE MISSING FROM THE LIBRARY AND I ASSUMED YOU WERE HERE INVESTIGATING.
BEING QUIET WHEN I NEED TO BE IS PART OF MY JOB.
I DIDN'T SEE THIS VIAL, AND I ASSUME NEP DIDN'T, EITHER.
EVERYTHING WAS TASTED AT THIS POINT IN THE BAKE.
MOST OTHER THINGS WERE PREMADE, SO THE GLAZE HERE WAS A WINDOW WHERE THE POISON COULD HAVE BEEN ADDED...
...OUR SUPPLIES WERE ALSO CLEARLY LABELED, SO THEY COULD HAVE BEEN TAMPERED WITH.
COULD MELONHEAD HAVE DONE IT?
AND USED ME TO CREATE AN ALIBI?
COULD NEP...
COULD SHE REALLY HAVE DONE THIS?
OF COURSE NOT.
I TRUST HER.

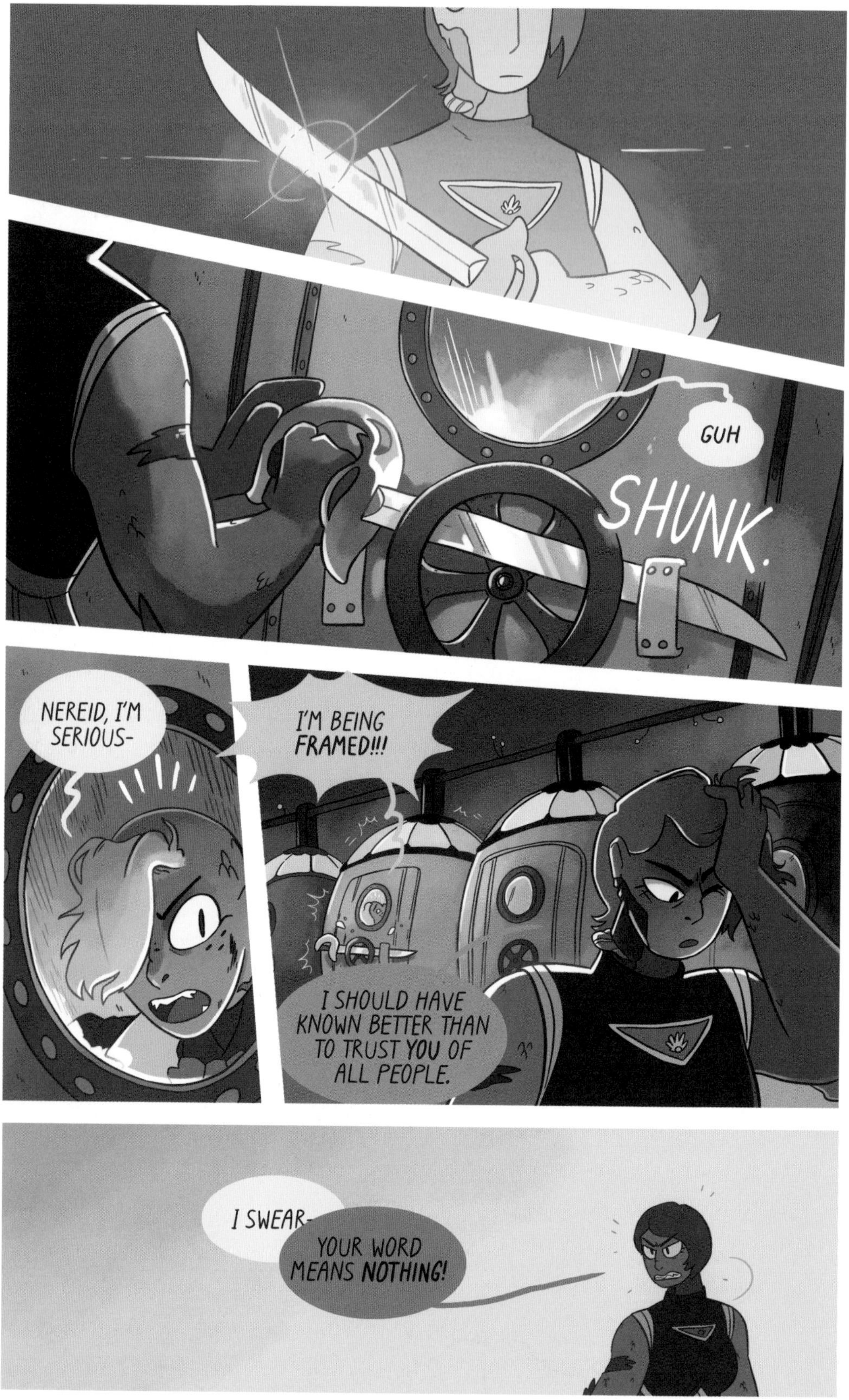
GUH
SHUNK.
NEREID, I'M SERIOUS-
I'M BEING FRAMED!!!
I SHOULD HAVE KNOWN BETTER THAN TO TRUST YOU OF ALL PEOPLE.
I SWEAR-
YOUR WORD MEANS NOTHING!

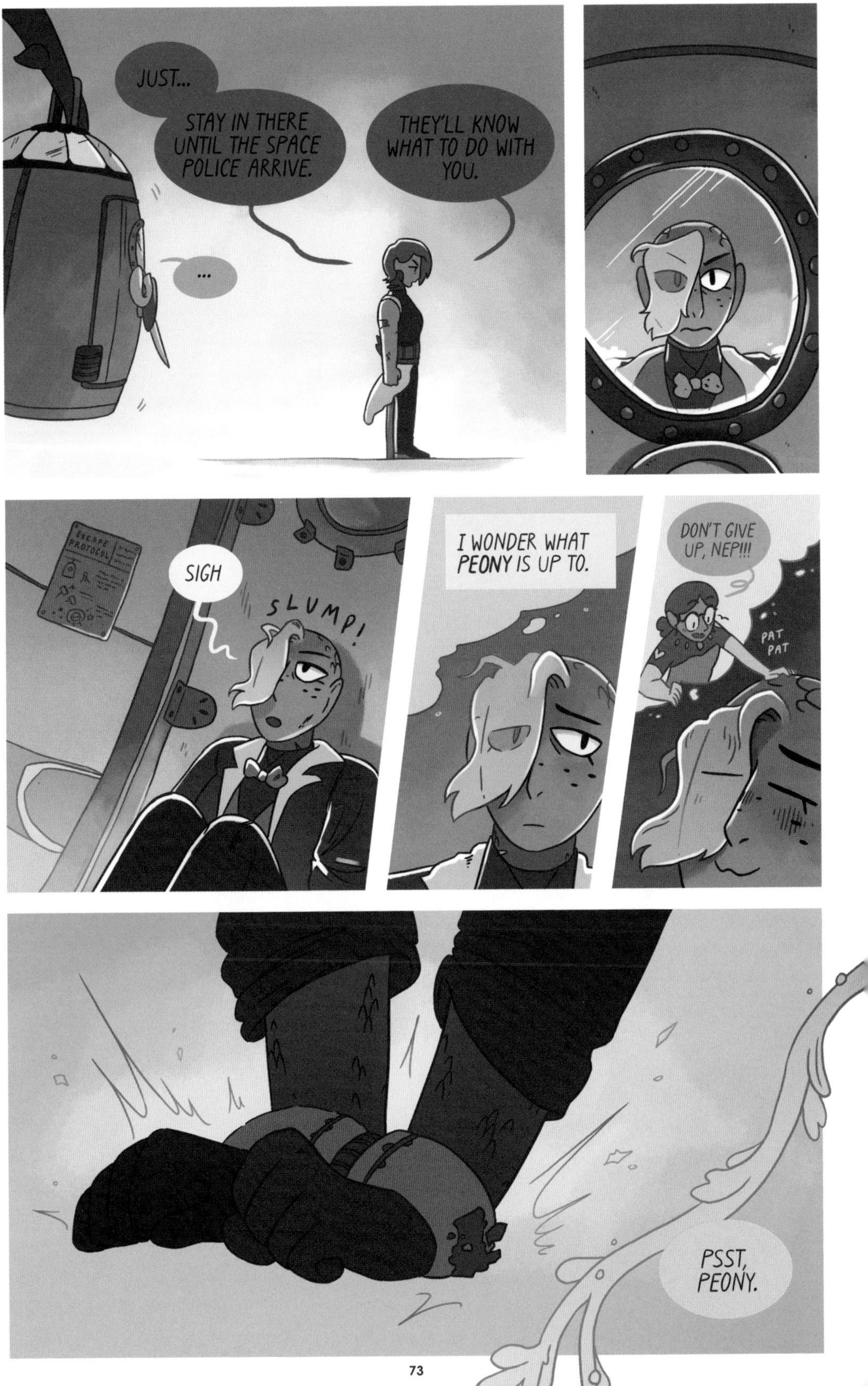
JUST...
STAY IN THERE UNTIL THE SPACE POLICE ARRIVE.
...
THEY'LL KNOW WHAT TO DO WITH YOU.
ESCAPE PROTOCOL
SIGH
SLUMP!
I WONDER WHAT PEONY IS UP TO.
DON'T GIVE UP, NEP!!!
PAT PAT
PSST, PEONY.

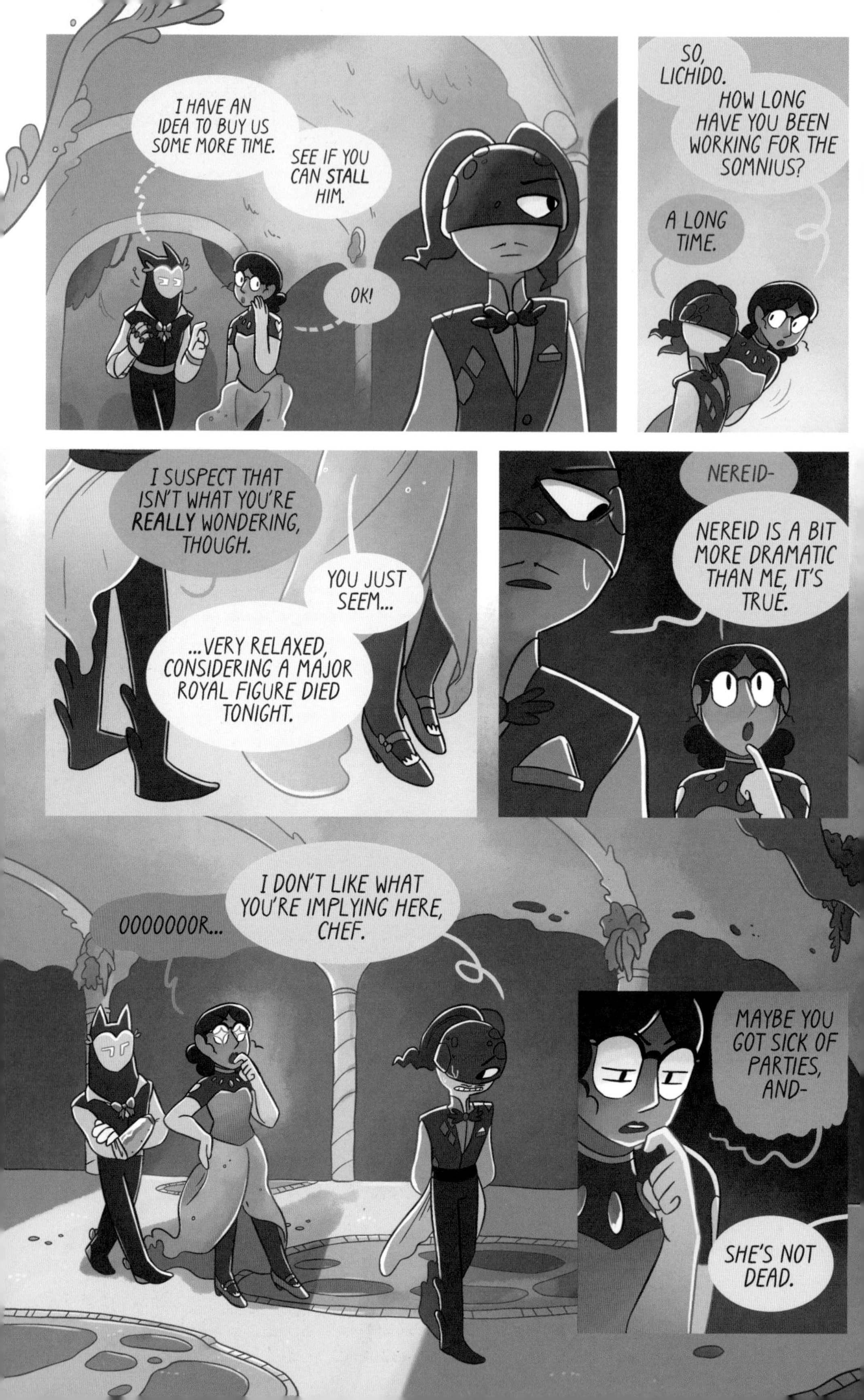
I HAVE AN IDEA TO BUY US SOME MORE TIME.
SEE IF YOU CAN STALL HIM.
OK!
SO, LICHIDO.
HOW LONG HAVE YOU BEEN WORKING FOR THE SOMNIUS?
A LONG TIME.
I SUSPECT THAT ISN'T WHAT YOU'RE REALLY WONDERING, THOUGH.
YOU JUST SEEM...
...VERY RELAXED, CONSIDERING A MAJOR ROYAL FIGURE DIED TONIGHT.
NEREID-
NEREID IS A BIT MORE DRAMATIC THAN ME, IT'S TRUE.
OOOOOOOR...
I DON'T LIKE WHAT YOU'RE IMPLYING HERE, CHEF.
MAYBE YOU GOT SICK OF PARTIES, AND-
SHE'S NOT DEAD.

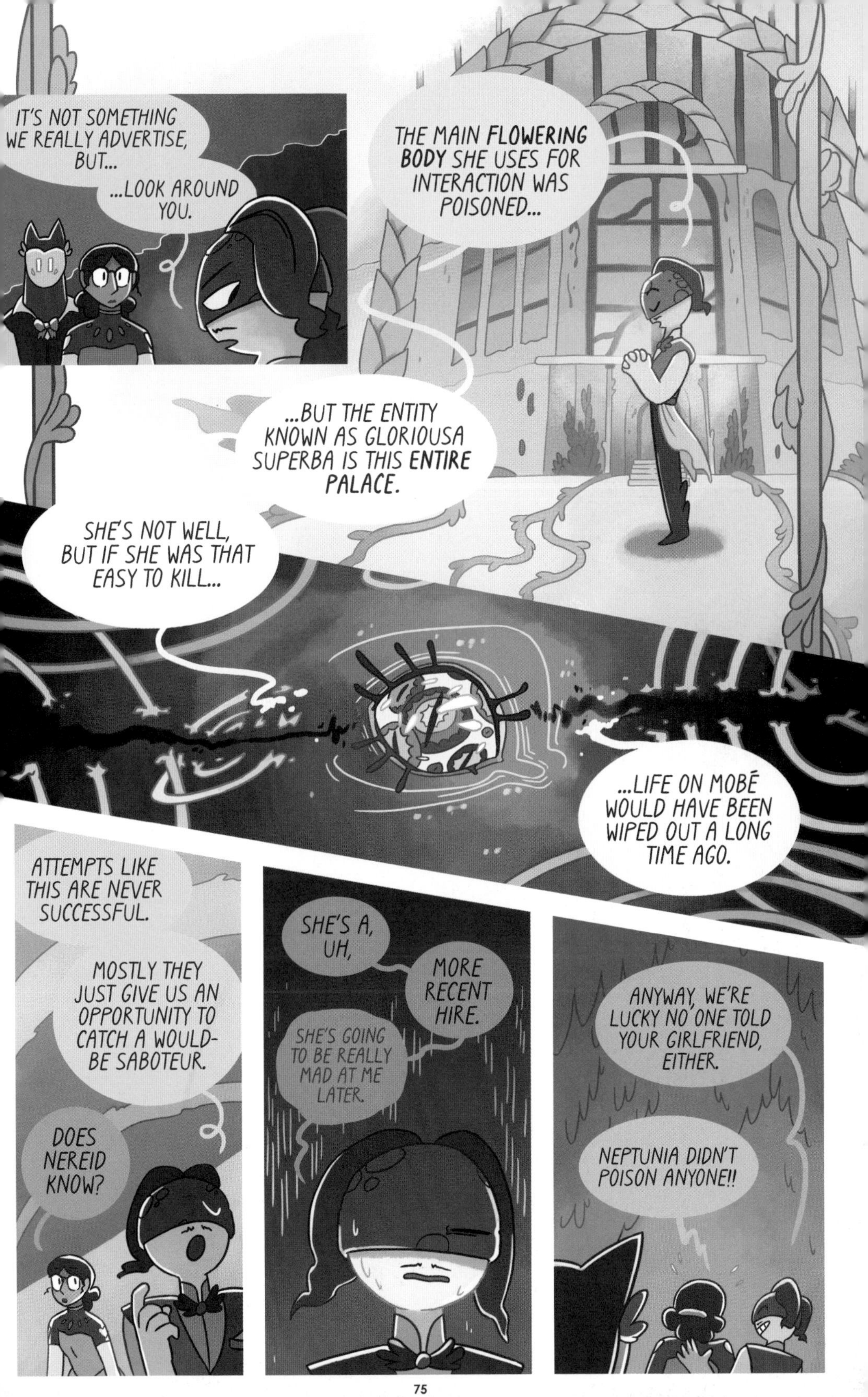
IT'S NOT SOMETHING WE REALLY ADVERTISE, BUT...
...LOOK AROUND YOU.
THE MAIN **FLOWERING BODY** SHE USES FOR INTERACTION WAS POISONED...
...BUT THE ENTITY KNOWN AS GLORIOUSA SUPERBA IS THIS **ENTIRE PALACE.**
SHE'S NOT WELL, BUT IF SHE WAS THAT EASY TO KILL...
...LIFE ON MOBÉ WOULD HAVE BEEN WIPED OUT A LONG TIME AGO.
ATTEMPTS LIKE THIS ARE NEVER SUCCESSFUL.
MOSTLY THEY JUST GIVE US AN OPPORTUNITY TO CATCH A WOULD-BE SABOTEUR.
DOES NEREID KNOW?
SHE'S A, UH,
MORE RECENT HIRE.
SHE'S GOING TO BE REALLY MAD AT ME LATER.
ANYWAY, WE'RE LUCKY NO ONE TOLD YOUR GIRLFRIEND, EITHER.
NEPTUNIA DIDN'T POISON ANYONE!!

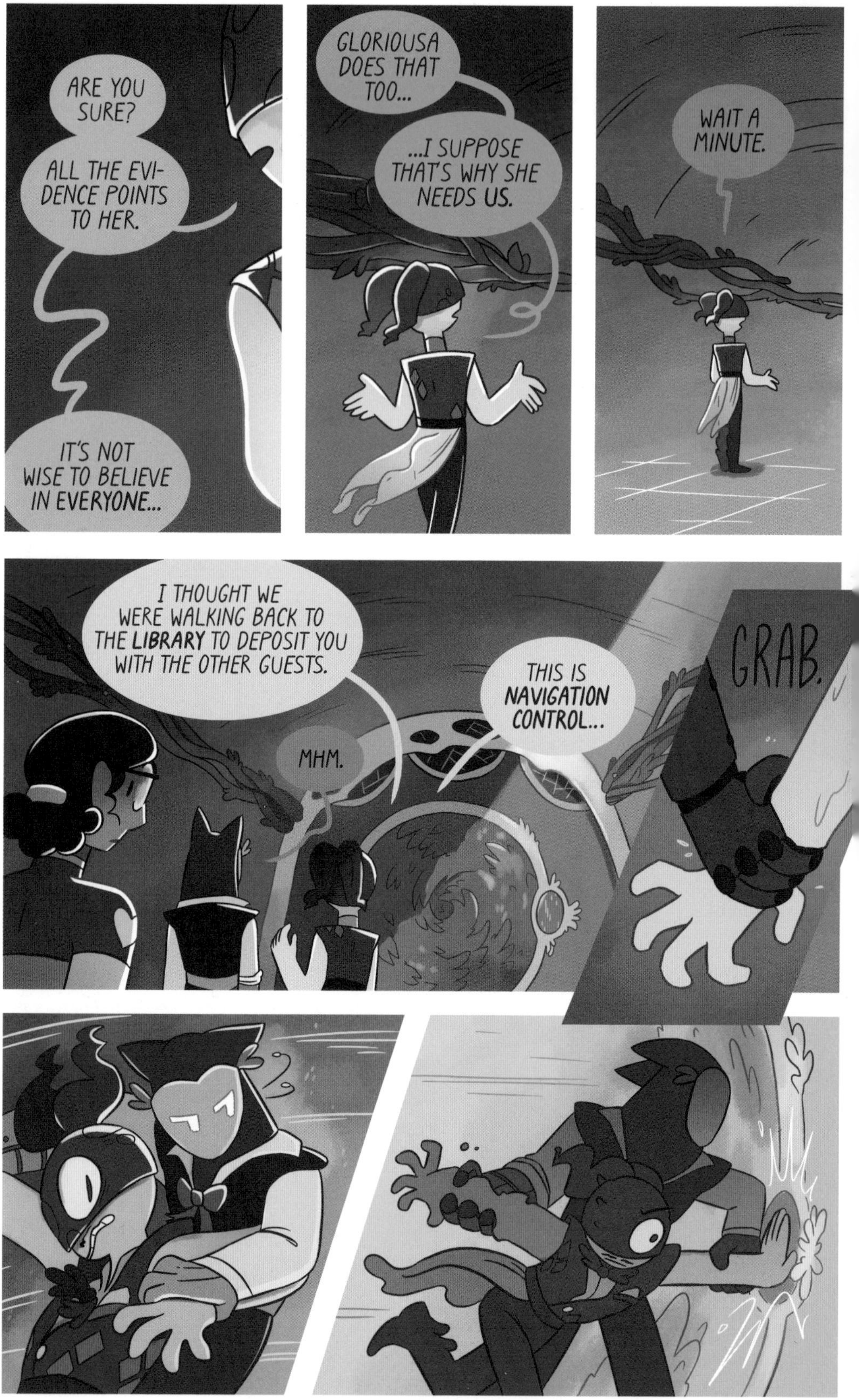
ARE YOU SURE?
ALL THE EVI-DENCE POINTS TO HER.
IT'S NOT WISE TO BELIEVE IN EVERYONE...
GLORIOUSA DOES THAT TOO...
...I SUPPOSE THAT'S WHY SHE NEEDS US.
WAIT A MINUTE.
I THOUGHT WE WERE WALKING BACK TO THE LIBRARY TO DEPOSIT YOU WITH THE OTHER GUESTS.
MHM.
THIS IS NAVIGATION CONTROL...
GRAB.

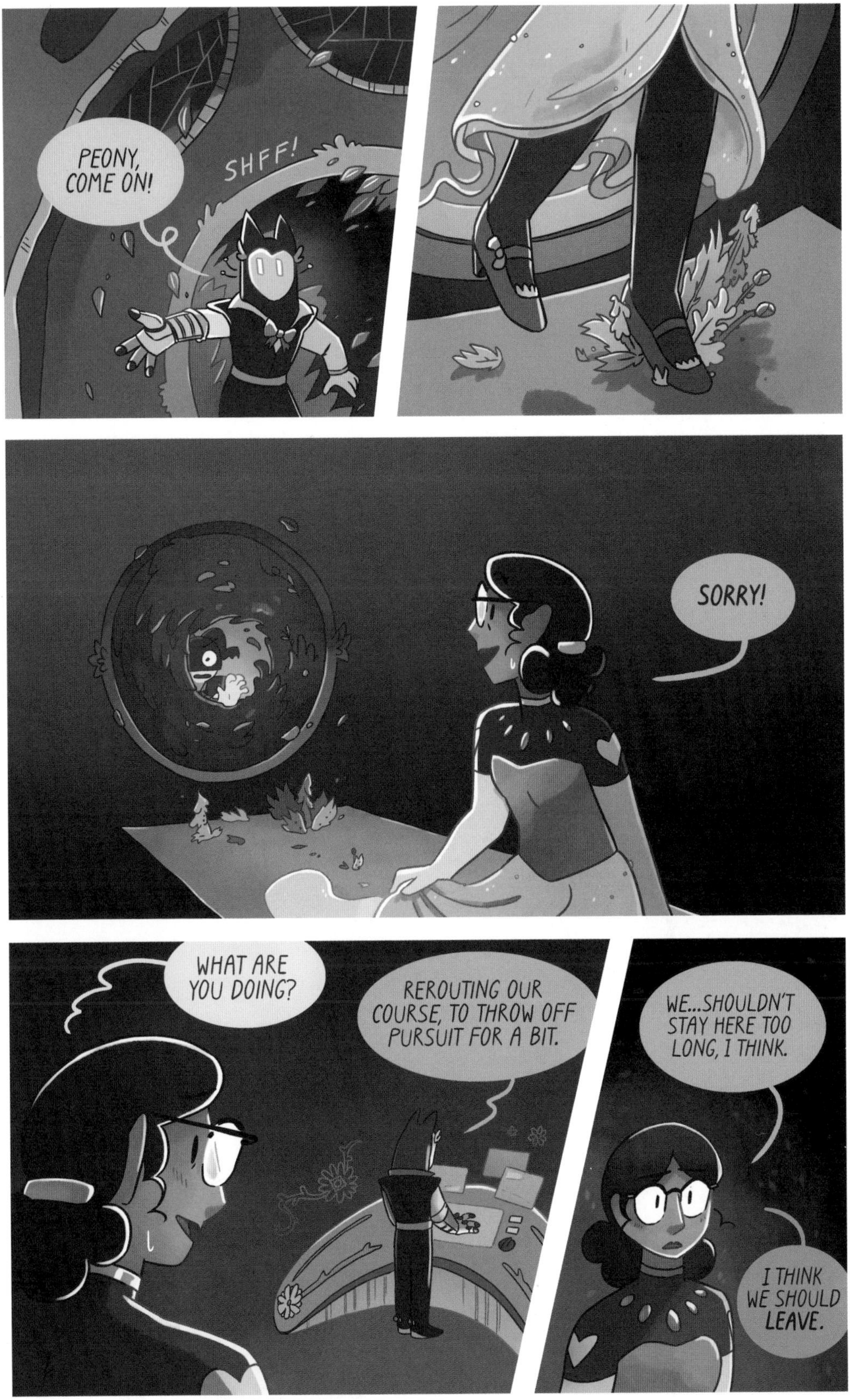
PEONY, COME ON!
SHFF!
SORRY!
WHAT ARE YOU DOING?
REROUTING OUR COURSE, TO THROW OFF PURSUIT FOR A BIT.
WE...SHOULDN'T STAY HERE TOO LONG, I THINK.
I THINK WE SHOULD LEAVE.

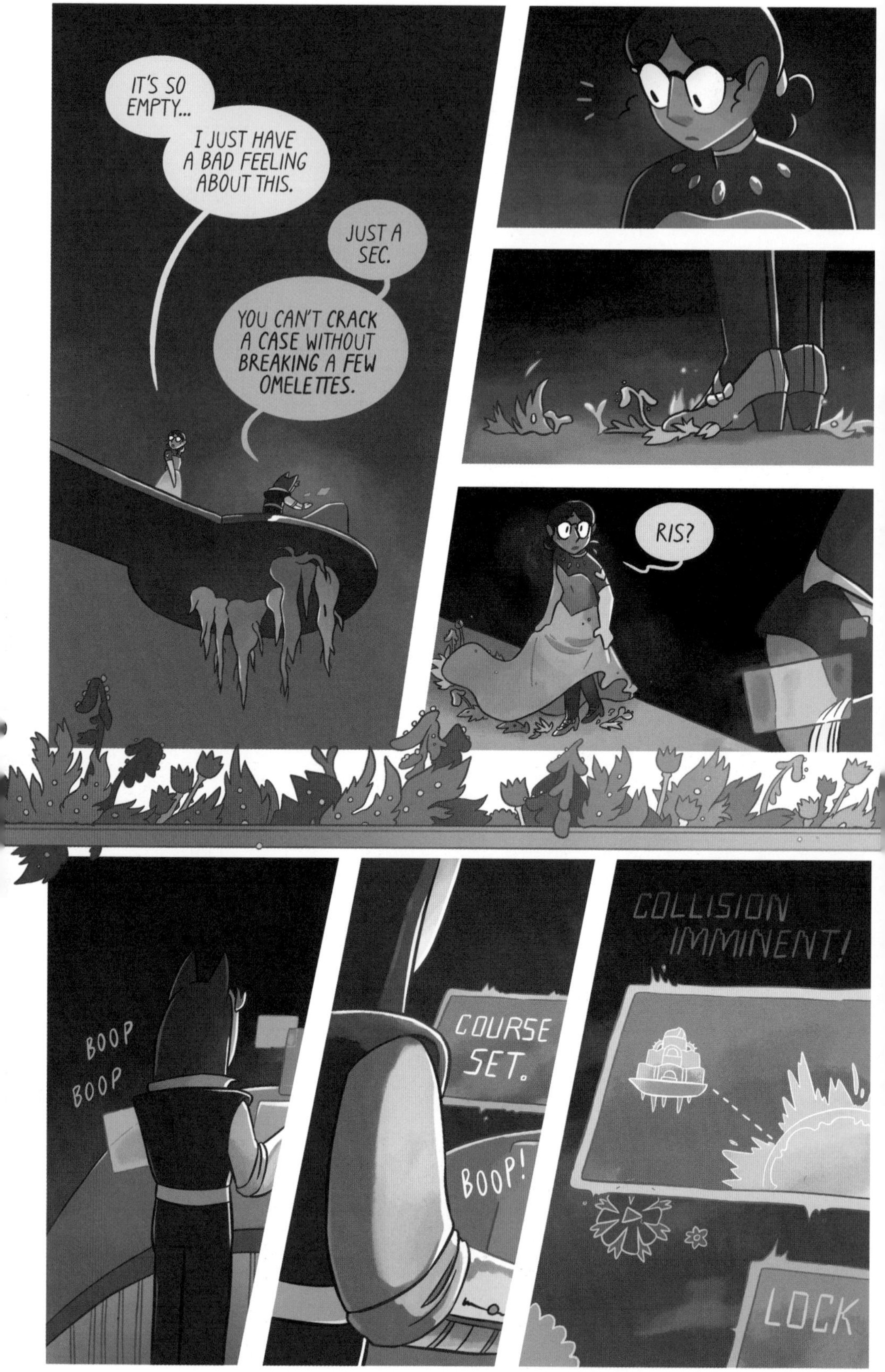
IT'S SO EMPTY...
I JUST HAVE A BAD FEELING ABOUT THIS.
JUST A SEC.
YOU CAN'T CRACK A CASE WITHOUT BREAKING A FEW OMELETTES.
RIS?
BOOP BOOP
COURSE SET.
BOOP!
COLLISION IMMINENT!
LOCK

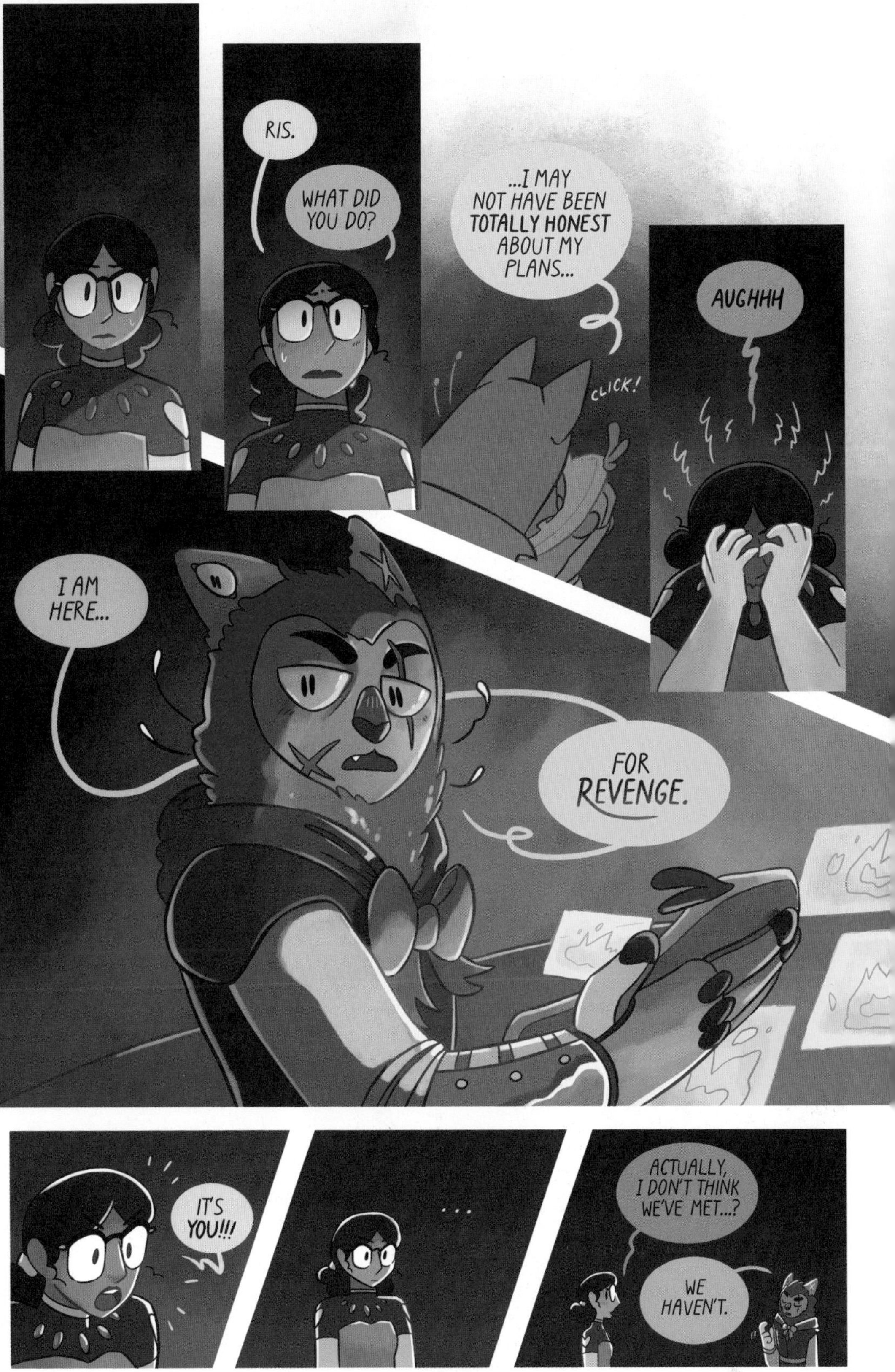

RIS.
WHAT DID YOU DO?
...I MAY NOT HAVE BEEN TOTALLY HONEST ABOUT MY PLANS...
CLICK!
AUGHHH
I AM HERE...
FOR REVENGE.
IT'S YOU!!!
. . .
ACTUALLY, I DON'T THINK WE'VE MET...?
WE HAVEN'T.

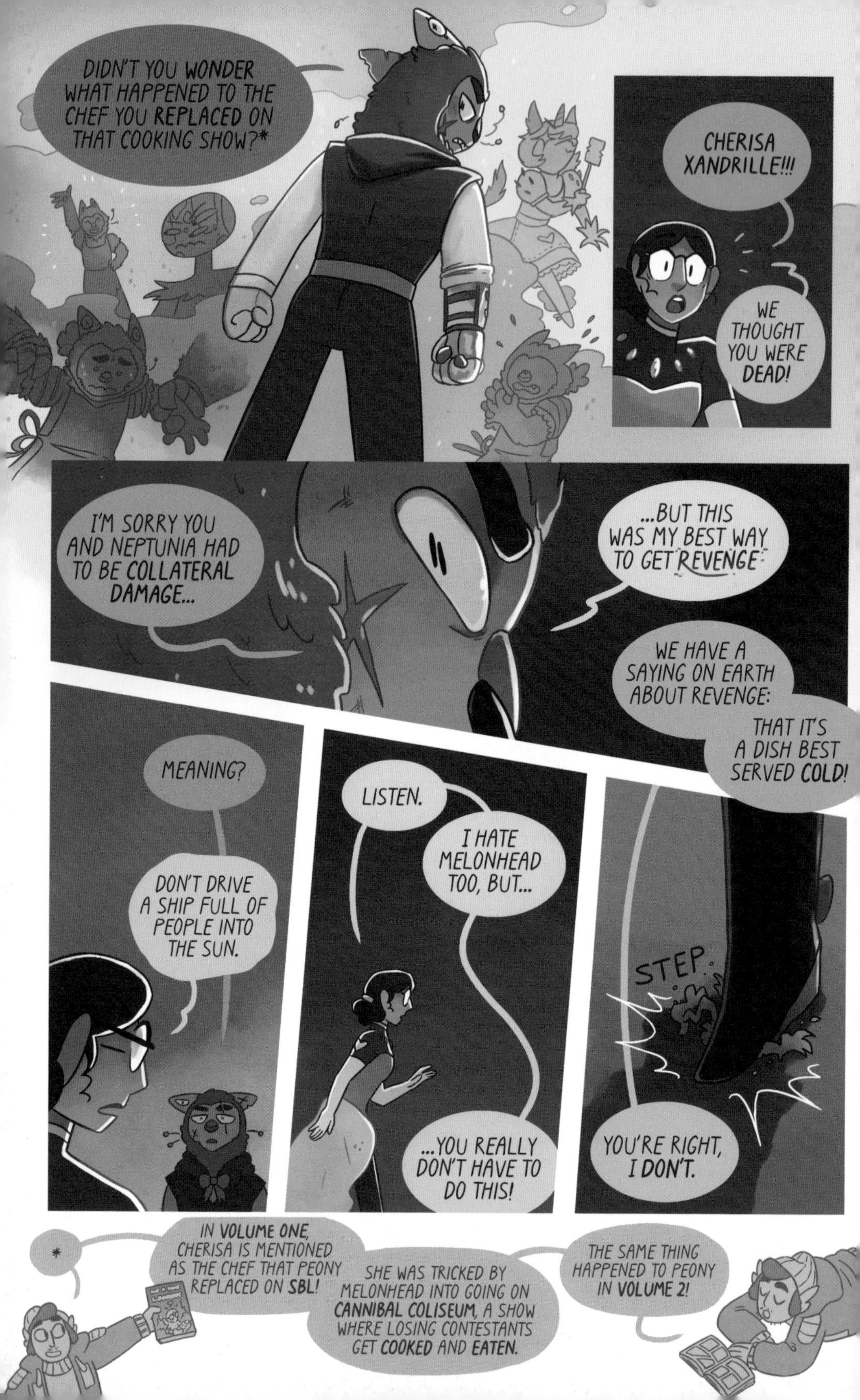
DIDN'T YOU WONDER WHAT HAPPENED TO THE CHEF YOU REPLACED ON THAT COOKING SHOW?*
CHERISA XANDRILLE!!!
WE THOUGHT YOU WERE DEAD!
I'M SORRY YOU AND NEPTUNIA HAD TO BE COLLATERAL DAMAGE...
...BUT THIS WAS MY BEST WAY TO GET REVENGE
WE HAVE A SAYING ON EARTH ABOUT REVENGE:
THAT IT'S A DISH BEST SERVED COLD!
MEANING?
DON'T DRIVE A SHIP FULL OF PEOPLE INTO THE SUN.
LISTEN.
I HATE MELONHEAD TOO, BUT...
...YOU REALLY DON'T HAVE TO DO THIS!
STEP.
YOU'RE RIGHT, I DON'T.
*
IN VOLUME ONE, CHERISA IS MENTIONED AS THE CHEF THAT PEONY REPLACED ON SBL!
SHE WAS TRICKED BY MELONHEAD INTO GOING ON CANNIBAL COLISEUM, A SHOW WHERE LOSING CONTESTANTS GET COOKED AND EATEN.
THE SAME THING HAPPENED TO PEONY IN VOLUME 2!

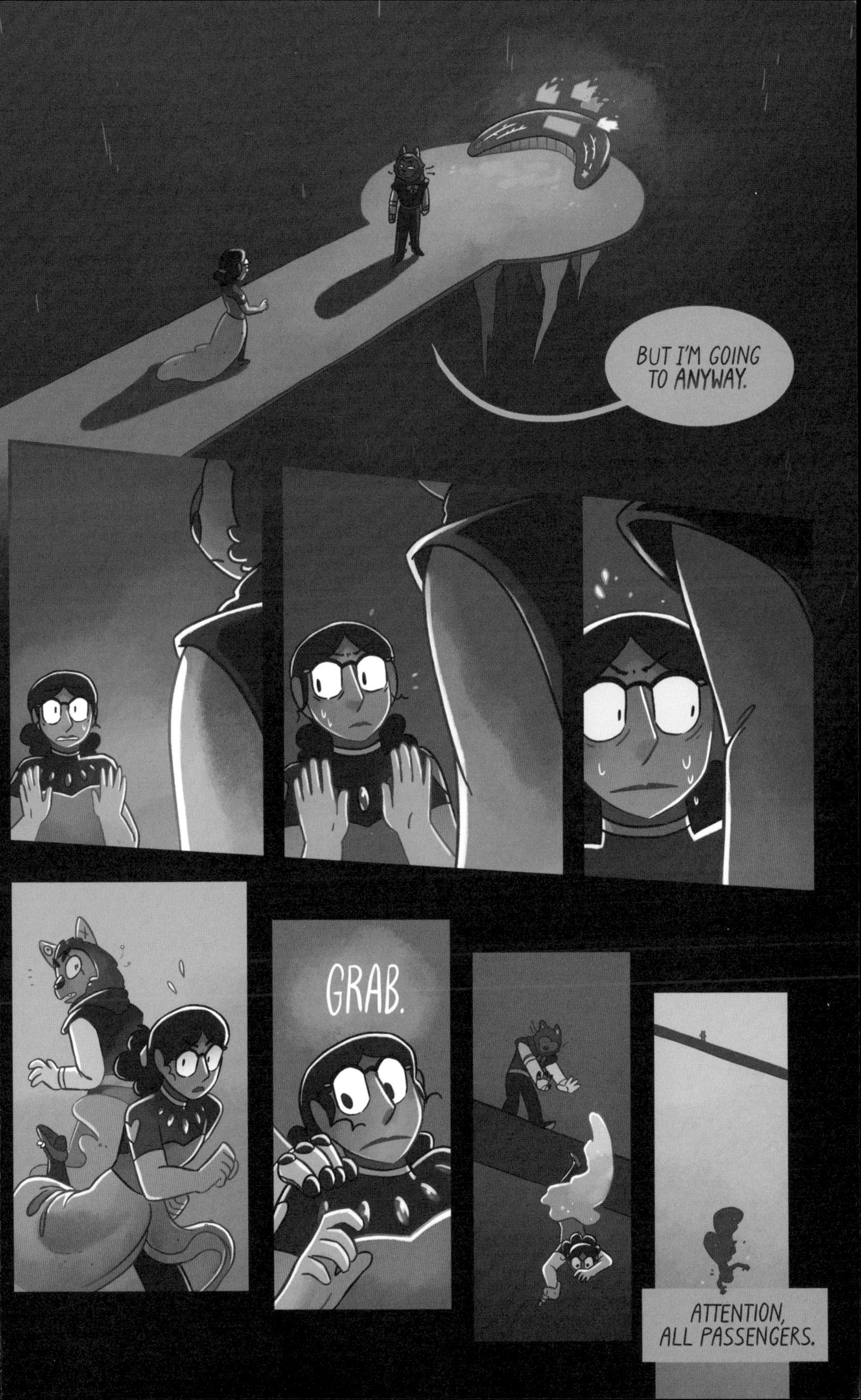
BUT I'M GOING TO ANYWAY.
GRAB.
ATTENTION, ALL PASSENGERS.

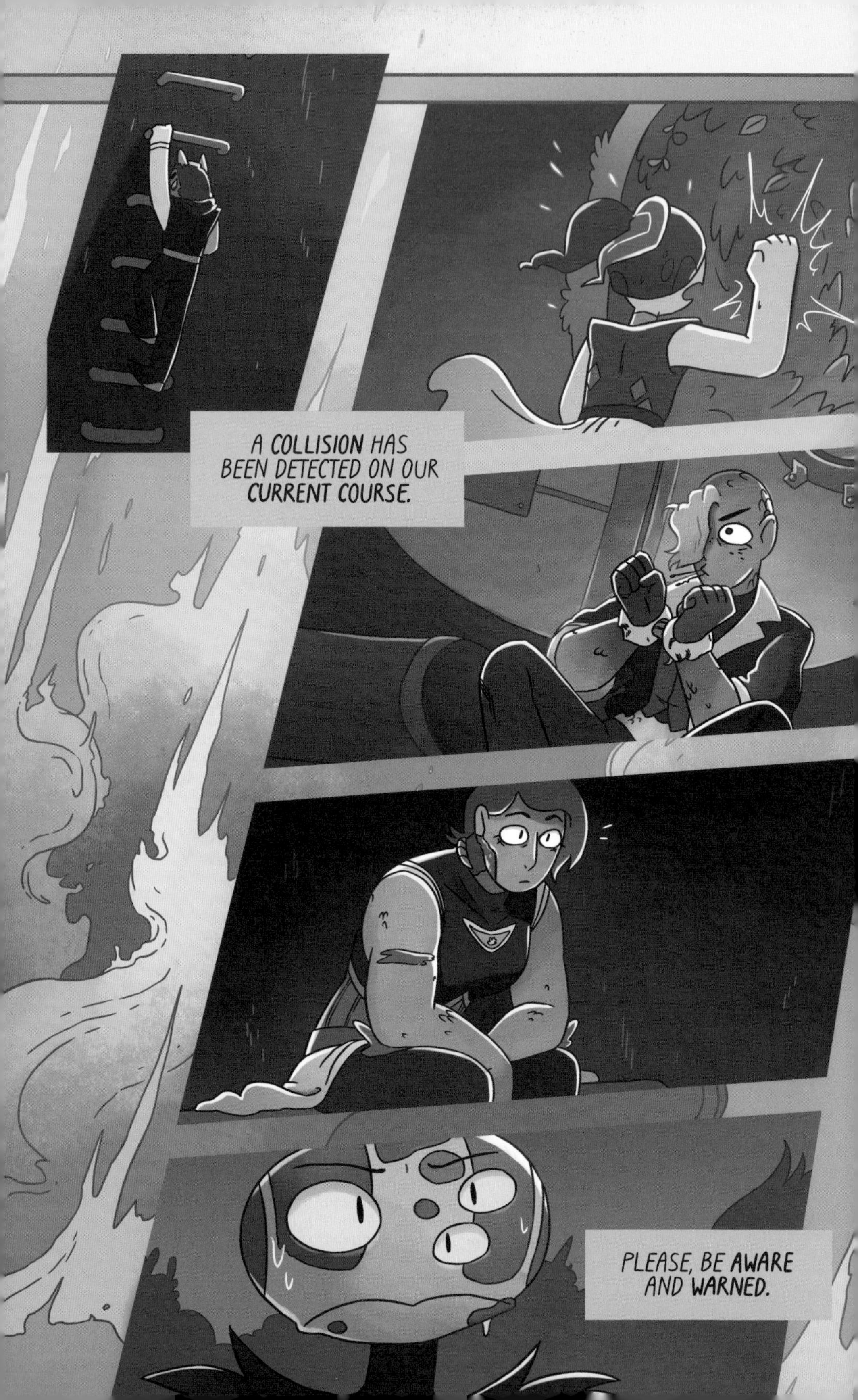
A COLLISION HAS BEEN DETECTED ON OUR CURRENT COURSE.
PLEASE, BE AWARE AND WARNED.

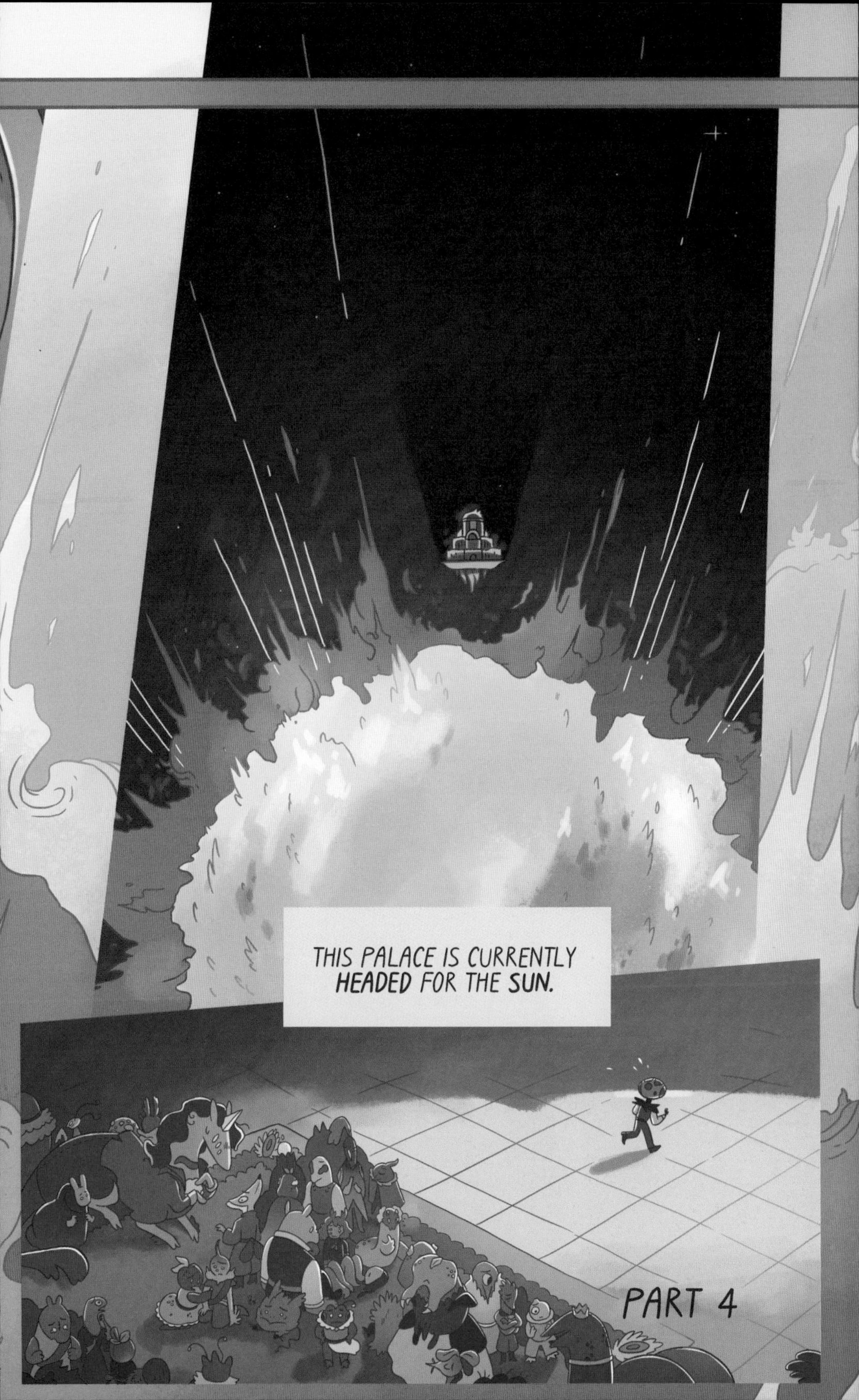
THIS PALACE IS CURRENTLY HEADED FOR THE SUN.
PART 4

ESCAPE BAY...

ESCAPE BAY...!

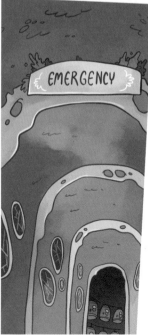

EMERGENCY

IS SOMEONE OUT THERE?

BOP
BOP
BEP
BEEEPT!
BOP

WHAT'S GOING ON WITH THE PALACE?

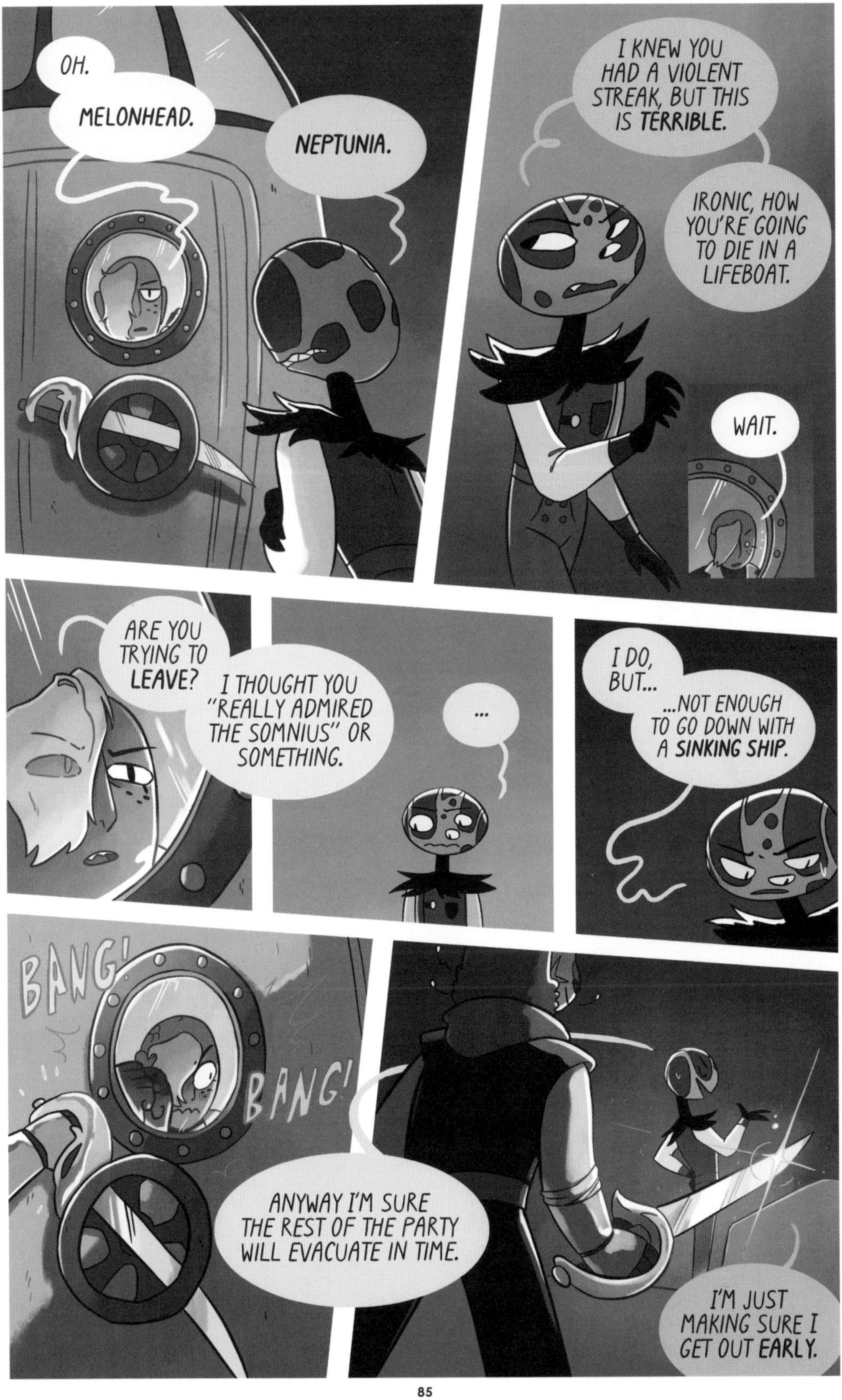
OH.
MELONHEAD.
NEPTUNIA.
I KNEW YOU HAD A VIOLENT STREAK, BUT THIS IS TERRIBLE.
IRONIC, HOW YOU'RE GOING TO DIE IN A LIFEBOAT.
WAIT.
ARE YOU TRYING TO LEAVE?
I THOUGHT YOU "REALLY ADMIRED THE SOMNIUS" OR SOMETHING.
...
I DO, BUT...
...NOT ENOUGH TO GO DOWN WITH A SINKING SHIP.
BANG!
BANG!
ANYWAY I'M SURE THE REST OF THE PARTY WILL EVACUATE IN TIME.
I'M JUST MAKING SURE I GET OUT EARLY.

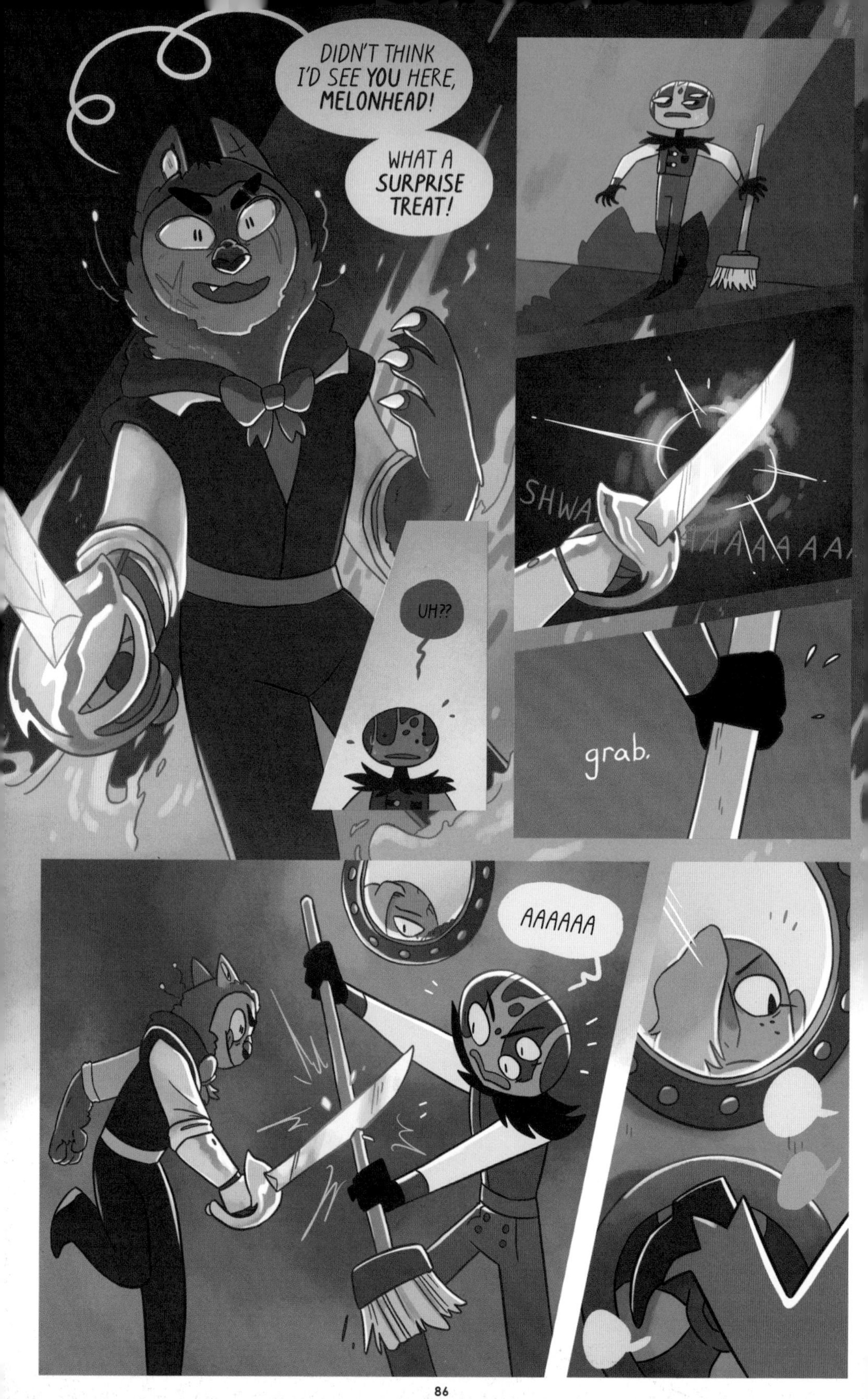

DIDN'T THINK I'D SEE YOU HERE, MELONHEAD!
WHAT A SURPRISE TREAT!
SHWA
AAAAA
UH??
grab.
AAAAAA

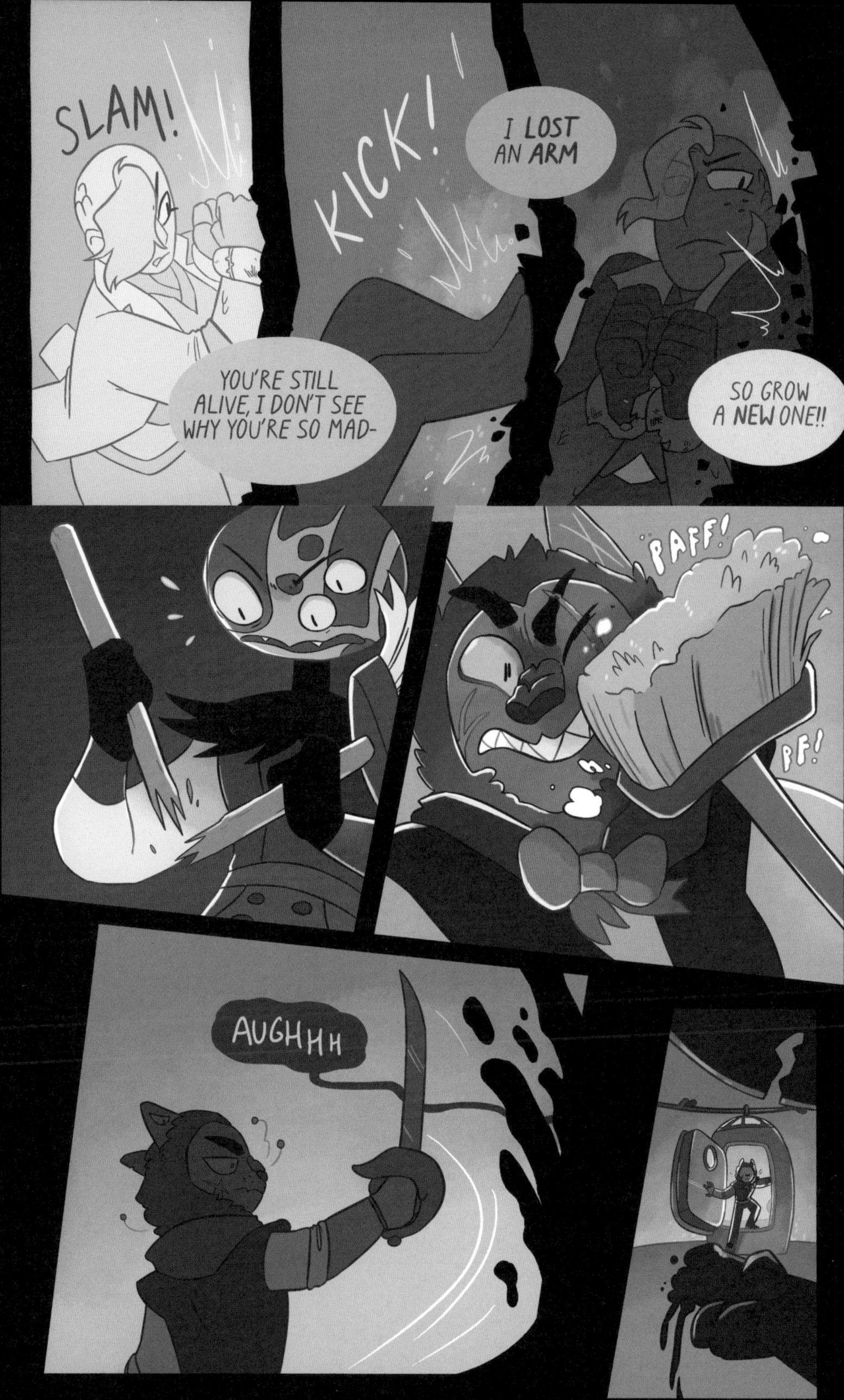
SLAM!
KICK!
I LOST AN ARM
YOU'RE STILL ALIVE, I DON'T SEE WHY YOU'RE SO MAD-
SO GROW A NEW ONE!!
PAFF!
PF!
AUGHHH

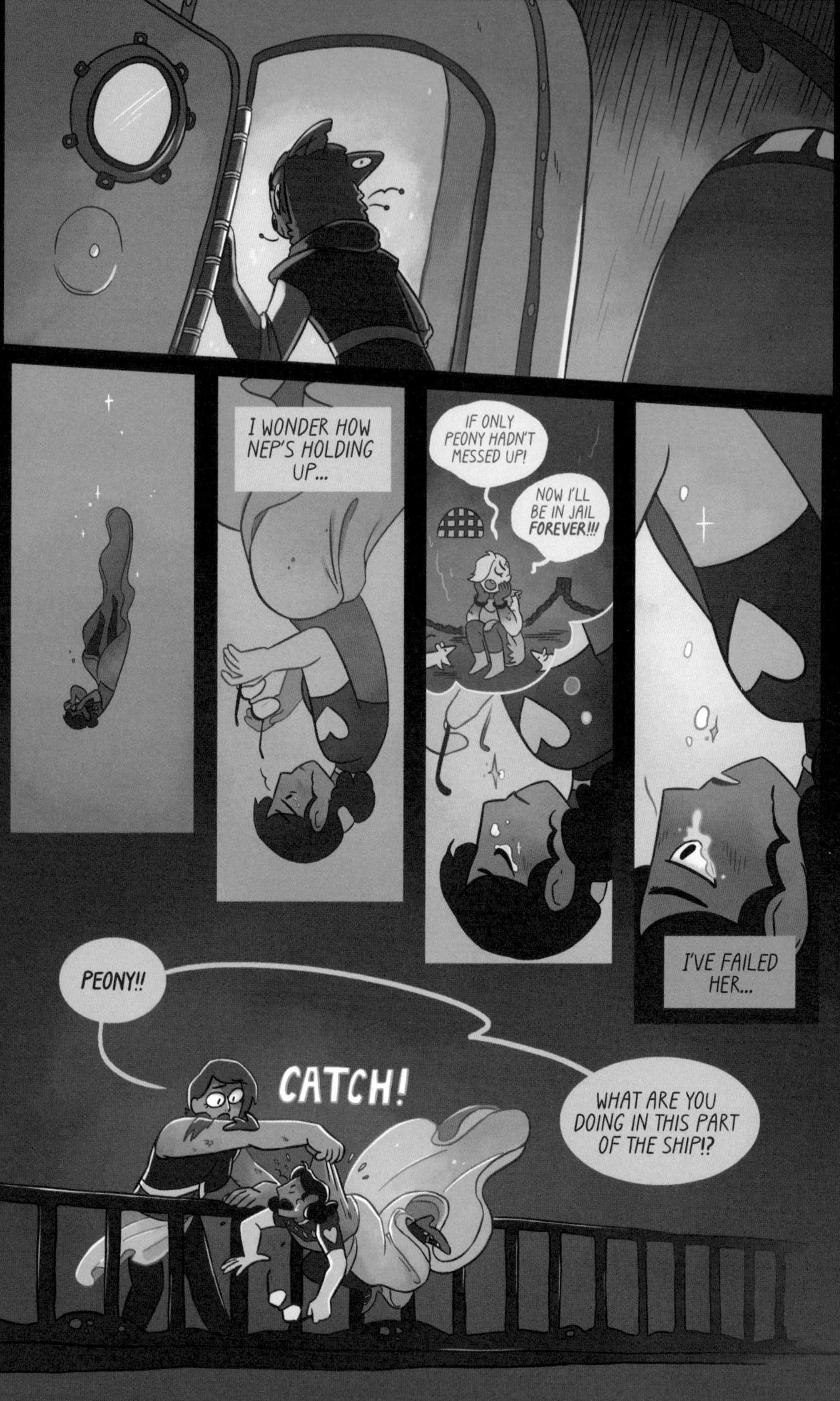
I WONDER HOW NEP'S HOLDING UP...
IF ONLY PEONY HADN'T MESSED UP!
NOW I'LL BE IN JAIL **FOREVER!!!**
I'VE FAILED HER...
PEONY!!
WHAT ARE YOU DOING IN THIS PART OF THE SHIP!?
CATCH!

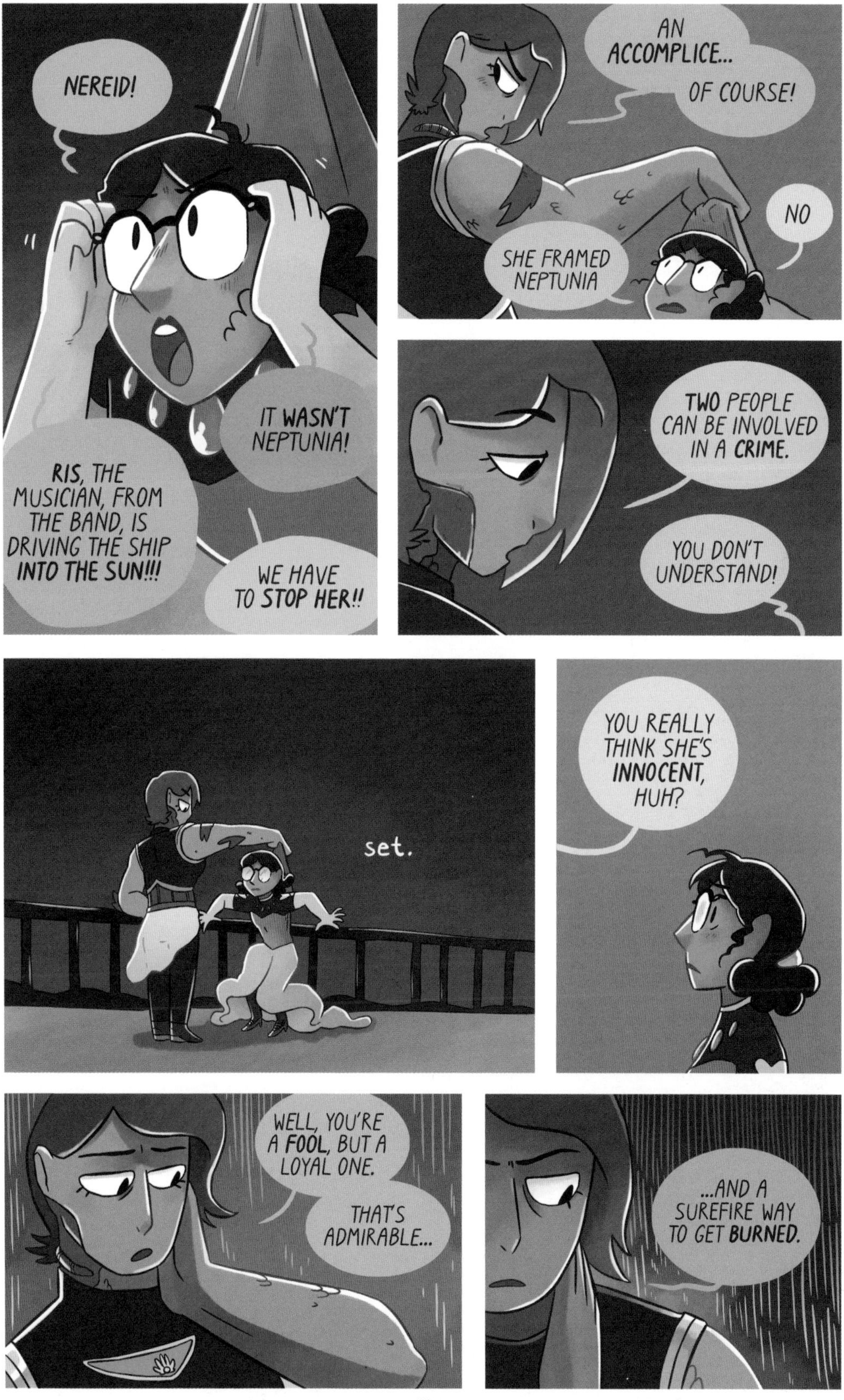
NEREID!
AN ACCOMPLICE...
OF COURSE!
SHE FRAMED NEPTUNIA
NO
IT WASN'T NEPTUNIA!
RIS, THE MUSICIAN, FROM THE BAND, IS DRIVING THE SHIP INTO THE SUN!!!
WE HAVE TO STOP HER!!
TWO PEOPLE CAN BE INVOLVED IN A CRIME.
YOU DON'T UNDERSTAND!
set.
YOU REALLY THINK SHE'S INNOCENT, HUH?
WELL, YOU'RE A FOOL, BUT A LOYAL ONE.
THAT'S ADMIRABLE...
...AND A SUREFIRE WAY TO GET BURNED.

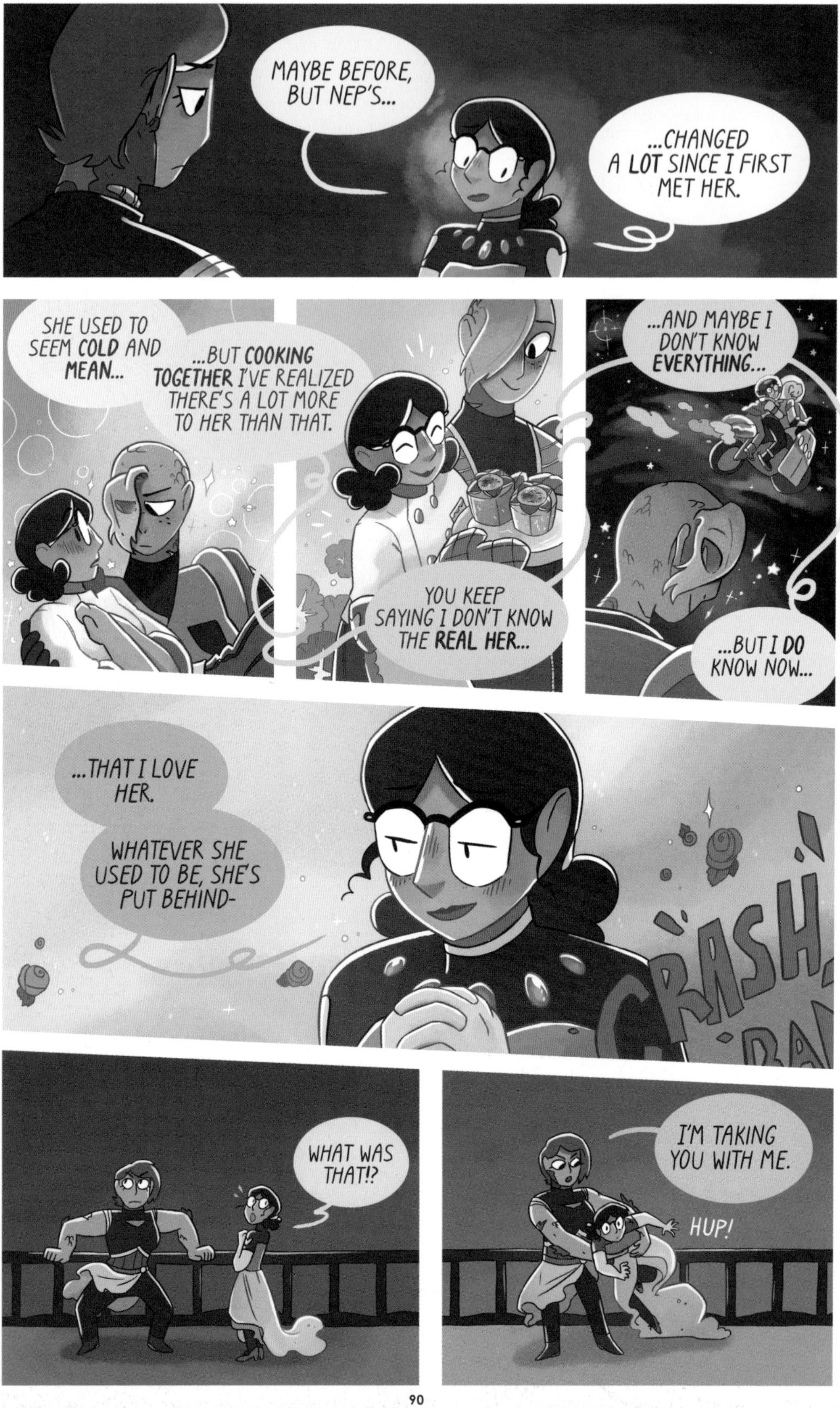
MAYBE BEFORE, BUT NEP'S...
...CHANGED A LOT SINCE I FIRST MET HER.
SHE USED TO SEEM COLD AND MEAN...
...BUT COOKING TOGETHER I'VE REALIZED THERE'S A LOT MORE TO HER THAN THAT.
YOU KEEP SAYING I DON'T KNOW THE REAL HER...
...AND MAYBE I DON'T KNOW EVERYTHING...
...BUT I DO KNOW NOW...
...THAT I LOVE HER.
WHATEVER SHE USED TO BE, SHE'S PUT BEHIND-
CRASH
WHAT WAS THAT!?
I'M TAKING YOU WITH ME.
HUP!

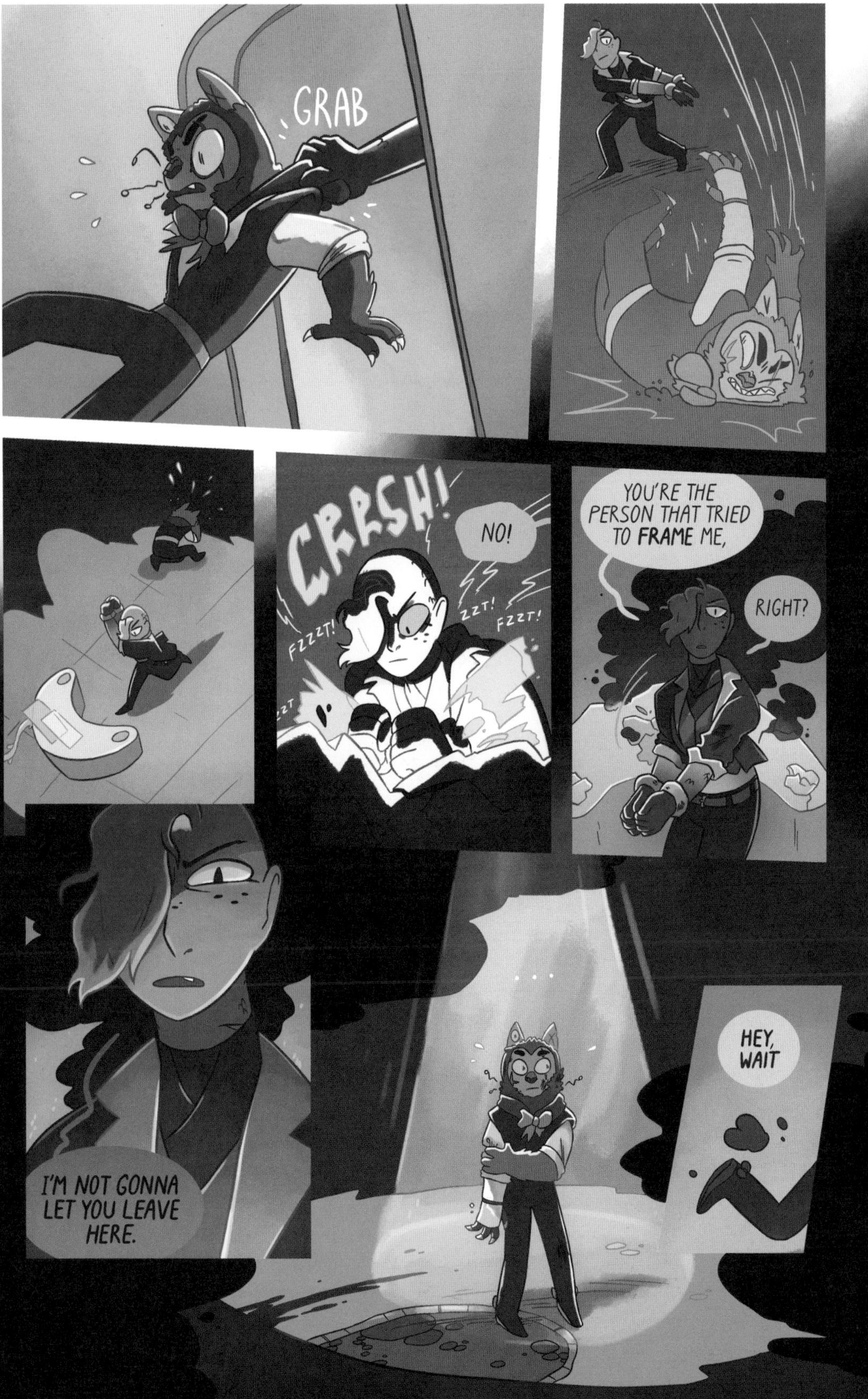
GRAB
CRASH!
NO!
FZZZT!
ZZT!
FZZT!
YOU'RE THE PERSON THAT TRIED TO **FRAME** ME,
RIGHT?
I'M NOT GONNA LET YOU LEAVE HERE.
HEY, WAIT

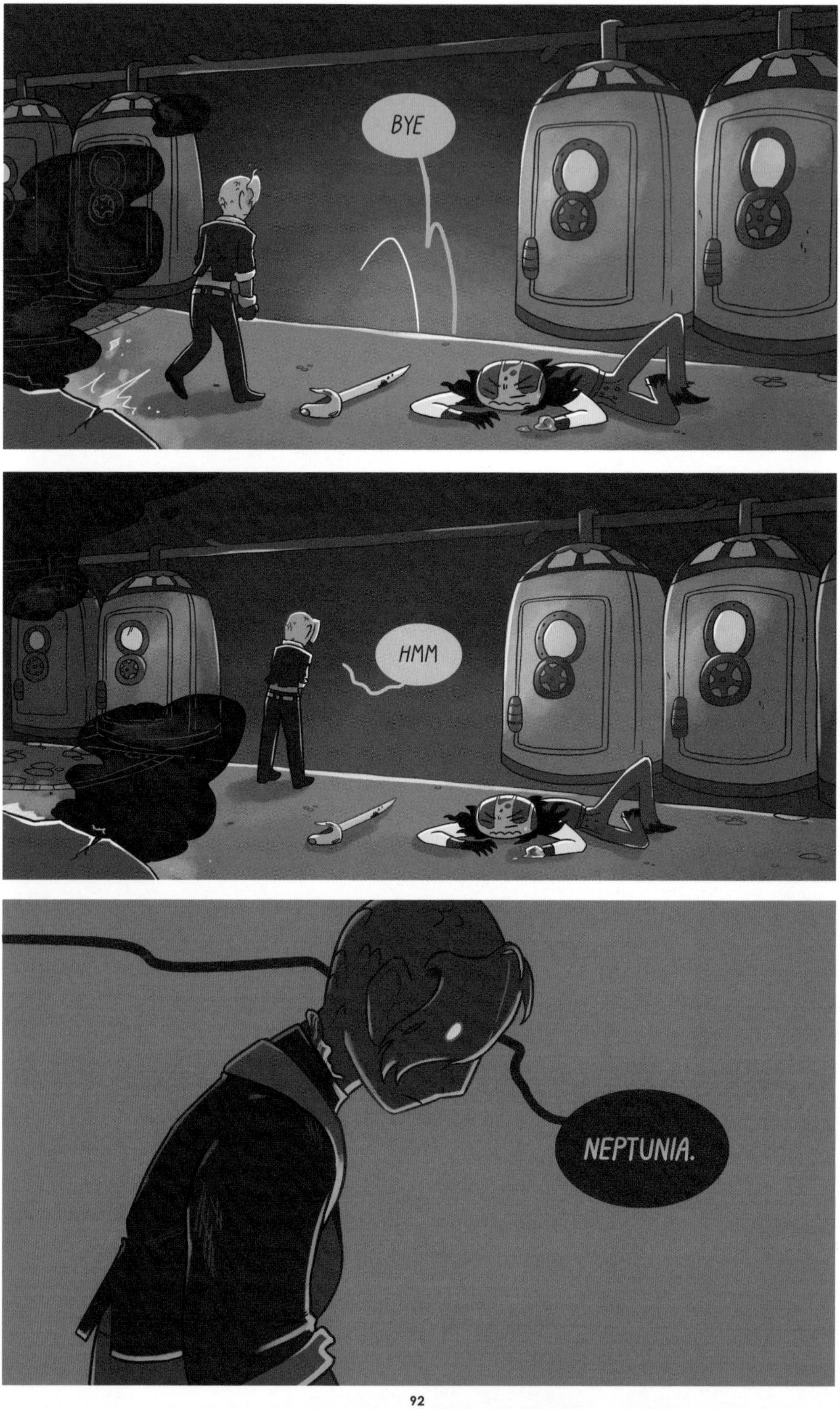
BYE
HMM
NEPTUNIA.

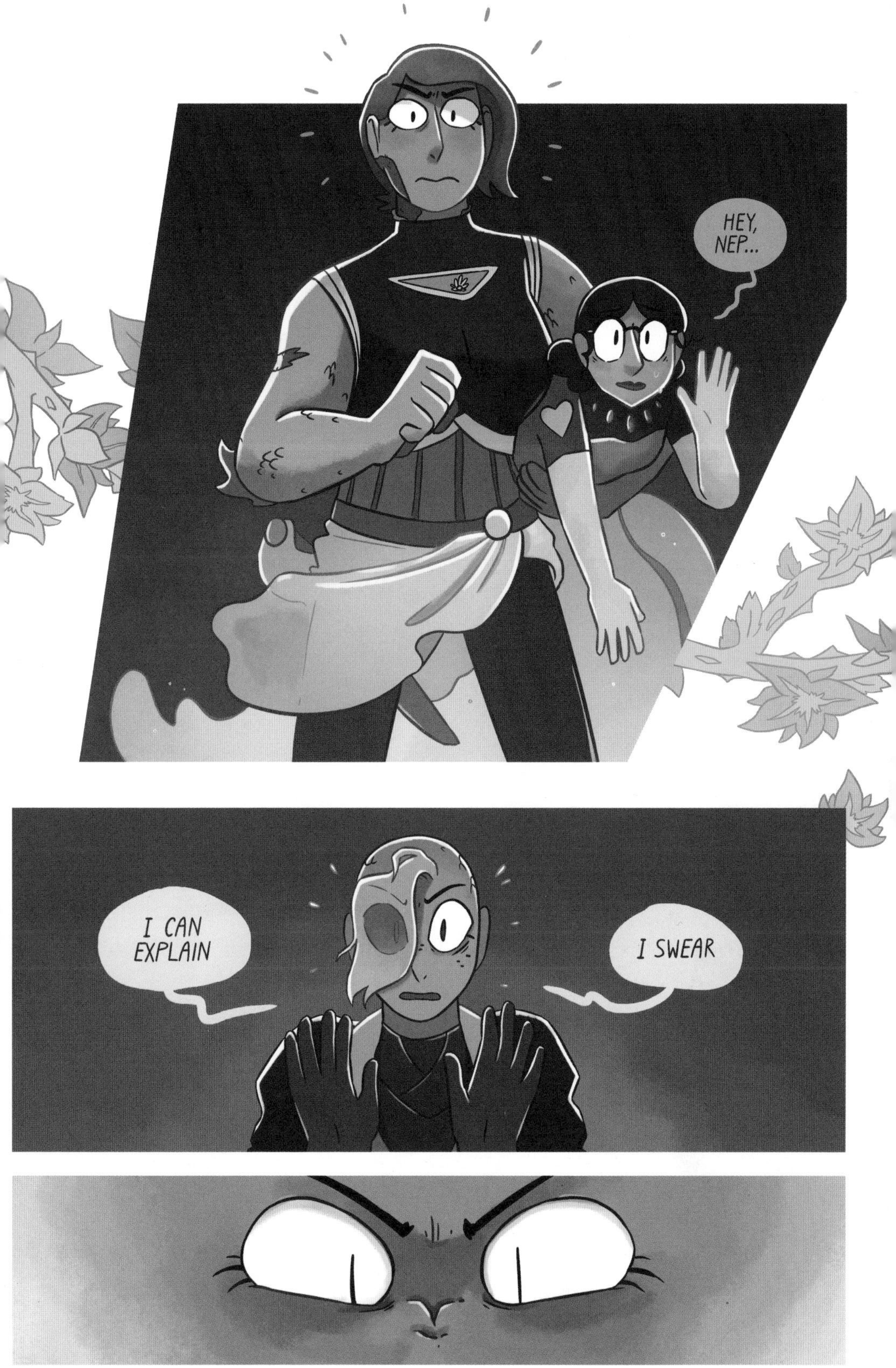
HEY, NEP...
I CAN EXPLAIN
I SWEAR

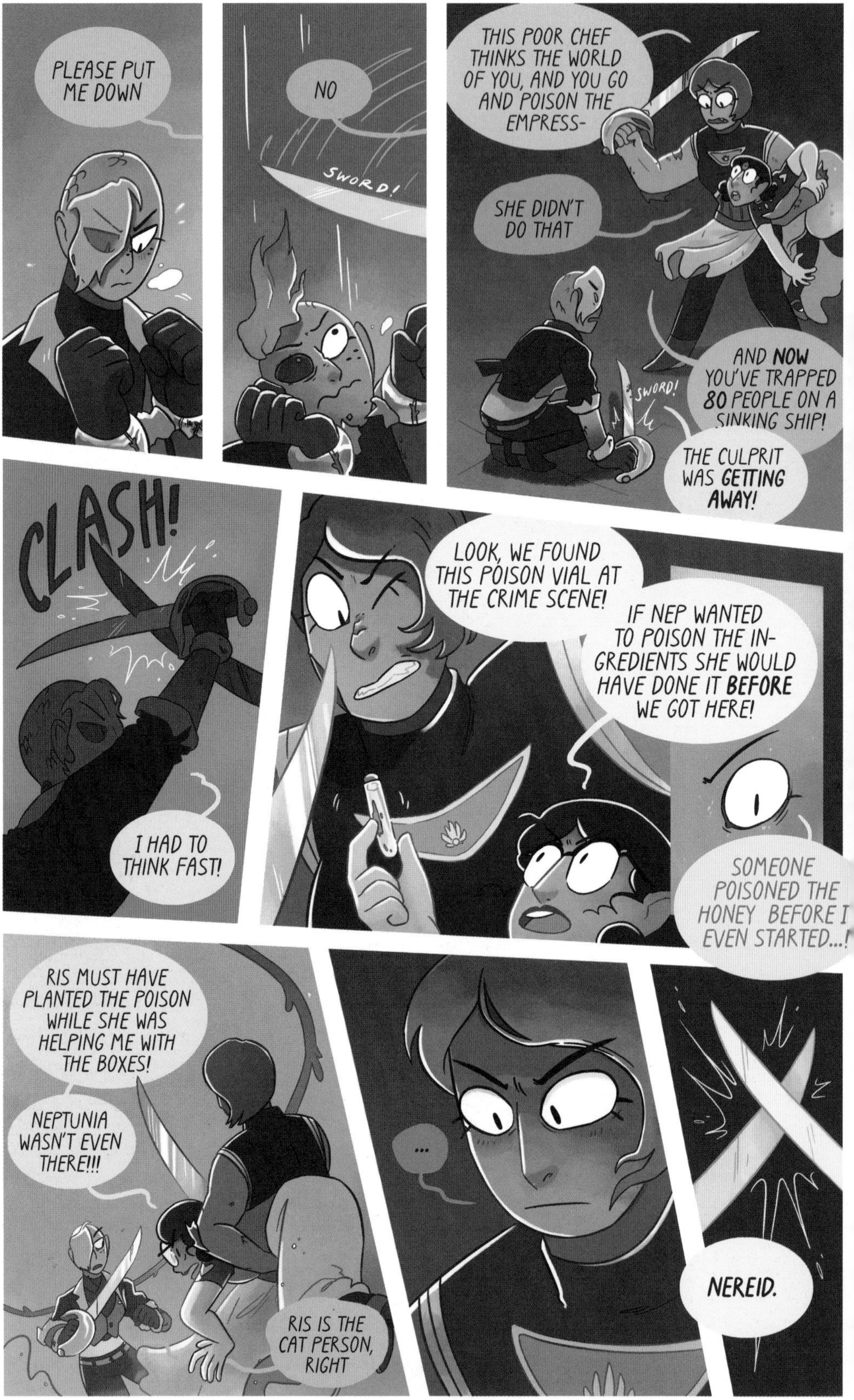
PLEASE PUT ME DOWN
NO
SWORD!
THIS POOR CHEF THINKS THE WORLD OF YOU, AND YOU GO AND POISON THE EMPRESS-
SHE DIDN'T DO THAT
SWORD!
AND **NOW** YOU'VE TRAPPED **80** PEOPLE ON A SINKING SHIP!
THE CULPRIT WAS **GETTING AWAY!**
CLASH!
I HAD TO THINK FAST!
LOOK, WE FOUND THIS POISON VIAL AT THE CRIME SCENE!
IF NEP WANTED TO POISON THE IN-GREDIENTS SHE WOULD HAVE DONE IT **BEFORE** WE GOT HERE!
SOMEONE POISONED THE HONEY BEFORE I EVEN STARTED...!
RIS MUST HAVE PLANTED THE POISON WHILE SHE WAS HELPING ME WITH THE BOXES!
NEPTUNIA WASN'T EVEN THERE!!!
RIS IS THE CAT PERSON, RIGHT
...
NEREID.

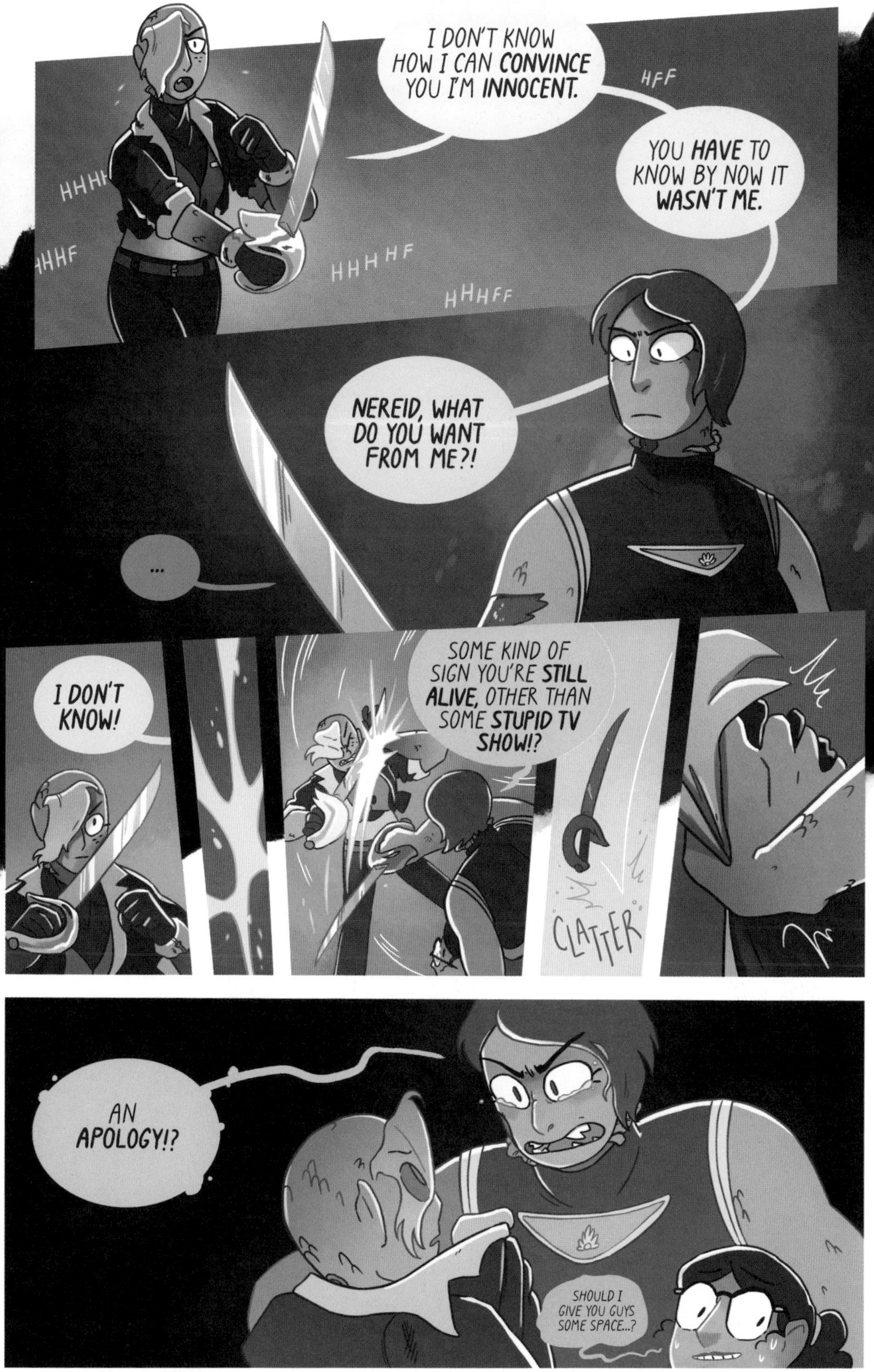

I DON'T KNOW HOW I CAN CONVINCE YOU I'M INNOCENT.
HHHH
HHHF
HHHHF
HHHFF
HFF
YOU HAVE TO KNOW BY NOW IT WASN'T ME.
NEREID, WHAT DO YOU WANT FROM ME?!
...
I DON'T KNOW!
SOME KIND OF SIGN YOU'RE STILL ALIVE, OTHER THAN SOME STUPID TV SHOW!?
CLATTER
AN APOLOGY!?
SHOULD I GIVE YOU GUYS SOME SPACE...?

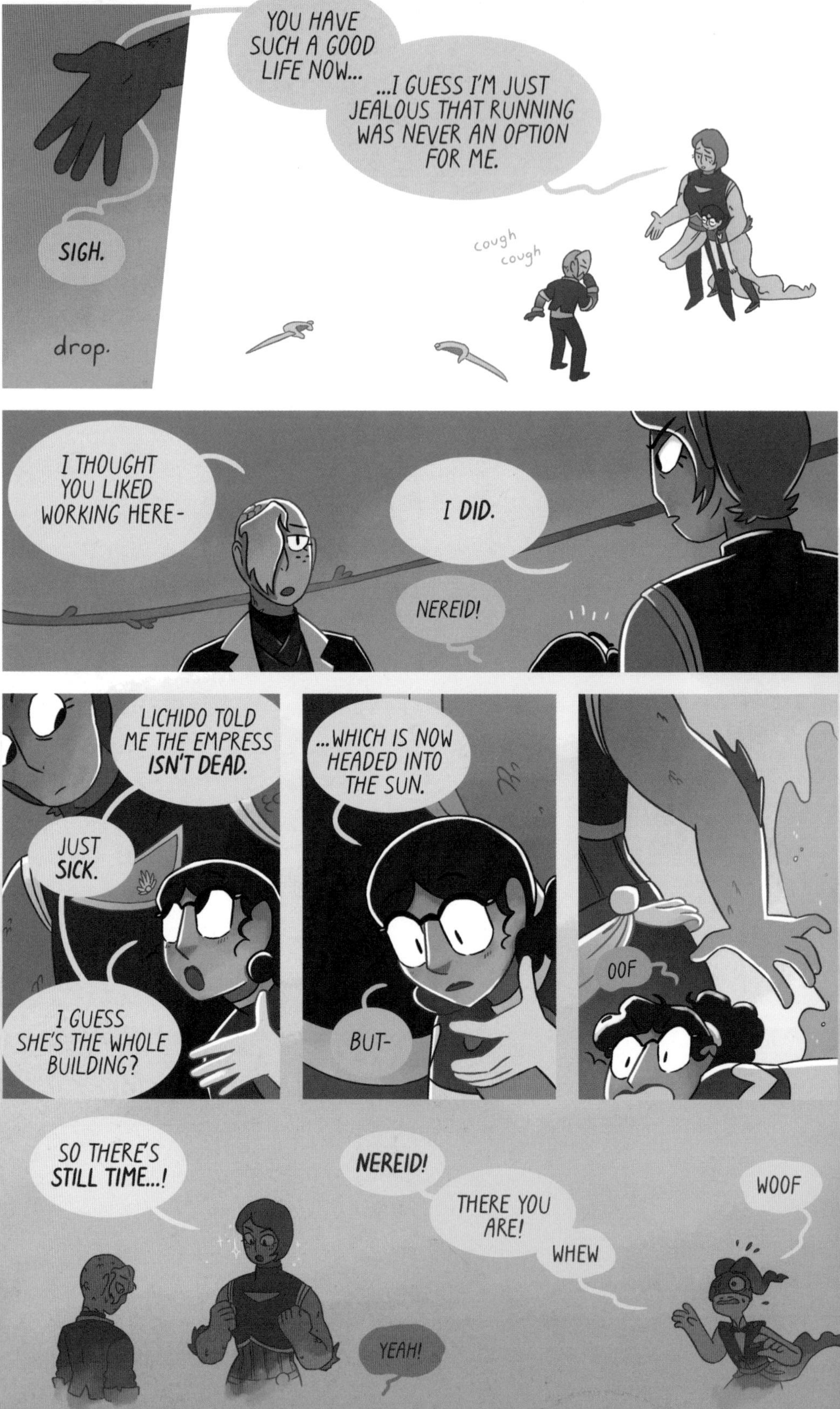
YOU HAVE SUCH A GOOD LIFE NOW...
...I GUESS I'M JUST JEALOUS THAT RUNNING WAS NEVER AN OPTION FOR ME.
SIGH.
drop.
cough cough
I THOUGHT YOU LIKED WORKING HERE-
I DID.
NEREID!
LICHIDO TOLD ME THE EMPRESS ISN'T DEAD.
JUST SICK.
I GUESS SHE'S THE WHOLE BUILDING?
...WHICH IS NOW HEADED INTO THE SUN.
BUT-
OOF
SO THERE'S STILL TIME...!
YEAH!
NEREID!
THERE YOU ARE!
WHEW
WOOF

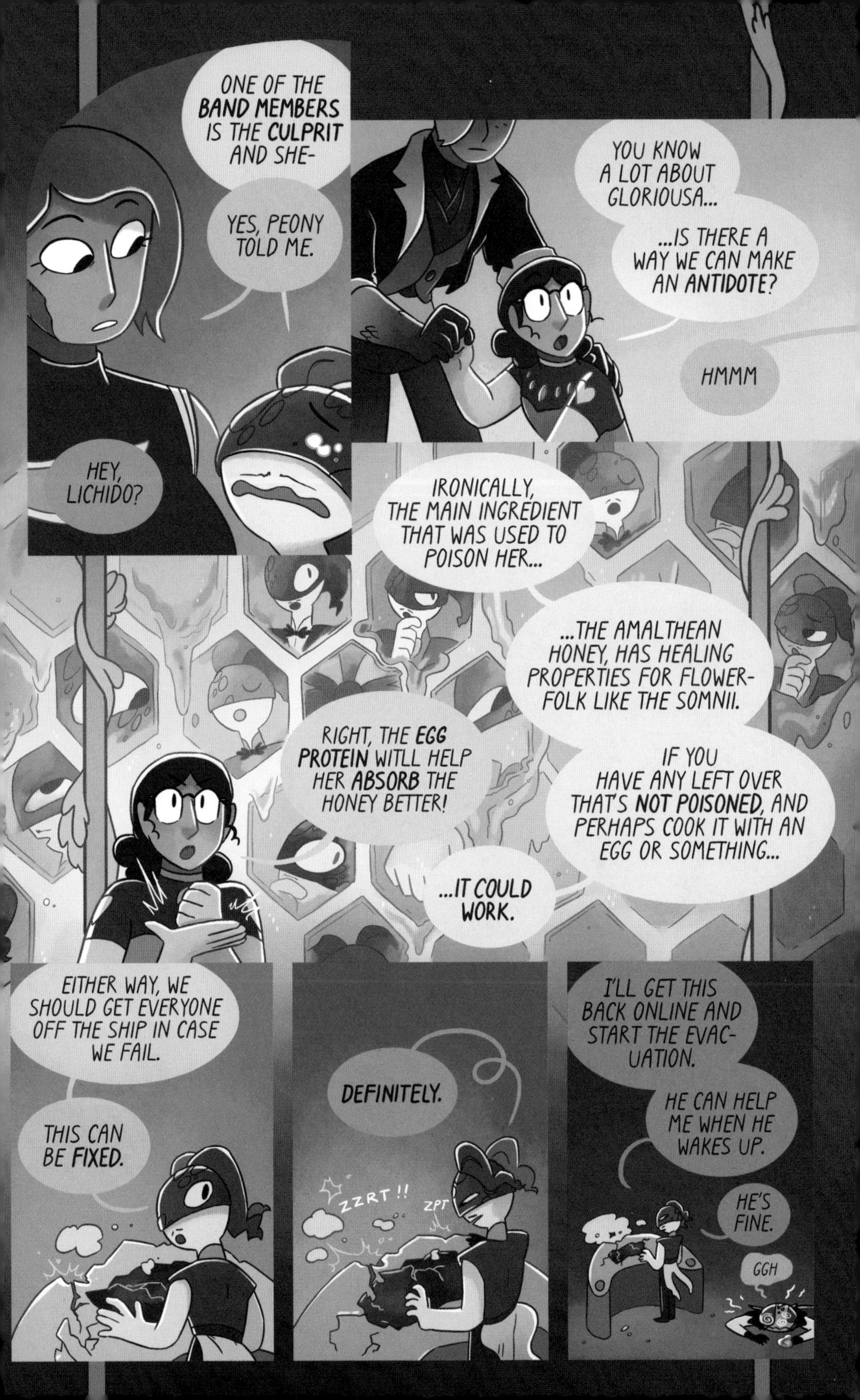
ONE OF THE BAND MEMBERS IS THE CULPRIT AND SHE-
YES, PEONY TOLD ME.
HEY, LICHIDO?
YOU KNOW A LOT ABOUT GLORIOUSA...
...IS THERE A WAY WE CAN MAKE AN ANTIDOTE?
HMMM
IRONICALLY, THE MAIN INGREDIENT THAT WAS USED TO POISON HER...
...THE AMALTHEAN HONEY, HAS HEALING PROPERTIES FOR FLOWER-FOLK LIKE THE SOMNII.
IF YOU HAVE ANY LEFT OVER THAT'S NOT POISONED, AND PERHAPS COOK IT WITH AN EGG OR SOMETHING...
...IT COULD WORK.
RIGHT, THE EGG PROTEIN WITLL HELP HER ABSORB THE HONEY BETTER!
EITHER WAY, WE SHOULD GET EVERYONE OFF THE SHIP IN CASE WE FAIL.
THIS CAN BE FIXED.
DEFINITELY.
ZZRT!!
ZPT
I'LL GET THIS BACK ONLINE AND START THE EVAC-UATION.
HE CAN HELP ME WHEN HE WAKES UP.
HE'S FINE.
GGH

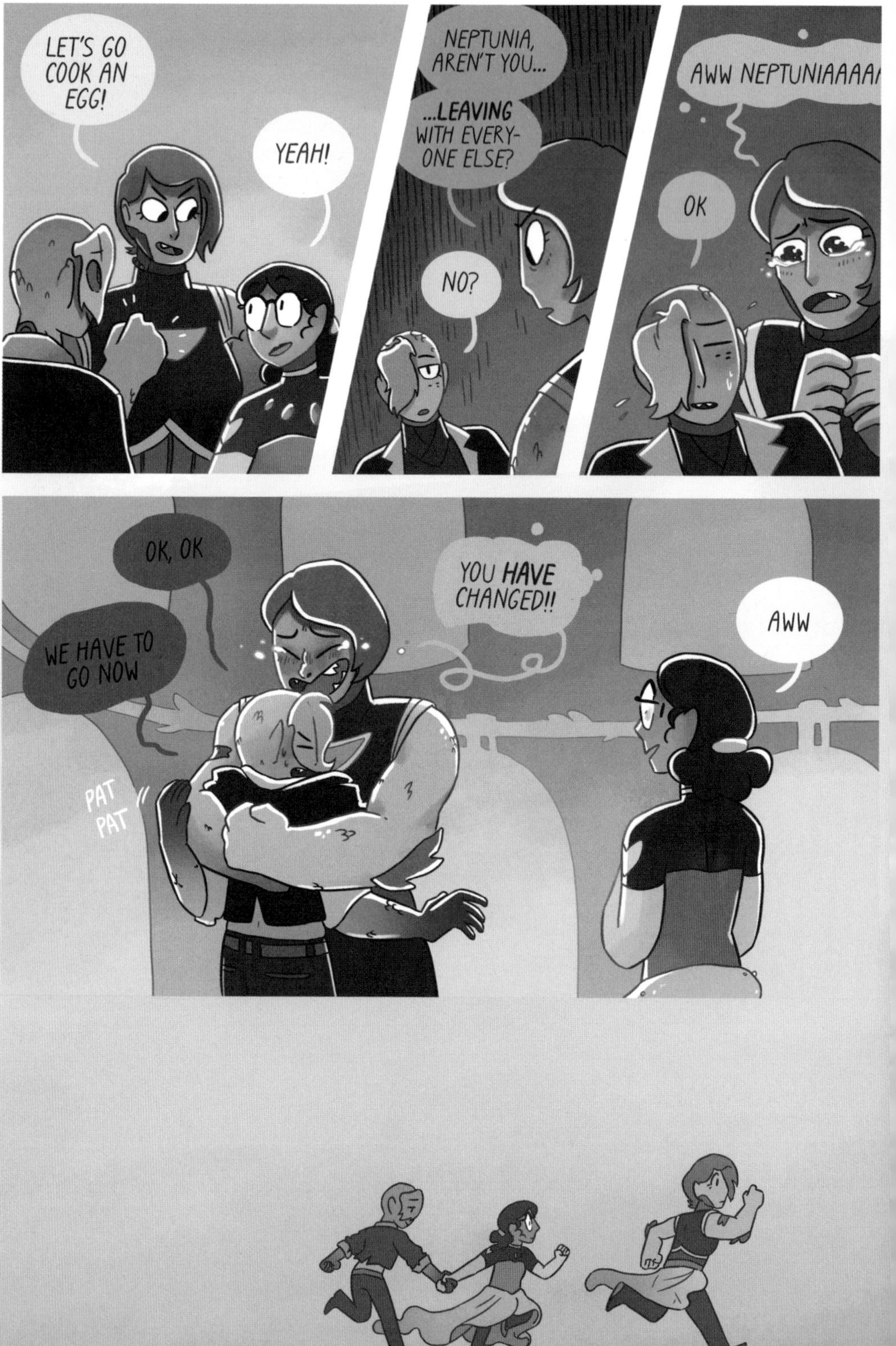
LET'S GO COOK AN EGG!
YEAH!
NEPTUNIA, AREN'T YOU...
...**LEAVING** WITH EVERY-ONE ELSE?
NO?
AWW NEPTUNIAAAA
OK
OK, OK
WE HAVE TO GO NOW
YOU **HAVE** CHANGED!!
AWW
PAT PAT

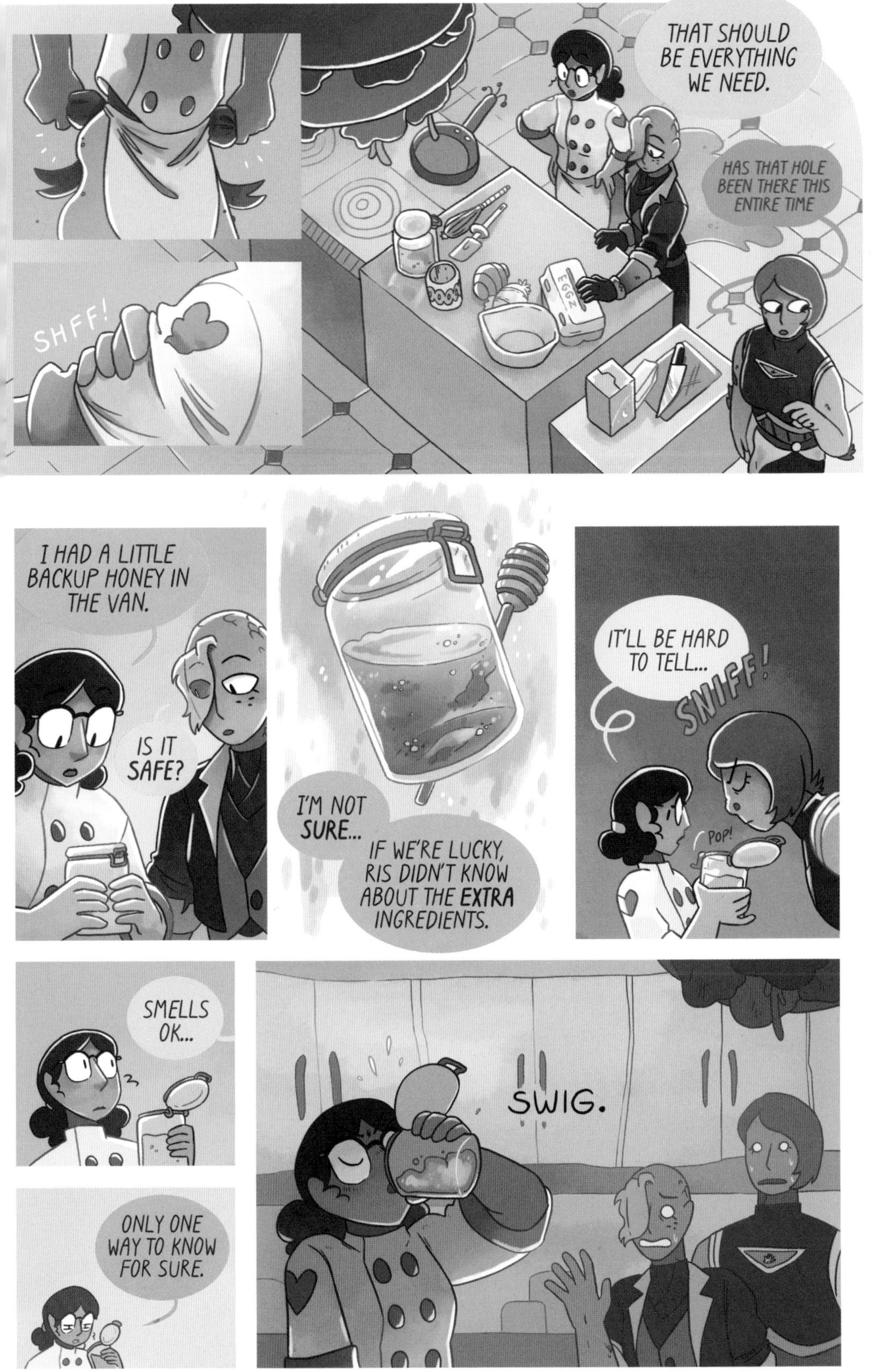
SHFF!
THAT SHOULD BE EVERYTHING WE NEED.
HAS THAT HOLE BEEN THERE THIS ENTIRE TIME
EGGZ
I HAD A LITTLE BACKUP HONEY IN THE VAN.
IS IT SAFE?
I'M NOT SURE...
IF WE'RE LUCKY, RIS DIDN'T KNOW ABOUT THE EXTRA INGREDIENTS.
IT'LL BE HARD TO TELL...
SNIFF!
POP!
SMELLS OK...
ONLY ONE WAY TO KNOW FOR SURE.
SWIG.

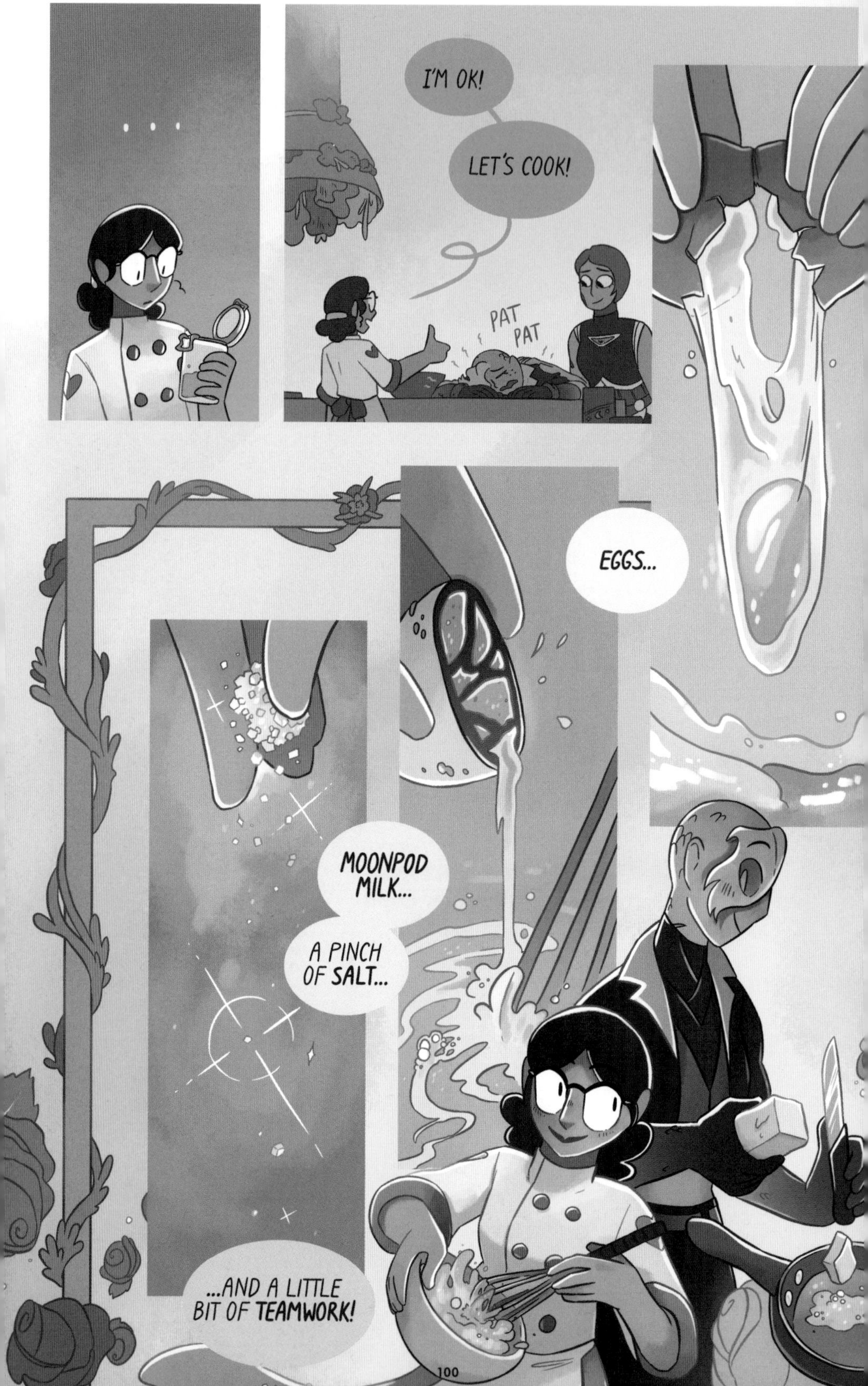
...
I'M OK!
LET'S COOK!
PAT
PAT
EGGS...
MOONPOD MILK...
A PINCH OF SALT...
...AND A LITTLE BIT OF TEAMWORK!

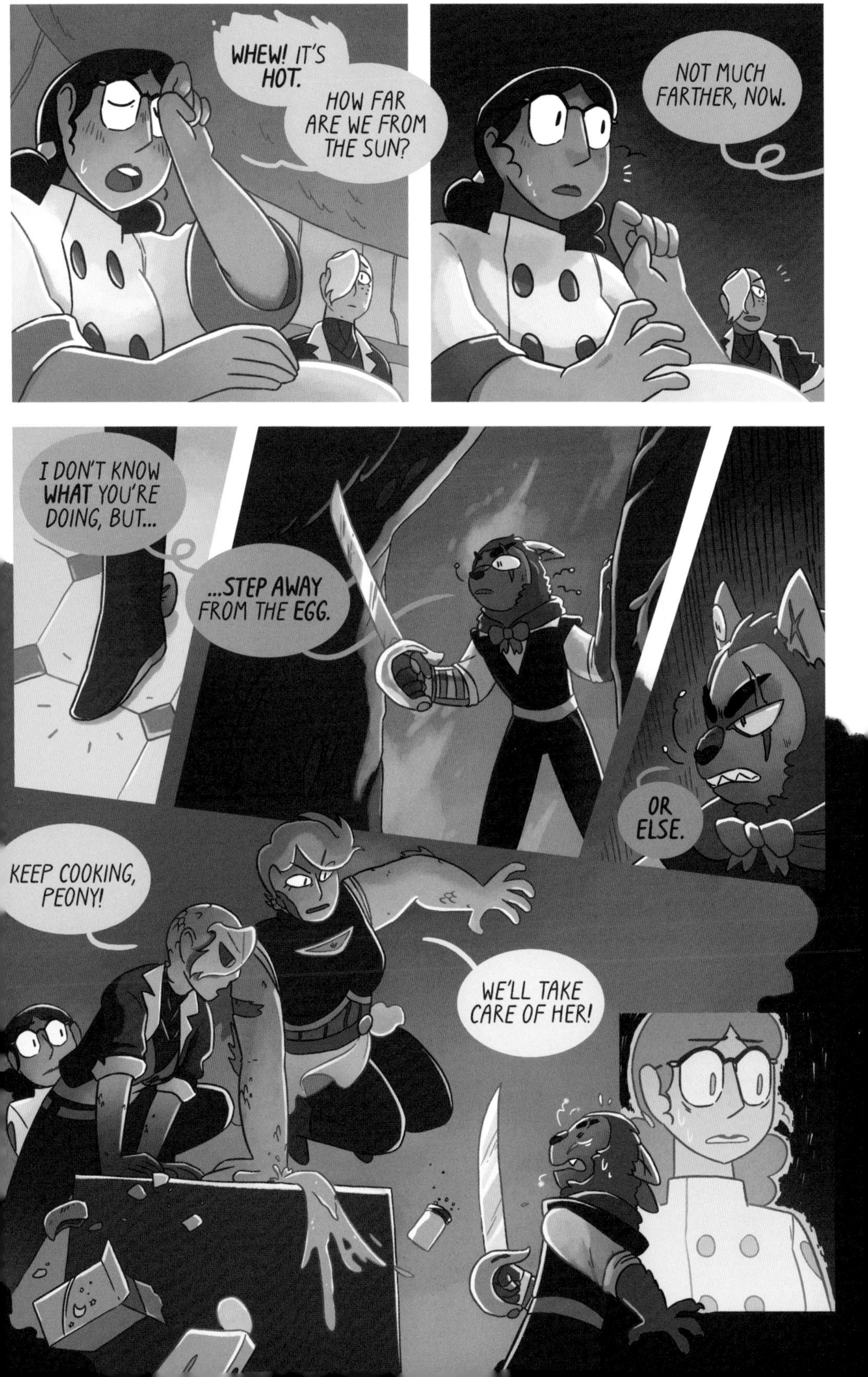
WHEW! IT'S HOT.
HOW FAR ARE WE FROM THE SUN?
NOT MUCH FARTHER, NOW.
I DON'T KNOW WHAT YOU'RE DOING, BUT...
...STEP AWAY FROM THE EGG.
OR ELSE.
KEEP COOKING, PEONY!
WE'LL TAKE CARE OF HER!

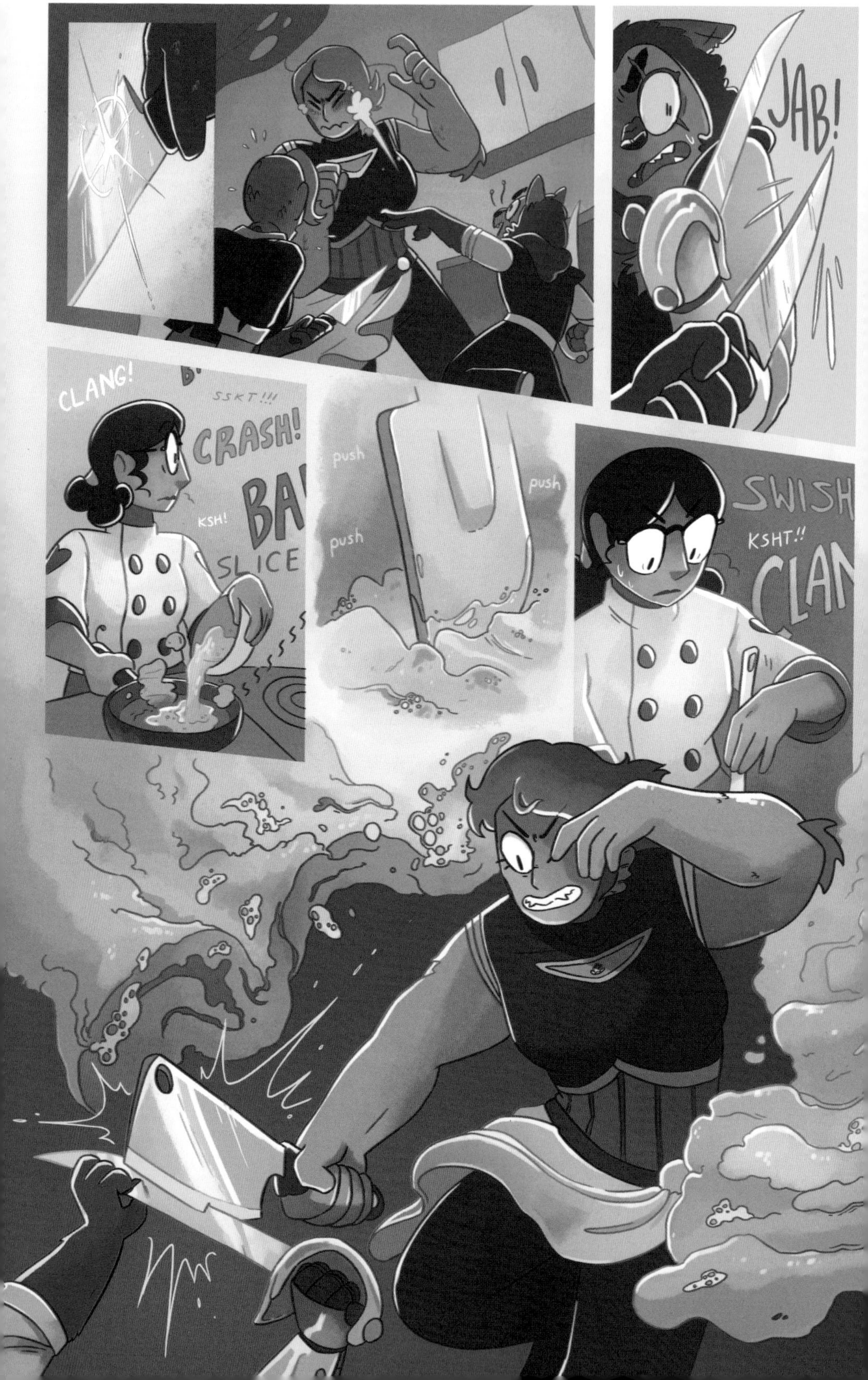
JAB!
CLANG!
SSKT!!!
CRASH!
KSH!
SLICE
push
push
push
SWISH
KSHT!!

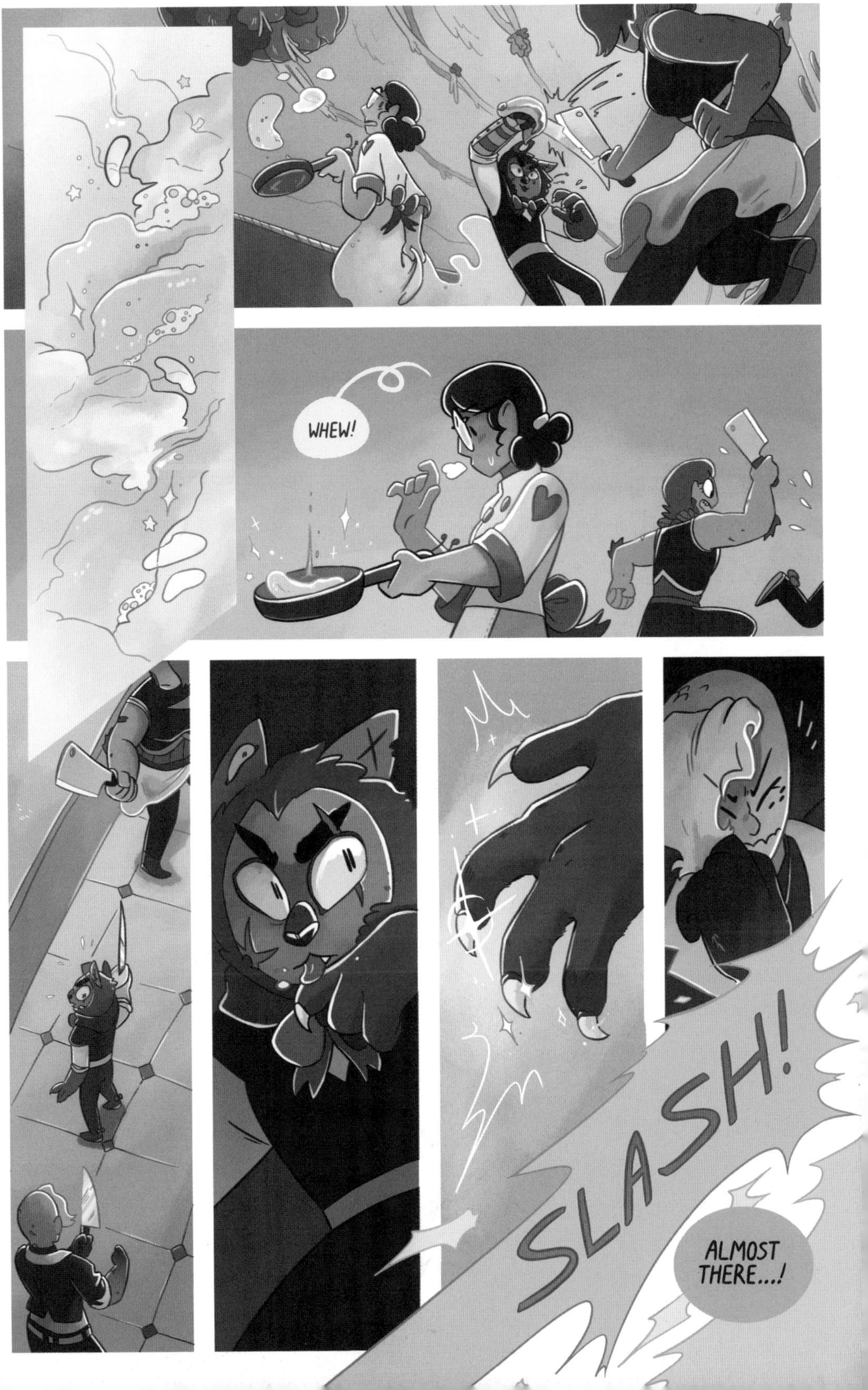
WHEW!
SLASH!
ALMOST THERE...!

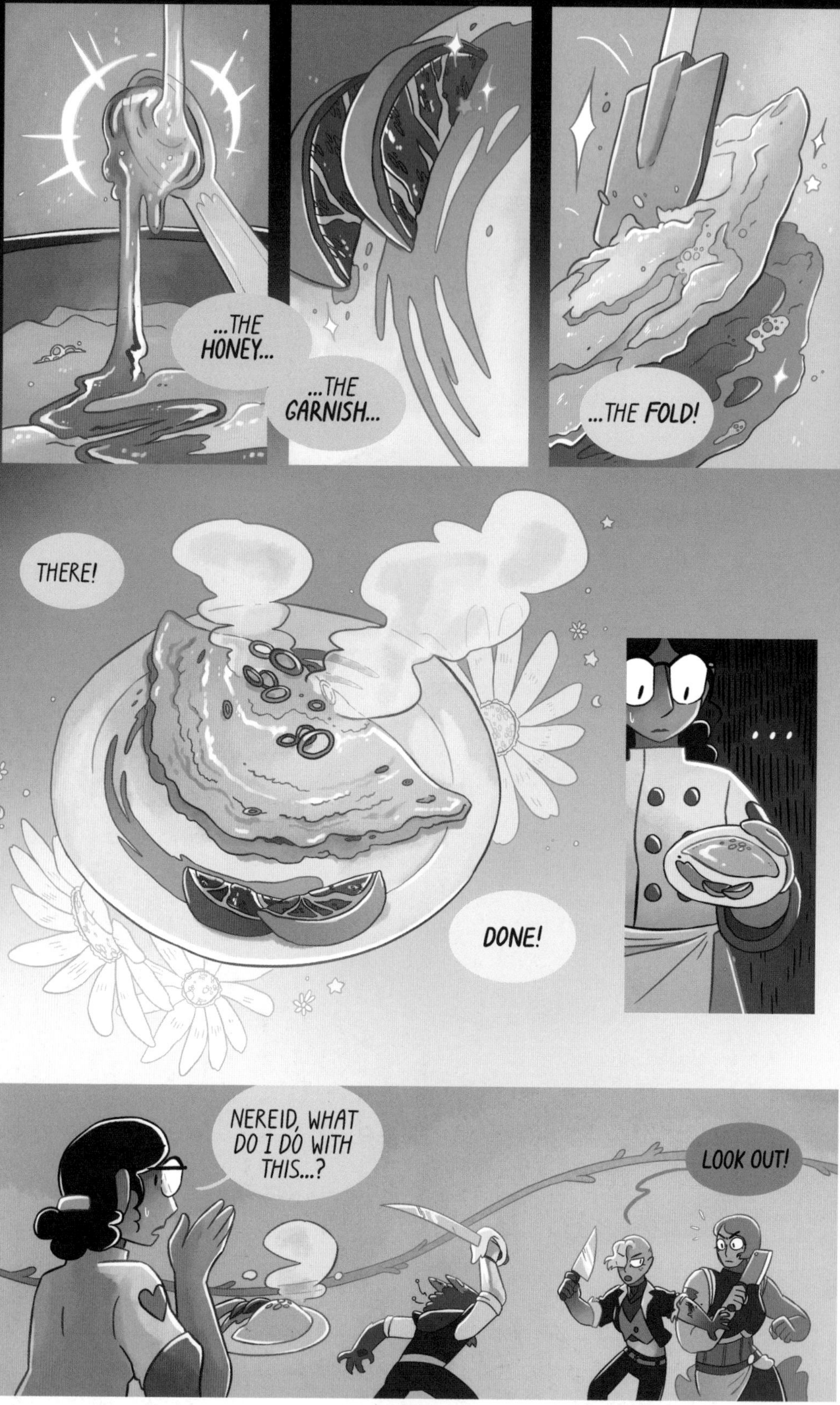
...THE HONEY...
...THE GARNISH...
...THE FOLD!
THERE!
DONE!
...
NEREID, WHAT DO I DO WITH THIS...?
LOOK OUT!

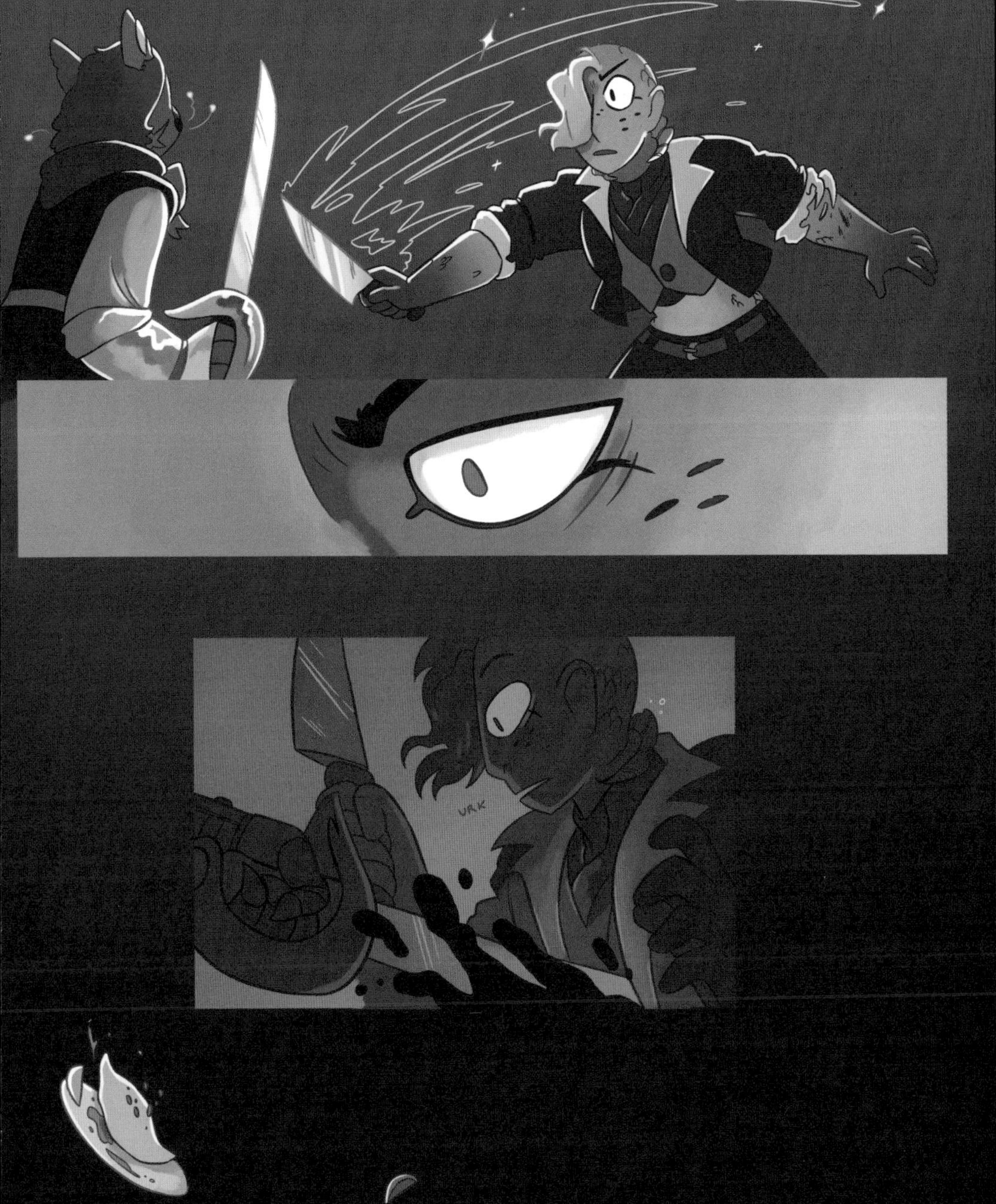
VRK

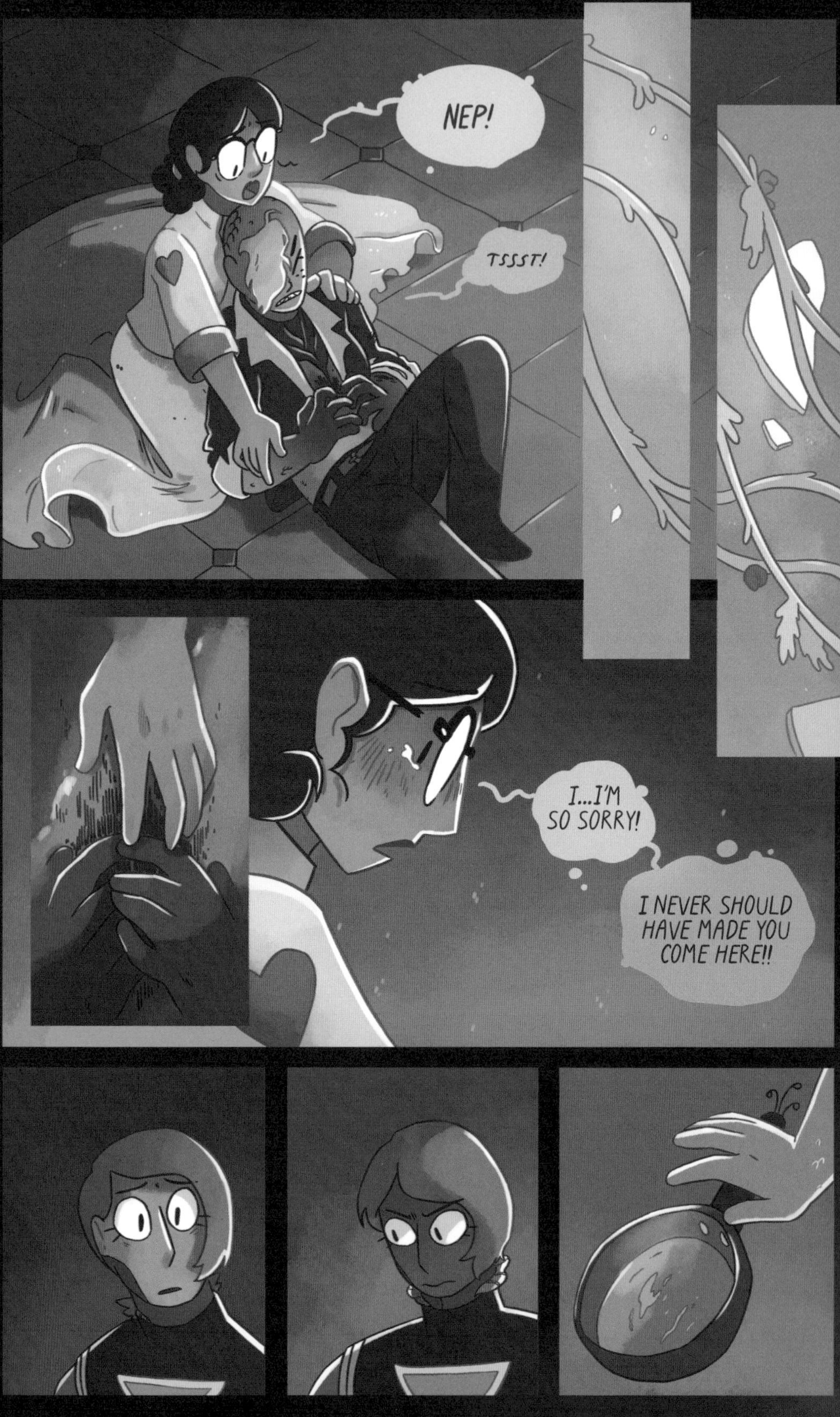
NEP!
TSSST!
I...I'M SO SORRY!
I NEVER SHOULD HAVE MADE YOU COME HERE!!

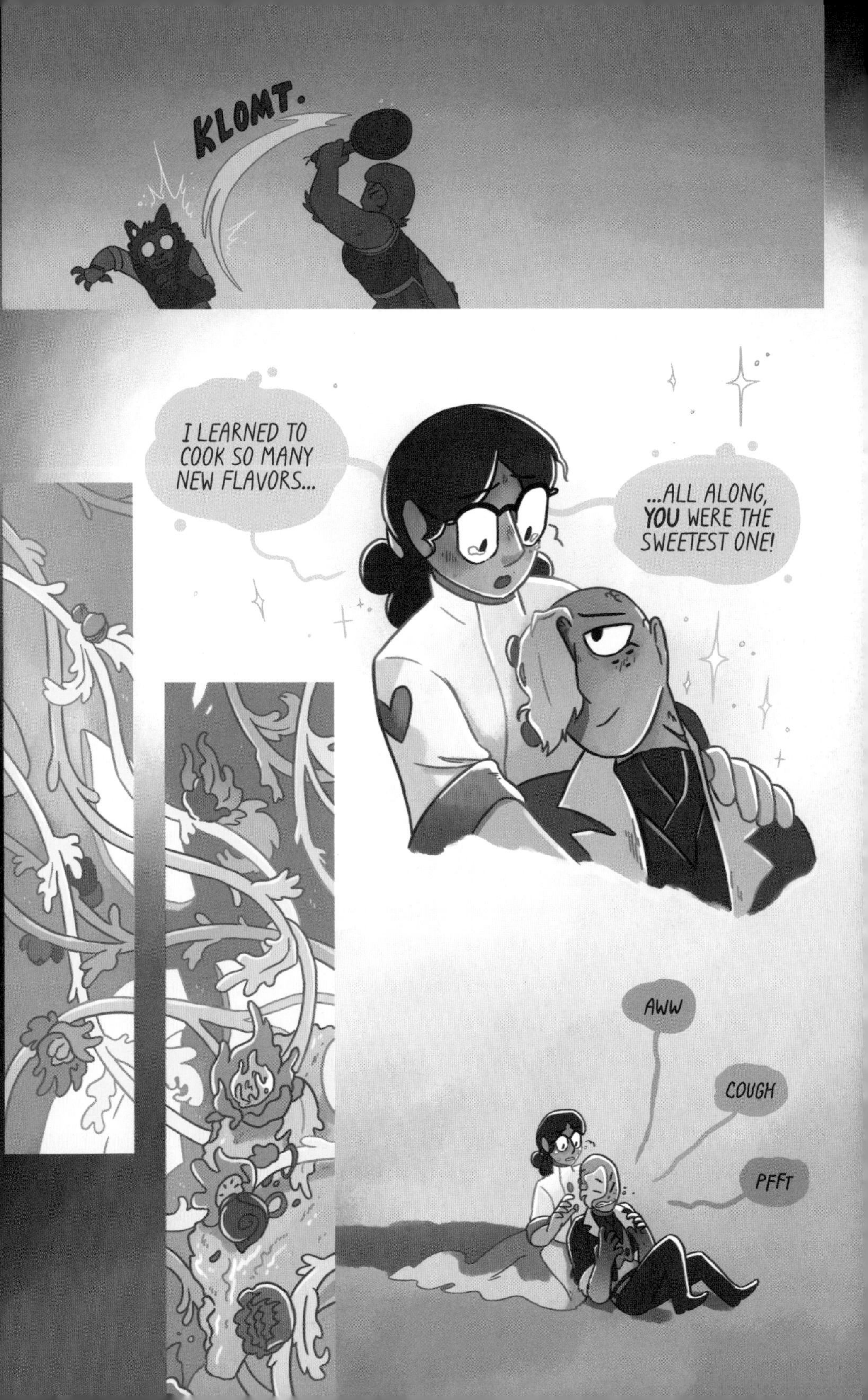
KLOMT.
I LEARNED TO COOK SO MANY NEW FLAVORS...
...ALL ALONG, YOU WERE THE SWEETEST ONE!
AWW
COUGH
PFFT

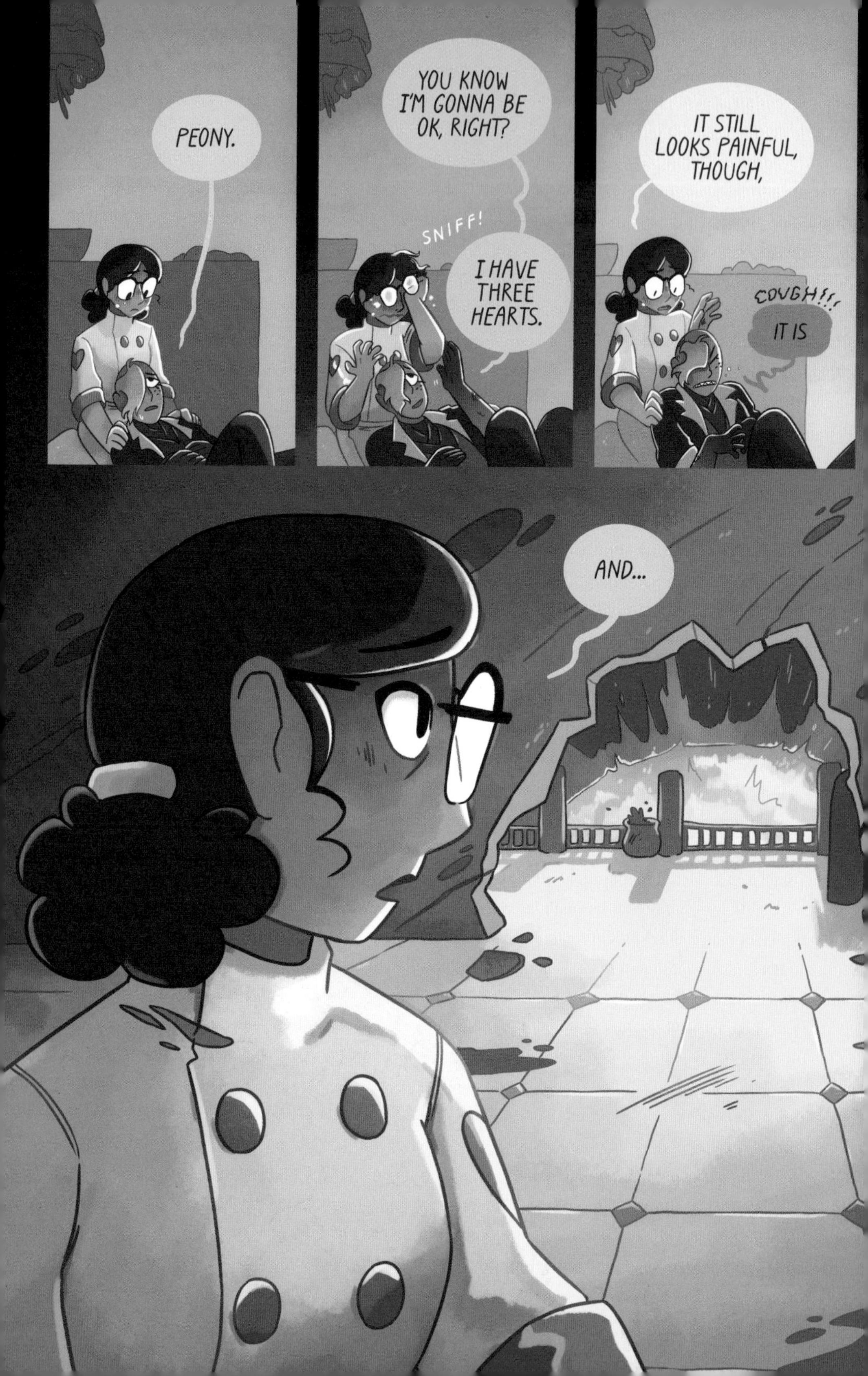
PEONY.
YOU KNOW I'M GONNA BE OK, RIGHT?
SNIFF!
I HAVE THREE HEARTS.
IT STILL LOOKS PAINFUL, THOUGH,
COUGH!!!
IT IS
AND...

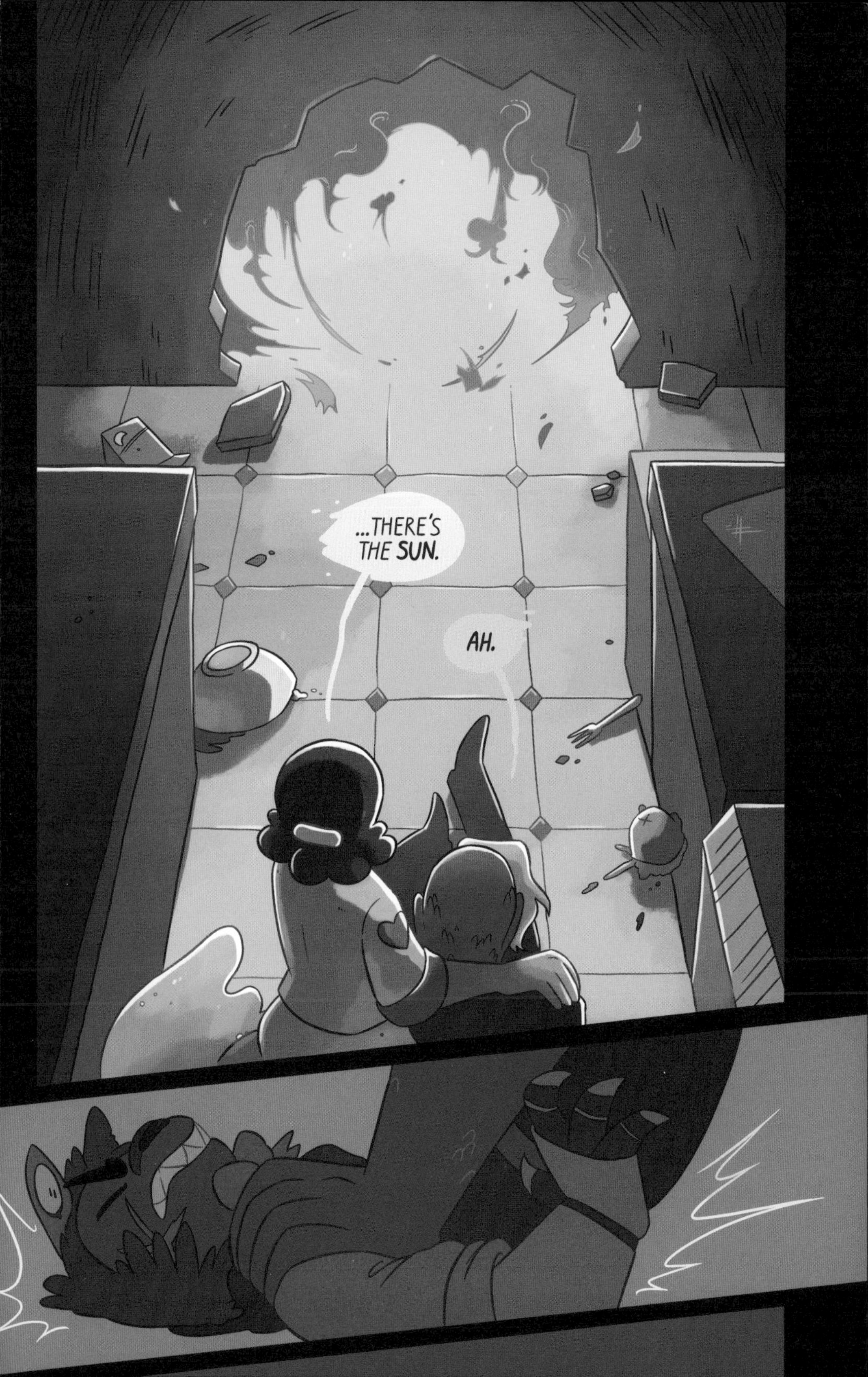
...THERE'S THE **SUN**.
AH.

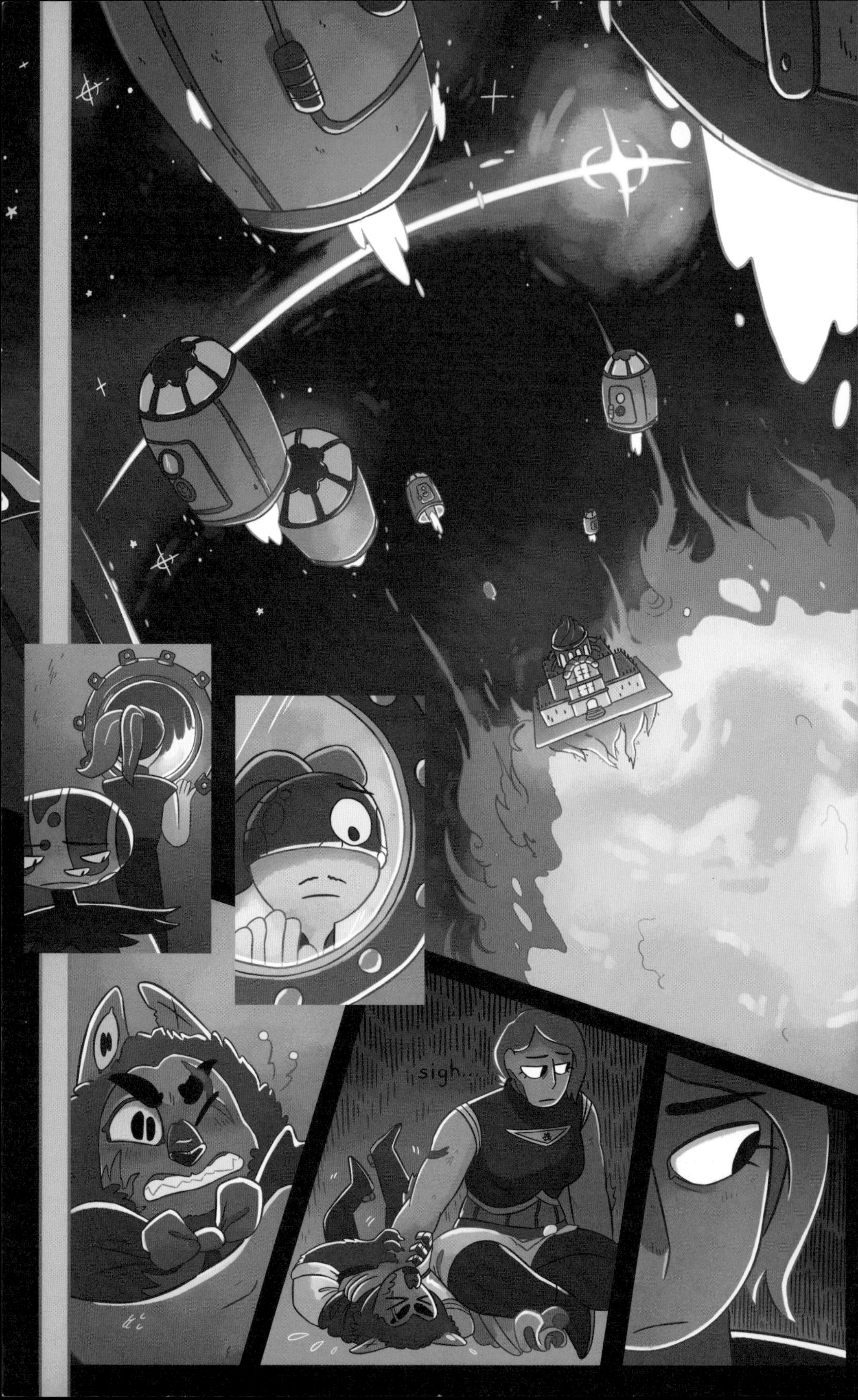
sigh...

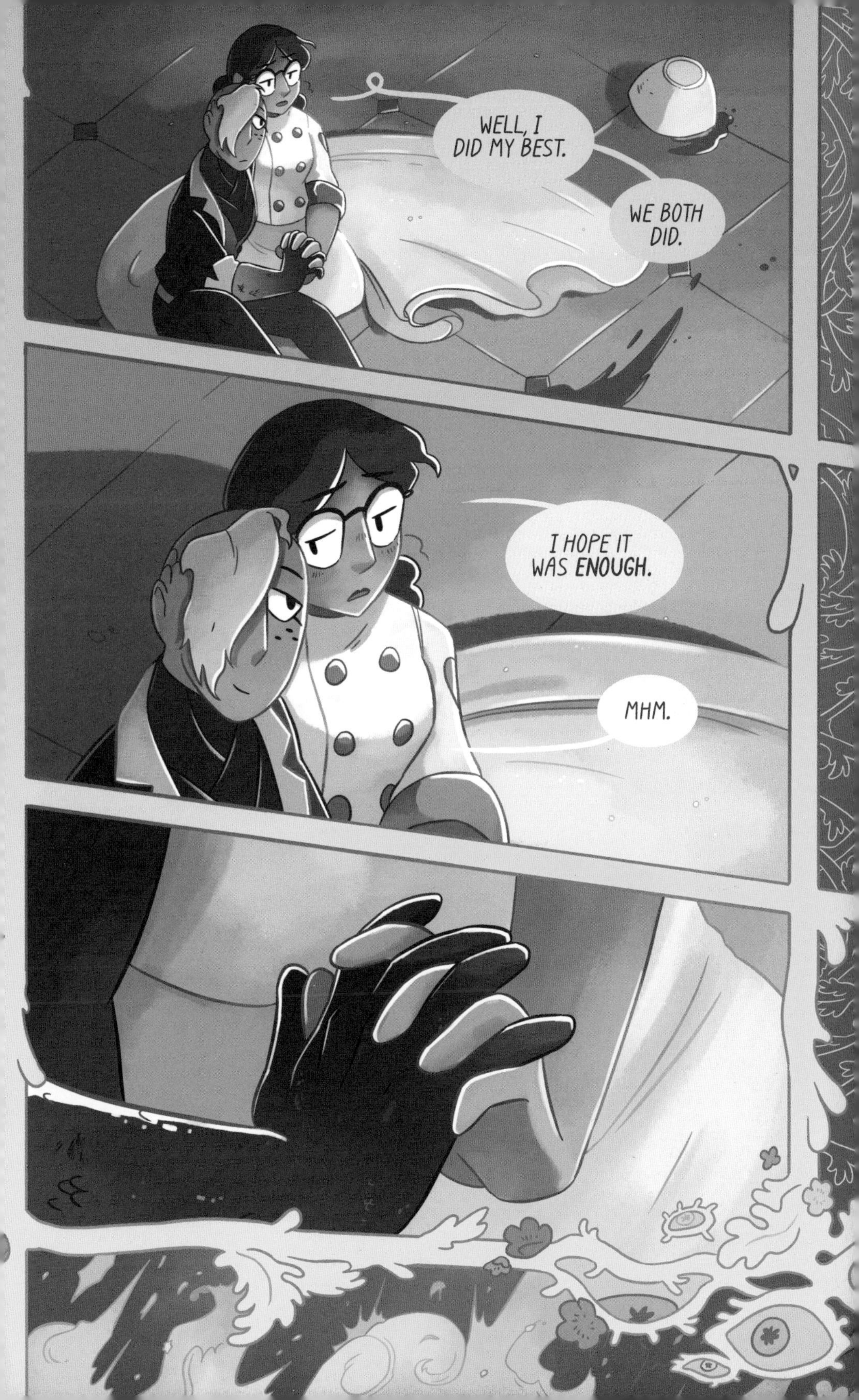
WELL, I DID MY BEST.
WE BOTH DID.
I HOPE IT WAS **ENOUGH.**
MHM.

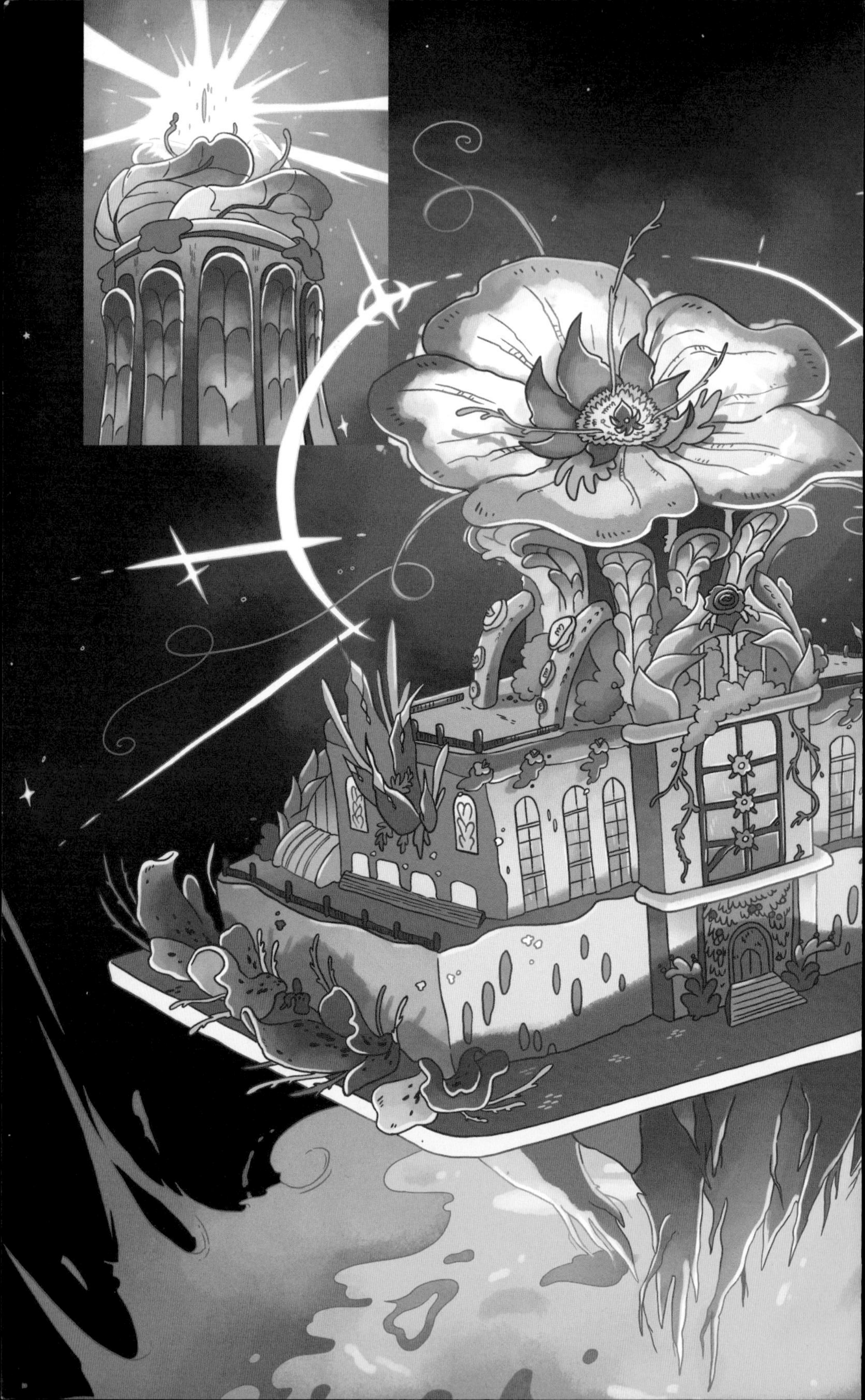

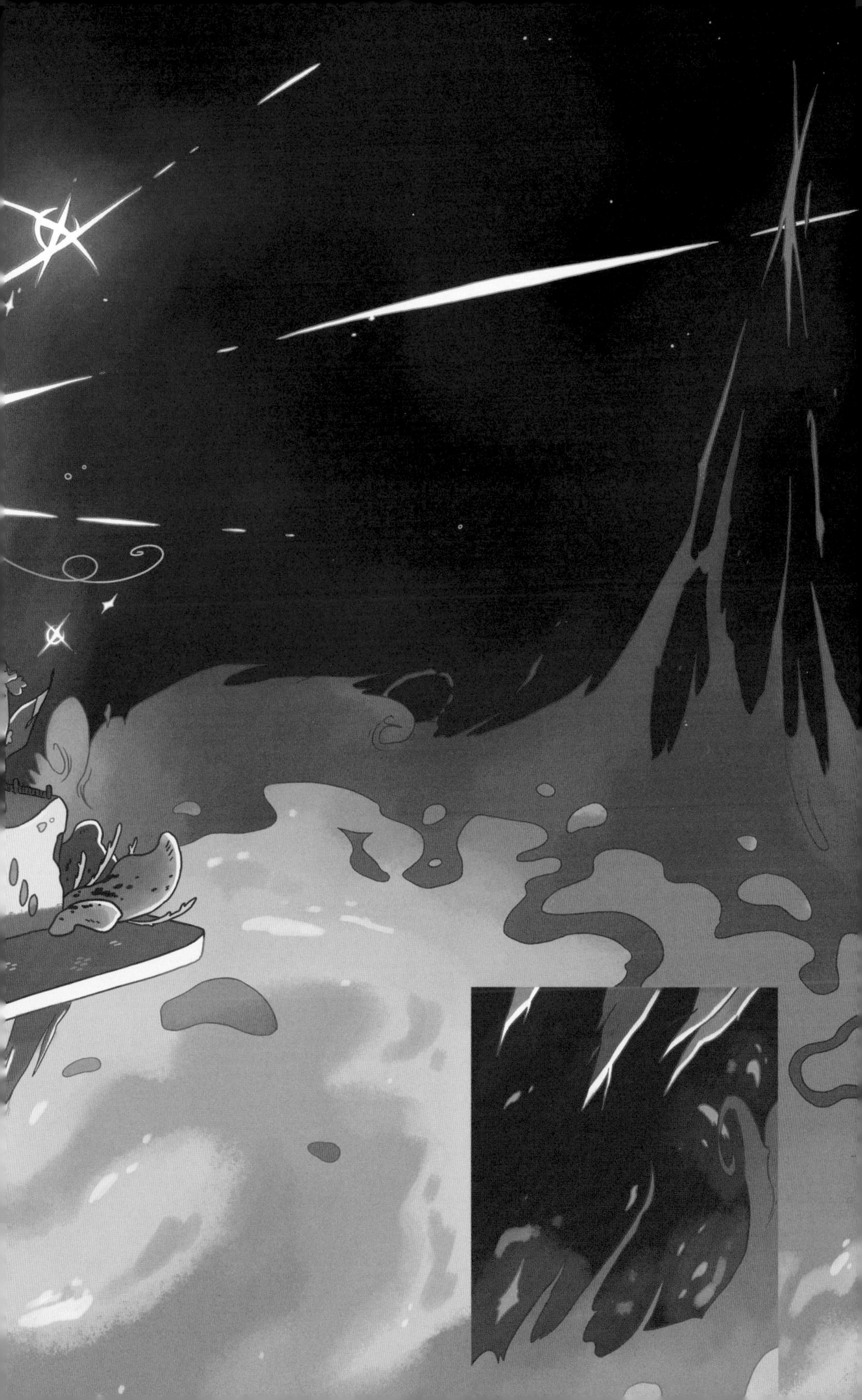

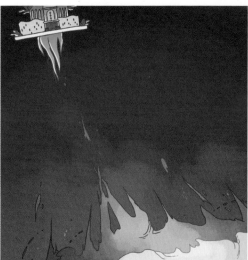

DID WE MAKE IT?

I THINK SO.

LOOK!

THE WHOLE PALACE IS **BLOOMING**...!

OH!

WOW...

HELLO?

ARE YOU BOTH OK?

THE CULPRIT GOT AWAY FROM ME IN THE CONFUSION, AND–

VVVRRRRR

THAT SOUNDS LIKE...

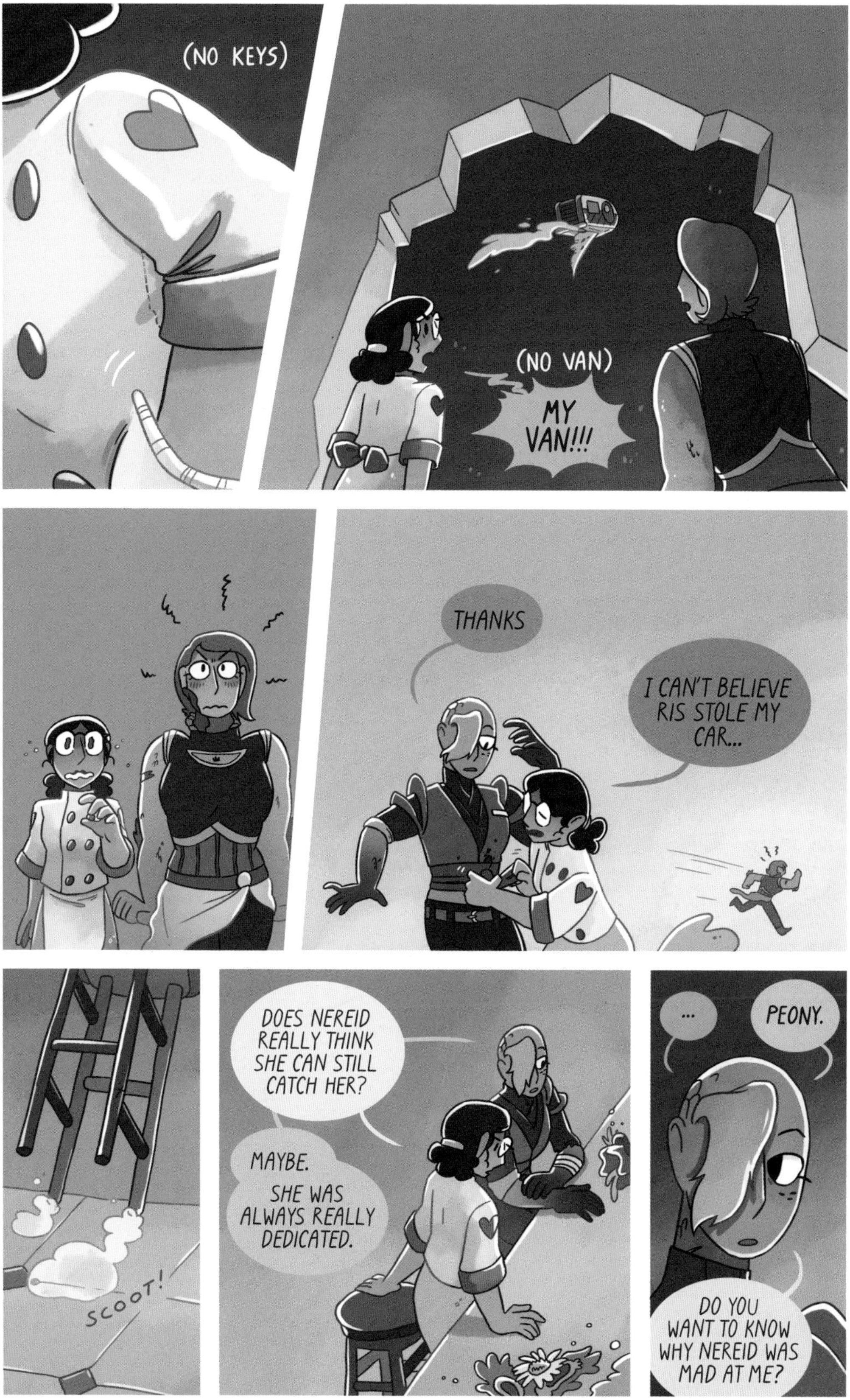
(NO KEYS)
(NO VAN)
MY VAN!!!
THANKS
I CAN'T BELIEVE RIS STOLE MY CAR...
SCOOT!
DOES NEREID REALLY THINK SHE CAN STILL CATCH HER?
MAYBE.
SHE WAS ALWAYS REALLY DEDICATED.
...
PEONY.
DO YOU WANT TO KNOW WHY NEREID WAS MAD AT ME?

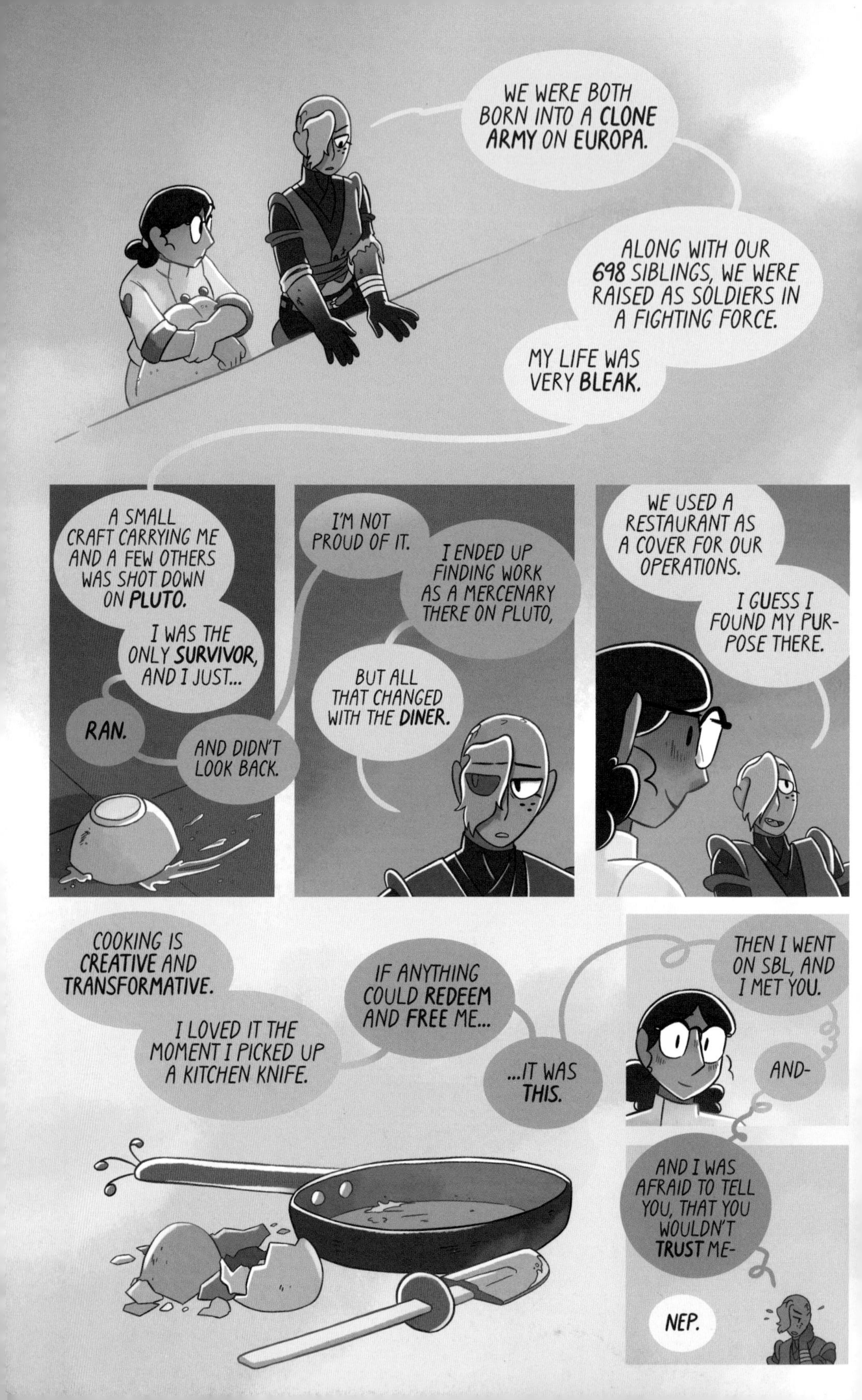
WE WERE BOTH BORN INTO A CLONE ARMY ON EUROPA.
ALONG WITH OUR 698 SIBLINGS, WE WERE RAISED AS SOLDIERS IN A FIGHTING FORCE.
MY LIFE WAS VERY BLEAK.
A SMALL CRAFT CARRYING ME AND A FEW OTHERS WAS SHOT DOWN ON PLUTO.
I WAS THE ONLY SURVIVOR, AND I JUST...
RAN.
AND DIDN'T LOOK BACK.
I'M NOT PROUD OF IT.
I ENDED UP FINDING WORK AS A MERCENARY THERE ON PLUTO,
BUT ALL THAT CHANGED WITH THE DINER.
WE USED A RESTAURANT AS A COVER FOR OUR OPERATIONS.
I GUESS I FOUND MY PURPOSE THERE.
COOKING IS CREATIVE AND TRANSFORMATIVE.
I LOVED IT THE MOMENT I PICKED UP A KITCHEN KNIFE.
IF ANYTHING COULD REDEEM AND FREE ME...
...IT WAS THIS.
THEN I WENT ON SBL, AND I MET YOU.
AND-
AND I WAS AFRAID TO TELL YOU, THAT YOU WOULDN'T TRUST ME-
NEP.

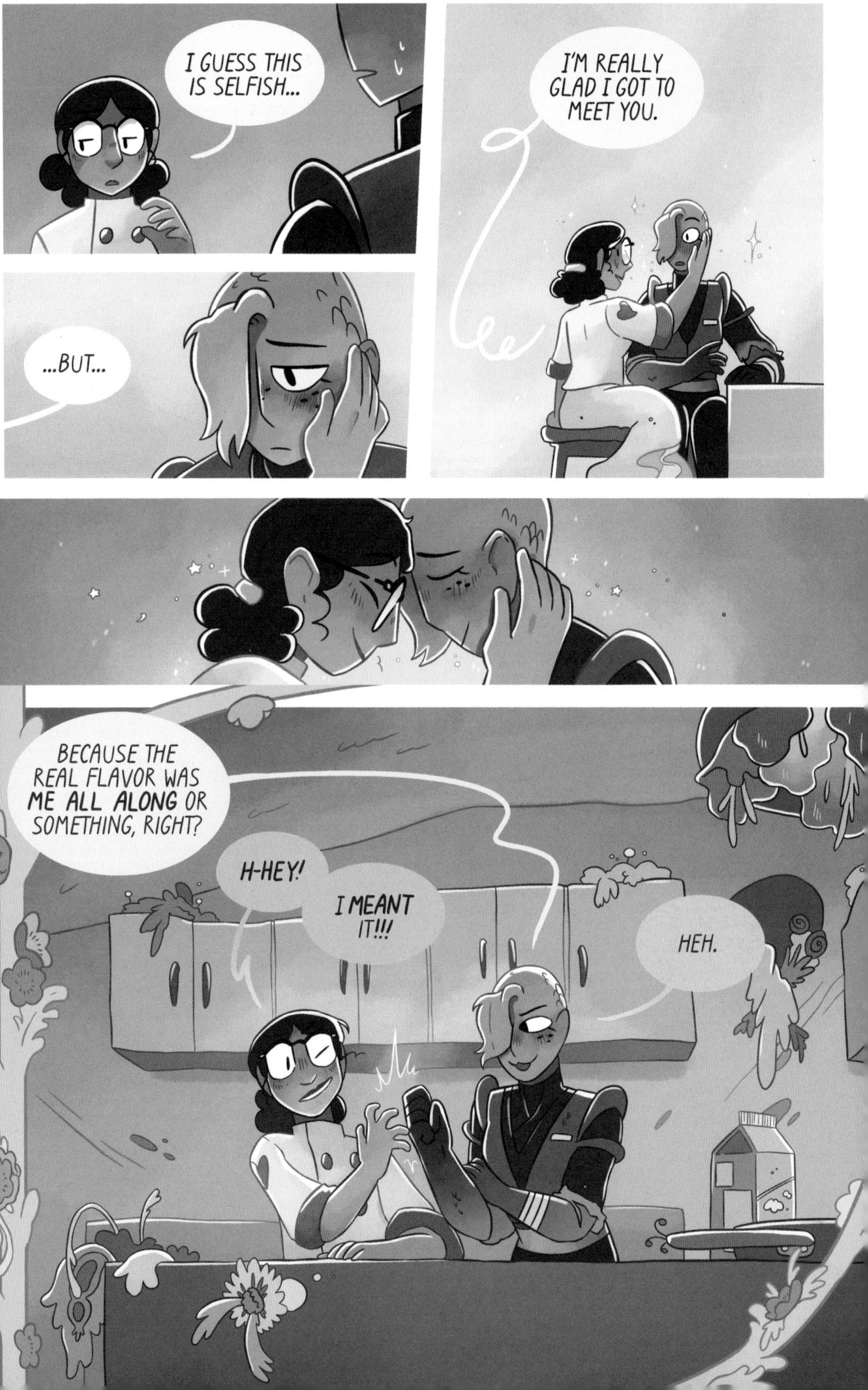
I GUESS THIS IS SELFISH...
...BUT...
I'M REALLY GLAD I GOT TO MEET YOU.
BECAUSE THE REAL FLAVOR WAS **ME ALL ALONG** OR SOMETHING, RIGHT?
H-HEY!
I MEANT IT!!!
HEH.

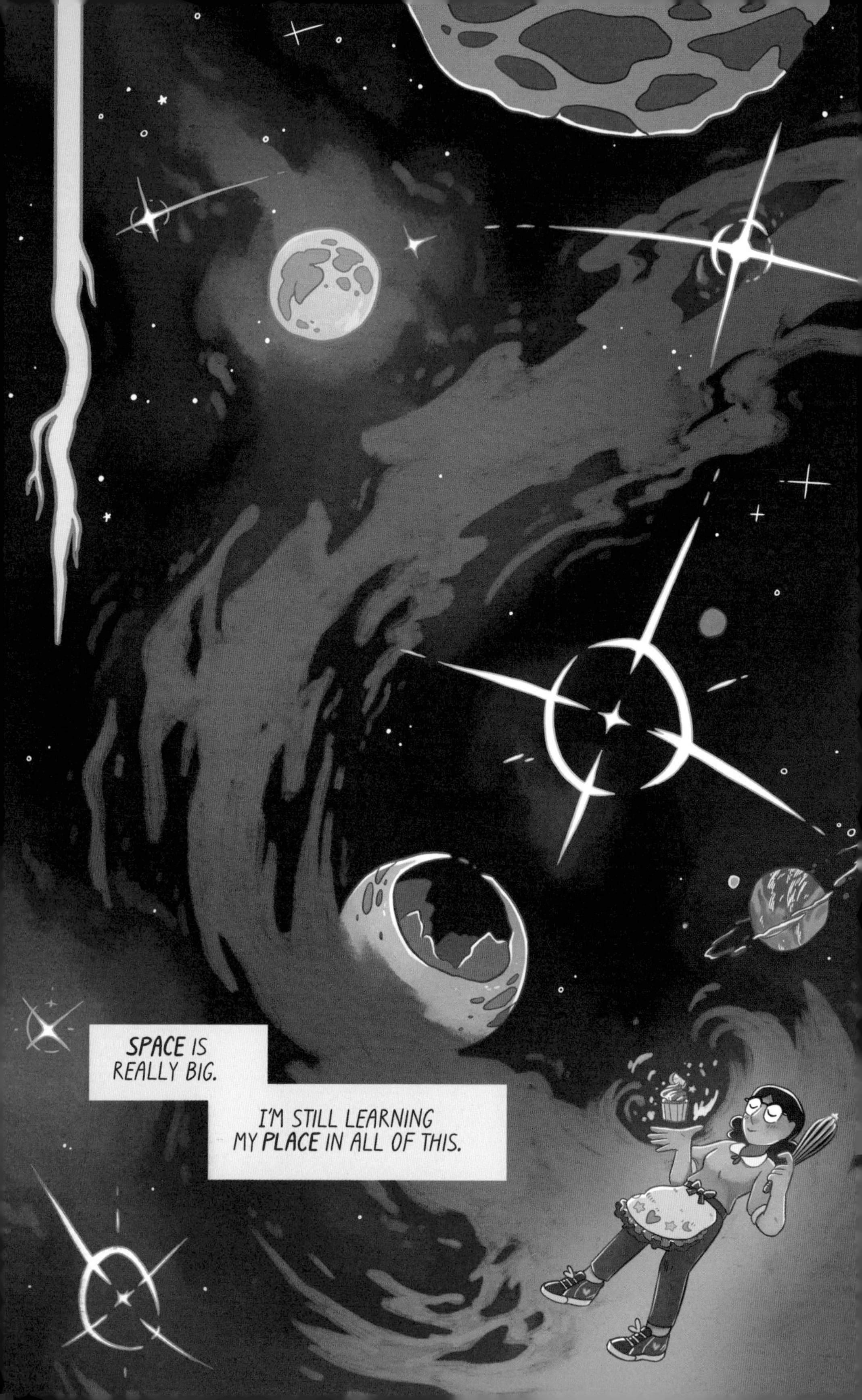
SPACE IS REALLY BIG.
I'M STILL LEARNING MY PLACE IN ALL OF THIS.

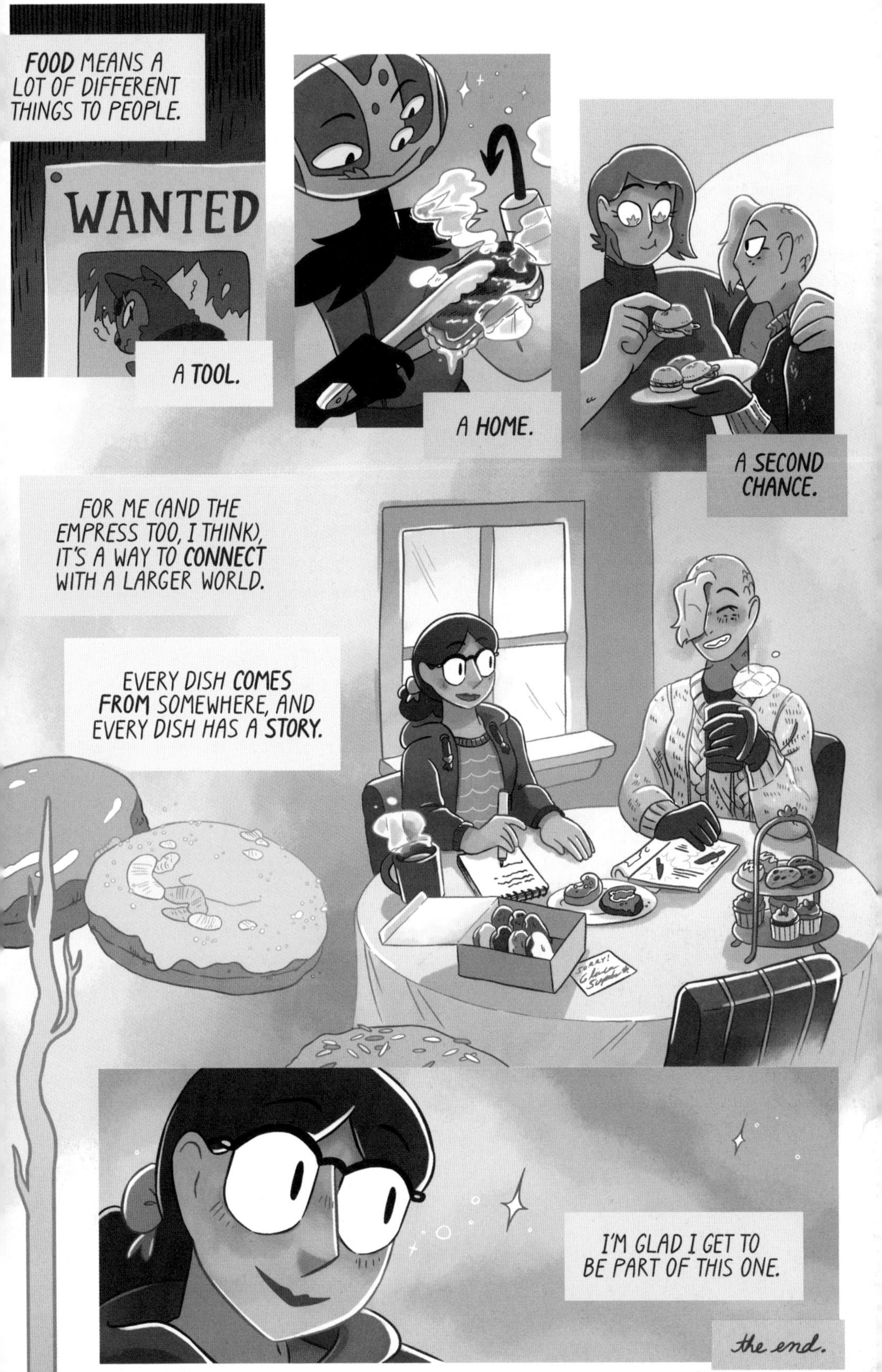
FOOD MEANS A LOT OF DIFFERENT THINGS TO PEOPLE.
WANTED
A TOOL.
A HOME.
A SECOND CHANCE.
FOR ME (AND THE EMPRESS TOO, I THINK), IT'S A WAY TO CONNECT WITH A LARGER WORLD.
EVERY DISH COMES FROM SOMEWHERE, AND EVERY DISH HAS A STORY.
SORRY!
I'M GLAD I GET TO BE PART OF THIS ONE.
the end.

COLOR SCRIPT

TO GET AN IDEA OF HOW I WANTED TO COLOR CERTAIN SCENES, I USED WATERCOLOR TO PAINT A FEW LOOSE KEY SKETCHES TO WORK FROM.

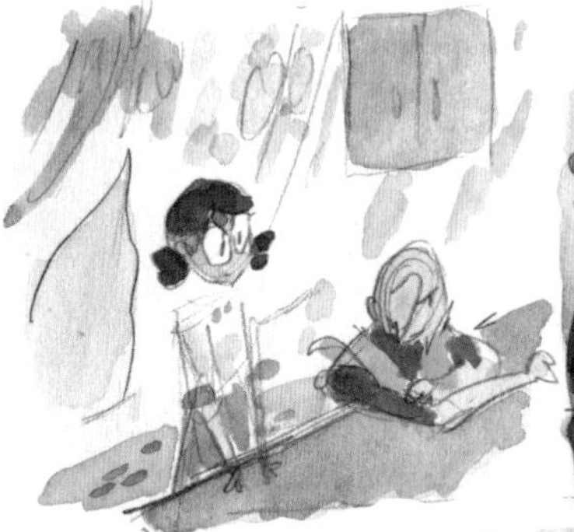
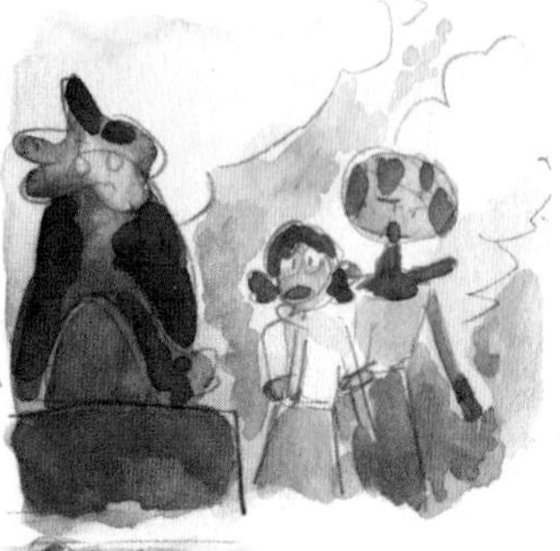
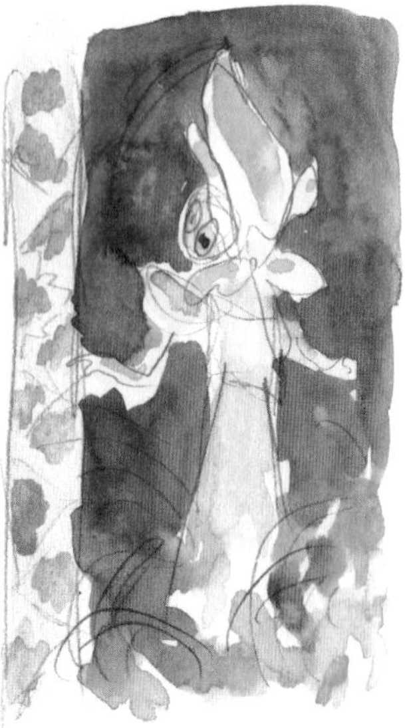
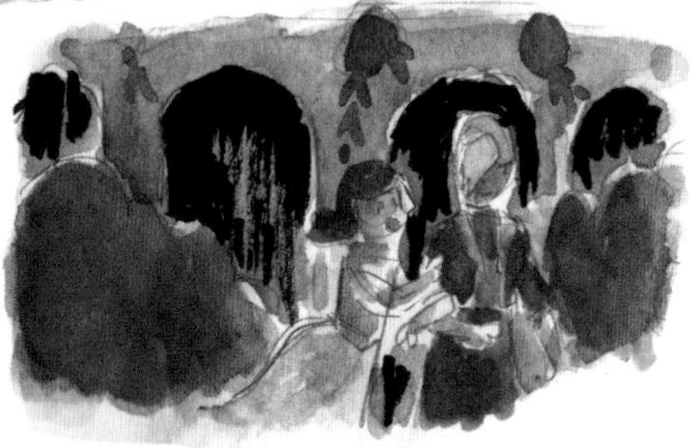
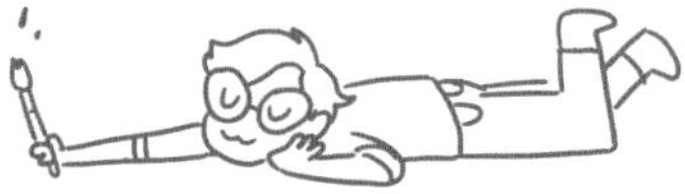
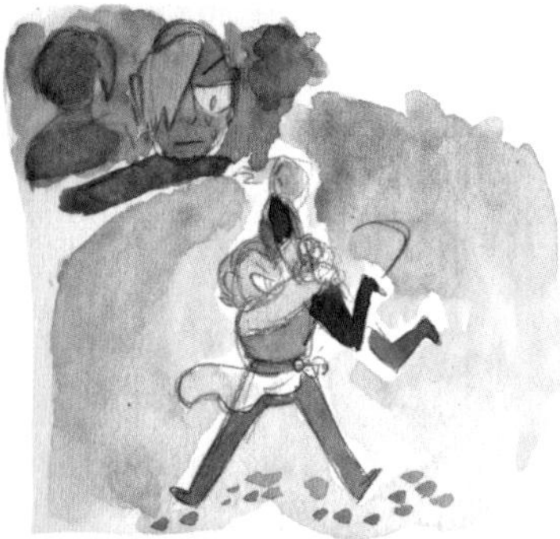
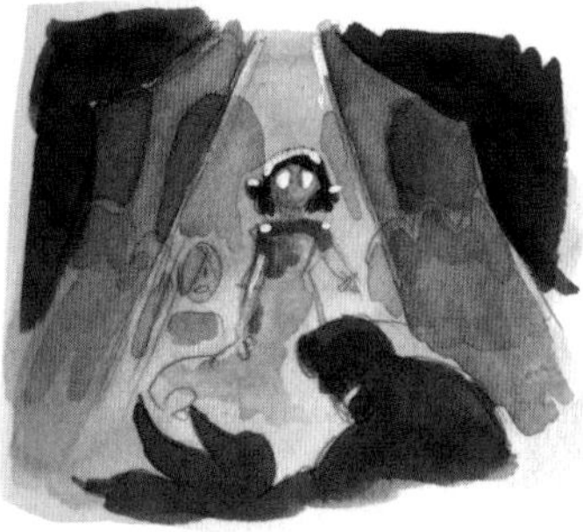
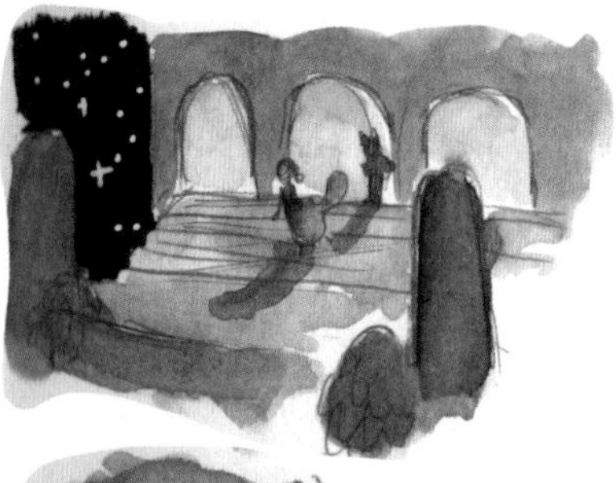
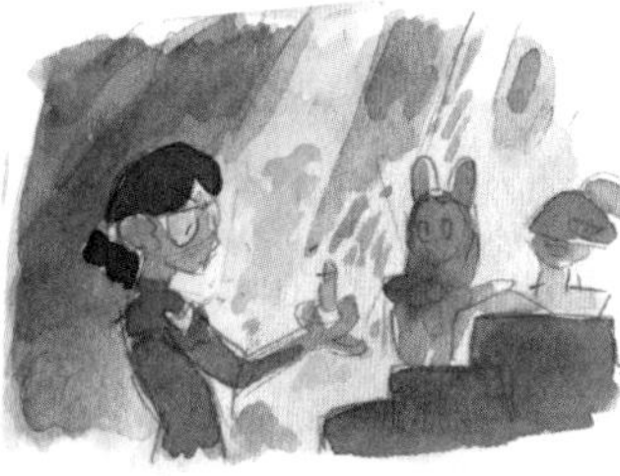
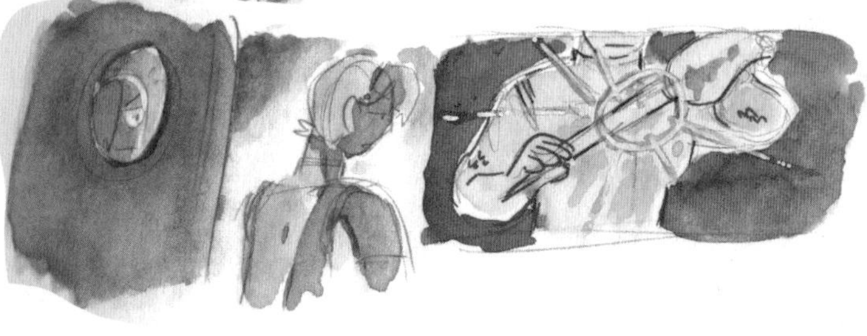

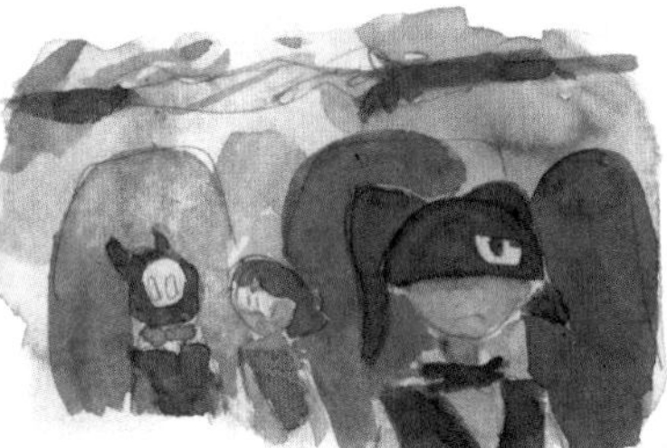
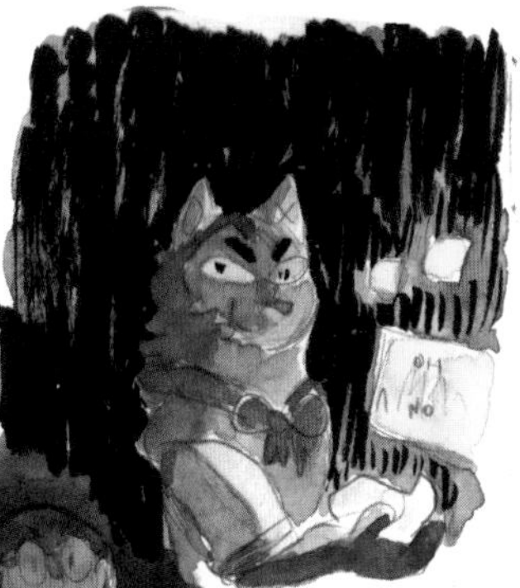
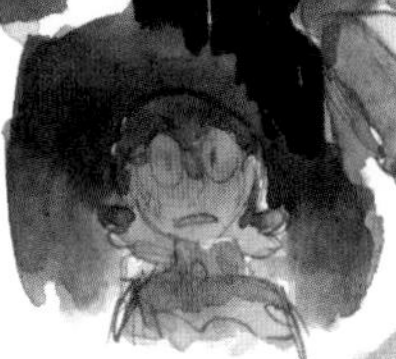
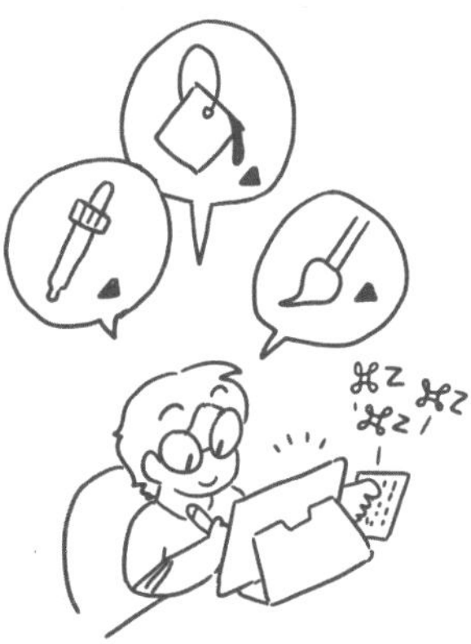
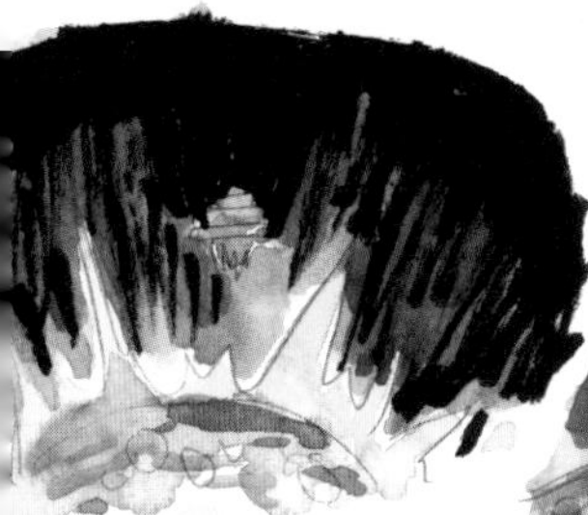
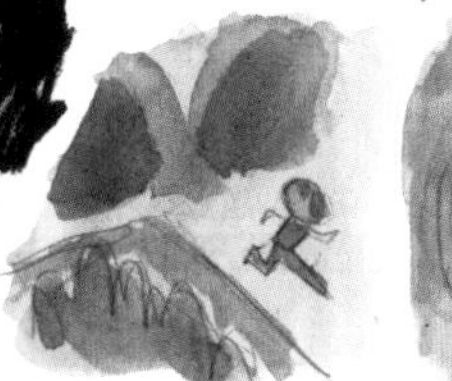
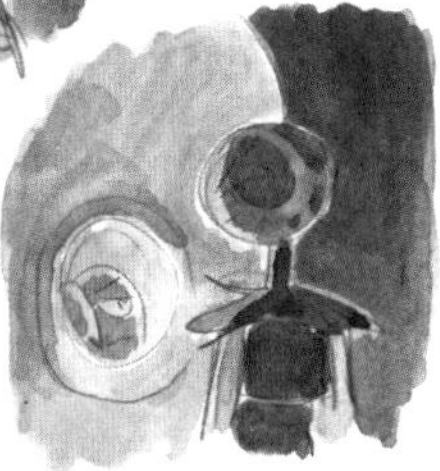
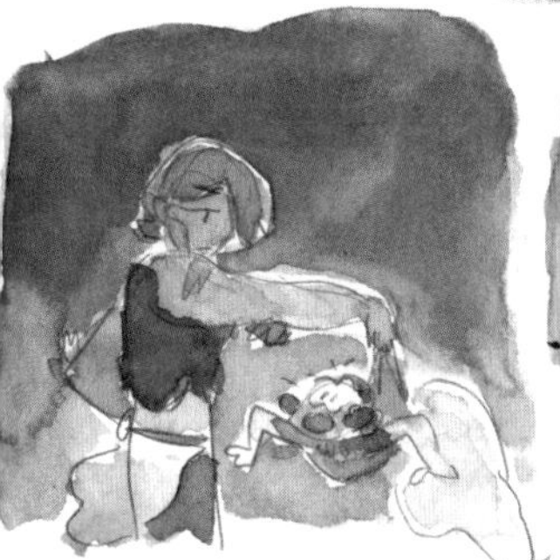
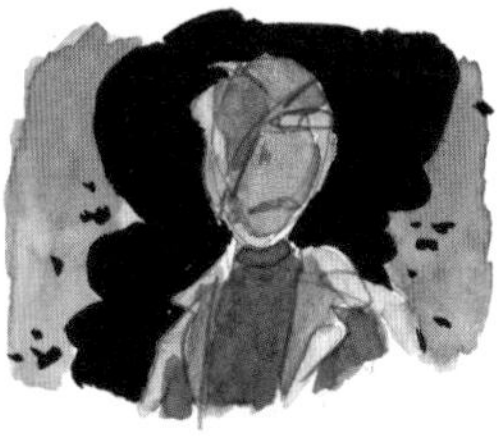

SINCE I MAINLY
USE A COMPUTER TO COLOR,
IT'S EASY TO ADJUST THESE
AND USE THE EYEDROPPER
TOOL TO GET THE COLORS
I WANT!

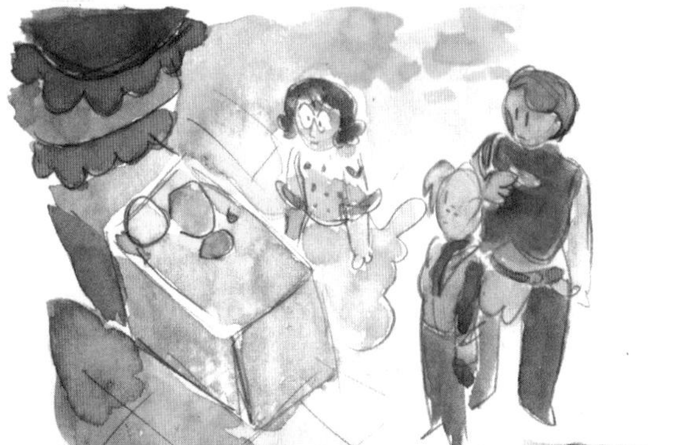
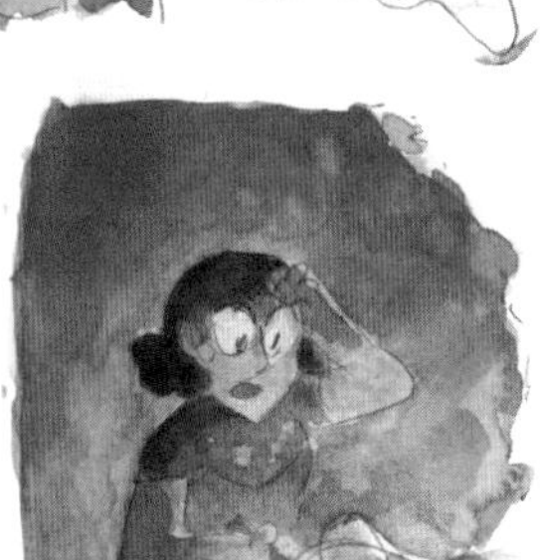
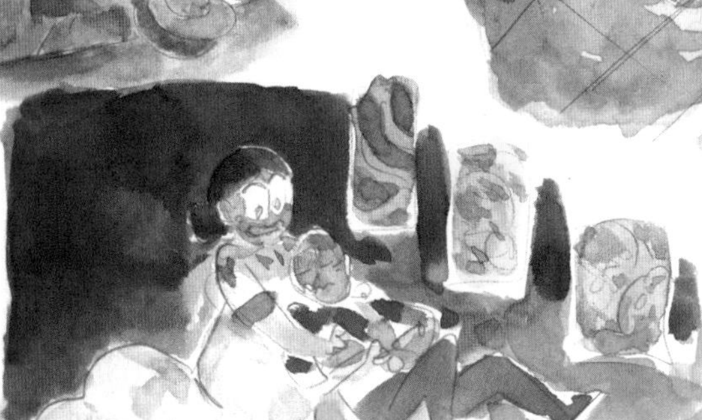
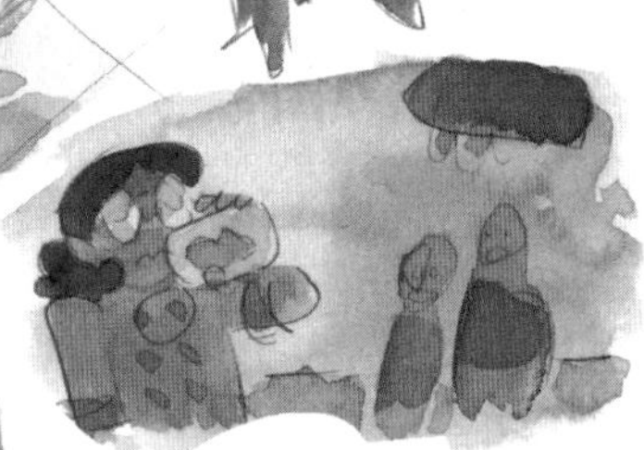
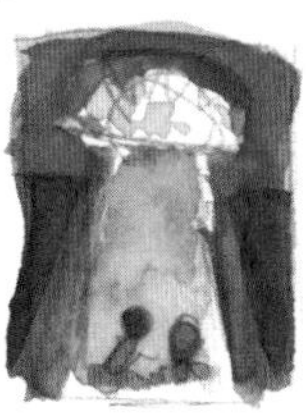

MISC. CONCEPT SKETCHES

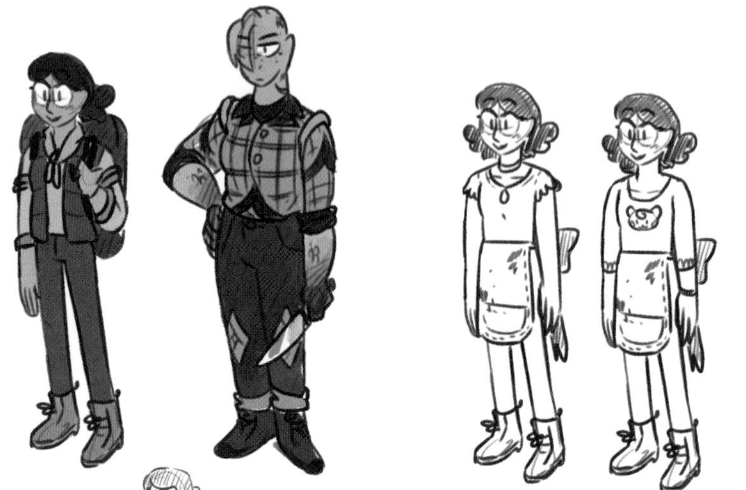

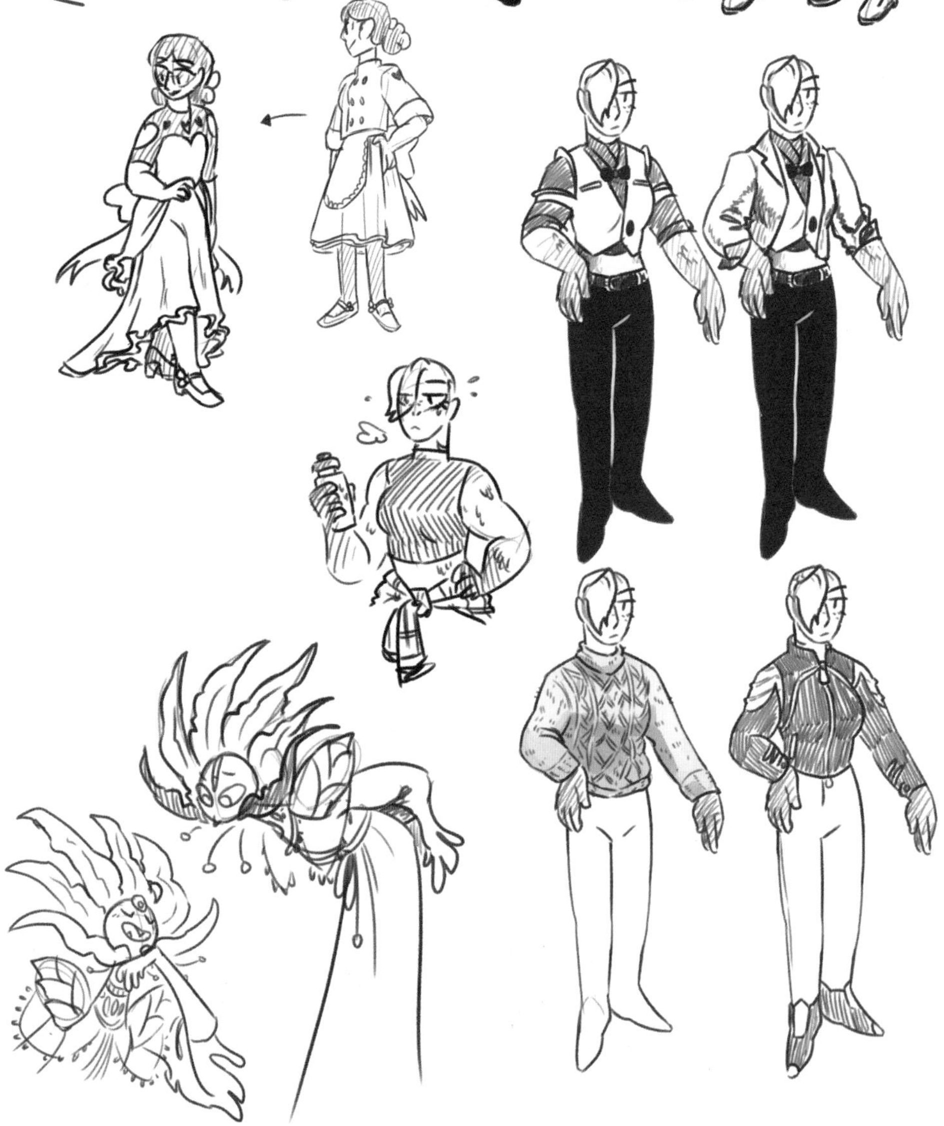

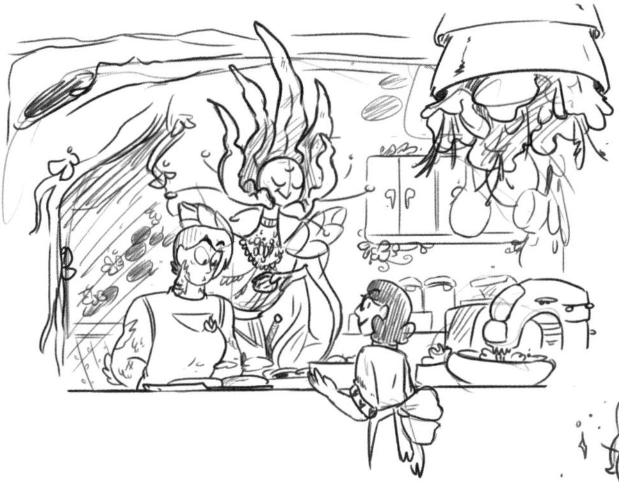

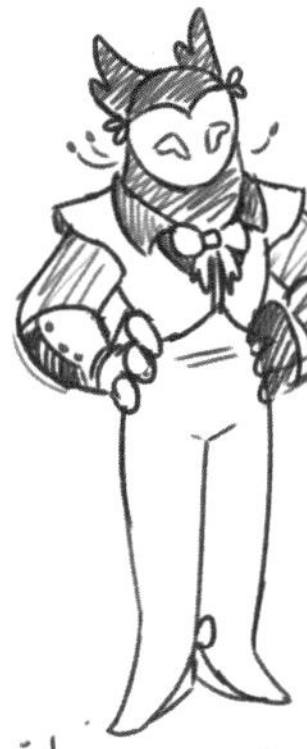

UNUSED COVER CONCEPTS

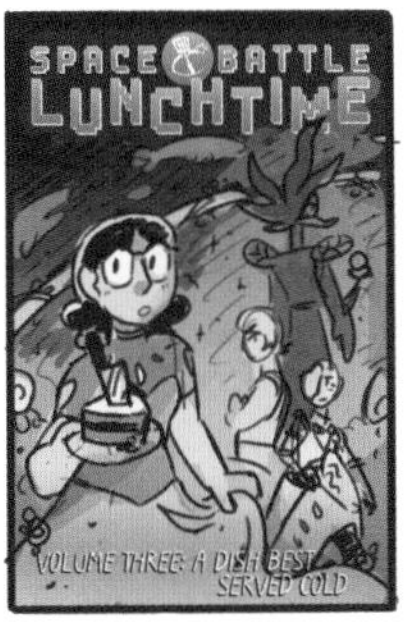
SPACE & BATTLE
LUNCHTIME
VOLUME THREE: A DISH BEST SERVED COLD

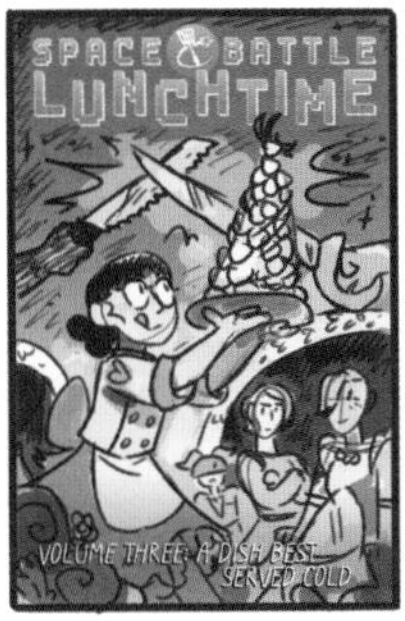
SPACE & BATTLE
LUNCHTIME
VOLUME THREE: A DISH BEST SERVED COLD

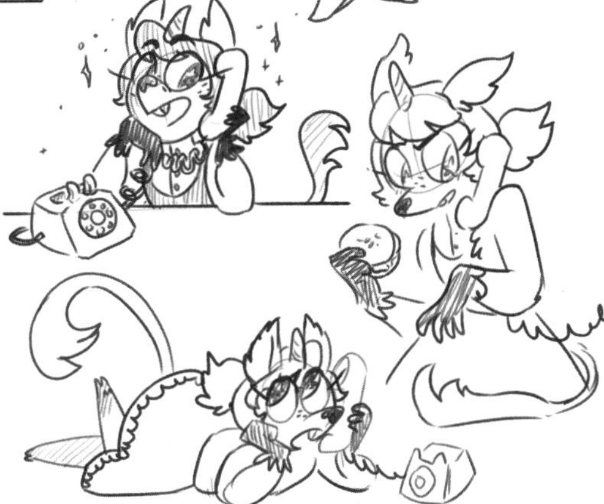

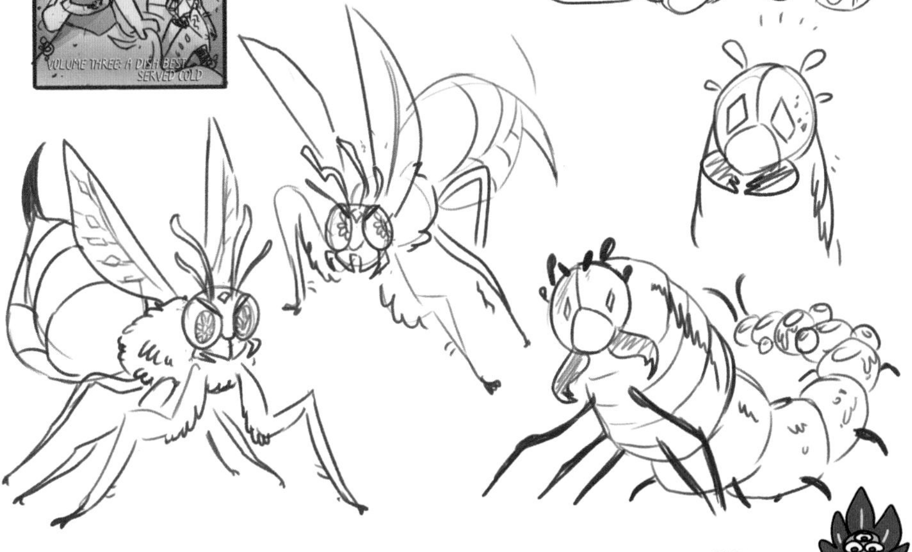

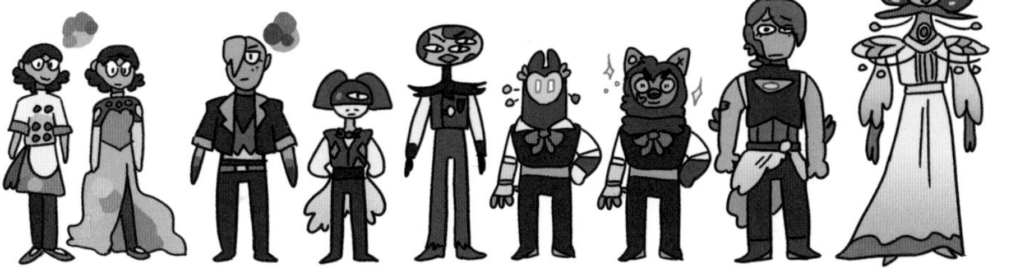

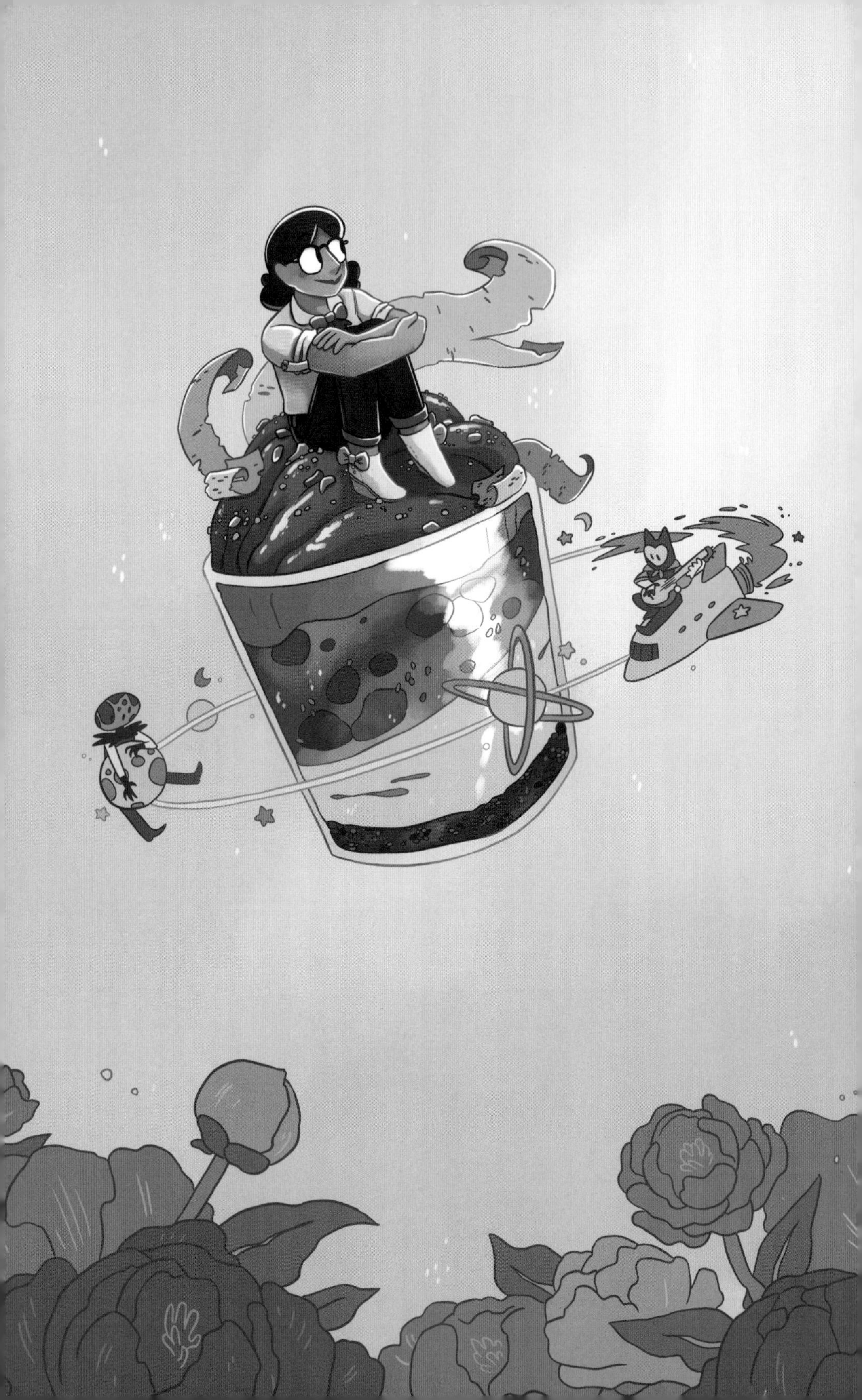

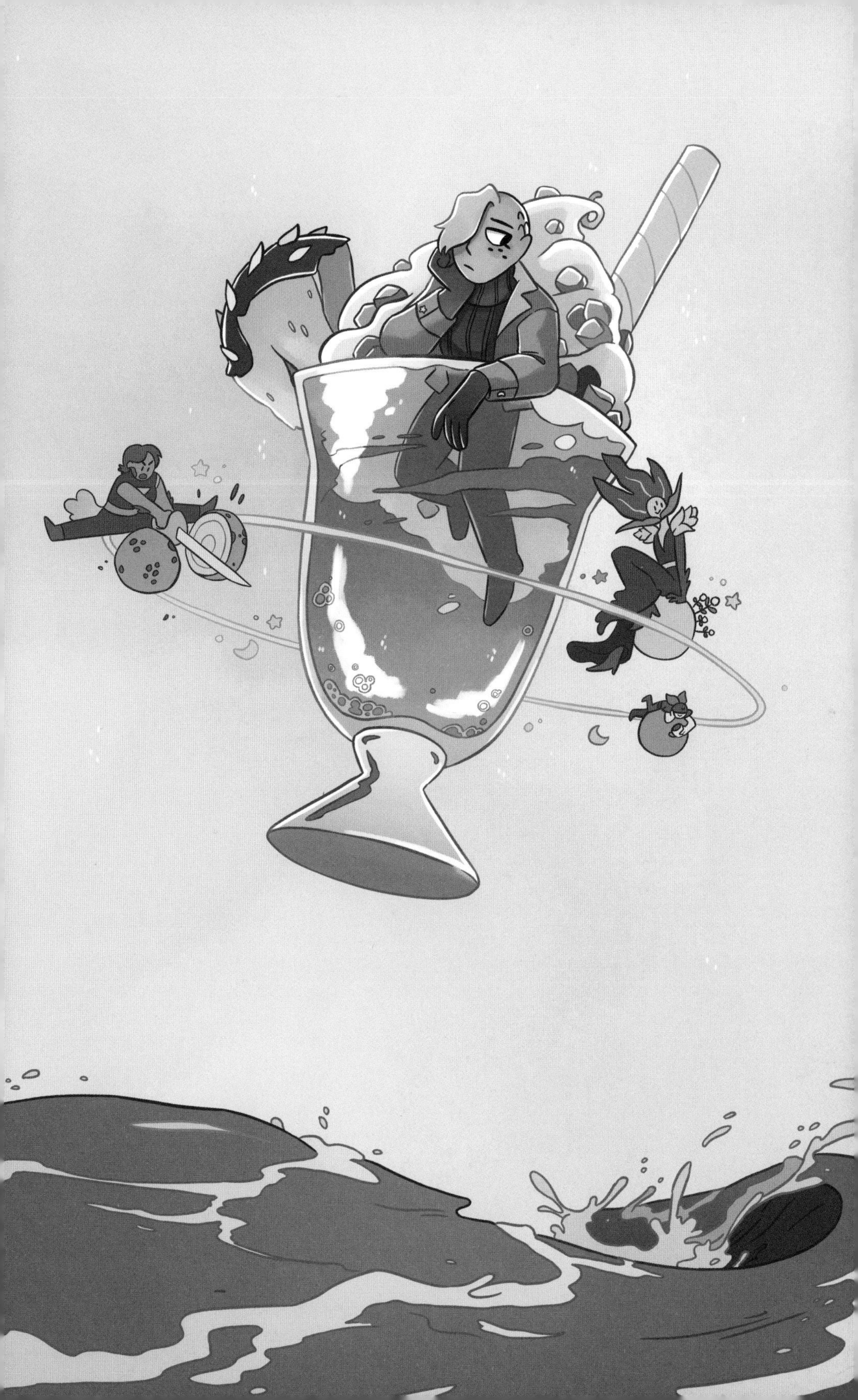

NATALIE RIESS is from a distant, unknown star. Her motives are unknown, but she seems to enjoy drawing food and making comics. She lives in Texas with her girlfriend and her girlfriend's cat.

YOU ARE A CONTESTANT ON THE INTERGALACTIC COOKING SHOW: *SPACE BATTLE LUNCHTIME!*

A BRAND-NEW CARD GAME

FOR 2–5 PLAYERS

based on Natalie Riess's delectable comic series!

Includes 116 cards & 6 tokens!

Collect and combine flavor cards, create prize-winning dishes, and impress the judges!

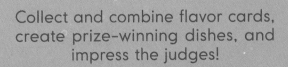

SPACE BATTLE LUNCHTIME
VOLUME 3: A DISH BEST SERVED COLD

WRITTEN AND ILLUSTRATED BY Natalie Riess
COLOR ASSISTANCE BY Sara Goetter
EDITED BY Robin Herrera
DESIGNED BY Hilary Thompson & Sonja Synak

PUBLISHED BY ONI-LION FORGE PUBLISHING GROUP, LLC

James Lucas Jones, PRESIDENT & PUBLISHER · Sarah Gaydos, EDITOR IN CHIEF
Charlie Chu, E.V.P. OF CREATIVE & BUSINESS DEVELOPMENT · Brad Rooks,
DIRECTOR OF OPERATIONS · Amber O'Neill, SPECIAL PROJECTS MANAGER
Harris Fish, EVENTS MANAGER · Margot Wood, DIRECTOR OF MARKETING
& SALES · Devin Funches, SALES & MARKETING MANAGER · Katie Sainz,
MARKETING MANAGER · Tara Lehmann, PUBLICITY · Troy Look, DIRECTOR OF
DESIGN & PRODUCTION · Kate Z. Stone, SENIOR GRAPHIC DESIGNER Sonja
Synak, GRAPHIC DESIGNER · Hilary Thompson, GRAPHIC DESIGNER Sarah
Rockwell, JUNIOR GRAPHIC DESIGNER · Angie Knowles, DIGITAL PREPRESS
LEAD · Vincent Kukua, DIGITAL PREPRESS TECHNICIAN · Jasmine Amiri,
SENIOR EDITOR · Shawna Gore, SENIOR EDITOR · Amanda Meadows, SENIOR
EDITOR · Robert Meyers, SENIOR EDITOR—LICENSING · Grace Bornhoft,
EDITOR · Zack Soto, EDITOR · Christopher Cerasi, EDITORIAL COORDINATOR
Steve Ellis, VICE PRESIDENT OF GAMES · Ben Eisner, GAME DEVELOPER
Michelle Nguyen, EXECUTIVE ASSISTANT · Jung Lee, LOGISTICS COORDINATOR

Joe Nozemack, PUBLISHER EMERITUS

ONIPRESS.COM LIONFORGE.COM

FIRST EDITION: OCTOBER 2020
ISBN 978-1-62020-785-0
EISBN 978-1-62010-806-2

1 3 5 7 9 10 8 6 4 2

LIBRARY OF CONGRESS CONTROL NUMBER: 2016937918
PRINTED IN CHINA.